BISON FRONTIERS OF IMAGINATION

PHILIP WYLIE

The Disappearance

Introduction by Robert Silverberg

UNIVERSITY OF NEBRASKA PRESS
LINCOLN AND LONDON

Grateful acknowledgment is made to Shapiro, Bernstein & Co. Inc. for permission to reprint lyrics from "The Last Roundup," copyright, 1933, by Shapiro, Bernstein & Co. Inc.

♾

First Nebraska paperback printing: 2004

Library of Congress Cataloging-in-Publication Data
Wylie, Philip, 1902–1971.
The disappearance / Philip Wylie; introduction by Robert Silverberg.
p.   cm.
ISBN 0-8032-9841-2 (pbk.: alk. paper)
1. Man-woman relationships—Fiction.   2. Married people—Fiction.
3. Segregation—Fiction.   4. Sex role—Fiction.   I. Silverberg, Robert.
II. Title.
PS3545.Y46D57   2004
813'.52—dc22   2004008329

ROBERT SILVERBERG

Introduction

Philip Wylie (1902–71) is not a name that comes readily to mind when one is listing the great science-fiction writers of the twentieth century: Robert A. Heinlein, yes; Isaac Asimov, yes; Arthur C. Clarke, yes; Ray Bradbury, yes. But Philip Wylie? Those who remember him at all remember Wylie, whose active period as a writer ran from the mid-1920s until his death in 1971, as a best-selling author of quasi-sociological polemics aimed at the hypocrisies of middle-class American morality, not as a denizen of the shadowy pulp-magazine ghetto out of which most of the best modern science fiction has emerged.

But Wylie seems to have regarded himself as a science-fiction writer. He characterized himself as such in "Science Fiction and Sanity in an Age of Crisis," published in *Modern Science Fiction* (1953), an important collection of essays (whose other contributors included Asimov and Clarke) edited by Reginald Bretnor.

> We science-fiction writers—most of us—have taught the people a little knowledge, but such a little and in such a blurred and reckless fashion that it constitutes true and factual information in the minds of very few. More than that, we have taught the people to be afraid—because most of us are afraid, and do not realize it. That man is a positive force, evolving and maturing, responsible for his acts and able if he will to deal with their consequences, we have not said.

In that statement Wylie made explicit what was demonstrated throughout nearly the entire course of his literary career: that he was not only a professional storyteller but also a man of ideas, a societal gadfly, an *agent provocateur*. Like Jonathan Swift, like H. G. Wells, like Olaf Stapledon, like Heinlein and Bradbury and Clarke, he saw the branch of speculative fantasy that we call science fiction as the vehicle through which to convey his philosophical beliefs. In such works as *Gladiator*, *When Worlds Collide*, *Night unto Night*, and *The Disappearance* he used the techniques of science fiction with great effectiveness for passionate didactic purposes and won himself a wide reading audience while doing so.

Gladiator (1930) established him immediately. It was his third published book, though actually the first one he wrote. His publisher, Alfred A. Knopf, held it back because of its fantastic theme, preferring to bring out two works of general fiction first, *Heavy Laden* (1928) and *Babes and Sucklings* (1929). *Gladiator*, a novel about a superman, was in fact the direct inspiration for the comic-strip character created a few years later by Joe Schuster and Jerome Siegel. In Wylie's story a scientist doses his pregnant wife with a chemical that provides their unborn child with extraordinary qualities: he is impervious to bullets, can leap so high that he seems almost to be flying, is capable of killing a twelve-foot-long shark with his bare hands. But Wylie's superman leads a lonely, troubled life and comes to a tragic end, for the primary purpose of the book is to dramatize the plight of a truly superior being in a world of ordinary humans.

That novel was followed quickly by *The Murderer Invisible* (1930), a work clearly indebted to Wells's *The Invisible Man* (1897). Marked by what began to emerge as Wylie's characteristic theme—isolation of the superior man—the scientist, who learns to make himself invisible, seeks to gain power over others through use of his secret and is ultimately destroyed by his own special abilities. A few years later Wylie would be hired to work on the screenplay of the famous James Whale film of Wells's novel into which he incorporated material from his own book. (Wylie had written the screenplay for *The Island of Lost Souls* (1932), a film version of Wells's *The Island of Dr. Moreau.*)

In 1932, also, came the publication of the novel for which he is best remembered by science-fiction readers: *When Worlds Collide*, written in collaboration with Edwin Balmer, one of the magazine editors for whom Wylie had been a prolific contributor. This tense and carefully realized tale of cosmic disaster vividly depicts the collapse of civilization in the face of the oncoming catastrophe and the escape of an elite group of survivors—led by that now-familiar Wylie character, a man of superior attainments—to another world. A sequel, *After Worlds Collide*, followed in short order, carrying the story onward to show the challenges of reestablishing civilization on the newly settled planet. The two books met with enormous commercial success and eventually, after nearly twenty years of delay, the first of them was transformed into a successful motion picture.

The Savage Gentleman, yet another Wylie novel published in the busy year of 1932, deals with the withdrawal of an American millionaire, his infant son, and a few trusted associates to an uninhabited Pacific island. Eventually the son, now grown, returns to the United States. He is a Tarzan figure but equipped with an unusual philosophical education that places him in sharp conflict with the mediocrity and insincerity of civilized life.

Famous now, Wylie allowed himself the indulgence of *Finnley Wren* (1934), a quasi-autobiographical novel with none of the trappings of fantasy in its plot. He made use of experimental techniques—including some Joycean prose pyrotechnics and the use of himself as a character—to attack his now-favorite targets of bourgeois morality, cheap journalism, modern education, and what he saw as the pretensions of the feminist activists of his era. Wylie even tucked into the text two unrelated science-fiction stories, a pair of lively if irrelevant satiric pieces. The book was extremely popular but was perceived by many readers as a scathing attack on women, giving Wylie a reputation for misogyny that he would never fully escape.

That reputation was, if anything, intensified by his ferocious collection of essays, *Generation of Vipers*, published in 1942. That book had a multitude of targets, but the attack that drew the most attention was his excoriation of the modern American mother—the "Great Emasculator," he called her, in the course of a vigorous onslaught against what he called "Momism." He appeared to be saying that all the faults and weaknesses of twentieth-century American culture could be traced to the smothering embrace of mom—an indictment harder to understand or accept in our times than it was sixty years ago, when society's concept of appropriate roles for women was far different from what it is today.

In the years immediately following *Generation of Vipers*, Wylie maintained an active career as a novelist, essayist, and social critic. His next novel, *Night unto Night* (1944), was, among other things, a fantasy about life after death, into which he once again inserted a self-contained science-fiction story, "The Snibbs Phenomenon," about Martians who had infiltrated the world during the war years, and also an odd fragmentary story called "The Cyfer Phenomenon," dealing with a man who awakens one morning to discover that he has someone else's leg in place of one of his own. In *Opus 21* (1949) Wylie returned, in fictional form, to the themes of *Generation of Vipers*, once more with fantastic embellishments.

But it was in *The Disappearance* (1951) that Wylie gave fullest expression to his ideas about the relationship of the sexes, and, yet again, he used the medium of speculative fantasy as the vehicle for his thoughts.

The Disappearance is often loosely categorized as science fiction, but true science fiction requires at least an attempt at rationalizing the fantastic event that is the mainspring of the story, and Wylie does not even try to offer an explanation for the startling phenomenon at the core of this novel: One day, suddenly, all the women and girls on earth disappear, leaving the men and boys alone in a purely masculine world. The women, in that same moment, have the equal but opposite experience: the men and boys have vanished, and they must cope on their own with all the challenges of existence. (No such sex-linked disappearances, however, strike animals of the lower orders.) There is, of course, no plausible scientific explanation for an event of that sort. Some of Wylie's characters suggest halfhearted theories about mass hallucination, others express the thought that it is the arbitrary and incomprehensible doing of God, and so forth, but ultimately neither Wylie himself nor the philosopher who is his chief mouthpiece in the book take any conclusive position on what has occurred. It is simply set down as a given. Thus *The Disappearance* must be classed as fantasy, not the sort of elf-and-wizard fantasy that is so popular today, but a kind of didactic fable, a speculative "what-if" fantasy that brings it close to the method of science fiction but without the pretense of a legitimizing theoretical rationale that science fiction in its purest form demands.

Wylie sets his story in motion very quickly. There is a preliminary passage on the daily preoccupations of midcentury America, which, with just a little updating, would sound amazingly familiar to twenty-first-century ears: "worries concerning 'the Russians,' the diminution of American liberties, hydrogen bombs, the distressful effect of civilization upon the so-called resources of nature, the growing gap between what education was supposed to accomplish and what it consisted of, the national debt and its intimate aspect of high taxes, the problem of the excessive cost of medical care, and the like" (6). But then the men suddenly and inexplicably lose sight of all the women, the women similarly lose sight of all the men, and from that point on two parallel but separate stories unfold against the same Florida background as men and women struggle to go on with their separate lives in a vastly altered world.

In telling his double story, fantastic though it is, Wylie employs a central technique of science fiction: the methodical and systematic exploration of all the implications of a single speculative hypothesis. Of course, the events that inevitably unfold would not be so inevitable in our own day, for *The Disappearance* is very much a book of its era, and that era was one in which most American women were housewives or secretaries or nurses or schoolteachers and it was the men who filled the roles of political leaders, corporate executives, doctors, firemen, coal miners, and absent-minded professors. Therefore what we see unfold reflects this polarity of function: the women, on their own for the first time, react to the crisis mainly by running in confused circles and screaming, while the men, once they realize that they are no longer to be held to "feminized" standards of behavior, relapse quickly into slovenliness, drunkenness, looting, and brutish machismo. We see harshly satirical scenes in which a group of Washington wives, attempting to reconstitute the government their husbands once had run, begin their deliberations with a five-day debate over the design of an appropriate costume for the new all-female Congress; the men, in their world, unleash an immediate rampage of crime on the lower levels of society while the best and the brightest gather at the president's behest for a bloodless and useless scholarly attempt at discovering the causes of the world's transformation. Then the Soviet Union responds to the vanishing of the women by launching a nuclear attack on the United States—a plot twist that makes little sense to a modern reader but is very true to the atomic paranoia that was rampant in the United States in the 1950s. And so it goes as the two story lines take us down widely diverging paths of parallel development.

The great surprise that emerges, finally, from this powerful novel is that the supposedly misogynistic Philip Wylie has actually written something approaching a feminist tract. Yes, he shows his female characters mostly to be silly fluttering things incapable of dealing with the fires, explosions, commodity shortages, and epidemics of the world they have so unexpectedly inherited. But he is even-handed in his depiction of most men as inherently amoral creatures who devolve into cruel little boys, dirty and dirty-minded, as soon as the restraints of a sexually balanced world are lifted. He expresses scorn for the women who blandly allow themselves to be turned into idle sexual objects, but he is equally scathing about the men who demand such objectification. Thus Wylie, the irascible cultural critic, demonstrates the folly of an educational and social system that condemns most women to a kind of permanent girlishness, while turning responsibility for the institutions of civilized life over to a male sex that wears only the barest veneer of civility over the primordial bestial urges of uninhibited savages. What emerges, ultimately, is a powerful statement about the interdependence of the sexes: we are each incomplete without the other, and we have failed (at least as of 1950) to provide women with the sort of training that would bring about a more rational division of the tasks of daily life, thereby preventing proper integration of the two halves of humanity and a complete sharing of adult responsibilities.

The Disappearance, which attained wide popularity in its day, was the last great success of Philip Wylie's career. As the issues that were of such importance to Wylie ceased to be central in the 1960s, his career waned and his life grew darker. Faced with a decline in readership, in intellectual interest in his work, and in the income that had supported a lavish lifestyle, he gave way to depression and alcoholism. Yet he continued his campaign against the follies of society in such bleak, pessimistic works as *The Sons and Daughters of Mom* (1971), and he called attention to encroaching environmental disaster in the posthumously published *The End of the Dream* (1972, co-authored with John Brunner). But his influence was profound in his own time, and in such books as *Gladiator, Finnley Wren, Generation of Vipers*, and *The Disappearance* he has left us a lively and disturbing record of American cultural attitudes in the first half of the twentieth century.

CONTENTS

Part I: The Hand of God

Part II: Armageddon

Part III: The Unloved

Part IV: Dream and Dimension

PART I

The Hand of God

A GENTLEMAN OF EMINENCE IS INTRODUCED AND A CURIOUS
EVENT TAKES PLACE BY WHICH HE, AND OTHERS, ARE
BAFFLED.

The female of the species vanished on the afternoon of the
second Tuesday of February at four minutes and fifty-two seconds
past four o'clock, Eastern Standard Time. The event occurred universally at the same instant, without regard to time belts, and was
followed by such phenomena as might be expected after happenings
of that nature.

To Dr. William Percival Gaunt, as to a large portion (if not a
majority) of males, the catastrophe was not immediately, or at least
not clearly, manifest; by him, as by multitudes of others, the ensuing
incidents were understood only gradually.

It is true that he was watching his wife, Paula, but he was
doing so absent-mindedly. For more than two hours he had been at
work in the study of his winter home in the suburban environs of
Miami, Florida—at work only in the flimsiest sense of the phrase.
Several large books, many with a secondhand look about them, lay
open on his desk. Amongst and around the books were slips of
paper which bore notations in his large, plain script. Before him
was a typewriter. In its carriage stood the upper halves of three sheets
of paper, one white, one yellow, and a carbon between. Upon these,

3

at the top left-hand corner, was the numeral 7, and the ending of a sentence evidently begun on page 6:

". . . in consequence of which it may be said that the Hegelian position, the Taoistic opposites, 'Parallelism,' and the other dualistic theories, while rising from the same observed causes, do not reflect identical or even similar formulative attempts."

Beneath this was a space. After the space, Dr. Gaunt had typed: "Prolix."

There were several more spaces, then:

"The dopes won't get to first base with it!"

Beyond that, the paper was barren.

The partial sentence and the two deprecatory comments implied much about the man at the desk—a philosophical bent, for example. Dr. Gaunt was, indeed, a professional philosopher; in the past he had taught his subject at various universities. He was, moreover, what the *American Magazine*, in a long article, had termed a "successful" philosopher. The word was employed in its commonest connotation: Gaunt's books, when he wanted them to be, were very popular. In addition, a comedy concerning a philosopher, which he had written during the winter after his marriage to Paula, had run on Broadway for more than two years. It had also been purchased by a motion-picture company for a six-figure sum, toured lengthily on the road, and enjoyed a revival in 1946. Gaunt was well-to-do.

His colleagues regarded the term "successful," thus applied to a philosopher, with semipolite hilarity. They tagged him with it and referred to it whenever they could. Their mirth, however, was tempered—sometimes by envy of Gaunt's fiscal achievements, but more often by awareness that Gaunt towered in the realm of academic philosophy even higher than he loomed in the company of mortal men. Gaunt himself sometimes said his "headier" hypotheses were so hard to understand that even he had to read them over and over to recapture their meaning.

His intellect was richly endowed and versatile; unlike many

brilliant men, he had achieved not only fame and fortune but, besides that, owing to his gregariousness and his tact, he had been of considerable use to his country in the recent war, sharing the councils of the military, administrative and scientific elect. Toward it all he showed a casual and often slangy indifference. That attitude, of never quite taking either his thoughts or other men's responses to them with absolute seriousness, was also plainly implied by the comments that interrupted the composition before him:

Prolix, he had said of his writing, and:

The dopes won't get to first base with it.

The work was a lecture intended for a fusty, highbrow seminar to be held in St. Petersburg in March. An abrupt realization that too much fustiness and too little brow height was going to limit the understanding of what he had already written had halted his endeavors shortly before three o'clock. He had not actually labored since that moment. Instead, he had worried, frittered and fumed—although, for most of the interval, he had presented the very image of genius wrestling in difficult speculation. The truth was other.

Gaunt had noted with a frown that his elder daughter, Edwinna (temporarily "living at home" after her second divorce), was persistently trying to sing the "Italian Street Song" from *Naughty Marietta*, a feat of which she was not quite capable.

He had observed that Edwinna's three-year-old, Alicia, was pattering unsupervised around the living room—and prepared his mind to hear something break.

Hester, the maid, was upstairs, running the electric waxer—a further frowned-at circumstance.

The philosopher had watched a mockingbird persecute two thirsty palm warblers when they had made pathetic forays on the birdbath.

He had lengthily examined a small scab on the tanned, roughened back of his left hand, wondering how he had come by the injury.

He had also entertained, one by one, a round dozen of the vague but nonetheless numbing worries that were the lot of intelligent persons in the period—worries that concerned "the Russians," the diminution of American liberties, hydrogen bombs, the distressful effect of civilization upon the so-called resources of nature, the growing gap between what education was supposed to accomplish and what it consisted of, the national debt and its intimate aspect of high taxes, the problem of the excessive cost of medical care, and the like.

He had gone to the kitchen for a drink of ice water, patting his granddaughter on the head benignly as he passed both ways.

So an hour had been spent, in dawdling.

He was thinking of his lecture again—of starting it over on, perhaps, a lighter topic—when Paula appeared.

She was freshly coiffured. Her figure, Gaunt observed pridefully, was as well proportioned as Edwinna's; Paula was, if anything, suppler and more graceful than her daughter. Her body knew more, knew it better, and showed both. His gaze went, as always, to his wife's hair; that too was youthful—radiantly so—and as red as the day, twenty-seven years before, when he had ordered her to stay after class for a reprimand and wound up by burying his fingers and his lips in the spicy opulence.

Paula had not minded.

On the contrary. Six weeks later, at a precocious nineteen, she had graduated; he and she had then signed the same marriage license.

Gaunt sighed and wondered why he sighed. Perhaps it was because he presumed it his business to analyze every scrap of thought or of emotion even though it gave rise to no more than the slightest exhalation. The notion vexed him.

Damn it, he thought, when a man is fifty-five and his wife is forty-six and when she looks like Paula and he feels as I do, a sigh is no more than minor prayer. It is a bead falling on a long rosary of passion and affection and good living. Let it go undefined! I loved the wench; the woman moves me still!

She moved him, then, differently.

She had been standing at the corner of the house gazing attentively at a gardenia that grew in a tub. It was a handsome bush with glittering leaves that here and there bore a blossom of incandescent white. A perfumed flower—and Gaunt had expected she'd choose one and put it in her red curls which, for the moment, were mathematically arranged. Arranged, he reflected, by some chatty pansy who knew how to fix female hair but not what it meant. But she bent forward and thrust her fingers into the earth among the gardenia's roots. Quickly she combed out several coral rocks and what appeared to be the casing of a very large insect. Next, she reached around a corner, picked up the end of a hose, bent again to turn the faucet and, digging with her fingers, watered the bush.

At that point, still smiling to himself, Gaunt gathered up the opening pages of his typescript with the intention of taking them out on the lawn and reading them to Paula. He rarely made a speech that Paula had not heard, at least in outline; he seldom sent off an article, or even a technical monograph, that his wife had not first read. Sometimes they did not agree about what he said or the way in which he said it. In such cases, Gaunt had formed a habit of sleeping on Paula's criticism; if it seemed valid the next day, he made changes; if his own attitude still held, he let the words remain.

Paula was especially sensitive to the levels of understanding in the varied audiences he addressed. That capacity, he knew, related to her aptitude for languages. He had been pleased and proud, but perhaps slightly patronizing, when she had continued, in the early years of their marriage, to study languages—ancient and modern, practical and esoteric: Sanskrit, Latin and Greek, Russian—and even, for a year, Chinese. His feeling was still indulgent; but he made use of her talent without apologies.

She could tell him whether or not "the dopes would get to first base" with what he had composed.

Besides, it would be pleasant to leave the study and sit in the sun, to smell gardenias instead of stale cigarette smoke, to talk to Paula instead of listening to sibilant anxieties in his own mind.

Also, his typewriter ribbon was getting dim and Paula would change it. Gaunt was not adept at such tasks. Whenever he undertook to replace a ribbon, he finished with his fingers inky, his hands shaky and his temper disheveled. He would then rancorously assert that the color film in his motion-picture camera could be changed without a hitch—a much more complicated proceeding. But, he would go on, after fifty-odd years of typewriters, no progress had been made in the matter of shifting ribbons. He then might rail against the Machine Age as a whole and all who took pride therein. If he had new auditors, he would describe other "obsolete booby traps in the American home"—his favorite being the "Rube Goldberg artifact" inside the tank of a flush toilet; man had learned to make airplanes, Gaunt would protest, but not valves. Paula could change his ribbon, with scarcely the smudging of a finger, before he'd got well into such a harangue.

He now grinned—glanced again at his wife—and abruptly put down the papers.

With the back of her hand, Paula had wiped at a tear. He saw her shoulders lift; she sniffled; she was crying.

She'd had a day—he knew that. A hard day. A day of those trivial unpleasantnesses which, taken separately, amount to nothing but, added together, form a weight that may depress the most buoyant spirit. She'd run over the list in the morning. It had included the dentist, the beauty parlor—which Paula disliked, a necessary argument over a bill with a bullheaded merchant in Coral Gables, and a session with the tax expert. Besides that—there was Edwinna. And Alicia.

Gaunt drummed on a pulled-out leaf of his desk for a moment, considering whether to comfort her. It was no time, in any case, to put his intellectual problem before her or to ask her aid in ribbon changing. Not that she would refuse to listen or to help—she would gladly do both—but that Gaunt's sympathy and affection caused him to discard all notion of adding his problems to hers. He watched a moment more and saw that she seemed to be diverted by the gardenia.

That supplied his answer. Paula was dealing with her small troubles and no doubt wanted to be alone, doing just what she was doing.

He looked at his work again—chagrined by his dawdling. The lecture would also be published, after he had delivered it. So, he decided, he might as well go on with it in the form he had chosen. If some listeners failed to understand, others might—and many of those who read it surely would.

He was aware of the noises all about him as he stared, unseeingly, across the palmettos and through the pines. But he accepted them and half understood why he allowed them to invade his workroom: they were evidence of his family—close by and in voluble being—and his family was the center of his existence. If he was sometimes distressed by the clamor, he was also, in another way, stimulated and consoled. That feeling came unphrased to Gaunt as he detached his mind from Paula and concentrated upon abstract philosophical ideas.

It was then that she disappeared.

He did not see her go, precisely. What he saw was that she had gone. He had assumed he was looking at her or, more accurately, at a point in space beyond her which included her. When she disappeared he did not say to himself, "Why! Paula's vanished!" He thought, instead, that he had been momentarily mistaken in the angle of his view and that she had stepped around the house.

At the same time, by a bit of good fortune he did not analyze, his daughter abandoned her experiment with light opera. The clear but not flexible soprano broke off in the middle of a note. And little Alicia ceased to patter about the living room—ceased suddenly, as if her staccato trot had taken her up on a soft staircase visible only to the young and accessible to them alone.

Silence did not follow. Hester's electric machine continued to hum upstairs and other, distant sounds replaced the stilled disturbances: the gardener's chopping at vine roots, the hammering of a carpenter in a house being built nearby and the far, lofty mutter of a private plane—caused, doubtless, by some student who took his lesson over a residential area where it would inconvenience, annoy (and thus attract the attention of) the largest possible number of persons. Nevertheless, the increase of quiet was appreciable.

He thought out new sentences rapidly and swiftly set them down, ignoring the two lines of rude self-criticism. His secretary would smile over the slang—and delete.

"What I have called 'opposites,'" he wrote, "rise from the reflection, in the psyche, of the 'oppositenesses' universally observable in nature. 'Oppositeness' is a rudimentary condition of existence. It is seen in myriad phenomena—none is properly seen without it. If heat be, cold is. If motion, rest. If height, depth. Thermodynamic process takes place between differences that are 'as if' opposites. Evolution is, again, a process involving paired opposites: what is, is destroyed, that what comes next may exist, to be destroyed for the sake of the ensuing form. That is the classic opposite: life and death—which, in turn, infinitely ramified and adorned with images, become the substance of love and hate in the mind and are transmuted to all the tropisms of the human soul, all ecstasies, all compulsions, and all the revulsions that the mind expresses as fears or in fear forms. All entity, including life, is found in states of tension between opposites. Progress —or evolution—is but *motion* amidst' these states, toward order, toward integration, toward individuation. The individual mind *reflects* a certain sum of them and the more it is aware the greater the sum of opposites it comprehends. To say . . ."

He stopped writing.

His household was, once again, interfering with his tranquillity although—as Paula had pointed out a hundred times—he might have shut the door to his study, and the windows besides, and installed air conditioning into the bargain, thus immunizing himself from the rackets for which he sometimes showed a peevish allergy. (His answer to that was to say he *liked* to work with an open door.) It was a stylized impasse of his demesne, a wasp in a peaceful room, a thimbleful of tempest where, in general, the landscape was calm. Paula understood it: he enjoyed the "feel" of having his family close; but she could never get him to admit as much.

Edwinna's dog had commenced caterwauling—an orange-colored cocker spaniel, Rufus by name, an appealing animal that was not given to doleful sounds. Gaunt supposed it distressed him particularly to hear the dog moan and yeowl in this fashion because it was Edwinna's dog and because he was disconcerted by his daughter's second, unexpected divorce and her self-righteous return to the parental abode. Not that Charlie Emmert had been perfect, or his successor, Billy Tackley, either—but a philosopher ought to be able to raise a girl who could pick and stick to one adequate spouse. He had been fond of Charlie and detested Billy. So it was not the loss of the latter but Edwinna's general attitude toward marriage that galled him. His pique at the dog reflected a displeasure with his daughter, which brought in turn self-reproach.

No man enjoys self-reproach save a masochist, and William Gaunt was not that. He called, "Rufus! Quiet, please!"

The dog entered the study, looked at the man, moaned again, and made to leave.

"What's the trouble, boy?"

The dog lowered and seemed to shake its head. It departed.

By now Gaunt was far removed from the thought train of composition. It was getting on toward half-past four, he perceived. Paula should have announced tea—which consisted of coffee in his case. Besides, Hester's waxer had settled to a steady buzz that indicated it was standing in some corner, carelessly left going and probably eating away layers of shellac.

Gaunt left his book-lined sanctuary. "Paula!" he called.

There was no answer.

"Edwinna!" he shouted, facing the corridor on the opposite side of a long porch.

Silence.

"Damn it to hell!" He strode between heavy glass sliding doors into his living room, crossed it, and ran up the staircase. As he had surmised, the untended waxer was whizzing in a corner where, apparently, it had arrived after zigzagging over the polished oak. He switched it off, went downstairs again and swung back the kitchen door. He had drawn a breath to expostulate but found no opportunity. The kitchen was empty. No signs of brewing coffee were visible.

No Paula, no Edwinna, no Hester, and for that matter, no Alicia.

Gaunt removed his tortoise-shell spectacles and ran his fingers through his thin hair. He did that in the automatic manner of a man spitting into a river simply because he has leaned over the rail of a bridge. But the latter is merely idle and wishes to make a splash while the man who rakes his hair expresses something definite: his bafflement. Gaunt looked at the spectacles, appreciated the gesture he had made, and only then became aware of the fact that he was befuddled.

He frowned, folded the earpieces, pocketed the glasses and went outside, stooping and dodging to avoid a door-shutting device which had gouged his scalp in the past. He yelled loudly: "Paula!"

Sun streamed over the sloping roofs of his modernistic house, making straight, angular shadows on the grass. Sun pricked through the live oaks and filigreed his curving driveway. Sun fell upon, but failed to penetrate, a rank curtain of wild vine at which the gardener still hacked.

"Byron!"

The colored man rested his heavy hoe and turned.

"Seen Mrs. Gaunt?"

"No, sir."

"She was there, at your corner of the house, a while ago."

"Seemed like she just plain disappeared," Byron replied, chuckling. "I see her—an' a second later—I don't. Nor ain't since."

Two voices now invaded the warm afternoon—those of young Gordon Elliot and his father, Jim. The Elliot house, beyond the oaks and the narrow boom-time street on which Gaunt lived (and which the jungle had all but reclaimed), was out of earshot for all but the most vigorous sounds. Father and son were now bellowing unashamedly:

"Mother! Where are you?"

"Bella! *BELLA!* Where the devil are you?"

Wherever she is, Gaunt thought, Paula and the rest of my womenfolk must be there too. And where, he asked himself, would that be? He started walking down his drive, rapidly—and heard, on the not-distant boulevard, the sound of a siren. It approached from Cocoplum Plaza, shrill and disturbing as it brought alarm closer—and merely provocative as it revealed by passing that the trouble it spelled belonged to others. Like every man, Gaunt had quailed slightly at the crescendo and tingled faintly with the diminuendo; unlike most, he reflected for a guilty instant upon the minor inhumanity of that process.

And then he saw Elliot—a man almost as tall as himself and even thinner, a Yankee with cavernous eyes at once faded and piercing, a lawyer who would have made a better mystic but who did well enough at law owing to a memory for detail that was like the index of a great library. Jim Elliot was, indeed, the most knowledgeable of all men concerning titles, grants and old land claims in the surrounding area and he had turned his information to good account. He was retained by some of the largest landholders and the most acquisitive corporations of the region—even though he was a Northerner and though it was known he had practiced Yoga, belonged briefly to the Rosicrucians, claimed to have made "astral" voyages outside his body, and although he had once journeyed in person to the monasteries of Tibet.

Jim Elliot trotted awkwardly, with his son, on the tree-roofed pavement of the ruined street, calling for his wife. He did not notice Gaunt until the boy yanked at the flapping tail of his plaid shirt and pointed. Then he changed his direction and ran up to the philosopher.

"Bella's been *taken!*" he said in a panting, sepulchral voice. "Gone!"

Gaunt said, "Nonsense! Paula's gone too! So's Edwinna. Hester. Did you hear that siren just now? Probably a fire or a car smash on Sunset Boulevard. Probably the women learned about it and ran to see—the way they always charge out for trouble."

"No!" The young boy said that—his dark eyes wide open and the flesh around them white. "I *saw* her go! She was watering the poinsettias—the big bush—and she disappeared—and the hose dropped and squirted the lawn!"

Jim Elliot glanced down anxiously at his son, then gazed at Gaunt. "That's what the boy says. And he doesn't lie. And it could happen, Bill. It could! The women of ancient Laecocidiae, in the reign of King Lestentum the Third, are said to have—"

"The hell with King Lestentum! Let's go over to Sunset and find out what all the excitement is!"

They might have gone. For a second they stood still, facing each other, in the slopes of sleazy sunlight. Then, from a distance, came a thudding explosion. They turned that way and looked again, uneasily, at each other.

The boy called dolefully, "Mo-o-o-ther!"

The lawyer's eyes dropped. He shook the craggy head that contained them; he brushed at his fuzzy, dark hair. "Let's go inside and see if there's anything on the radio."

"It can only be some local mishap—" Gaunt began. But he followed.

They went up the back steps and entered a stew-savored kitchen which Jim Elliot himself had outfitted. On the end of a table he had built, in the breakfast nook, under a pot of begonias, stood a small radio. The lawyer switched it on. Gaunt noticed a tremor in his hand. Gordon sat tensely on a stool.

The hand turned the dial slowly—passing through the hiss of stations on the air but not broadcasting—hurrying over a station that was sending dance music—and finding at last a human voice. A voice ragged with the effort of its owner to maintain control.

"I repeat," it said. Elliot turned up the volume so that the kitchen vibrated with hysterical noise: "At four-oh-five this afternoon, now forty minutes ago, the event took place. Confirmed by local observation—confirmed by phone calls—confirmed by the ticker. At present there is not much to add. The ticker is standing still. This station is endeavoring to contact the networks. Newspapers in Miami, reached before the phones became jammed with calls, said they only knew what everybody knew. It is believed there will be advices from the White House presently. It is rumored that the event may be due to enemy action. Stand by—and keep calm. The event . . ."

"Event!" Gaunt hit the Formica surface of the table with his palm. "In God's name, *what* event?"

"The women," Elliot replied almost softly. "Their—going."

"Man—make sense!" Gaunt choked off to listen.

"The event," the radio went on, "is at present totally unexplained. New York City, like Miami, reports that at four-oh-five all women on the street and elsewhere disappeared. All girls. All female babies. Wait a minute! Stand by!"

Silence—save for the crackle of wasted electricity.

Gaunt found himself seeking a chair. He felt his back hit it. He became aware that the lawyer's eyes were boring into him. Jim Elliot expected him to say something—to comment—to react.

And Gaunt began commenting. "Impossible! Mass hypnosis! Hardly such a thing as could be accomplished by what that jittery booby calls 'enemy action'! A moment of universal schizophrenia—the collective result of pent-up anxieties . . ."

"Do *you* feel schizoid?" Elliot smiled as he said it.

"What about Sarah?" Gaunt asked.

"I went upstairs as soon as Gordon told me what happened to Bella. Naturally. The baby had been in her play pen. Gone."

Young Gordon began to cry quietly. His father reached out and touched his shoulder.

"Go ahead, son. Cry. I could cry myself. We've lost them. It's not what I expected—but it's no more than we deserve."

The philosopher realized the inanity of his attempt to find a reasonable hypothesis for a situation he did not understand. No such thing could happen as appeared to be happening, *ergo*, it was an illusion. If not mass hypnosis, his own dream. He was asleep somewhere and this was a particularly real and upsetting nightmare. (But he did not believe he was asleep.) He had lost his reason, then, and this was a philosopher's madness. (But he was not mad. But that was what the mad believed, always.)

It was true, then.

But truth is never preposterous.

A miracle? But miracles—even to those who credit them—are never *evil*.

The radio spoke again in the tone of a crazed Jove. Jim Elliot reached out and cut down its volume:

"Here's a bulletin—the first one through in some time! Paris, London, Mexico City report their women vanished also. All Soviet and Soviet-controlled stations have gone off the air. Soviet women broadcasters are reported by authoritative sources to have ceased talking abruptly at the same instant women vanished elsewhere. The President has called his Cabinet, also Congressional leaders and others. Advisory! Men are urged immediately to go to the rescue of all children who might have been depending on women for their care as these—probably boys only—will now be without any adult." The announcer's voice broke. "My God! Will somebody hurry—please—to 808 Evedado Street, Coral Gables, where my twin boys are— probably in the nursery on the second floor! Please! Nearest listener! Number 808 Evedado Street, Coral Gables! Two boys, nine months of age! In yard or on second floor!" There was a pause and a gulping sound. "Bulletin! Car crashes reported everywhere as women drivers vanished from behind wheels. Fires breaking out. Advisory! Warn all survi . . . all men—to see to it that stoves, lamps, backyard fires, irons and other electrical equipment are checked or cut off immediately. Investigate all homes. Break and enter if necessary. Two gas explosions in Miami already reported as result of ovens turned on but not lighted. Inspect all homes. Use caution. Bear in mind that looting will be punished. Martial law expected at once. Bulletin! . . ."

Gaunt signaled by twisting his hand and Elliot cut off the radio.

For some moments the two men and the boy were speechless.

Then Jim Elliot glanced at the stove. A double boiler simmered there. "Bella was having stew tonight, Bill. Better join us."

Gaunt said slowly, "Good God. Yes. Maybe I should go over to my place and make sure it won't catch fire or blow up. I'll be back."

As he went out the door he heard young Gordon say plaintively, "But they'll come home soon, won't they?"

And his father answered, "Never, my boy. For us—this is the end of the world!"

Gaunt cut through a hedge of hibiscus and walked up his drive. He was glad to be alone. Alone, he might at least ascertain whether or not he was sane.

2

Paula Gaunt was a woman of warmth, of engagingly varied moods, and of many capacities. She was perceptive and sympathetic —as a rule. She had one minor vanity: she dyed her hair the shade of red she'd been born with. As far as she could tell, Bill had not caught on, although she'd begun to dabble with henna fifteen years ago when the first gray strands had appeared. She called the original color "copper pink"—and henna had not restored it. But other chemicals had been effective. Through frequent visits to expert hair-dressers she had maintained to the age of forty-six the hue and luster of her unusual adornment. The trouble was, not to know whether Bill knew. Since this was a matter of pride, and slightly obsessive, she gave it undue importance.

On a Tuesday, the second in February, and her regular afternoon at the beauty salon in Coral Gables, Marcel had been absent and Francis had performed the chromatic ritual. Francis was competent at cutting and setting; but, as Paula saw immediately upon taking the mirror he gave her, he had used the wrong shade. Her hair was, actually, a deep auburn with an opalescence which, in daylight or even lamplight, gave it another surface shade, a semitransparent beige, or a dusty rose, or even a mistily bluish pink, so that when she turned her head, or walked, or when the wind blew, men —and women too—looked at her not just because she was lovely but because of the unusual and fascinating climax of her good looks.

Paula's troubles that day did not end with the discovery that Francis had altered the hue so that her locks were too pale and Bill, this time, would certainly discover that his wife was vulgarly dyeing her hair.

She drove home to a continuation of bother.

Edwinna had left her roadster in the drive at such an angle that to pass it Paula was obliged to cut across a stretch of newly planted monastery grass. Upon entering her kitchen, Paula found that Hester, who should have finished the wax polishing and started tea, was still buzzing away upstairs. Edwinna—who might have taken over, since she knew the routine—was asininely, fatuously giving forth with song in her room. Little Alicia, untended, had executed on the terrazzo in the living room crayon work which would take hours to remove.

The child saw her grandmother as she opened the Kelvinator door to get a drink of cold water and came running to the kitchen in one of those elfin, tiptoe, eye-cutting moods that men love and women rightfully suspect. Before Paula could get back to the refrigerator door, Alicia had reached in, grabbed an open jar of jam, and dropped it.

Paula had a strong impulse to spank the little girl. She resisted. She was not a child swatter and it was not Alicia's fault that she was spoiled and meddlesome. It was her mother's. The faults of Edwinna, moreover, could be ascribed in the same way to Edwinna's parents. Paula felt guilty and sad.

She took a dustpan from the broom closet and a damp cloth from a hook. She began cleaning up the spattered jam and the broken glass. She wondered if spanking would improve Alicia: authorities differed on the matter—as they differed about everything concerning children. Paula also reflected on how much Alicia resembled Theodora at the same age. Theodora would be eighteen now—if there hadn't been a polio epidemic when she was six. For a moment, Paula thought of the child she and Bill had lost and she tried to imagine whether or not Theodora would have grown up to be difficult, like Edwinna.

Alicia meanwhile began trying to help and Paula smiled gently at her.

"It's a terrific mess," the child said.

"It sure is!"

"I'm hungry."

"Well, dear, I'll soon have tea ready. And there's more jam."

Edwinna pushed through the kitchen door so suddenly that it rapped Paula's knuckles. She rubbed them.

Edwinna was wearing a cocktail dress—a new one, of Paula's, which Paula had tried on only at the store. Edwinna's blonde hair was combed in its smooth, *femme fatale* zigzag, to a point that just touched the dihedral arch of her brows. Her dark eyes—eyes like her father's, but without their patience and repose—perceived the splashed preserves and shattered glass. The winged brows rose. But no apology came from her beautiful, crimsoned lips. She looked at her daughter with malice and said, "Poltergeist!"

"What's that?" Alicia asked.

Paula felt angry—and resigned. She had never been able to understand her daughter. And this was, in any case, one of those days. One of those days when you had to go to the dentist and the hairdresser and when you had to argue about a bill, spend an hour and a half with a tax accountant, give up a lunch appointment that would have been fun and eat a sandwich instead. On such days the mayonnaise in the lonely sandwich would be rancid—it had been— and the lettuce brown. On such days your daughter would help herself to your newest frock and bang your hand with the swinging door. Paula felt almost superstitious about "sequences."

The only thing to do was to stay calm. If you lost your temper you felt more miserable than before. They were all little things. Life was, alas, mostly little things. Occasionally she wished trifles would lump themselves together to make one big calamity—something worthy of her mettle. But she shied from that thought too: big troubles were just worse troubles. Not trouble but pettiness was the occasional bane of her days, excepting, of course, Edwinna. Adult, unsatisfactory offspring are tragic.

Edwinna, having rebuked her daughter by calling her a name, now pirouetted like a dancer. "How do you like your new dress?"

"I thought," Paula answered patiently, "you were going to stay home tonight? You said so—and Bill and I made a date to play bridge with the Claytons."

"They can come over here just as well, can't they?"

Paula sighed. "They wanted us to see their new slathouse. Bill's thinking of having one."

"I'll bet if Dad starts raising orchids, he wears 'em! I've seen men do it around here. In their lapels."

"Why shouldn't he?"

"Drippy—that's why." Edwinna's eyes narrowed. "Alicia! Get away from that spider! It might be a black widow!"

Paula rose, with the dustpan and the cloth. She looked. "It isn't —and why scare the child? It's a house spider. Don't—!"

She was too late. Edwinna had already crossed the room and set her smart sole on the frightened spider.

"They catch other insects," Paula murmured. "They're harmless. And we've never seen a black widow around here. Just on the Beach, at the other house."

"Oh, fiddle! How can a child tell a harmless spider? Alicia! Sit *down* somewhere! You make me nervous. Look, Paula. A perfectly darling-sounding man phoned me, earlier. A pal of Toby Newton. He asked me to go over to the Woods' for cocktails, and dinner afterward, at Ciro's." She scraped the dead spider from her shoe on the tile step that led down to the laundry. "I didn't have anything decent to wear—which brings up another point."

"Not *money*?"

"Yes, *money*! Charlie, that twerp, hasn't sent Alicia's monthly check yet. And Billy is behind, as usual. I haven't a cent."

It had never occurred to Edwinna that she could work. That

she was highly educated. That she had energy, youth and intelligence. That a twenty-six-year-old woman, twice married, twice divorced, with alimony from one man and child maintenance from the other, might—by the exercise of a little resourcefulness and from a sense of self-respect—make up any difference she wanted (she actually required no more money) by her own efforts.

"Do you realize, Edwinna, that Bill has to earn three dollars, these days, to keep one? And the one he keeps will only buy about half of what it used to."

"Is it my fault Dad's in the upper brackets? Should I cry?"

"What I mean is, the upper brackets aren't really upper any more. Didn't you ever feel *responsible* for yourself? For *anything*? *Anybody*? Do you actually believe that all a gal has to do is streamline her outside—so she looks like something built to attach to a plane —and from there on in it's the sole duty of the male sex to see that she has no wants? Do you really imagine that—"

"Mother!" When Edwinna used the word "mother," it meant that she did not care to hear any more. She was fed up. She looked at Paula thoughtfully, and shrugged one modish shoulder. "Mother," she repeated. "I mean *precisely* that! As long as I can get away with it. Why not? Was I consulted about being here? No! That was *your* idea—yours and Dad's. You had all the fun. And the social praise for having kids. *Twins*, even! Maybe all the virtues went into Edwin and I got what was left over. Anyhow—it *wasn't* my idea to start with. And I *don't* have a good opinion of this world. The men I marry in it go soft and jittery, like Charlie—or mean, like Billy. I did not make the world, or the men here, or choose to be here. So I feel entitled to do what I can to compensate."

"That's certainly one beautiful—"

"—philosophy. I know. Or is it just—not kidding yourself? Have *you* had such a wonderful life?"

"Yes, I have. With certain exceptions—"

"Phooie! Twenty years of hard studying to learn a lot of things you've never used. Twenty-seven years of being Dr. Gaunt's house-keeper and errand boy. An M.A. and a Ph.D. in languages—and all you do is write grocery lists in plain English and add drugstore bills and count dirty clothes. That—definitely—is not for your Edwinna. Look. I need dough and the point is—will you give me some—or do I have to bust in on Dad?"

"I'll give you some," Paula said. Her face was pale; her eyes were indignant. She would have to explain later, to Bill, and he would be annoyed—at her. But not so annoyed as he would have been if Edwinna had interrupted his work. Paula opened her pocketbook, which lay on one of the stainless-steel counters, and took out two twenty-dollar bills.

"Is that it?" Edwinna asked.

"That's all there is."

Edwinna said, "Thanks," and started toward the living room.

"You better take Alicia along," Paula said, "because I'm going outdoors. She made some crayon marks on the terrazzo. Maybe you'll start rubbing them out. On second thought—leave them. It's my dress you're wearing."

The tall, blonde girl whistled at her child as if she were a pup and took her hand. "Come along, dear. Mummie'll tell you some stories about wolves."

In the sun, outside, Paula trudged along. "Damn, damn, damn!" she muttered. Edwinna didn't *care*—and when people didn't care, you had no means of moving them, influencing them, reaching them. She'd been that way even as a child: stony, emotionless and often cruel. *Why?* Envy of her twin because he was a boy? Sibling rivalry? Paula dismissed that up-to-date idea with irritation. Somewhere inside Edwinna there was a person with courage and brains—lost under layers of hardness, of selfishness, of pleasure seeking, of contempt for everything and everybody. A swell person nobody would ever meet —in this world.

Paula picked yellow leaves from the solanum vines.

The local anesthetic had been absorbed and her tooth ached where the drill had bitten deep. Her knuckles still ached, too, from the door swung open without warning. She walked around the house and saw that Byron had failed to follow her instructions concerning the gardenia; it was wilted at the tips and soon the buds would begin dropping. He'd put in some stones to hold the peat moss—too many—but he hadn't watered the plant at all.

She went to work.

What did we do wrong? She asked herself the question sorrowfully—as parents have asked it through the ages. Her answer was Edwinna's recommencement of the "Italian Street Song": a mocking answer. Edwinna thought she could sing; she thought she could have been trained as a coloratura; she was like a million other girls who had good looks and who, owing to that accident, considered their potentialities unlimited. A dope.

Paula shook her head and thrust her hand into the peat moss to speed the wetting of the roots. She glanced at Bill's windows and saw his silhouette. She wanted—she needed—his solace. A wretched day —the wretcheder because its miseries were mostly trivial. She was impelled toward her husband; but he was working. He wouldn't like being interrupted by a sobby wife whos tears were caused by nothing new and nothing important and nothing that could be remedied. She pulled herself together with a strength she invariably summoned when things reached this low pitch. *Typically feminine,* she said furiously to herself, and it helped.

But if Bill looks out, she thought, I'll wave. And maybe he'll come and talk; we've spent years talking about Edwinna to no purpose—but, at least—it's better to share the shambles.

And she thought, with another momentary sag of her spirit, that the bright sun would certainly reveal the change in the shade of her hair—if Bill did look. She fought through a panicky instant of wanting to run away. It was replaced by a sudden assurance. Probably Bill had always known about the dye. Probably he understood, exactly, why pride and middle-aged anxiety made her try to keep it a secret. Probably he wouldn't think it vulgar—funny, perhaps; or wistful.

For, after all, he loved her. She was sure of that.

Very sure and very much comforted. She gazed toward Bill again, ready to give a cheerful salute and a smile if he noticed her.

While she looked, Bill disappeared.

Paula ran into the house.

He was gone, all right.

Edwinna was sitting on the porch, still singing, watching Alicia patter about and waiting, in a false "sweet-mother-wife" pose, for her blind date to arrive.

Paula came out of the study and asked in a thin voice, "Did Bill leave his room?"

"No."

"That's what I thought! He just vanished!"

"Did you look in his bathroom?"

"Of course."

"Well—he didn't come out—I've been here. And there's only one door. So probably he simply evaporated."

"Yes. That's what he did."

Now Edwinna looked up. "Mother. You're pale as a *ghost!*"

Paula leaned against the edge of the maple-topped table where her collection of potted plants bloomed gaudily. "He must have thought of something, after all! He must have made some *discovery!* He must have *been* thinking, after all! Though it's more the sort of thing Jim Elliot would do . . .!" She ran back through the study door and tensely addressed the empty room while Edwinna, and then Alicia came to watch.

"Bill!" she whispered. "Bill *darling!* Come *back!* Or say something!"

Edwinna shook her mother. "Snap out of it!"

From beyond the lawn, beyond the palmettos and the tall Caribbean pines, came a tremendous crash.

Both women immediately rushed to the windows and peered through slats of the Venetian blinds. A power pole several hundred yards away slowly fell over, bringing wires with it and causing a blue flash and a soft explosion. Smoke, then flames, sprang up at the base of the pole from the wreck of the car or truck that had hit it. Palmettos prevented them from seeing the vehicle.

"Somebody's been hurt!" Edwinna started to run.

"Wait!" Paula yelled upstairs. "Hester! Stop waxing and take care of Alicia! There's been a car smash!" She turned to her daughter. "Bring the fire extinguisher from the guest-room closet. I'll get the two in the car porte! We'll go in your car—since you blocked the turning place!"

Within a minute they were on the way. Paula raced down the curving drive in first gear; she shifted to second as she shot along the bough-tunneled street; she shifted again, stepped on the accelerator for a moment, and braked hard to turn into a shortcut bulldozed through the Gaunt palmetto land. She emerged on a straight, white coral street lined with pines. On her left was Teddy Barker's bungalow—on her right a blazing car, its staved nose hard against the stump of the fallen pole. Paula leaped out and directed a white stream from the extinguisher on the fire.

"You might get killed!" Edwinna said frantically. "Short circuit!"

"This stuff is a nonconductor. When mine's out, gimme yours."

Edwinna did so and stood by until her mother effectively put out the fire. "We've got to get the doors open," she said, "and the people out."

"What people? Nobody's in it!"

The younger woman ventured nearer the smoking, hissing wreck. She looked. "That's a fact! Somebody must have left it in gear, and it must have started up—by itself."

Paula put down the fire extinguisher and looked at her daughter with an expression of interested disapproval. "Is that what you think?

Then why didn't Teddy Barker come over? He's home. His car's in his garage."

Edwinna turned, stared at the bungalow, noted the car, and shrugged. "That Lothario! Probably he has company."

"And where was Byron when we drove past?"

"Probably lying in the weeds, sleeping. I've seen him do it before now."

"Then—why hasn't anybody come? You could hear that crash a mile!"

"Somebody is," Edwinna answered. "Your pal Katie."

Kate West was, indeed, running from her home farther up the coral street. As she ran, one of her long, black braids fell from a none-too-secure hairdo. She didn't try to put it back. She called, "Oh, Paula! Thank heaven, you got here! I heard it and I was scared to look. Is anybody killed?"

"The car was empty, ninny!" Edwinna yelled back.

"I phoned the police right away. The line was busy! Then I saw the blaze start up and I dialed the South Miami Fire Department and *it* was busy! Then I tried the County Fire Department— and *they* were busy! I was simply beside myself! And in the midst of that, George had to go and disappear! He'd been playing in the yard—and he's wandered off! Oh, *dear!*"

Kate's dark-blue eyes rested on Paula, waiting direction, comfort. She held the fallen braid in her hand and bit the end of it, as no doubt she had done in times of stress when she was a much younger girl and had worn braids down her back.

She still looked, Paula thought, like a kid—not a wife and mother. Like a sixteen-year-old—a plump, implausible facsimile of feminine maturity—frightened, appealing, hoping she'd done the right thing. Her eyes were worried. In shorts, with her tumbled, Indianlike hair, Kate was wholly out of place on a street in a city at the instant of unguessable (no, guessable) cataclysm. A bonfire at some teen-age girl's camp where everybody was a little shuddery as ghost stories were told—that would be fitting for Kate.

Paula had always felt maternal toward her young neighbor. Now the feeling overwhelmed her and she wanted very much to soothe Kate. But she didn't know what to say. She didn't even know, precisely, what it was that she felt—or felt most.

The three women stood there for a matter of seconds—Kate panting, Edwinna frowning slightly over the discovery that she had extinguisher fluid on her dress. (Paula's dress, thank the lord!)

"All the lines were busy," Kate repeated in an anxious, apologetic tone. "I couldn't *bring* myself down here till you came! Blood makes me sick—and people *burning* . . . !" she shivered.

"Never mind," Paula answered. "You did the best you could. Lots of girls wouldn't even have tried to get the fire engine, or cops."

The very blue eyes were grateful. "I've got to find Georgie, now. You'll pardon me . . ."

"We'll help you look," Paula said. "But I'm afraid . . ."

From far away came the roar of a great explosion. Black smoke, inflamed at its heart, bulged into the sky. While they watched, not speaking, a smaller explosion occurred near Cocoplum Plaza and smoke rose from that place also.

Then at last another person appeared. It was Bella Elliot and she came down Forty-seventh Court in the green shade, slowly. She was weeping. In her arms she carried young Sarah; she kept patting the child. She did not seem to have noticed the heavy blast in the distance or the smaller, nearer explosion. When she recognized the three women she smiled, because she always smiled when she first encountered people she knew.

"A thing has happened," she said, almost as if she were reciting a piece, "that I don't know how to stand. Jim's gone—on one of those astral voyages—only he went bodily this time and he took Gordon along. I saw them. They were in the yard together, though Jim couldn't see me. I was watering the poinsettia. And they went before my eyes—just in a flash! Completely."

"I know . . ." Paula murmured.

Bella didn't hear, or notice, or stop talking. "I've always worried about the—thoughts—Jim has. And the cults and things he investigates. But I've always felt too—like your Bill, Paula—that they were mostly in his imagination. He was only interested because he wanted to know all the truth and because he wanted to be sure he was being as *good* a man as possible! As if there could be any better! But he went away—with Gordon."

Kate murmured, "My Georgie . . . !"

Edwinna interrupted coldly. "I've got a date who's due any minute! And I've got to change, since we had to put out this fire. Paula—that was *your* idea—the old Girl Scout emerging!—and if it's ruined your dress you can blame yourself! And I hope you'll get over this crazy idea that Dad and Mr. Elliot have vanished off the earth, by the time I come home again!"

She walked over to the convertible.

She didn't ask the others if they wanted a lift. She simply backed, cut the wheels hard, and drove home.

Kate looked with increased fright at Bella and at Paula, again murmured the name of her one child, and turned toward her house.

Paula crossed to a dip in the concrete-topped coral wall around Teddy Barker's garden. She pushed herself up on it with the heels of her hands. She took Sarah from Bella and set the child on the wall. "They're *all* gone, I think," she said. "*All* the men."

The younger woman shook her head. "Just Jim—and Gordon."

"Bill too. I was looking right at him—the way you were. Byron's missing. Then, there was nobody in the car that crashed. It must have been going along, and run pretty straight for quite a ways after the driver—went. In the ruts. Then hit. And Georgie's missing too. And Teddy's car is here and he never walks anywhere if he can avoid it, except golf—but he didn't come out when the accident happened. Then you. And of course the explosions."

"You aren't making any sense, Paula! Do you know that?"

"Were you?" Paula shook her head. "Bill would have figured it out in a split second. It took me—a little time." Her voice was steady, reasoning, patient with its owner. "Things *would* blow up, after all, wouldn't they? Things men were doing that had to be watched. Like filling a truck with high-test gasoline. The only question is, how much area does it cover? No! There's another. *What* happened?"

"I told you . . ."

The redheaded woman spoke sharply. "Listen, Bella. *Listen.* What happened to your Jim and your Gordon happened to my Bill and it has evidently happened to lots of other men and boys around here. Now let's go back to your house or my house and turn on the radio."

When they did—when they had walked down the lane and through the hibiscus hedge and put Sarah back in her playpen— when they had switched on the radio under the begonia in the kitchen where the evening's stew simmered, they heard no meaningful sound. No music, no commercial, no voice.

"That car," Bella said, still fixedly. "The pole, switch it to the battery."

Paula shook her head, but complied. The radio still was mute. "Try a light."

The other woman snapped a switch. Lights went on. She cut them off. "What is it, then?"

"The engineers," Paula whispered. "They're all men, so far as I know. Without them, they can't broadcast, can they? Women?"

"You mean—men *everywhere*—just—" Bella gestured.

"Around here, anyway."

"Maybe they'll be back—in a minute."

"I don't feel as if they would."

"What'll we *do*?"

"God knows," Paula replied. "Put out fires, tonight, probably—if we can. Hunt for women who can run power plants and things like that. There can't be many!"

Bella tried to smile again. Her wide, mobile mouth turned up at the corners. The vestige of a familiar radiance came into her eyes. "Maybe it's only a dream."

"Or maybe life until now was."

"Maybe . . ."

"What?"

Bella shook her shiny brown head and began to cry.

Tears filled Paula's eyes. By-and-by she spoke again. "You stay here with Sarah. I'll walk over to Sunset Boulevard and see what it's like there. Perhaps I can find out something."

"Do you really think it's real?" Bella's voice wept the words.

Paula asked a question that her philosopher husband had not so immediately and usefully put to himself: "Maybe not, but what use is it to believe anything else?"

"Could it be something the Russians have done?"

Paula was momentarily startled. "I don't believe so." She pondered and shook her head. "It's more like something—"

"Something *what*?"

"God did. Though I never believed in that kind of God."

"A cruel one?"

"One who'd violate natural laws. But of course we don't know all the laws. Perhaps not even many of them."

"I feel so utterly helpless."

"Maybe that's the idea." Paula's voice now had a grim edge. "Maybe we always were. Maybe we just stopped being aware of the fact."

"Don't go, Paula!"

"I'll be back soon. If you want, you could call people we know. The dials are probably still working."

"I will! Everybody!"

A few minutes later Paula stood at the point where her street emerged from the Australian pines, the cabbage palms and the strangler figs to join the wide boulevard. She saw several cars in the distance, on lawns, crashed into houses, or piled up against trees. Around one, women were bending over a prone figure. Farther away, an unidentifiable house was burning. There was no fire engine and no crowd. As she stood, cars screamed crazily past. All were driven by girls and women; all the drivers were pale and possessed with an emotion that made their eyes glitter. Horror. Hysteria. Panic.

She walked back rapidly to her drive and up to the house.

Edwinna, in a red silk print—her own—was pacing the porch. "That jerk!" she said. "He's an hour late!" She shook her smooth shoulders angrily. "Mother, for heaven's *sake* stop going around as if you'd seen spooks!"

Paula found that she wanted to laugh. But she was afraid that if she laughed a little she would laugh too much. "Your date," she said, "isn't coming. Not now. Listen, Edwinna. You've always been difficult to instruct. But maybe you can learn this one thing." She set forth calmly, almost monotonously, the relevant sights and events of the past hour. "So you see, darling, your date probably won't arrive. Maybe you'll *never* have another date. The men—even the boys—are gone."

"That," said the daughter, "is utterly unthinkable!"

"As your father used to say, Edwinna, it is only the unthinking mind that finds anything unthinkable. To use the word is just to show your membership card in the society of morons."

"It can't be *everywhere*," Edwinna said, making a concession against her instincts.

"I was going to try to find out," Paula replied.

She went to the hall, picked up the phone and dialed. She waited for minutes, lighting a cigarette with one hand, her elbow on the packet of matches. She wondered how long cigarettes would last.

Finally she said in a swift tone, "Long Distance? I want to call New York." She waited and Edwinna, at last in a state of cogent emotion, waited queasily beside her. Paula said, "Yes? . . . . . Are they? . . . . . Is it? . . . . . Thanks." She hung up. She breathed out smoke. "According to Long Distance—the circuits are jammed now— but the men vanished in New York too, and in every other city they can reach. They can't reach many, because the wires are down in most places. They found out by radiophone."

"How could she just calmly sit there—?" Edwinna asked in a raging tone.

"The operator? Habit. Training. She's telling people—as fast as they decide to make calls on Long Distance."

Edwinna's hysterics began suddenly. She screamed that if it was true and there were no men she would kill herself. She ran from the hall. She grabbed up Alicia and shook the child, bawling into her face that her daddy was dead and everybody's daddy. Paula reached her at that point, hit her as hard as she could with an open palm, caught the relinquished, appalled three-year-old, and sat down, holding Alicia until she stopped howling.

The sun went lower.

Edwinna sat quivering in a porch chair for five minutes. Then she left for a moment and returned with a glass and a bottle of whisky.

Paula looked at her. "That's the first sensible idea you've had all day. And it's only half an idea, at that."

The younger woman was crestfallen. "Oh, mother!" she said. She started out for another glass, halted, poured a drink in the one she had brought, handed it to Paula, and left. When she came back, tears had streaked her mascara and she was sobbing, very softly, at long intervals.

Paula gazed at her with a kindness she had not shown Edwinna that day. Sip by sip, while she watched her daughter weep, she finished her drink. She kept patting Alicia and murmuring to her. And she wondered, while she did these things, what had really happened, and why, and whether or not she had acted sensibly from minute to minute, in view of what appeared to have occurred.

She couldn't be sure.

But who could be?

3

A PHILOSOPHER IN A QUANDARY—A CITY IN DESPAIR.

Before the Disappearance, persons who called themselves intelligent and were generally presumed so to be would doubtless have imagined that any such event would throw the world into instant and permanent chaos. But the very limitations of persons regarded as intelligent by Western society (or by the Orient, for that matter), along with the unprecedented nature of the phenomenon, produced other and different results from those which even the most informed might have anticipated.

There was panic, to be sure, in abundance—catastrophe upon catastrophe, murder and arson and insurrection. Looting became a way of life for multitudes. Entire nations (small ones) fell prey to a variety of ritualistic hysterias. But in some larger, better organized societies the shock was partly counterbalanced by habitude, and the very frightfulness of what had happened stunned millions into a sort of awed supernormalcy. The further fact that it was not what had been fearfully anticipated prevented other myriads from behaving in the ultraterrible way they had subconsciously expected to behave in, following the detonation of the first atomic bombs.

The Disappearance also precipitated such a multitude of alarms and emergencies, which required swift action for the mere preservation of life, that nearly every man, as William Gaunt and his neighbors were soon to discover, was soon busied to the point of exhaustion.

At first, however, Gaunt continued to act from the inertia of his own personality and from private habit—as did innumerable other persons. The fact that so many did just that, preserved, through the early hours of crisis, a skeleton of familiar organization and behavior.

Firemen, although they could not immediately deal with all the sudden fires that ensued upon the vanishing of the women, went hooting and clanging to such fires as they could. The operators of "wreckers" rushed hither and thither through landscapes of smashed cars, setting back on the road whatever vehicles were usable and hauling others to repair shops. Emergency crews, frightened like all men about their loved ones, nevertheless hurtled to the nearest points of disaster and commenced to string new lines on telegraph poles, mend bridges, shut off gas mains, and the like. Habit, indeed, influenced even the most highly placed persons. It was later reported that the first question asked by the President of his hastily assembled Cabinet concerned the possible effect of the absence of all women upon the next elections.

Professors and teachers, in many cases, continued to hold (if not to instruct) classes suddenly and incomprehensibly reduced. Surgeons, inexplicably bereft of nurses, went on as best they could with operations. Ordinary laymen turned from the inexplicable to the salvage of boy babies who had been dropped onto floors and bare earth, down flights of stairs or into fishponds. The news reached embattled troops. Firing ceased on the earth's face. Guerrillas fraternized with the enemy. Soldiers straggled from the line.

Gaunt, naturally enough, at first philosophized.

He walked up his drive, forgetting it was his intention to check his house for incipient perils. Unconsciously, he may have noted the absence of smoke or of ominous electrical humming and so dismissed that errand altogether. Certainly he was aware that a sense of tragedy and loss would sooner or later overwhelm him. But he was even more aware (at that point) of his possession of a mind both potent and unique and of the duty to bring it to bear upon the problem.

Characteristically, he went to his study and, characteristically, he determined to jot down his thoughts in the form of notes. Tens, hundreds of thousands began diaries soon after the Disappearance and regular diary keepers continued to make their routine entries. But it is quite possible that Gaunt was the first man of all to do so after what the radio announcer had repeatedly called, in a fatuous, quasi-military fashion, "four-oh-five."

At five-oh-five, or thereabouts, in his bold, tidy hand, Gaunt set down a fairly detailed description of the events to which he had just been witness and of his impressions. At some time after six, aware that the room had grown quite dark, he turned in his chair and switched on the lamp behind his back. The fact that it lighted and that its steady glow meant many things (such as, that the power plant in Cutler was operating and that the lines between his residence and the plant either had not been knocked down or had been repaired) never entered his head. He took the light for granted—at the moment. He was focusing the full powers of his mind elsewhere.

He had selected, to write in, a large "dummy" of blank pages bound in leather like a book—a handsome affair, a gift from the dean of Wake Forest College which Gaunt had saved for some special writing occasion. On the page he had numbered 16, he wrote: "Hypotheses."

He sat awhile.

He underlined the word—and sat again, scowling. Finally, swiftly, he set down the following:

A) A nightmare. Objection: I respond to every test for being awake.

B) Insanity. Objection: None—in fact. No man can test himself for sanity. Intellectually plausible but emotionally unacceptable.

C) Mass hypnosis—mass, posthypnotic suggestion, and so forth. Objections: No hypnotist has ever been successful with the whole of any audience, even a small one; no person, group, or entity known on earth has access to everybody—I, for instance, have not listened to radio until this day for weeks, rarely read a paper, and so on; if the force of *mind* is here involved, it can hardly be *human* mentality.

D) Enemy action. Objections: Those above; also—what point, if "enemy's" own females also have vanished? If not, why did their radios cease, their women broadcasters fall silent at the critical moment?

E) A space-time, i.e., "physical" phenomenon. Objection: Again, none. Quién sabe? Certain legends, Rider Haggard's *She,* William Sloane's *To Walk the Night,* suggest imaginatively a bizarre connection between the conscious (or unconscious) entity of *femaleness* with mathematics, space, time, and the mystery involving these. No scientific material exists in respect to either the legends or the fiction.

F) Lysistrata. A trick, that is, learned by and disseminated amongst women to bring to heel the currently idiotic activities of men. Objection: Tenable as an idea but beyond the capacity of women to agree upon, to keep secret, and to perform unanimously and simultaneously.

G) Precedent, i.e., Elliot's "Laecocidiaean women." Objection: Never heard of them—or King Lestentum. More of Elliot's probing into pseudo history, myth, intellectual balderdash.

H) God. *Well?*

Gaunt set the journal aside. Having got to that point, he felt for the moment that he could carry theorizing no further. He went out of his study, across his porch and onto his lawn.

The night was clear with a tuft of cloud here and there. There was no moon. The stars, as they so often did on warm Miami evenings, held perfectly still without sign of shimmer, so that it was as if they were all planets; Sirius, which was high, could not be told from

Mars, which would rise later, save that Sirius was bluish and Mars would seem reddish. Gaunt looked up at the stars for some minutes, thinking about God.

Many times in the past five years he had also looked at the great, round rock of the moon with the thought that the earth might soon resemble it—or looked at the remote, secretive stars with the idea that the earth might soon blaze as they did. In the midst of such reflections he had often wondered if God—if *any* Consciousness in Universe—would be disappointed over the collapse of so interesting and nearly successful an experiment as that of Life on Earth.

Probably not. Probably, if there were more Awareness in Cosmos than man owned (instead of, as Gaunt sometimes suspected, only colonies of such consciousness as man and his animal antecedents had painfully brought into being), that Vast Awareness, having tried Life under terrestrial conditions, would decide (if Life exterminated itself) that the local conditions had been wrong. An atomic dissolution of the earth would then be merely a short cut to a new mixture. Man, or other life forms that might be waiting to supersede him, did not matter. It would always be what Life became aware of, and what Life did owing to such awareness, that mattered. Man unco-operative, afraid, hateful, suicidal, was, after all, death-incipient. If the trend went too far that way, human hope was vanity. The wisest hope in such a case was for a recooled planet and new germ plasm, to try it all over in a new two or three billions of years.

Now his thoughts ran parallel but were of different content. He paced his deep lawn, smelled the opened jasmine and heard unheeding the early call of a chuck-will's-widow.

Perhaps the masses, the energies, the light years overhead (and underfoot and all about) could *intervene* when some valuable experiment went awry. And perhaps such intervention would be as strange as this one.

He had pocketed his spectacles in order the better to look at the stars, and like a boy who is about to enter a classroom or to walk up on a platform to receive a prize, he carefully smoothed his thin, undistinguished hair. With just such embarrassment, he pinched his long nose, tweaked it, pulled it. But finally, with reluctance and in humility, he knelt. He did not pray. He did not even shut his eyes. Instead—a minute node in the presence of the stars, the illumined engines of infinity—Gaunt looked almost straight up—at things that might not be there, things the very light whereof had left them thousands of centuries before—and said, "I hope so."

He hoped, he meant to signify, in all his inconsequentiality, that what lay about him was concerned a little with him and with the planet that was inhabited by others like himself.

The expression relieved him.

It was as close to prayer as he'd come since adolescence. It was, he felt, such an expression—and only such—that men of honesty had any right to utter: not even Faith, but only Hope; and Hope in the mere unknown and undiscovered, the undefined and the uncomprehended. To imagine one's self made loftier or more knowing by any "Faith" was, Gaunt believed, the stuff of Original Sin itself.

A racket broke off this effort at communion.

Gaunt stood.

A gray car, unknown to him, jolted toward the house, missing the driveway turns. It slid to a stop, its bumper buried in Paula's solanum, inches from the brick wall on which the vine grew. Out leaped a man, and the breadth of his shoulders in the gloom, the easy gait with which he ran, identified him as Teddy Barker before he called, "Bill! You here?"

"Out in front."

"Horrible thing happened to me! Horrible! Don't know what to make of it! Came straight to you and Paula—cleverest people I know!" These words issued from Teddy as he rushed up the walk, through one screen door of the porch, out the other, and onto the lawn. They were spoken loudly, with a nervous punctuation between them, a giggling. The accent was that of a well-bred Easterner, an affected

quasi-British. He held out his hand, which Gaunt first shook and
then used as a lever to turn him back toward the house. They sat
down together on the porch; the older man switched on a lamp.
"Well, tell me about it. Paula's not here, though. Didn't you know
. . . ?" His voice trailed off. Evidently Teddy did not know.

The younger man—Barker was thirty-six—looked, in the lamplight, like that prototype of manly handsomeness, of groomed virility,
of go-getting geniality, for which magazine illustrators strive and
which is realized more often in full-color, full-page advertisements of
such luxury goods and services as yachts, round-the-world tours, dude-
ranch vacations and expensive dinner clothes. Deep-chested, broad-
shouldered, tanned—in all but flagrant "good condition"—he had the
guileless but direct blue eyes, the bronze, cropped, curly hair, the
prominent chin, a boyishness belied by a baritone voice, the immaculate profile and even that slightly characterless aspect which prevents magazine readers from discovering in the pictured males traces
of individuality that might be identified unfavorably with real persons and so reflect upon the illustrated story or the advertised product.

Gaunt stared at him and he had ample opportunity to do so for
Barker was busy with pipe lighting—taking his time, while, apparently, he decided how, or whether, to go on with his tale.

Gaunt thought with an inner smile that Teddy was what another generation would have called a cad: broker, bachelor, a former
backfield man at Dartmouth, a customers' man—a ladies' man above
all else—perennial fourth at bridge and an eternal third in countless
triangles, whispered about but never quite becoming the subject of
open scandal. Never, Gaunt knew, because husbands had long since
come to regard Teddy as the nearest thing to harmlessness in the wide
range of wifely harm. His sins had a juvenile innocence about them;
they partook of the nature of misplaced good deeds. Besides, they
were so numerous and evanescent that the involved ladies, flattered
but rarely overwhelmed, regarded their own part as mere indulgences
—like new, unneeded (but pretty) frocks. Furthermore, for various

married males, Teddy had supplied the unspoken *quid pro quo* which eased hidden matrimonial tensions in matters of night-club blondes, tailored secretaries, others among the selfsame wives, and less reputable young ladies too.

There was, Gaunt next reflected, a Teddy Barker in every sizable social "set" and in nearly every country club, simply because the handsomest philanderer in each became accepted as the facsimile. That, in turn, implied several things, such as a general need, the immaturity of a society that could turn out innumerable Teddys to supply the immature need, the divergence between code and conduct, and so on. The special appreciation Teddy showed for attractive women past thirty, and chic ones past forty, added to his unspoken but acknowledged value. It could also be construed, the philosopher went on to himself (noting the pipe was at last in full, cherry-red bloom), as evidence that Teddy's libido was oriented toward the unconscious memory of his mother, though to have told Teddy that would have been to invite a knockdown, if the teller were virile enough, and ending of all friendship, even if not.

Gaunt wondered why he and Paula had found Teddy likable and seen much of him. Not because they were neighbors—the friendship had begun long before. But because, most likely, in his own way Teddy was sincerity itself. He played his part, stuck to his code, and imagined himself the soul of chivalry and romance; he was invariably good-tempered and kind and possibly had saved many worth-while marriages certainly without ruining one. He amused Paula, and if he sometimes bored Gaunt, that was a matter of degree only—for most persons sometimes bored Gaunt owing, he felt, to the fact that where his main interests lay—in speculative philosophy—few persons any place (and almost none in Miami) were capable of conversing. Teddy amused Paula and therefore pleased Gaunt. She'd always had a sisterly feeling about him—advised him in his quandaries and helped him redecorate his bungalow after the Gaunts had built their new home across the palmettos and pines.

It was time for Barker to speak. "I'll tell you what happened—
what I think happened. I've made up my mind to—though I never
did such a thing before. In confidence, understand."

"Of course."

"You know Myra, Mrs. Jay McCantley?"

Gaunt felt a slight shock. Surely Myra, for all her serene allure,
was above reproach! Surely a superficial chap like Barker would not
interest her! His mind's eye conjured her up in many situations—on
platforms, at banquet tables, in booths at charitable bazaars: pale brow,
pale skin, pale-amber eyes, and long ash-blonde hair knotted heavily
at the nape of her neck. Her husband—banker, church warden, civic
leader—always at her side. And the four children too—particularly in
the annual Sunday newspaper features about "Miami leaders" which
generally started off with the McCantleys, their Spanish-type home
on the Bay, their offspring and their good works. Gaunt thought all
that—and nodded.

Teddy now took his pipe from his even, polished teeth and
looked at its bowl. Very male, very diffident, very—pseudo sensitive,
Gaunt thought. *An act.*

"You're a man of the world," Teddy said.

Few would deny that label and certainly not Gaunt. He smiled
as (he noted with self-annoyance) a man of the world should smile,
and nodded a second time.

Teddy smoked again. "A bachelor—gets about."

"Why not?"

"And—it gets around that—he gets around." Teddy chuckled at
that little joke of phrase.

"Bound to."

"There are some women—mature, sophisticated from the—well
—the bookish standpoint—whose lives are pretty—bleak. Tame.
Maybe merely a touch too monotonous." Teddy, as he talked, became
calmer. It was the subject most familiar to his thoughts—with the possible exception of stock quotations. "Such women are sometimes at-

tracted to the type of man I just referred to. One who—gets around."

"Why not?"

"The point is"— Teddy hesitated—"they rather go after them, at times. In a snooty way, of course—no matter how badly they get the old burn on."

Gaunt felt impelled, from a sense of his admiration of Myra, to better that banal description. "You mean, they reach that point in wisdom and experience at which their imaginations become active— that point, after completing their major duties as wives and mothers, at which a certain private indulgence seems not unworthy? And if they happen to meet a suitably appealing male, who is unattached and available, they're not above giving him a sense of their feelings?"

Teddy beamed. "*Right!* What I was trying to say! Anyhow— not long ago—bridge-tea at the Island Harbor Yacht Club—Myra asked me to take a turn down the dock to talk over plans for the St. Patrick's Day party—and I suddenly realized she was—well—she put her hand in mine and—wiggled her fingers. You know. I won't say I wasn't surprised. The statuesque type—one worships them from afar. I was on the dubious side—even me." Teddy paused, flushed faintly and went on. "Looked at her—and you could see it. There we were, leaning against a blob of pilings—wind blowing, Bay blue, people all over the lawn and veranda behind us—and Myra with her fingers in my hand, looking at me—the *way*. Do you know what?"

"What?" Gaunt asked, feeling depressed by the story.

"Women like that, leaders, women used to commanding—are sometimes terribly direct, Bill. Most exciting! She simply said, 'Yes?' in an asking way and I said, 'Wonderful,' or something of that sort. She said it would have to be very very hushy because her husband's a Texan, for one thing, and her reputation couldn't even have the old breath of what-not on it. She had one friend she trusted, gal we both know who'll be nameless. Cute apartment. I thought of the idea of driving home—to seem to be at home—and sneaking out through the hedge and using a rented car—the one in your drive—myself."

Gaunt, who had known approximately what was coming, now knew precisely. "I see."

The younger man sucked on his pipe. "Might as well fess up. Today was one of the days." He smiled candidly, delightedly. "What a woman! Used the old beauty parlor stall—it's about the best—"

"I'm afraid I'm unfamiliar with it."

"Ye gods!" Teddy chortled. "A husband—unfamiliar with *that* one! Lookee, Bill! A woman can spend three-four hours in one of those superbeauty parlors. Right? Hair, nails, massage, steam bath, reducing exercises, the works. Or, she can get things fixed up in an hour, with a bevy of minions fussing on her at once. But can you tell—can anybody tell—whether she put in one hour or four? No. And that gives the dolls three good hours, not even 'shopping'—where they might get crossed up because some catty pal wouldn't have seen them where they said they were. In a place like the Salon of Youth, in the Gables, for instance, a girl gets privacy from the minute she goes in. Cubicles. No checking up possible. See?"

Gaunt saw. He was a little weary with the detail. "You and Myra then, were in the cute apartment of the nameless friend at four this afternoon, and she disappeared."

Teddy leaped to his feet. "Good God, man! You *know!*"

"I suspected."

"But—how? What happened? I've been going nuts! Stark nuts! The thing was simply impossible! If I'd been in another room—well— they run out sometimes. If I had even been dozing—well—one does. If—well, to put it absolutely on the line—"

"Very embarrassing!"

"*Embarrassing!* Look here, Bill! I've shot grizzlies! I've roped mountain lions with ranch pals! I flew a P-38 all over Europe when we moved across France. I've been shot down in flames. Bailed out right into an alley, not a scratch, café a block away and a pretty waitress, as I've told you. I *think,* I mean, I've always known what it is to be scared. But never *that* scared! There I was—

"I can clearly imagine." Gaunt sought to avoid further confession.

"You can't possibly imagine!" Memory had started Teddy's shakes again. Glowing coals and dottle spilled from his pipe. "There she was. I mean—there we were. We couldn't have been more there. She even just—well—put all that ash-blonde hair over us both. And then . . ."

"Gone."

"Gone," Teddy whispered. "Gone," he repeated hoarsely. "I thought I'd had some lapse of the brain. Maybe fainted a minute. Got up pronto and looked. Called—not loud enough to attract anybody. Purse was there. Clothes there. No Myra. Seemed impossible. Still does."

There was, Gaunt felt at that moment, a good deal of justice in the predicament. Yet, while he noted its ironical merits, he could still sympathize with the other man. "What did you do?"

"I waited. What the devil else could I do? Helena . . . There! I've spilled that! Too damned upset! Well—Helena was due back at five-thirty. The apartment house has six floors and I was on the third. Fire escapes at the end of the hall. Elevators—automatic—two of 'em. I whipped into the old gabardines, stashed away the purse and clothes—and sat around. Figured even if I'd conked out for a sec, she'd hardly run down the fire escape or use the elevators—skinny, like that."

"Skinny?"

"In the buff, old fellow. The *au naturel*. Myra is a levelheaded dame, if anything. And really something, for forty-two she admits and four more I know about—and four kids besides. That milk-white skin —and a figure like the best in the old Metropolitan Museum of Art! Anyway, I stashed things—and sat—and stewed. Had a drink. Went to the bathroom and looked myself over—thought possibly somebody had sneaked in, socked me on the beezer, and shanghaied Myra. Somebody such as her husband. But no lump on the Barker bean.

Thought maybe the drinks we'd had when she got there were
Mickeys. But no head, no thick taste, no aftereffect. And the worst
thing—so far as I could figure, if I was out, it only lasted a minute or
two. Because we'd been talking about what time it was—just before—"

"I'm not surprised," Gaunt said.

Teddy's voice was thunderstruck. "You're—not—*surprised!*"

"No. All the women vanished at four-five this afternoon."

"You're kidding."

"No."

Teddy sat down. His frown was convincing to the extent that it
indicated an immense effort to think, if not actual thought. "I don't
get it."

"That was four o'clock. It's nearly seven now. What did you do
in between?"

"I told you. Fizzled around the apartment. Decided to wait till
Helena came back. She never did. By six o'clock or so, I was nuts.
I put Myra's things in one of Helena's bags and scrammed. Got in
the rented car. Drove out over a few back roads—wanting to cogitate.
Decided to come over here—finally—since this seemed like something
that needed a pile of gray matter and a lot of the kind of cautious
finding out that Paula's so good at."

"I suppose she is."

"Paula?" Teddy stared at his host. "You should know! At in-
trigue, that girl makes old Machiavelli look like a first-time canasta
player!" He shook his head. He paced. He sat down. "I tried parking
and applying the noodle. No dice, as I said. So I came here. Back
roads most of the way—felt like keeping out of sight, somehow. Nearly
got held up once, though. Been an accident. Can't figure it." Suddenly his voice rose. "You *mean* it—that *all* women disappeared?"

"Girls, girl babies, women—all over the earth. The whole female sex."

To Gaunt's surprise, Teddy relaxed visibly. He stretched out his feet. He looked at the perfect whiteness and the shining brownness of his two-toned, wedge-soled shoes. "You know," he said soberly, "in a way, it might be a relief. Atomic stuff, I suppose?"

"*What!*"

Teddy was still occupied with personal reactions—especially with his relief from immediate fear. "Isn't that it? Understand the rays sterilize people. Probably they tested something—and it just did a full job—on the women."

"Look here," Gaunt began, and realized he did not know precisely what he intended to say. "Look here," he repeated. "It isn't the atomic bomb. Nothing like that is atomically possible. Radiation isn't selective."

"What is it, then? Will they come back?"

"Nobody knows."

The pipe was out. Teddy relighted it. "They all went—like Myra? Whoosh!"

"Not even a whoosh. Just gone."

"Clothes and all?"

It was a matter Gaunt had not thitherto considered. "In, I suppose, whatever they were—or weren't—wearing at the time."

"You suppose we're next on the list? Men?"

That, again, was another point, and this time a cardinal point, which Gaunt was ashamed to realize he had so far failed to consider. His shame was greater because Teddy Barker, rather than Jim Elliot, had hit upon it. "Can't say. Nobody knows why or how they vanished. So there's no way to conjecture about males."

"It'll rack hell out of the Market! Close it awhile, most likely."

"No doubt."

Teddy pulled his ear lobe. "Well—I came to the right place. Found out. Guess I'll go over to the Hunt Club for supper. Got a date—no, thank God—had a date with Bessie for late tonight. Glad it's off. If the Market shuts the old doors, and the dames stay gone, I think I'll run down to the Keys and catch up with my fishing. Want to tag along, Bill?"

The philosopher stared for a moment at the other man and slowly smiled. "No, thanks, Teddy. Be busy. You may be, yourself."

"Suppose so. Still—they'll probably pop back tomorrow. Be a pity. I could stand a couple of weeks without 'em. Couldn't you?"

Gaunt put, with vehemence, a question that tormented him. "Look here, Teddy, before you go. Tell me how in hell you manage to take a piece of news like this almost as if you expected it?"

"Expected it?" Teddy was startled. "If you'd seen me this P.M. you know how damn'd *little* I expected it! But you tell me it happened to *all* the dames—and consequently I say—so what? *All* dames —is different. Ever since those atom boys got fiddling with the forces of nature, we've known some cockeyed thing would sure as hell happen, sooner or later, haven't we? Poison the air. End of the world. Destruction of the whole map. People tinkering with powers they don't understand, right? Well? The dames vanish. Whango— and they're gone! Some long-hair with more know-how than good sense pulled one that slipped a few cogs—right?"

"I hope," Gaunt said softly, "others are as sanguine. Still—that opinion might make things go hard with chemists and physicists—"

Teddy rose. "It should." He sliced the flat of his hand across his throat and winked cheerfully. "The self-important, stuck-up, know-it-all, I-dood-it-and-you-shove-it so-and-sos! Well, I'll scram along to the club and see what the other fellows have to say. It should be rich! And if the dames are gone for good—*brother!*—will I be Miami's most envied man! The only one who really got . . ." He broke into pleasant laughter. "What sourballs they'll be! Thanks for everything, Bill! The news sure relieved me. Did right to come straight here. Be seeing you."

Gaunt, who confined himself as a rule to "damn" and "hell," sat motionless until his guest had started the motor of the rented car and swept buoyantly down the drive. Then, with great deliberation, he said, "Well, I'll be *God*-damned!"

He was hungry. He realized that Jim and young Gordon were doubtless waiting for him.

It was a short and mournful meal—the boy silent, his face taut and occasionally tremulous, the flesh around his eyes as pale as chalky water—the father in a trancelike state. When Gaunt arrived, Jim did trouble himself to report such news as the radio had supplied but it was the kind Gaunt had anticipated and discounted.

Nation-wide martial law. The mobilization of all emergency services. At the Departments of State and Defense secret conferences were in progress. The President had spoken at six o'clock. The situation, he said, was world-wide, although Soviet Russia had not officially admitted the disappearance of its women. No one, he added, knew what had occasioned the awesome circumstance. People were advised to go to churches, to stay calm, to refrain from looting, to care for all handicapped persons and children. News of any surviving female, anywhere, was solicited urgently. A "Committee of Savants" was being summoned to Washington for "discussion and investigation." Local and national news had flooded in, after the President's speech. Many cities were fighting sizable fires—Chicago, in a blizzard. Hordes of half-crazed tourists thronged Miami's railroad stations and airports but accommodations were unobtainable.

That sort of thing, Gaunt thought.

After his summary, Jim returned to his trance—serving the stew in bowls and eating automatically. For dessert, there was icebox cake. When Jim sliced it, he dropped a solitary tear into the whipped cream, plainly remembering that Bella had prepared it only hours before. He had made coffee and the two men drank it.

"Maybe," Gaunt said, as they carried the dishes to the sink, "you two would like to get in my car and ride around?"

The child's sad eyes showed a momentary eagerness.

But the lawyer shook his head. "I want to think, Bill. And I

want no part in tonight's holocausts. It would probably be dangerous
to go into the city, in any case. There's some key to this, Bill—and
the route to the key is meditation."

"Then I'll see you in the morning—and thanks for dinner."

Gravely, Gaunt shook hands with both of them, and gave the
boy a pat on the back. "Take care of your dad. Keep your courage
up, Gordon. That'll help him the most of all.

His porch light was reflected from the boles of pines beyond the
T-shaped house and it silhouetted indistinctly the roofs and walls of
two wings. So recently welcome and joyous, so new—the house
now loomed as bare and bleak as an abandoned factory. Its awning
windows (he thought) were exactly like factory windows and the
flat roofs had an industrial look. The rectilinear shadows were un-
homelike, suddenly, and not even functional, since all significant
function was now lost to the structure.

Gaunt got in his car, one of the two family sedans, and morosely
avoided Edwinna's coupé as he drove away.

At first he encountered little traffic. What cars there were either
dawdled uncertainly or shot by drunkenly. Along LeJeune Road,
men and boys were standing on their lawns, sitting on porches, talking, calling to each other. Everywhere, radios gibbered. The Dixie
Highway was without illumination, a dark hall cut through banyan
trees. The jam of city-bound cars began on Brickell Avenue. Gaunt
realized that if he approached Miami much closer he would find no
parking place and might later be unable to extricate himself from
the crawling, honking river of vehicles. He was, at the moment, near
a girls' school his two daughters had attended. There would be no
school on the next day, he thought. With that he turned into the
play yard and parked in such a way he could readily drive out.

He walked with other walking men and a few boys under
flowering trees to the summit of the drawbridge. Ahead of him, the
skyscrapers, boulevards, streets and parking yards of Miami glittered
as usual, sidewalks crowded with males, streets packed with beetlelike

cars. No boats moved below on the gleaming river; none moved at sea excepting far out, where the lights of a tanker inched against the dark horizon. Gaunt wondered if they knew.

He strode into the maelstrom of people. Every sort of man walked there, drove, ran about. The poor in the clothing of the poor, the well-to-do in the business suits they'd been wearing at four-oh-five. The men who had gone meaninglessly home to dinner and returned. The men who had stayed in town. Tourists in such clothes as only tourists wear. On the varied faces, all kinds of expressions: shock, foremost; overt weeping and sobbing; horror and fear; plain excitement, commonly: wonder and awe; a look, here and there, of secret amusement or relief or even of thinly guarded bliss—an inscrutable and ominous expression. Many of the men were drunk and the bars roared so specifically that they could be located, in any block, above the general pandemonium.

Papers were being dumped in bundles from trucks; the bundles were ripped open and the sheets sold from fast-melting heaps, papers with enormous black headlines: WOMEN VANISH.

Gaunt's stride slackened because of the numbers of pedestrians, somewhat, and more because of the dreamlike sensation that seized him. Men and boys snatched at him, said something or other . . .

"Hey, mister!" A young Latin. "Want to buy a watch, cheap?"

"Hello, Gaunt." A familiar face but unplaceable. "Horrible thing, isn't it?"

"Come on in here, pal." A weeping, bleary citizen with a dirty shirt. "Buy me another drink—I'm out of cash!"

An old man, bald, with nasty eyes: "This is the Last Judgment of American capitalism!"

Gaunt said peevishly, "Nonsense!"

The old man sneered. "You wait! The ships of Marxist destiny will wing over us before dawn!"

The philosopher stared at the cranky derelict. "Crap," he said.

A crying child. "Mister! Mister! Please, mister! My dad went in there and I can't even get in so he can find me."

Gaunt looked at the boy and at the dozen-deep press of men around the seedy bar. He picked up the child, pushed into the place ferociously, and finally reached the swilled wood surface. He stood the child there and thundered, "Whose boy is this?"

It took repeated efforts to get any attention but finally a flat-chested man held up a hand. "Mine." He seemed ashamed.

The kid yelled, "Daddy!" and dove at his father, spilling his beer.

Gaunt went on.

Ahead, beyond the alabaster walls of a tall building and the yellow-brown arch of a tawdry arcade, he saw some men and a few boys moving up a stairway and realized, after a puzzled moment, that they were entering St. Paul's. He thought of the Reverend Connauth, smiled fleetingly, and forged ahead.

The organ, as he entered the vestibule, was hammering insistently while a huge congregation sang, "Faith of our fathers, Holy Faith, We will be true to thee till death. . . . In spite of dungeon, fire and sword. . . ."

The church itself—Gothic, shocking in the middle of Miami's medley of the modern, of nineteen-twenty nondescript, and what someone had termed William-Jennings-Bryan-Spanish—glowed with pinkish lights set behind pointed arches and downhanging festoons of concrete molded to look like stone. It was filled almost to the last row with men who torrentially expressed the faith of their fathers.

Gaunt was led to a seat by a young usher who had been weeping. A fat bullock, a man whose cheeks were flooded by tears and whose breath poured forth in a sweet, gin-flavored tenor, held out a hymn-book, pointing to the place with a clean, conical finger. Gaunt knew the hymn—it belonged to his childhood faith more than to the minister's denomination.

On the platform, Connauth sat in the panoply of his dark robes. Behind him rose another wall of ornamental cement that terminated in stalagmites—crosses and fleur-de-lys and other such ornaments as, no doubt, the Goths had carved better in better cathedrals. High overhead the vaulting jumble came together above a rose window of colored glass which surged with intermittent light as neon signs outside flashed on and off again. But the groins, where the rocketing concrete came together, were as gloomy and complex as the roof of a limestone cave.

It was apparent that the congregation had greatly moved itself by its own singing. Gaunt could feel the sensation—the zeal, the supplication, abandonment in the hope that mere abandonment would bring relief. He could feel, too, a speciousness.

Outside lay the city, the mechanistic city, the shoddy city, the workaday city, the city of technical ingenuity, of penny-snatching glamours, of petty sports and games and gambling, of ten thousand greasy dishes seasoned to vulgar taste. But here, in its soul, for all the rosy glow and sumptuous cement, for all the incense, real gold of cross and chalice, glimmer of valuable tapestries and silks, he found only a false replica. Here, the very attitudes and sensations were not germane to the disaster but to woes of ignorant, impassioned folk five hundred and more years dead. Goths.

The hymn ended, bringing peace to vibrating eardrums.

Connauth rose and moved to the pulpit with slow steps. He spread his silk buzzard's wings and spoke in his voluptuous, paternal voice—the voice, Gaunt had often thought (he knew the minister well), that the Redeemed and the Saved no doubt expected to hear issuing from the lips of Jehovah on the Day Gabriel loosed the Trump.

"Let us pray," Connauth intoned.

The heads went down.

"Oh, Lord, oh, great, omnipotent Heavenly Father"— pause—"in this mighty hour of crisis, of the Unknowable"— pause—"we who inhabit the humble footstool upon which Thou hast seen fit to situate us all—"

He is going, Gaunt thought, to see to it that God gets blamed, in part anyway. I wonder if he misses his Berthene? I don't imagine I would. She should have been a man. She should have been a blacksmith. Big as she is, it's hard to imagine how she can contain quite that much righteousness.

Could.

Could have contained.

It was then, curiously enough (and probably because, since he knew prayer *per se* so intimately, his mind wandered away from nonessential listening), that Gaunt was struck by the *fact* of missing Paula.

The bemusement of some five hours fell away from him.

His viscera drew together as if in response to a deep stab.

His breath caught. He had the self-possession, or the false pride, to glance once at the fat man beside him before he leaned forward as if in attentiveness or humility and became paralyzed by his sensation of loss. It was literal paralysis. He could not budge or even breathe. His mind was set upon by such a pain as might ensue if serpents could strike the soul direct and bring it down writhing. His long, tough hands grew white with hanging on the pew ahead. He gasped, finally, and no one turned, though he did not look this time to see. He was aware, for a minute, of nothing save the terrible fury of grief.

Out of it, or in its midst, he made an attempt to fight back. The very aggressiveness of his emotion required such an effort.

My children, he said to himself. But his children had become their own selves long since. Edwinna in her marriages. Edwin—Edwin had been given leave by his father when, a very boy, he had flown away to the wars. It was Paula alone who still belonged to him and who had been torn from him. There was no surcease. Paula was gone. The accepted, the expected companionship was ended. What remained?

The world, then, the stricken world?

But there was not, in that interval, any compensation to be had from thinking of how the world shared it with him. He broke into sweat and his breath raked back and forth through dry lips. But he did not hear it or feel it or still its harsh suction. Yet he tried to deal with himself.

Why *now*? Why *here*? Why in this crass travesty of a cathedral? Was God actually present in so indecent a chamber? And why ask that?

Paula, Paula, Paula, his heart wept.

The unquenchable flicker of his forebrain went on:

There is a *guiltiness* in you over this matter. The church has reminded you of the primitive essence of guilt. You should have felt it earlier this evening. (But when? At what instant? For what reason? He could not recollect.) Your sorrow is a double sorrow, for you have brought about a portion of it, yourself.

That sensation. . . .

It left him.

There was organ music.

Connauth had stopped intoning. God had been blamed, appeased, entreated. Now they would sing again.

Gaunt straightened up, sobbing unreservedly, unnoticed. He looked at the angels and prophets and saints on the stained glass and at the golden gleam of the Cross. He watched the minister in his medieval costume turn the pages of a prodigious Book older than the Dark Ages.

"The Lord is my Shepherd."

Gaunt did not want to hear the Twenty-third Psalm at that moment. He took a clean handkerchief from his hip pocket, wiped his long, narrow face, blew his nose, and stood. No one paid him any heed as he walked down the aisle still dabbing at nose and eyes.

Green pastures . . .

Fear no evil . . .

He was on the steps again. *Outside.*

But through the small, impalpable sensation of guilt within himself he had found, mystically, Jim Elliot would have said, the beginning of a way to bear his anguish.

Now, somehow, the roar of the city, the soft, sweet air of the Miami night on his wet brow and two sea gulls winging unnaturally in
the starlit air between the church and the loft building across the
street, enabled him to go on, to go ahead, wherever *that* might lead.

The streets, as he continued through them, had taken on an aura
of madness. Vehicles were at a standstill, blatting helplessly. Some, he
saw, had been abandoned in the middle of a fixed stream of traffic—
which explained why none could move. No police were to be seen,
though he heard sirens in the distance.

He went toward the park and the waterfront.

The lobbies of hotels were packed with men—men talking, men
yelling, men drunk, men with drinks in their hands. Radios with
thicker clusters of men around them were drowned out at a few
paces. Gaunt passed the window of a jewelry shop. It had been staved
in and ominous teeth of plate glass showed around its empty cases. No
one tarried to observe this evidence of plunder; all edged away, rather,
as if they half felt suspect. Through the palms, across the water
(where more rows of headlights stood motionless upon the causeways)
he saw the shimmer of Miami Beach, and, at three points, the orange
gleam of buildings afire.

Presently, moving down Biscayne Boulevard with the interweav-
ing thousands, he came to a congestion of men and pushed in to
see what held them there. They were spilled roundly into the street
and even standing on the cars of strangers in front of a night club
called "The Powder Puff." Gaunt, who was very tall, soon saw the
reason. Under the name of the club was a gaudy sign showing what
appeared at first glance to be women entertainers. But over the pic-

ture were the words "World's Most Famous Female Impersonators."
At the entry of the club a small stage had been improvised and on it.
as he looked, two of the "impersonators" suddenly appeared, dancing, nearly nude, in the manner of burlesque girls, a manner old
before there had been any civilization.

The crowd cheered.

The two men dressed as women, dancing as women, now hoisted
a sign:

"We're all you've got, boys! Come up and see us sometime!"

From the crowd rose catcalls and whistles, fountains of noise as
obscene as fountains connected with sewers.

Gaunt stared, listened and shuddered.

He decided to go home. . . .

The journey, normally a walk of fifteen minutes and a drive of
twenty, required more than two hours.

Toward midnight, however, he sat again on his porch.

The images faded, lunatic crowd, shattered windowpane, wriggling impersonators, concrete-Gothic interior of the compromise ca--
thedral—the half portion of a deceased reality: nave, section of a
transept.

Remembrances of Paula eased his barbarian visions:

Paula in certain dresses at particular places, in situations engraved on the mind, and Paula's shaped lips making phrases as fresh
now as her breakfast conversation that morning.

Paula giving birth. *Twins, darling! What a husband!*

Or nursing in the elegant, the voluptuous, the somehow en-
viable. . . . *Obviously, Bill, twins are the thing nature planned. As
you can figure out for yourself!*

In Paris and Vienna and Lucerne and Verona and in Venice
and in London too, when the V-2's began to fall. *They're like a lot
of people I know: you only realize they've arrived after the damage
has been done.*

Paula in the flat they'd occupied when they'd been married. And then, Paula as mistress of the fine house they'd rented after the success of his play. *How swell to change overnight from a professor's wife to something like a trustee's kept woman!*

Paula turning the leaves of the first copy of his first book. *How much more acceptable the royalties will be than the reviews!*

Or at Edwinna's second marriage. *The groom will learn nothing from this; the bride might, though—when it's washed up.*

The first time he'd seen Paula.

She had arrived early for class—a girl of eighteen, looking many years older and much younger—even childish: a face saved from over-much passion by piquancy, and embellished with that insolent red hair. *I took your course so as to be sure to learn everything about everything.* And she had winked.

A cry now escaped him, a forlorn sound, embarrassed even by his lamplight and escaping quickly into the jasmine-scented dark beyond the screens:

"Paula! Dear! You must find your way back to me!"

There was, for answer, the confused reverberation of some fresh, unguessable disaster in the distance.

But this, he thought, was not the agony of the church. He could stand it.

He could, he found, even turn from it.

For now his mind went to Edwinna, the Family Problem. And to little Alicia, who had appeared to be a new deevlopment in the same field. To Edwin also. Edwin would be—where? In Manhattan, certainly. With his wife, Frances, and with their daughters, Jean and Carlotta—and the three of them gone, also. What, then, would Edwin do? The sturdy thing, the audacious thing, whatever it might be. Gaunt hoped he would soon see his son. Maturity, marriage, or the wars had led him to create in his mind an independence for the boy —for both his children—and it stood him in good stead now.

But toward Paula, he would never have a similar sensation of discreteness. He found himself wondering, momentarily, at the fact that he had not thought (since the disaster) of the dead Theodora; to that old tragedy he was accustomed.

Where his dreaming next would have led, he never knew. His phone rang.

4

WHEREIN THE END OF THE WORLD AS THEY KNEW IT REVEALS
TO MANY GALLANT LADIES THAT THE WORLD ENDED WAS ONE
THEY DID NOT KNOW.

The Disappearance required imagination for its understanding. Women deficient in the quality were unable to assimilate the event and, as a result, their responses were unsuitable. To deal with problems that immediately arose required vast imagination, as well as logic, and also a variety of informations which are popularly referred to as "know-how."

These three—know-how, logic, and imagination—are all that distinguishes man from beasts. The first is the product of the other two; it is the ranging imagination that suggests new concepts and brings to awareness concepts thitherto buried in instinct; it is logic which sifts true imaginings from the merely fanciful and practical ideas from the merely bizarre, aimless, or wanton. The employment of the two thus furnishes humanity with its occasional increments of knowledge, or know-how.

Imagination without logic is worthless. It conceives uncritically; pursued for its own sake, it but deforms the mind. Logic by itself is only futile; without imagination it can only reprove the proven and so discover nothing. The integrated person needs to develop both and to use both, equally and constantly.

Unfortunately for his own good, man has placed above those two divinest attributes another property: his vanity, his ego. Through that inflated organ (an organ which, as men multiply, multiplies itself into the ego of groups and nations and becomes identical with a culture) men create the misshapen patterns of their societies. *The tendency to establish a pattern is innate and absolute,* whether it be done in the name of Zeus, Moloch, Jehovah, or Marx. But, wherever men set aside their imagination and their logic to insist upon patterns that originate in vanity, they obey the rules of conceit and not truth. At the same time they shut themselves away from their best opportunity to learn. So all that distinguishes them from beasts is diminished and they inevitably grow more toward beastliness and less toward the humanity for which they are truly shaped.

In Western society, and particularly in American society, imagination is stultified from infancy. The imaginative child is discouraged and upbraided. He is told that the process is mere dreaming, that it wastes time and leads nowhere. It is said to be "impractical." As the child grows and its imagination inevitably leads it to express unconventional ideas and to try new behavior, it is chided and even viciously punished for such signs of unorthodoxy.

In America, the child is schooled, if a boy, toward fiscal endeavor. It is taught to want to be a "good provider," if not a millionaire. From babyhood it is pursued by advertisements and commercials which give it the aggregate impression that the aim of life is to acquire funds wherewith to obtain all it hears recommended. The American media of communication hypnotize it into a set of special desires. A girl, of course, takes up the same doctrine. Her aim becomes to find a mate with money to act on every radio commercial or, at the very least, to set herself up in a career which will enable her so to act, independently.

Thus American imagination is directed—as if in the whole of life no other aims or satisfactions could be found than those of being a consumer, avid, constant and catholic. Logic has not, of course, anywhere far advanced, as witness the fact that twentieth-century man has several thousand different descriptions of the nature of Nature, which he calls religions, and that he is nevertheless able to regard the preposterous circumstance as rational. His own "faith" is, of course, the one he regards as "logical" and he submits neither it nor, as a rule, any other to either imagination or reason.

Wherever distortion is cultural the deformed are either blind to their enormities or proud of them and the latter is the dismal rule. The old Chinese were vain about the miniature feet their binding produced in women; Flathead Indians admired the slope given the brow by a board lashed to the infant skull; and the Ubangis set great store in their teased-out plate lips. Persons not in those groups are generally revolted (and not surprisingly) by all such customs.

But the practice of constraining and deforming the personality—of binding the imagination, of strapping a set of fixed rules arbitrarily to logic, and of teasing out only one sort of know-how—is the common, daily vice of *every* culture.

The American mind, its imagination channelized, its logic limited, its know-how hugely and uncritically specialized, is footbound, flat-headed and plate-lipped psychologically. It presents a personality with so little room for normal function and so much atrophy that the nation itself has no clear idea of what a person might, could or ought to be. As savages gloat over their induced deformities, so Americans dote upon the warped intellect of the public. A Babbitt is the envied norm here; a Nazi, or a Communist, elsewhere; a normal man would be anathema. So civilization has advanced but one step where two need to be made. It has ceased the arrogant, savage tricks of misshaping itself biologically but it has as yet not even much investigated its equally savage rituals of psychological deformation. Indeed, the general populace is not in any way aware that what it thinks, feels, dreams and employs for motive is often monstrous.

In women, cultural inclination had all but ruled out the possibility of imagination and logic. Females are regarded as "naturally" deficient in both. That attitude, which rose in the paleolithic, is part of man's inordinate self-assertion and he was able to establish it then simply because he was stronger. The abuse was never corrected and women of the twentieth century usually accepted it; fifty millenniums of indoctrination are bound to have an effect.

Hence women, presented with the instantaneous vanishment of males, were in an extremely poor psychological condition to deal with the aftermath. Whatever pattern innately existed in them, what faculties they owned as individuals, what promptings, urges, intelligent ideas, logical extrapolations and valid hunches they were capable of were hidden; they found themselves without a tradition, without experience, without confidence, and without know-how.

Here and there, of course, a few exceptional women rose as best they could to the desperate occasion. Paula Gaunt was one of them. If her own life had been circumscribed by such "womanly" chores and attitudes as were general, she had nevertheless enjoyed the advantage of association with a man who, however conventional his behavior, had a mind of some originality and did not allow orthodoxy to inhibit expression. In speculation, if not experience, William Gaunt was less misshapen than most of his fellows. Paula had vicariously learned the sensation of that. She was, besides, a woman of native abilities. Also, she had the best education obtainable—although education distorts more even than it informs. It could not be said she was in any way "prepared" for the aftermath of the Disappearance, however. She was merely less unprepared—so she did what she could where she was and as the need appeared.

Greater Miami, a community of a half million souls before its males vanished, fared better than most megapolises. It was spread over a larger area; its residences were less intimately mingled with its business buildings; waterways dismembered it; the local construction codes required its edifices to be able to withstand hurricanes; and its slums were segregated, owing to the fact that their tenants were Negroes and this was the Deep South. Still—

Still—

Within minutes of the Disappearance, a host of major catastrophes occurred. Any one of them would have made front-page news across the nation if newspapers had been printed on the day following and if greater and more numerous calamities had not taken place elsewhere.

Fires broke out, of course. They broke out where gasoline, pouring untended, encountered sources of heat. They broke out in factories and in power plants and where machines continued to operate, threw sparks, hotted up, short-circuited, smoked and burst into flames. In cleaning establishments, upholstery shops, laundries, and stores—the fires began. Here and there in the infestious sprawl of South Florida's "colored towns," a flame moved from its supervised source to an unpainted wall, a scrap of curtain, or some heap of old rags and papers that had been the family pallet. In Miami proper, forty thousand persons dwelt in one square mile of stinking shanties. These took fire. No engines, of course, raced to the rescue.

Approaching and departing planes of many airlines, small ships on local flights and huge, four-engine liners coming in or gathering speed for the long, clean hop to New York, Chicago or the West Indies, were suddenly pilotless. Most of them crashed, at sea, in the Everglades, in the midst of business blocks and residential areas. Swaths were ripped through the pale, tropic stucco of neat houses; valleys of fire were left behind. A few planes escaped, brought in by cool-nerved stewardesses who, unaware of the world's situation, knew only that their own pilots, copilots and male passengers were gone; the stewardesses were able to crash-land the ships successfully in fields and on shallow lakes.

The civilized earth became a shambles of wrecked motor vehicles.

Trains ran on, in many cases, their locomotives unsupplied with "dead man's" brakes.

Thus the Golden Comet, luxury express, having made its appointed stop at Palm Beach, rushed toward Miami an hour behind schedule. Of a sudden, there were no men aboard it and no little boys playing tiredly in its handsome aisles. There was, even, another sort of palpable loss on the train, as everywhere.

Genevieve McCracken, in the observation car, hurrying home to bear her third child, suddenly found the mound of her abdomen relaxed, caved in, all evidence of pregnancy vanished. She hastily rose, clutching her slipping skirt. In her compartment she disrobed and stared with horror at the slack folds of skin that only minutes before had harbored a viable child, a son, she had hoped. She pressed and kneaded herself with a quivering hand. But the fact could not be denied: her child was gone, and she had not borne it.

She whimpered. She bit her nails and worried. She took medicine. She tried to sleep. At last she put up the curtain an inch, bent forward and peered to see how soon she would be in her husband's arms. Suburbs now hurtled past the windows—an ugly huge Navy warehouse, a lumberyard, a smoldering city dump, a junk heap, and a trailer park set in the midst of tall bamboos and pink oleanders. One after another, grade crossings flashed before her eyes and twice, down long street vistas, she saw women running.

Presently the train passed a boulevard she recognized, buildings she knew, and soon, to her horror, it sped through the station, roared into a switch, heeled, came level again, and thundered on. Genevieve had a glimpse of the people waiting to meet the train—all women, it seemed, milling about, their eyes lifted only at the last instant to look with a unanimity of horror at the flashing express.

Beyond Miami, the tracks led to Homestead, following the Dixie Highway and passing the Gaunt residence at a distance of about half a mile.

As Paula sipped her Scotch, she could hear in the distance the rumble of the afternoon freight, coming up from the growers' area, loaded with oranges and winter vegetables. Its dreary whistle spread rings of sound over the flat landscape and Paula thought of the long cars filled with crates of good things to eat, things people would eat, would have eaten, in snowbound cities to the north. But now she heard another sound: the fast clatter of an unscheduled train approaching from Miami.

In that way, crewless, on a single track, the two engines met head on. The cars behind the freight locomotive leaped crisscross into the air and crashed upon each other, bursting thousands of crates of oranges, bowling grapefruit along the tracks and drenching the right-of-way with the dribbled juice of tomatoes. Human beings, women and girls, were dealt with in the same fashion by the opposed cars: their bodies, arms, legs, rolling heads and blood commingled in the steel and the dust.

"Great God!" Edwinna whispered. "What's that?"

Paula was already running for her car. She passed Hester and Alicia. The old colored woman had turned saffron and her eyes held a wild look. Paula stopped long enough to hug her. "We'll soon be back, Hester! Remember—you've got Alicia to care for. *You, alone!*"

The wild look receded.

They sped over a bridge that crossed a canal along the banks of which were terraces cut in the coral. Flowers bloomed on the terraces; boats rode at anchor nearby. They rushed by scenes, already familiar to Paula, of crashed cars. Edwinna gaped. They followed a curving thoroughfare past large houses in the yards of which spathodeas and bombax trees were bent with big scarlet blossoms. Soon they crossed the highway and stopped near the screaming avalanche of wrecked passenger cars.

Other women were there already, some trying to help, some merely staring. One or two whom Paula first thought were casualties had only fainted, and lay like dolls on the weedy grass. "You drive," Paula said to the cowering Edwinna, "to the new hospital. There might be a few women doctors available. And the nurses! Tell them that—whatever they've got on hand—this is worse!"

Paula strode to the closest group of girls and women. "Which of you live around here?"

Most merely glanced at her and gazed back at the shrieking, moving objects amidst the shattered metal. But there was an authority in her tone which caused two or three to reply. "I live down yonder." "Our place is two blocks away."

"Well, then," Paula said in a clear, positive voice, "go home! Get some of these other women to go with you! Bring boiling water here—all the iodine you've got—bandages—clean sheets—everything for first aid! Get beds ready! We've got to take care of this—*ourselves!*"

The women looked, talked to each other, and began to move.

Some, now, were venturing into the steel and the glass and the gore where they could see other women and children.

Paula stared up and down the long stretch of track, parkway and wide road. Cars moved on the latter but of these most went by frenziedly with no more than a quick braking for a look. A few slowed and stopped and their occupants got out. In the distance she saw the low sun glittering on the many slanted windows of the university dormitories. It gave her an idea.

At the same instant a hand touched her shoulder. She turned and saw Emma Bradley, the secretary of the South Miami Women's Club, with tears in steady, gray eyes. "Paula—what is it?"

"God knows! The men are all gone. We've got a horrible wreck here. Emma! Take charge—will you?" Paula outlined the directions she'd given and the further plans she had made.

Emma hiked up her sleeves while she listened, retied the purple kerchief over her gray hair, and went toward the nearest women without a question.

There was pandemonium on the campus when Paula drove up to the Student Club. Clusters of hysterical girls, and girls running without purpose, made eerie drama against the modernistic architecture and the sunset-tinted calm waters of the lagoon beyond. Paula parked, ran up the steps and out onto the terrazzo of the open-air dance floor where she could be seen.

"Listen!" she shouted. *"Everybody! Quiet! Listen! Silence!"*

By and by, save for sobs and peripheral running, she had the attention of about a hundred girls.

"I'm Paula Gaunt," she said loudly. "Some of you may know me. All of you know who my husband is—William Percival Gaunt. He's taught courses here in past years and you've put on his play at your Ring Theater and you read his books. *Look, girls.* I don't know why what has happened has happened. But I do know the men are gone. Everything is *up to us*—and how we come out is going to depend on *how we behave now.* You girls are the most able and intelligent of the whole bunch in *all this area. Start using your heads!* Get everybody together! Form a committee to register what everybody can do. We've got fires to fight. There's a terrible train wreck down the Dixie Highway. People are hurt everywhere. We've got to figure out *how* to organize. *How* to locate qualified women and doctors and get them where they are needed. We've got to find all girls studying engineering—all people who can run power plants, repair power lines, everything of that sort. Nobody is going to take charge of anything tonight unless *you do!* We'll need girls who can shoot—to guard things. Girls who can run fire engines—or who would volunteer to try!" She talked on . . .

As darkness fell, the sky lit up around the horizon, with the widest and most intense glow in the middle of Miami where the shanties of forty thousand Negroes were mingling flames to make a single, mile-square pyre. . . .

Paula did not keep her promise to return to Bella Elliot's for supper. She went without the meal. And she did not see Edwinna again that night.

The girls and the women professors at the university had needed only the focusing of their scattered minds to set them in action.

What she did, Paula said afterward, they would soon have done by themselves, without her. In ten minutes she was ensconced at a table in the outdoor restaurant beside the dance floor and the lagoon. Girls were lining up chairs as if Paula were going to lecture them. Pens, paper, cards, bulletin boards, the materials for making lists were being assembled.

Next, in rapid succession, girls—nominated from waving hands —rose to suggest who should head up firefighters, engineers, rescue workers, nurses' aides. Those suggested, if not present, were sought immediately by runners. When they appeared, they quickly formed their own committees, set out to commandeer such equipment as they could after registering for whatever action they had undertaken. Within two hours, working now by the headlights of sedans driven into the open court of the building (for the power was off at the university), Paula had dispatched some fifty "crews" on various missions, most of which had been suggested by the students.

In a good many other towns and cities, other Paulas had leaped into similar situations, women with good nerves and minds, women with the organization know-how of club officers, but women who, like Paula, were faced with uncountable dilemmas they were not equipped to handle. They did their best.

Toward eleven o'clock that night, a girl with black bangs, her face smudged and the smell of smoke on her jeans, raced up the steps of the Student Club and reported to "headquarters" in a staccato southern voice: "Niggertown's burning to ashes! We headed the women and the children to Bayfront Park and the other parks, like you said. We got guards around. People are abreaking in everywhere, though. Gettin' food and gettin' jewelry—ahead of the fire! It's driving down the main streets, now."

Paula said quietly to Professor Aveley, one of the women who had become a chief lieutenant in the passing hours, "We can't stop it. I asked about dynamite. Nobody knows how to use it—or even where men keep it. It would be silly anyhow to try to blow up rows of skyscrapers, when we haven't got a soul who can blast a stump!"

"We'll just have to continue trying to evacuate." Professor Aveley was large, mousy and homely. She taught math; no one would have thought, unless they had thought very carefully, that she had the mind of a field general. "I understand there are a dozen different groups working in Miami now—with our girls. And more in the areas around here. They'll have to spread the word to pull people back —ahead of the fires, getting everybody out of the houses. By morning—" She shrugged.

"I know," Paula said. "There'll be less than half the population —and probably far less than half the housing."

Professor Aveley nodded. "Then we can thank the Lord for a climate you can sleep in! Imagine Minneapolis! I've been! I was brought up there. Ice cold! Snowing, maybe!"

"I think—" Paula said, and stopped. She looked at the girls working at tables, the girls coming and going from the street, the graceful buildings in the alternate glare and darkness of headlamps and shadow; she looked at the orange circle of fire on the horizon. While she looked, lights went on everywhere on the campus.

The woman beside her murmured, "Thank God for Alberta and her gang!"

Paula nodded. "I think one of us ought to go down there . . ."

"Right. You. I'll hold the fort."

Paula demurred. "Perhaps I should, after all—"

"Go on," the professor said. "Fire scares me."

Paula was forced to stop at the foot of Brickell Avenue. She parked on somebody's front lawn, took out the keys of her car, locked it and ascended the drawbridge.

Miami's skyscrapers were silhouetted against seas of flame that rose to the north and the west. There was no electricity. In the nearer streets, women were running—many with children, nearly all carrying suitcases or bundles. Women were trying to drag trunks from the two nearest hotels.

While Paula watched, a motorboat started near the bridge and made its way downstream in the glaring light. It had outriggers. These hit the bridge, splintered, and crashed into the river. Paula leaned over the rail and saw the women in the boat begin to hack at the debris. The cruiser pushed on under the bridge and headed toward the Bay. As it passed, Paula saw that two of the women in the stern wore evening dresses—and all of them, with the possible exception of the pilot, appeared to be drunk. They waved glasses and bottles at her.

She left the bridge and ran through frantic, heedless women to Flagler Street. Here the smoke was thick and choking. There were not many people. Light flooded down the side streets in a baleful yellow-orange tide. An august roaring accompanied the conflagration as it ate toward the city's heart. It was not so loud, however, that she could not hear a plate-glass window shatter some yards away. She turned. A dozen women were hurling things at the glass. Then they poured into the hole they had made and began stripping garments from the mannequins. Paula realized that the futility, the imbecile greed, should have enraged her; but it did not. For a fleeting instant she thought instead that these women doubtless had never owned such clothes—and she pitied them. Then she saw two girls with drawn revolvers, university girls probably, hurry up the street. The looters shouted to each other and ran, carrying armloads of fluffy fabrics.

Paula was coughing now, choking. She turned down Flagler Street toward the waterfront. The park that bordered it was crammed with people, most of them black. They faced the pyre of their homes, their "town," and they seemed to be almost wholly silent, overcome with the loss not just of their men, their sons, and their houses but, no doubt, of many relatives and friends trapped in the square-mile tinderbox.

Paula stood awhile at the corner of Biscayne Boulevard and Flagler Street, gazing from the masses of people to the great buildings and wondering whether or not fire in these nearer edifices would cook the multitude. Probably not. The boulevard was wide, the park of some breadth, and the light wind blew from the ocean. White women and a few colored, several of the former wearing what evidently were the old air-raid warden helmets of their husbands, patrolled nearby streets. Some had pistols, some shotguns, and some rifles. But it seemed to Paula that there was little need for arms at this point. The looting of a few stores had lost all meaning; what was important— the temper of the crowds—was controlled by the awesomeness of the catastrophe. The people were not in physical panic, whatever the state of their minds might be.

Nothing, exactly nothing, Paula decided, could be done to check the mammoth fires. Those in the park would survive. Those out of the direct fire path would have time to get away. Those in immediate peril were being warned by volunteers. The whole roaring situation was under such management as could be contrived and the human beings who lived now would mostly be saved for the morning.

She walked back along the boulevard, passing individual women and groups of women hastening with their burdens toward the park at the waterfront. Babies in carriages. Myriad suitcases. A scraggly creature with cropped hair carried nothing but a violin case; it hung open and was empty, which the woman obviously did not know. A fat blonde raced along the street with a young girl and, between them, a hamper jammed with bottles. A thin, dark girl pushed an old woman in a wheelbarrow. Paula helped them across the street. It was not very difficult: in the center of Miami, no vehicles were moving.

A blast came from somewhere behind Paula, in the fire, and a murmur rose from the park. For one lurid moment Paula thought of Hersey's account of that night in Hiroshima. Well . . .

They'll need—Paula thought.

Water, her mind said.

Water to drink.

But how? She remembered the luxury cruiser. There would be girls who could run boats—and there were boats in the canals and boats anchored off Coconut Grove. There were wells—if the city pressure failed. Drums could be found. By morning, the people in the parks would be very thirsty.

She hurried back across the bridge, looking over her shoulder once, like Lot's wife, at the burning metropolis.

She took her keys from her pocketbook and started her car. She drove across several lawns and through two hedges to avoid a new, croaking snarl of traffic.

We must keep any more people from coming into town to see what it's like—the curious jerks! she thought.

She drove carefully. There weren't many cars but there were no street lights either, and of the cars on the road most were operated in a reckless and alarming fashion.

The campus looked almost normal, with lights burning in the buildings and students, girl students, commencing to use the classrooms. For injured people, Paula realized, as she saw four girls carry a stretcher from a laundry truck into one of the buildings.

Professor Aveley was sitting in the center of a table that, by the addition of similar tables, had grown to a length of fifteen feet or so. Other women—some from the university and some not—sat flanking her. In front of each was a hand-lettered placard that designated the service in her charge: GUARDS, FIRE FIGHTERS, FIRST AID, NURSES, TRANSPORT, RUNNERS, ENGINEER—ELECTRICAL, ENGINEER—WATER, and so on. Girls came and went, bending briefly over the desk chiefs.

It had grown like that, Paula thought, in just a few hours. A fast-operating, integrated Thing. And it couldn't do much. They didn't know how to do much. Or even how to imagine what to do. They'd collected perhaps twenty thousand people in Bayfront Park, for example, and not remembered drinking water. Let alone, Paula's

mind went on, sanitary facilities. But they could use the Bay for that
—it wouldn't matter. The sewers emptied there anyhow.

Paula's chair was still vacant. She sat in it.

"What?" asked Professor Aveley.

Paula told her in short phrases. "Water," she finished, "to drink."

"Lord! Never thought of that! We'll start a new division. Sue!
Mollie! Listen—!"

Somebody passed sandwiches and coffee. Paula took a cup of
coffee but she wasn't hungry. Women would, she thought; right off;
start making sandwiches.

"*Bakeries,*" she asked of the woman beside her.

"Got a division on it," the other replied. "There's a big bakery
right near. No power, though. Some of the girls think they could
get a cable from the university, down there. They're already running
it on the poles—using ladders. We've got a hundred volunteer bakers
and not one damned girl who can climb a power pole!"

That was when the rain began—just before one o'clock. Some
said later the fire caused it. Others said it was the usual spring rain—
mercifully early that year.

In Miami—as anywhere in a typical "palm forest" belt—it can
pour as hard as in the "rainy forest" regions: an inch in a few minutes. During the next hour three inches fell on the area and in some
spots even more. That was not unprecedented. Spring, summer and
fall, Miami can turn itself in a matter of minutes from a balmy, blue-
sky day or starlight night to a dark deluge that floods the flat streets,
stalls cars, backs up the storm sewers, spreads acres of lake over pavement, curbing and lawn, and sets rivers raging where man had never
intended.

At the university, the effort continued in the downpour. As energetically as ants faced with a sudden new threat to the colony,
students began to move tables, signs and personnel from the patio into
the cafeteria. All the women, including the crew chiefs, were soaked;
all ignored it. Work was resumed under fluorescent lights in a vast

hall amid steel tray rails, steam tables, and an orchestra podium where the uncouth mechanisms of music gleamed meaninglessly.

Curtains of rain miles thick cut off the volcanic horizon. The women at first hoped and soon knew from incoming runners that the deluge was saving the city.

When, at the end of an hour, it lifted, they could see only here and there in the distances a stubborn glow where fire remained. The rain, as if dissatisfied, came again to complete the chore.

Other cities were not so fortunate. . . .

The east grew briefly gray, then disappointingly dark again. But the pearly undertone returned and stayed and was followed by such a vague light on the landscape as the moon makes. A strip of dull crimson flared above the Bay and at last it was morning.

Paula surveyed the scene in the cafeteria. New women, women who had learned the ropes in the night, had replaced many of those who first began to organize the students. Professor Aveley was still there, however, at a table now detached from the rest. She looked as if she would not need sleep for a month.

Paula went when they sent her away.

The trees dripped and glittered in the radiance. Sun would soon bejewel them. Birds sang . . . Paula stopped her car sharply to make sure that what she saw was a *pair* of warblers.

So birds were all right. And she recalled, now, the barking of a neighbor's puppy, Buster. *Dogs, too, then.* She drove slowly. Funny. She hadn't even wondered, until just this moment. Male birds, male dogs, just men. Male people.

Sunset Boulevard was no different, no different at all, save for the beneficence of the rain which seemed already to have made the grass greener and revived plants that stood in rows in the Hibiscus Nursery. Washed off the dust, she thought. Her driveway was just the same, too: puddles in it, the scent of night-blooming jasmine still drifting under the live oaks, tassels of Spanish moss swinging in the early currents of air and her own covey of quail running like chickens from the place where she scattered wild bird seed to attract them. Half the world had (she would not say "died") disappeared; many, maybe millions, had truly died (if *that* was the way to say it), but her own premises were just as they had been.

Edwinna's car was there, too, and parked beyond the turning place.

A curl of smoke from behind the brick wall startled Paula. She hurried, but even before she could see, she knew. She smelled bacon and was hungry. She rounded the vine-covered wall and saw Hester bending over a fireplace made of two cement blocks. The fire was crackling; she had put a large, copper-bottomed frying pan over it. Beside her, on the ground, were split-up pieces of a wooden box and a large coffeepot ready to replace the pan. Hester's large eyes were warm with relief.

"Alicia, she's asleep. Miss Edwinna, she's on the porch."

"Good."

"You look tuckered, Mis' Gaunt."

"I'll have some of that bacon—and some bread—if there's enough."

Hester nodded. She then carefully considered what she wanted to say and said it with as little emotion as possible. "All the cullud people, they got burned up, I suppose?"

"*Lord!*" Paula whispered. She walked across the grass and put her hands on the shoulders of the old, dark woman. "Hester, I wouldn't try to go down there right away. Maybe later in the day. Maybe we can get some word before night. But I think your people are all right. They went to Bayfront Park—all of them—and they're being taken care of."

"Most of them," Hester said, "aren't too much account. But my grandchillun . . ."

"I'm sure they must have got through, Hester." Paula could not bear to watch the controlled burgeoning of hope. The older woman wanted, needed, to be by herself. "The whole area burned—where you live—and where your daughters and grandchildren live. But the people got out. Perhaps we can find them all a place nearer here, soon."

She retreated around the wall.

Hester had dignity; above all else she hated to display her emotions. Contrary, Paula reflected, to what people say about Negroes, and in spite of any amount of evidence contrary to *that!*

Edwinna lay in a wicker porch settee, her feet hooked over its arm, her head propped against a pile of varicolored pillows, a drink untouched, beside her.

When her mother appeared she moved her eyes but not her neck and said, "I heard about you. We had a delegation—several, in the end—from your schoolgirls' rescue society. Not that they didn't help. One of them, some damned chemistry major, even ran a blowtorch and cut steel."

"You stayed at the wreck, then?"

"I stayed," Edwinna said.

There was no way to tell: she had bathed and changed her clothes. Paula smiled. "Good!"

"Not that you took any interest in what happened to me, after you sent me flying off to the hospital."

Paula sat. She picked up her daughter's drink and swallowed a third; it proved unwelcome. She hiccoughed. "No. I forgot all about you. You're twenty-six years old and should be able to look after yourself."

Edwinna lighted a cigarette, inhaled and blew smoke at the ceiling. Her wavy blonde hair was combed to its perfect point. She said, "I never knew before what color people were, inside. I never realized, when you split them open and burst them apart, the same things showed up that you see in butchershops."

Paula glanced covertly at her. The voice was even enough. But the words sounded like the edge of a new hysteria. "Oh?"

"No. I never realized a disemboweled little girl would look a lot like lamb quarters. 'Intestine' was just a word. 'Colitis' was something you got that made your gut ache. Now I know what it is."

"Edifying."

"Did *you* know?" Edwinna answered herself. "But, of course! The buzz bombs and V-2's in England. I suppose that train wreck wasn't anything novel—to you."

"I'd done a little volunteer nursing in hospitals before that," Paula said mildly. "The human interior wasn't exactly a secret to me."

"Dear old Red Cross! I always thought it was a social thing. Do you know what I did?"

"No, Edwinna."

"Vomited."

Paula turned her head away slightly.

"Did you hear me?" her daughter asked. "I yorked. Upchucked. Snapped my cookies."

"I did, myself—the first time."

"You did!" Edwinna marveled for a moment.

Paula watched fingers of the morning sun feel in amongst the Caribbean pines and the bristling, green palmettos. "I was—oh—about your age. I'd been to a hospital for a little repair surgery. Nothing much. A young surgeon that I took a fancy to, quite a fancy, wanted me to watch him operate. They dressed me all up and just at what he regarded as the most interesting point—well! I got out of the operating room in time, but not the hall."

The younger woman digested that. Twice, her eyes moved thoughtfully to her mother's face. "I never knew you—took a fancy— to any living male but Dad."

"Neither did your dad, thank God!"

"But you did?"

"All women do, sooner or later, often or rarely, more or less. Only, the ones who have been taught to kid themselves never realize it. Virtue's cheap, but the virgin heart is merely a blind condition of the brain."

Edwinna said gently, "What did you do about—those fancies?"

"That," Paula answered, the sound of remembering no longer in her voice, "would be telling!"

A long moment passed. Finally Edwinna spoke again. "I have never been so shocked in my life. Incidentally, Hester is cooking up some bacon and egg sandwiches. And I'm damned glad you're back. I was worried."

Paula said, "Thanks."

"Another thing. There's a kid in Alicia's nursery that I brought home from the wreck. Her mother was—her mother did what they call died in my arms. A mess. The little girl's all right. I gave her a sleeping pill. Her name, if she wakes up before I do, is Martha."

Paula said very softly, "Okay, Edwinna. Martha. I'll remember."

"I'm bushed," the blonde girl sighed. "I was waiting around for you." She rose slowly and lithely. She stretched. "I'll cadge a sandwich and cork off. Don't bother looking for the dress I was wearing. I buried everything."

Paula, left alone, sat smiling a little, while the intensity of the sunshine increased and until she heard Hester approaching in the paddle-footed way that indicated she was carrying a tray.

"I hope, Bill," Paula whispered, "you heard your daughter just now—wherever you are!"

5

A JOURNEY IS MADE TO AN ORDERLY BEDLAM.

"Gaunt—Gaunt—Gaunt—" said the President. "The name's familiar." He peered into the late night from a window of the White House office.

"A writer," said Clayton Mavoley.

The President grimaced and erased the expression so quickly he left his associate stranded with an answering smirk. "Wait a minute! I've read a couple of his books! Not a newspaper writer, if it's the Gaunt I'm thinking of."

In front of Mavoley, on a long table, were a half dozen sets of folders in filing cabinet drawers. With these were several reference books. He turned the pages of *Who's Who in America*, wetting his thumb. "Here," he said. "William Percival Gaunt." His eyes, enlarged by spectacles, jumped along the lines of fine print. "Born in Connecticut. Guilford. Eighteen ninety-five. Went to Yale *and* Harvard. B.S. and it says he was a mathematics major. M.A. in psychology. Ph. D. in philosophy. Sure covered the waterfront! Wife. Son. Two daughters—one deceased. String of honorary degrees. Written about four—six—eight—a dozen books. A play. There's a whole paragraph listing papers and monographs. He worked in Blake's co-ordinating group during the war—"

"By golly! I *know* the man!" The President was thinking back. He chuckled. "When I was in the Senate! A big, raw-boned gazebo. Long nose, long chin, forehead enough for three men, looks a good deal like a horse. Did a hell of a piece of work getting research teams together. Talks English like a human being. I remember—"

"He's waiting on the line," Mavoley said. "In Miami. Lives there. We got through on the Navy's circuit."

For the twentieth time that evening the President picked up the phone to talk personally with one of America's leading citizens. The President was tired. His body ached. It was necessary for him to draw a breath and conjure a smile so that his voice would sound the way he wanted it to. With the right sound of voice, suitable words would follow.

Of the twenty men he had reached, seventeen had agreed to come at once. One was ill. Two had refused. Of the two, one was hysterical and didn't believe he was talking to the President of the United States. The other was merely sarcastic.

In Miami, Gaunt, who had waited for a long time, finally said, "Yes, Mr. President?"

The reply was confident, courteous, even cheerful sounding. "Things getting under control in your area, doctor?"

"Apparently."

"I suppose sympathy's a poor offering—at such a moment. But I can imagine how you feel. Wife. Daughter."

"Thank you, Mr. President."

"You no doubt appreciate why I called—now, and personally. I'm trying to gather together—from every walk of life—top men— for a conference—starting tomorrow. I hope there's nothing so urgent in your area that it wouldn't be possible for you to join us?"

"As a matter of fact," Gaunt answered, "it's very quiet out here. Miami's a madhouse, of course. Not much real violence—and yet—"

The interruption was curt. "Thank God for that! In other cities . . . !"

"I'm alone. I've been trying to mull it over."

"Good man! Then you'll be here? I can't think of anything more effective than organized mulling, by all you experts." The President hesitated and then asked, "You haven't hit on a line of inquiry that might be profitable?"

"I haven't much data. May I ask—was it world-wide?"

"Absolutely. I can't go into it now, of course. And I'll switch you to the transportation people working here. World-wide—and —if it's any use to you while you fly, all the primates."

"All the primates!"

"So I'm told. Apes. Not monkeys. Will you ride a two-seater P-38? That's a fighter plane? In the morning?"

"Of course."

"Thanks, doctor, and good night." Gaunt heard the President say, "Switch him to Billings." A minute later, he found himself making arrangements to be picked up in a fighter plane at Miami Airport at seven the next morning.

He packed quickly and afterward walked down his drive to the Elliot house.

Jim was alone in his front yard—reclining in a deck chair, his face turned toward the sky.

Gaunt told him where he was going.

The reaction was curt. "Futile!"

Gaunt had felt stimulated by the invitation, the command—inasmuch as the situation most nearly resembled war and the President had the right to act in this crisis as the nation's commander in chief. Now he was momentarily irritated by the Yankee lawyer's skepticism. "Futile? Why? What else is there to do? It's intelligent! Even if nothing is learned—it will at least give the public the assurance that everything is being tried. That sort of assurance is vital!"

Jim Elliot laughed hollowly. "How can you assure anybody after a catastrophe like this?"

Gaunt's vexation ebbed. He sat down facing his friend. "You're right, Jim. You're dead right! Still—it's human to try to use such powers as we have, in *any* situation. See here! I want *you* to help us. I want you to outline and send me your own reflections. You've got an unusual mind, a background that's almost unique, in America. Give us the benefit of it."

Jim stood up then. Perhaps he was human enough to be flattered. More likely, Gaunt thought, his humanity was touched by the mere knowledge that another person respected his ways of thinking. In either case, he too had softened—his mood of hopeless melancholy had lifted a little. "If I have any thoughts, I'll mail them to you." The practical man went on, "What address?"

Gaunt shrugged in the darkness. "Care of the White House will do."

"Of course! What else? Anything I can take care of here?"

"Yes, there is. I'm going back to get a little sleep, if I can. I'll shut off the electricity in the morning. But keep an eye on my place. Have Byron stay there, if he will. He's due again at eight and

I'll bet he shows up. Edwin keeps some rifles and ammunition down here. They're in the closet off my study. You better bring them over here and lock them up. You might need firearms; and we certainly don't want looters or roving teen-agers to get their hands on such stuff."

"I'll hold the fort."

There was silence. "Gordon sleeping?"

Jim nodded. "At last."

"Well—"

They shook hands. The philosopher strode into the darkness under the live oaks.

Jim sat again, alone.

When Gaunt had checked what he had packed and put aside shaving things and a toothbrush for morning, and when he had set Paula's little gold alarm clock, he hunted in the medicine chest. Paula had some seconal somewhere; and he probably would have to be up all the next night. He found the red capsules in a bottle marked "Aspirin," wondered why women so frequently changed pills around, took a grain and a half of the barbiturate and lay down in his pajamas. He thought that probably he would not sleep at all. A heavy slumber overcame him before the drug could work but owing, no doubt, to the psychological effect of it. Once, during the night, he half woke with the awareness that it was raining thunderously. He thought of open windows and recollected that rain did not blow in through the awning type with which his house was fitted. He slept again. . . .

The pilot had a black mustache and small, dancing eyes. He spotted Gaunt on the fringe of the multitude at the airport and hurried up. Gaunt had been told to carry identification. The pilot asked for it, although he had recognized his man from the description given him. He took the philosopher's single, heavy suitcase and led him toward the baggage rooms.

A stranger snatched Gaunt's arm. "You got transportation?"

Gaunt, taken by surprise, said, "Yes."

The man held on firmly. A fattish man. "I have to make Meridan today! Three boys there! Mother gone! I've only got eleven-fifty in cash—but I'll make it ten thousand—check. I'm Armstrong—Armstrong Copper and Brass—"

The pilot had turned. "As you were, bud," he said. "This gent is going on a special plane to Washington—"

"Twenty thousand!" the man said in a shrill voice.

Gaunt pulled away.

It was neither a comfortable nor a revealing flight. The plane's extra seat was painfully small for a man of Gaunt's size; visibility, although excellent for the pilot, was poor for his passenger; and they flew at a great altitude.

Gaunt had glimpses of the green and white metropolis of Miami as they climbed and of smoke rising here and there. Two or three times, later on, he caught sight of other cities with similar pillars of smoke. But for the most part he could see only the pilot's head, instruments, blue sky, and stratified white clouds.

He did not think of snow until they wheeled down over Washington, but he had thought of his overcoat. He'd put it on, at the pilot's suggestion, before climbing aboard. The warm morning of Miami had become the chill of altitude almost within seconds.

Snow lay upon Washington, snow on the hard ground around the Capitol, snow on ice in the reflecting pool in front of the Monument and on the frozen rims of the brown Potomac. They came straight in; traffic was not stacked up here. The airport waiting rooms were almost empty. As Gaunt was escorted to a limousine he saw why: soldiers were intercepting cars at the airport approaches, asking for credentials, turning back slow, angry streams of men.

He was taken to a large hotel where room-and-bath were reserved for him. A clerk, pale and distracted, presented him with a letter; a bellboy, no more composed than the clerk, carried his bag.

"You're in the conference?" the boy asked.

"I guess I am."

"You help make the atom bomb?"

"Not directly—no."

"You think they'll get the girls back?"

Elevator, carpeted hall, door, key, room. "I don't know."

"You *gotta!*" the boy said in a strained voice.

Gaunt tipped him and sat down. He slit the letter. It was signed by the presidential secretary and asked him to present himself at two P.M. in the lobby of the hotel from which he would be driven to the opening assembly. That gave him time for a substantial breakfast, and since room service was functioning, Gaunt ate alone.

The meeting was held in Constitution Hall, as the auditorium of the D.A.R. obviously was not needed at the time by its owners. Limousines and private cars were discharging the conferees when Gaunt arrived. Inside, standards had been placed at various points among the seats so that the "delegates" could assemble by professions and trades. There were signs for biologists, physicians, surgeons, physicists, chemists, mathematicians, psychologists, economists, sociologists, industrialists of various sorts, federal and state officials, and so on. There were no signs for philosophers. But Gaunt's letter had told him to sit with the Co-ordination and Evaluation group. He located that sign and started down an aisle. On every seat, he noticed, was a pad, a number of sharp pencils, and a printed leaflet.

And on every hand, it seemed, a single word was being uttered. The word was, "Doctor!" "Hello, doctor!" "How are you, doctor?" "Fine to see you, doctor!" "Tragic moment, doctor!"

These remarks began to be addressed to him, and he began to utter them. He saw many men he knew, some he knew well, others he knew merely through reputation and press photographs. Mobley, Ascott, Tretter and Findlein were among those he recognized under the Co-ordination and Evaluation placard.

Gaunt greeted them and took a seat amidst the hubbub.

The printed leaflet proved to be a brief description of the aims of the conference along with a collection of miscellaneous information compiled for the "presidential guests"—information about eating places in Washington, a street map, a list of the hotels, the categories of guests assigned to each, and the names of the men who had been invited to the conference along with their professions, principal achievements, and home addresses.

Tretter, the anthropologist, leaned back and grinned. "Fine job! Fast organization, eh, Gaunt?"

"First rate."

"Got any ideas?"

"Nothing I'm proud of."

"Radley says they're going to ask for suggestions from the floor."

"Damned foolishness, if they do."

"Right! We'll see."

The din rose to a pitch higher than any, Gaunt thought, but that of a cocktail party. Then rapidly it tapered off. On the flag-draped platform a band began to play a march. The President entered quickly, with the Vice-President and Dr. Robert Blake, whose tweed suit looked slept in and whose boyish face wore a slightly abashed grin.

The band was silent for an instant and then began the National Anthem. The men—Gaunt thought there were five hundred by that time, not counting those in the area marked "Press-Radio-TV"—rose and began to sing.

Afterward, the President stepped briskly to the center of the stage, looked at the audience, peered momentarily at the microphones, and began to talk, without a manuscript.

"Thank you, gentlemen," he said, "for coming. For coming on such short notice, from such far places under such painful circumstances. Many of those invited will arrive later. I thought it best to convene you who have reached Washington at the earliest possible time. What is said here and whatever may be accomplished here now will be given to the rest in printed form. In a few minutes"—he looked at his watch—"I am to address a joint session of the Congress. What I have to suggest will be brief. Dr. Blake will take charge of this meeting, following my departure. Many of you know him, all of you know of him, and his contributions to atomic energy, to the fission bombs, and to theoretical science."

The President paused and gazed at the men before him as if he could see them one by one. "You know," he continued at last, "the problem. Yours are the best minds of the nation. I have no more knowledge of our situation than any other layman. If science has any particular information about it, I am unaware of that. The few details with which you may be unacquainted will be given to you by Dr. Blake. It is not necessary for me to tell you that I pray God you will find the reason for, and the solution of, this august catastrophe. As a man, as a husband, as a father, I can only wish you Godspeed in your efforts. As the President of this nation, I can and do offer you any and every facility at our disposal for such research as you shall embark upon. Each of your groups will presently elect a chairman. I shall be accessible, I assure you, to any of you who feels I may be of assistance."

Again he paused. He went on in a lower tone: "I, like the seventy-three million remaining Americans, wish you luck!"

Abruptly he bowed his head. He prayed briefly.

Then, to applause, he walked from the rostrum—walked quickly and disappeared through a tall doorway.

Robert Blake took charge of the meeting. He stood at a lectern, his weight on one foot, his other foot turned edgeways on a relaxed ankle. He leaned on an elbow. He coughed. He seemed not like a great scientist but like any college junior, with a crew haircut, standing in mild self-consciousness before a class. For a while he said nothing. Presently, absently, he fished in a pocket and produced a battered package of Chesterfields. He lighted one. The men before him laughed a little and several of them followed suit, Gaunt among them.

"Look!" Blake eventually began. The men laughed again and he grinned at them. "The President has told you that I will brief you on such details as you may be unaware of. They're skimpy—and skimpy is a generous adjective under the circumstances. We do know the event was universal. We do know it extended through the primates including gorillas, chimpanzees, and so on." That caused a murmur among those who had not heard it. "We have already gathered a considerable body of negative information, also. By that I mean, so far as instruments show, so far as *science* is aware, no unusual physical phenomenon occurred either before, at the time of, or after the Disappearance. No change in solar or cosmic radiation, for example. No observed electromagnetic disturbances of any kind. Nothing noted astronomically. So—"

He had tapped his ashes on the floor while he spoke. Now he looked about in vain for an ash tray, shrugged, dropped his cigarette and stepped upon it. "I hardly need to outline the sorts of work upon which we are expected to engage. The broad problems of economic adjustment and social organization will be submitted to the proper groups. The matter of research into causes, of probability study, and so on: the general attack on the mystery of why one sex of one family of terrestrial life should be eradicated in what appears to have been a period of time so short it was not measured—and here we have some interesting information from film and photographic plates of women, girls and female infants, exposed at the critical moment—will be the principal undertaking of us all. You have been divided into groups and before we adjourn today each group will elect its own chairman-spokesman. I suggest that each group meet separately to-night for discussion and that, at a joint conference, tomorrow morning, recommendations be made by each chairman of topics for general consideration.

"It was my thought that we should proceed directly to the election of chairmen, to separate discussion, and to framing reports. The President, however, has asked me to call for suggestions from the floor at this time. I have nothing to add and the meeting will therefore presently be open for such suggestion. Let us appreciate, however, that what is said here will be broadcast to the world and printed in the newspapers. That very fact is, doubtless, the reason the President wanted suggestions made now. By that, gentlemen, I intend to remind you it is our duty as scientists, as experts, as leaders, as citizens of a great and free nation, to display whatever keenness we have and whatever common sense and courage we possess. The world is listening to us. Your suggestions?"

Men stood. Hands went up. Blake waited awhile and finally chose. "Dr. Wendley?" He addressed the audience in general. "Dr. Wendley is a physicist—known to most of you—who has served United Electric Corporation, and this government, brilliantly for many years."

The old man had a straggling goatee, he wore half-moon spectacles; his voice showed his years. "As a Christian," he began agitatedly, "I suggest this meeting, and all others like it, be permanently adjourned and that we return to our homes for continuous prayer! We are dealing with the Lord's punishment—and not any working of nature!"

He sat down. The advice was followed by a slight, and slightly stunned silence, a mark both of respect and of surprise, and then by rising sound that was a mixture of protest, mirth, hissing and a few low-pitched boos.

But Blake took the old man's suggestion gracefully. "I'm sure," he said, "that feeling is shared by millions. In a sense, I share it myself. Unfortunately, we were assembled here not to pray, but to think. Yes? Dr. Averyson? Dr. Averyson, gentlemen, is professor of economics at Princeton University."

A flabby man in a gray suit with a dark-green corduroy waistcoat.

Pencils were ranked like miniature organ pipes in his breast pocket and numerous papers, folded lengthwise, bulged in his side pockets. He was clean-shaven, brown-haired, and he spoke in a high, important voice. "At Princeton University, gentlemen, we have found that the most satisfactory approach to the unknown is the pragmatic and the statistical. My eminent colleague, Peter Frehenfals, in association with"—he cleared his throat—"myself, offered in the year 1946 a treatise on the subject, entitled 'The Social Parallax,' which is regarded in, may I say, perhaps with undue immodesty, very authoritative quarters as the standard development of the procedure which I am about to recommend. The female sex has vanished from the face of the earth. Now, then. We ask ourselves, is this true? Do we *know* it to be true? Can we *prove* it? . . ."

Obviously, Gaunt thought, the jackass would continue in that vein for hours if allowed to do so. He watched Blake's sensitive face change from attention to an irritation which was the more evident because of the smile disguising it.

" . . . no *trend* toward the disappearance of women had been observed," Averyson was saying, "hence the initial methodology of ascertaining *trend* is not merely impracticable but offers no feasible approach whatsoever."

"Thank you, Dr. Averyson," Blake cut in as the man paused for rhetorical effect. "Now—"

"I have not yet made my point," Averyson retorted peevishly. "Some explanatory remarks are essential to lay the groundwork—"

Blake waved his hand. "Exactly. And you can make them initially to your group."

Blake quickly recognized a huge, melancholy-looking man who was standing in the midst of the biologists. "Dr. Steadman. You all know, gentlemen, of Steady's contributions to genetics. Dr. Amos Steadman, of California Institute of Technology."

The enormous, sad-visaged man had a somber voice. "Admitting," he said to the assembly, "that I haven't one single intelligent notion on the whole situation—and in appreciation of the fact that all of you are probably as tired as I am, as sleepy, as depressed and saddened —I move we elect our several chairmen, avoid blathering, get some rest, and go to work, as committees, tonight."

"Second the motion!" several called.

But others rose.

Blake smiled at the geneticist. "Gentlemen, I'm inclined to agree. However—Dr. Tateley? Dr. Tateley is an astronomer. I hardly need to tell you of *his* work."

The thin, white-haired scientist was in a front row so he turned to face the auditorium. "My friends, colleagues and associates," he began, "all the way down here from Boston, where I happened to be last evening, I reflected upon our dilemma. I had the opportunity, yesterday, to make various inquiries. I learned what you have been told. I learned that even ultraspeed motion-picture films being made of the posture of a female dancer, for instruction purposes, show the woman intact in one frame, gone in the next—a difference of something of the order of one one-hundredth of a second. I found that a female technical assistant engaged in temperature and pressure experiments at Radcliffe vanished, in a chamber equipped with many recording instruments, none of which showed any change whatever. Automatically registering stroboscopic devices under the control of women show the ending of their management to have been instantaneous. I realize that these are gross measurements from the standpoint of most of us. Nevertheless, I cannot help but reflect that this may not be a problem for physical scientists. Not, at least, one which will yield to our present formulations and instruments. I would like to suggest, therefore, that we have a word from another branch of scientific inquiry, namely, psychology, and a further word from a still more speculative field. Put it this way. With whom, I asked myself on the train, would I like most to converse at this time? My answers were swift and firm: Dr. Elgin Willis Tolliver, the psychiatrist, whom I know only by reputation, and my very good friend, William Percival Gaunt, who calls himself a philosopher, but who is as able a mathematician and nearly as good a theoretical physicist as anyone in this august body."

Tateley sat down. Heads turned.

Gaunt found himself overcome with embarrassment. He was glad that the astronomer had mentioned Tolliver first.

Blake, meanwhile, replied: "An excellent suggestion. Dr. Tolliver, would you care to contribute?"

The psychiatrist was very short and sturdy, five feet one or two. The thickness of his glasses denoted eyesight so feeble as to approach blindness. As he rose, a tic convulsed one side of his face. And when he spoke it was with so formidable a speech impediment as to make it difficult to understand what he said. His shyness was painful to behold. All in all, Gaunt thought, he looked in desperate need of psychiatric assistance rather than a man eminently able to render it. What he said, however, kept the auditorium in strained attention:

"I c-c-c-c-think, c-c-c-gentlemen, that Dr. c-c-c-Tateley is on the r-r-r-right track."

The mind itself, he went on, is capable of sustaining every imaginable kind of illusion, even of producing, in one and the same body, two discrete personalities. It was not inconceivable to psychology, as it appeared to be to the physical sciences, that some factor—psychic or physical or "j-j-j-j-call it what you may"—could set up a single illusion in a large group. That had been done, partially, often enough through hypnotism. Partial achievement suggested, at least, the *possibility* of complete achievement; that, in turn, hinted at a universal achievement. The world could be, he meant, in a state of total illusion, a state, perhaps, of actual hypnotic sleep, in which it merely seemed to each sleeping male that what appeared to have taken place was real.

Silence followed the statement.

"Are you prepared," Blake at last inquired, "to suggest how such a universal 'sleep,' as you call it, might have been produced?"

Dr. Tolliver shook his square, close-cropped head. "I am not."

Another silence. The man on the platform nodded, as if to himself. "Dr. Gaunt?" he then said. "Are you there, Bill? I haven't seen you."

So Gaunt stood—towered up, his six feet and three inches emphasized by the shortness of the previous speaker. Unlike some of those who had addressed the audience, he had no confidence in himself at this moment. He did not even know, he had been unable to decide, what he was going to say. For perhaps fifteen seconds his eyes ranged over the men, rested briefly on Blake, moved to the flags and the uniformed band behind them.

"I'm here, Bob," he said, "or—with Tolliver's correction—I *think* I am here."

They laughed a little at that.

Gaunt waited. "Shortly after the—Disappearance—I made a list of possible hypotheses. They include Tolliver's suggestion. They are, I fear, such ideas as have already occurred to most of us, with perhaps an exception or two. I hold with Steady—with Dr. Steadman—that we need rest, that we are wasting time here, and that we should divide into our several groups to set forth divergent plans of inquiry. However, I would like to make one suggestion. Let us not be too hidebound in the execution of any project. Let us examine, not just history, which has no precedent for our predicament, but the myths and legends, in which miracles and miraculous disasters abound. And let us try, as we bend ourselves to our task, to think, as Ouspensky has suggested, 'in other categories.' Neither we, nor women, and not sex itself, may be what we have assumed them to be. Mathematics and physics have reached the point where we can contemplate the effect upon a whole human being of a single quantum of energy touching an atom in one gene. But we know, actually, nothing of the relationship of sexuality to energy. We have, merely, a language that has skirted close to the border of formulations in the field. All I have to suggest at this time, therefore, gentlemen, is that we allow our *imaginations* full play and, while we check what we imagine empirically, let us not permit empirical methods to inhibit our minds."

Gaunt sat down. There was scattered applause. Blake was smiling "That," he said, "is the substance of what I'd planned as my own final advice for the day. And since it's been given, I'm ready to take a vote on the motion to elect chairmen and adjourn, pro tem. I hope there will be no questions. I nevertheless invite them."

One or two men rose. It proved that their questions related to matters of personal need—domiciling, financing, and the like. These were speedily answered and the meeting was recessed.

The men immediately broke into groups. Flashlights began to flicker in the auditorium. Gaunt, shaking hands with old friends and strangers who introduced themselves, was seized upon by a man who said merely, "Slack. *Chicago. Tribune.* How soon do you expect results, Dr. Gaunt?"

"How soon," Gaunt replied, "do *you* expect to have an inspiration, wake up with a sonnet written in your mind, or dream true?"

The reporter persisted. "All I could gather from the palaver was that you smart boys were as baffled as everybody else."

Gaunt grinned. "Anybody who gathered more would have invented it!"

"Apparently, you don't mind having the world told that its experts are punko in this crisis?"

"Not a bit."

"What about the Russian angle?"

"Ask a Russian." Gaunt laughed. The reporter gave him up.

Somebody handed Blake a gavel. He pounded for order again and ballots were presented to the members of the conference. In reasonably good time, nominations were made and votes were tabulated. To his discomfort, Gaunt found himself elected chairman of the group that was to appraise and integrate the work of all the others. Then the meeting adjourned.

It was a gray afternoon outdoors and sharply cold. In the

limousine assigned to him, Gaunt was hurried through guarded streets. As he rode, he looked at the winter-stained buildings, the cold sidewalks, the soldiers, and the few hurrying men and boys—at snow patches and ice that had been slush for a few midday hours, at the bare trees and the murk-hung distances. His world was ended. Yet if all men were dreaming, he and his colleagues were supposed to waken them. If men were paralyzed by some unknown force, he and his associates were expected to learn the nature of the force. If another planet had attacked, they were to find that out. If the women had vanished into immaterial and everlasting nothing, they were to deal with that. If humanity was dead and did not know it, his was the task of recognizing death for whatever *that* was.

He thought about it with melancholy. Never before, said his mind, in the echo of a desperate, old phrase, had man been faced with so much to think about and so little with which to think.

The Hand of God lay heavily on the land.

These words came from nowhere, from Space beyond the somber backdrop of the nation's capital, from Time, from his remembered youth.

The hand of God was heavier, by far, than the sternest of his Calvinist ancestors had guessed.

This was like Old Testament days: an epoch for prophets.

Gaunt supposed that in small towns, in the mountains, on winter-swept prairies, men with the faith of their forebears were looking at the plain beds where their wives had slept and into prim hushed parlors where their daughters had been courted, with just such sensations. Praying to a God they consciously feared (and hence often, unconsciously, so hated as to be themselves the lifelong and hateful responses) to lift His heavy hand, to ease the burden, the "burthen."

He felt something not far from fright at the thought that any attitude of the spirit called "faith" could breed such resignation; and his alarm grew even more real as he wondered if, perhaps, that masochistic-sadistic symbology were nearer to the truth than his own concepts.

The limousine waited for a red light as senseless as signals continuing after Doomsday. Nothing approached. Nothing crossed. The city was a wintry void; the wind intoned to itself; nude branches bent against a barren sky—not just beleaguered but abandoned. The car moved. Lights showed ahead. He felt relieved.

I'll talk it over as soon as I get home, he found himself thinking. With Paula. She'll have some suggestions.

And then, although he remembered that was impossible, he clung to the idea—as if by imagining what was contrary to fact he could somehow not delude, but refresh himself.

He let the notion she was beside him invade his mind—stirred with the spontaneous memories—pretended that, out of the corner of his eye, he could see her gloved hands folded in her lap. I do contain, still, something of her, he thought. And when she was here, what I then contained was (in many ways) little more—my own sense of her, not her sense of herself, and not, certainly, whatever she truly was that was perfectly sensed by neither of us.

What was she, then?

And what am I—what was I—that was able to capture in itself a sense of her?

And how did what I guessed and sensed, felt and knew of her, that held me, represent possession of her, and also, a thing possessed by her that she could use, as if part of herself was part of me and we both knew it?

How much, he went on thinking—trying to simplify the idea—of what I call "me" was made of her, belonged to her, and had a female essence?

There was something. He groped after it and had a rise of near-exultation, a sense of being on a significant Verge which was banished as the limousine braked hard to permit the passage of three soldiers in a jeep.

As he entered the ornate lobby of his hotel he heard his name chanted by the loudspeaker. He hurried to the bell-captain's desk and, after identifying himself, was ushered to a phone booth.

"Bill? Bill Gaunt?"

"Yes?"

"Bob Blake! I'm at the White House offices. There's been a new development. Something unforeseen—urgent! I've been requested to have the committee heads meet here right away!"

Gaunt had dismissd the limousine. He asked at the desk for a taxi, explained who he was and told where he wanted to go. A cab was procured.

He rode the short way, hurriedly and with agitation.

What else *could* it be? Bob was worried—or worse.

Soldiers, secretaries, Secret Service men, rooms, corridors, it seemed to take a long while. And then, with the others, he was wait-ing in a sitting room hung with pictures. The President himself ap-peared, with Blake, at the end of a long time.

A President lacking any sign of his customary cheer, even of aplomb. A desperate man. He stopped beside a table, put his hand on it, gestured to the men to sit down, for they had risen, and spoke mechanically:

"Gentlemen. I'll leave you in a moment with Dr. Blake. As the heads of the committees appointed this afternoon, I think you should be informed of everything. My Cabinet"— he jerked his head— "meeting with me now, disagrees. I overruled them." He smiled a little, snappily, without any amusement. "We have just received word from the Soviet government of a decision to destroy the free world on the grounds that the disappearance of Soviet women is un-questionably the work of the democracies."

Someone said, "Good God!" No other sound was made and soon the President went on.

"There is one very shocking matter in the statement handed to me a little while ago by the Soviet representative. The document claims that the harbors of several American cities—it does not say which ones or how many—have, for some time, been mined with hydrogen bombs. The United States of America is 'ordered' not to interfere in any way with Soviet operations on pain of the explosion of those mines. I may add that we have no idea whether the claim is true or a bluff. I would like your reactions."

He looked at them, stiffened his shoulders, and marched from the room.

PART II

Armageddon

6

THE ONSLAUGHT.

One man walked to a window and gazed out at the cold dusk. Because he moved, others looked at him and they saw, by and by, a shudder pass over his body. Gaunt let his eyes range over the walls which were solidly hung with paintings—paintings of many schools and with many subjects—gifts to Presidents who were remembered only through lists of names and gifts to Presidents whose words and acts had kindled flame in history's niches—pictures of people and ships and buildings, of flowers and landscapes and the sea.

"Well, gentlemen?" Blake said it softly.

Someone—Gaunt did not identify the speaker—muttered, "Retaliation?"

"At what price?" Blake asked.

Another man, an industrialist, Gaunt recalled, but he could not remember which one, said vehemently, "It's up to you experts, now, to sweep the mines from the harbors!"

Blake was impatient but he took a chair first, curled one foot upon the other, relaxed. "It can be tried, of course, Mr. Ames. But the bombs aren't, themselves, sufficiently radioactive to be detected by instruments. It would mean, simply, blind dragging, in big bays and harbors, in sounds and estuaries, where we've already dumped thou-

sands upon thousands of bargeloads of junk. Every sizable object encountered by the draggers would have to be raised to the surface
where the water was deep or inspected by divers where it was not. I
should say, for example, that to drag the waters around New York
City alone, if every available rig in the nation were concentrated
there, would take perhaps six months. And nobody could be sure
even in that period that one hydrogen bomb had not been missed."

"Evacuate, then," Ames said. He was a solid-looking man of
about sixty with gray eyes and a broad forehead. His manner was not
arbitrary or truculent, but very vigorous.

The other men were paying this discussion their concentrated
attention. Blake shrugged.

"Again—take New York. Weeks would be needed merely to get
the population of Manhattan off the island. And that population
would only be added to millions of fugitives from the Bronx,
Queens, Brooklyn, and elsewhere. Where would they go? By what
transportation? How would they be housed in wintertime? How
would they be fed? How would their sick be dealt with? If the full
facilities of the nation were used to handle them as well as possible, and it wouldn't be very well, how would the nation also
evacuate Boston, Philadelphia, Baltimore, Washington, here—the
West Coast cities—Chicago, Detroit, Cleveland—?"

"Those last," Ames interrupted, "aren't seaports."

"But they are ports." Blake tugged at his socks, thrust a finger behind the counter of a shoe, hunched his shoulders, waved his free
hand. "Have we checked every boat that has moved on the Great
Lakes, down to fifty-tonners, say, during the past few years? No. Have
we watched every truck and every freight car that might reach all
such vessels by land, during the same period? Of course not. We
haven't even had a radar screen around the continent." He smiled
faintly. "You will recall, Mr. Ames, that hundreds of tons of alcoholic
beverages were daily smuggled into this country during Prohibition.
I infer, from that, it would not be impossible nowadays to smuggle

objects weighing a few tons, either whole or piecemeal, into the same country. Note that I do not say it has been done. I do not say that there are hydrogen bombs on the floors of the harbors of our cities. I merely say that none of these things is impossible, theoretically."

"Do you propose, then," the industrialist asked, "to allow the Red armies to proceed without intervention?"

"No. I don't. I have made no proposals. I am waiting to hear what you gentlemen suggest."

Ames rose. He said nothing further. Locking his hands behind his back, he walked to the windows and joined the scientist who had shuddered.

"One thing."

Everybody looked at Gaunt. A smile showed on his elongated face and it was of a sort that made the appalled men feel there might be resources and hopes of which they were unaware.

"Obviously," Gaunt began, "this dilemma cuts two ways. Knowing my own country and my countrymen, I'm quite sure that the United States has not taken the step of mining any Soviet harbors." He glanced inquisitively at Blake, who smiled back faintly and shook his head. "But there seems to be no reason for admitting the oversight."

"Sly!" said one of the listeners.

"We should," Gaunt continued, "inform the Soviet immediately that we have similarly prepared certain of their harbors. Their neurotic suspicions of the democracies will tend to make them believe it and they will find themselves in an uneasy predicament, like our own."

"*Uneasy!*" someone murmured sarcastically.

"Next," Gaunt said, "in my opinion, we should endeavor, by submarine, or plane, to *carry out* precisely such mining. It would probably take time—"

"It would," Blake agreed grimly. "None of our atomic weapons has been prepared for use as a radio-detonated mine."

"Then we should prepare some," the philosopher said. "A rather elementary step that should have been tended to, long since."

Blake flushed.

"Beyond that," Gaunt finished, "my own inclination is—let us tell them to detonate their mines and be damned!"

A rumble came from the great, shaggy figure of Steadman, the geneticist. "Lord, man, do you know what you're saying?"

"I know."

Steadman got ponderously to his feet. "You're saying—go ahead! Wipe out millions of us, if you're not bluffing! Destroy our cities! Wreck our industries! Sicken and maim and injure and drive mad— sterilize and make cancerous millions more of us! Saying that, Bill— for the sake of a gesture!"

"A gesture?"

"What else is it?"

Gaunt sighed. He walked to a position more nearly in the center of the congregation of men. "What's the alternative? Europe overrun. England—probably hors de combat in a brief atomic blitz. It's such a little target, as weapons go nowadays. Then there will be our one nation, alone, facing a Soviet-dominated planet, with the mines *still* undetonated, the danger *still* as real as whatever its degree is now. We had our chance; we ignored it."

Blake was looking at the thick, worn, Oriental rug. He did not raise his eyes. "*What* chance, Bill?" he asked quietly.

Gaunt sighed once more. "I've talked about it, written about it, advocated it—for five long years. It's simple. Too simple for men with modern, complex minds to see, I guess. Gentlemen, most of you are scientists. What you and your fellow scientists have achieved has been accomplished through freedom and because all knowledge was made accessible to all men. Nucleonics, atomic energy, is only one special branch of human inquiry into the facts of nature. To allow it to be made 'secret' simply because it produced fabulous weapons was the greatest blunder in American history. We offered it to the world. Russia rejected our terms of freedom and openness. At that time, we in our own turn should have refused flatly to *let* Russia—or any nation—so act that we were obliged to restrict American freedom of knowledge. Instead, we accepted abrogation—like weaklings, like beggars! Like men who had forgotten that all we stand for is freedom, that freedom alone sustains us, we assented to a Soviet world policy which obliged us to abandon *at its heart* the very concept of freedom."

Someone said, "Fiddlesticks."

Gaunt peered in the direction of the voice. "Fiddlesticks? If we had seen that our own liberty had suddenly, through no fault of ourselves, become one with world freedom—if we had stood fast for it— we had the power to sustain our ideal without striking a blow. It was 1946. Russia had no bomb. Crushed, impoverished, starving, in chaos—Russia would have had to yield to the United States, the earth's most powerful nation. Instead, we closed the hatch on freedom and crash-dived into a sea of secrecy where our secrets were re-discovered—as was evident they could be—or leaked out—as some did—or were stolen. For five wretched years we blundered in the dark. Now, as we emerge, we find the picture changed and our strength matched by enemy strength which is more ominous to us than we are to them, simply because we are more vulnerable!" Gaunt paused to light a cigarette. "America stupidly turned its back on free-dom and this is the cost. So—if they mean to have war—I say, let us at least fight it in liberty's name—bravely and openly—and give up trying to compromise, to stall, to outwit."

"I protest!" Wendley, with the white goatee and half-moon spectacles, was on his feet. "We need Christian leadership here—!"

"We've been led," Gaunt said coldly, "without the knowledge or consent of the people, for five years, by a handful of politicians and physicists. Led to this humiliating condition. Led as an *unfree* people —a people who decided *not* to know. Blake, and some of you others, have indicated feelings of guilt. Of 'sin.' Well—the sin was to abandon freedom. Failing to create a free world, our men of science, by refusing to act in a secret world, could have forced the issue single-handed. But they are, alas, only men. They had—it proved—no more insight or morality, no greater loyalty to liberty or larger idealism, and no more readiness for sacrifice, than the commonest ditchdigger. They are not to blame for not being superior. But they can never think of scientists, from now on, as other than, or different from, or superior to, the blindest amongst us. I have said it all over and over. If, now, when war is almost academic, when death to masses is almost a joke, you *still* will not rally for freedom, then, I think, the species deserves its fate!"

Tolliver, the psychiatrist, said stammeringly, "C-c-c-he's right!"

The white-haired astronomer, Tateley, called, "I agree!"

"Surely," said Ames, the magnate, "there is another route—?"

"Prayer!" Wendley half shouted. "Let us disband these conferences! Let us say to the Soviet that we surrender—rather than that we shall be the authors of our own effacement! Then—let us put our case before God Almighty!"

"God Almighty," said Blake, swinging his foot a little, "seems to have judged our case already—and unfavorably. Bill Gaunt has hinted at one factor which we've overlooked in the immediate fear of hydrogen bombs. We met here this morning to consider a problem far more crucial and disastrous than which nation may win any war."

"I disagree!" Dr. Averyson, the Princeton economist, still carried his pencils and wore his green corduroy waistcoat. "I feel, and I move, that we regard the Russian threat as paramount. For several reasons. First, we seem unable to do anything relevant or cogent about the disappearance of the women. Second, since they vanished by means beyond our control, we may logically assume they can and will be restored by the same means. Third, there *may* be no future for us under Soviet domination! Fourth—"

"False logic," Tateley said sharply. "A war—a victory—is nothing compared with the catastrophe that has already overwhelmed us."

"There's this," Gaunt put in, "and we ought to consider it. We keep looking at everything from the viewpoint that the Soviet is powerful and we are vulnerable. Let us turn *that* about. Let us assume, for the sake of discussion, that the citizens of Russia, being even more primitive than our own, were even more disturbed by yesterday's cataclysm. What would their government do in that event? With insurrection threatening in a population of frantic males? It would make some fresh, unprecedented challenge to divert the public mind—to keep the machinery of military control in motion—to replace helpless bewilderment with disciplined, comprehensible action. We may be facing, not a recklessly opportunistic government, but one that has taken new steps owing to internal disintegration."

There was silence for a moment while that thought was turned over.

"V-v-very astute," Tolliver presently stammered. "Very! And in that case, our rejoinder should be—not words—but deeds. All-out atomic attack. An effort to abet Soviet chaos before increased discipline firms up their public attitude!"

"—which," Averyson said in a sickly whine, "would probably bring down total ruin, instantly, upon ourselves. This very city. Even this room!"

Mindebein, an anthropologist, who had not spoken until that moment, said, "God, how detestable a coward is!"

The economist whirled. "I resent that, sir!"

The thin little man came to his feet—for Mindebein weighed less than a hundred pounds. His large brown eyes were steady. "I believe," he said, raising his face to the economist's, "it is customary to ask if you would like to make anything of it. Would you, doctor?"

Averyson was furious enough to lunge. Men stopped him. He sat down.

Blake, who had leaped forward with amazing speed, now dropped back in his chair and threw a leg over its arm. "I don't want anything said here taken personally or personally directed. Presumably, we are soon to give the President the benefit of our collective advice. Some points have been made. Are there others?"

The talk went on.

And talk, Gaunt found himself thinking, was all it would prove to be. It was the trouble with these men, this century. Given time, months or years, and they would have come up with several brilliant, if theoretical solutions of the present problems. Faced with them in a single hour, asked for decisions intended to regulate action, they could only argue.

As the talk continued, food was served. The men ate, some even with relish. They mulled the ideas already presented and offered new ones. They theorized and they reminisced. They drew analogies and cited historical parallels. They described brilliantly to each other various processes—physicists making atomic energy understandable to economists—biologists making the mathematicians see what radioactivity did to human tissue—industrialists explaining the ingenuity and courage with which various great steps of warmaking had been financed and carried out in the past.

But when, toward nine o'clock, the President asked for a verbal report from Blake, he left the chamber wearing an expression of embarrassment which revealed to everyone what Gaunt had observed: how ineffectual they were.

He was gone for less than half an hour. When he returned, he was gray-faced. He sagged as he walked forward. The babble stilled. He looked from man to man, one by one, around the chamber.

"Gentlemen," he said, "any advice we might have had to offer would have been superfluous. At about four o'clock this afternoon, in a barn not half a mile from the center of Pittsburgh, a large moving van was discovered by some boys. They broke into the van. It contained what they described to the police as a boiler and a television aerial. The police investigated and summoned members of the university faculty. The 'boiler and aerial' have been examined and partially dismantled, at what personal risk to the professors you will appreciate when I say that it proved to be a very large uranium-lithium-tritium bomb, set to be detonated by radio signals. The Soviet statement that our cities have been mined is therefore not bluff. It is fact. The mine, in this case, was merely not in a harbor, as the declaration claimed. Its detonation would unquestionably have destroyed the Pittsburgh area."

Nobody spoke.

Blake went on: "This circumstance was followed by another. An apparently similar bomb *was detonated,* at seven forty-two this evening, our time, apparently in the Bay, at San Francisco." The young physicist shut his eyes and passed a hand over his forehead. "A few—disconnected—details—are coming in. Apparently all persons, buildings, and even the hills within some eight or ten miles of the San Francisco end of Golden Gate Bridge have been annihilated—vaporized—melted down. For another ten-mile radius not much life has been observed by planes cruising the area at suicidally low levels. Reconnaissance is continuing in planes carrying searchlights. Suburban areas not shielded by mountains, as far as thirty miles from the center, have been flattened and are on fire. A tidal wave inundated the towns above and below the bay—and, of course, across the bay. A cloud of radioactive steam, sea water, and mixed materials is blowing inland on a steady west wind and dispersing along the slopes of the Sierras. Its course and dispersal are being checked from the air by technicians and pilots who, obviously, will pay with their lives for their exposure to the radiation in the cloud."

Several men tried then to say something. Blake waved at them. "I have not quite finished. In view of these facts, and in view of extraordinary powers voted to the President by Congress in a closed session this evening, our bombers are taking off from bases outside this country, close to target areas, with nuclear bombs in their bays. We do not know how many will get through the radar, anti-aircraft and fighter screens protecting the Soviet Union. I think, however, you are entitled to be told that if even ten per cent of our planes reach their targets, it may be said with conviction that, before morning, Russia probably will be without a single, intact major city."

Toward morning, Gaunt found himself at the entrance of his hotel. . . .

By that time he knew that many of the American aircraft had not only delivered their bombs but returned to their bases. He also knew that no further explosions had occurred in the United States. He had sat talking, with the others and with various officials of the government, through most of the night—expecting, like the rest, to glimpse a flash of light before Washington and its broad environs vanished from the earth.

In the cold and the dark, he stepped from a limousine. But, instead of entering the dimmed-out lobby, he walked down the street a ways, pulling up the collar of his overcoat and stuffing his hands in its pockets. Few people could be seen. An occasional policeman or soldier. A rare jeep or military car. Once, a thundering procession of motorized antiaircraft guns came out of the night, shook the earth in passing, and roared on into the black city. Gaunt presently reached a small park and stood at a corner of it, looking at the sky where, now, the stars glittered.

His eyes moved to the Great Dipper and Polaris. While they were thus fixed he saw—suddenly and only for an instant, to the left of the North Star—a flame-colored light. It was as if some cosmic hand had switched on and off the Aurora Borealis. He went back to his hotel knowing that a city in the direction of Chicago or Detroit— with all its inhabitants and their works—had been destroyed by a tumultuous flare of atomic energy which had towered so high in the stratosphere as to be visible around the earth's curve, hundreds of miles away, where he stood.

7

IN WHICH CERTAIN LADIES TAKE LIBERTIES WITH THE LAW.

That morning, after the night of wreck and fire and God-sent deluge, Paula was tired, yet not so tired as Edwinna. She sat awhile, admiring the annuals which grew in the bed bordering the porch. She watched, as Bill had, the defense of the bath and the feeding station by the mockingbird that held it against jays, ground doves, and all comers in the warbler family. When Hester brought a bacon and egg sandwich and coffee, she ate slowly and drank peacefully, her attention on the bright burgeon of the planet's first morning without human males.

It was impossible to conceive of. If Bill had died suddenly, she thought, it would have been utterly different even in respect to Bill. The shock would have been intense, the initial woe and mourning hardly more than a style of reflex, and true grief would have followed, bit by bit, in all the remaining afterward. There was shock now, far more shock, in a sense, than even the death of her husband would have occasioned. No doubt grief would rise in her like a tide, each wavelet higher than the one before, in the uncertain future. Still—the mordant panoply, the tuberose smell of private death were absent here in spite of the ubiquity of death itself. That made a difference.

You cannot say *he is dead,* or *they are dead,* she told herself; you cannot say *Edwin's gone,* either, as he would have been gone if his plane had been shot apart in combat. It is so much *not-death* I can hardly feel that even the *really dead women* have really died. Their death seems more like another manifestation of what happened, a secondary effect; and that isn't reasonable at all since they were burned, crushed, and torn to bits. But what *is* reasonable now?

I will be, she thought.

Then for a moment it was as if she could hear Bill dissertate: "My dear, I don't know whether it's environmental or sex-linked, but the constant, observable unwillingness of women to *reason,* when they are faced by a problem that will yield to logic but not to emotion, has given the ladies their ageless reputation for intellectual frivolity."

Paula wondered if men were really better reasoners. In local, immediate matters they might be *more likely* to reason. But the net result of their collective attempts to be logical was a preposterous society, a pervading sense of embarrassment, a *lost* feeling amongst women (that they knew about) and amongst men (that they seemed unaware of), along with what they called a "civilization" which, in the near-fifty years of Paula's experience, had seemed not only heathen and barbaric, but blind to the fact, and getting worse every year. If *that* was the result of reason, she wanted something more than reason. And here, she thought, was an idea she might have used in rebuttal to Bill—and one Bill would heartily have denied. He would have said her list of particulars showed not where reason failed, but merely how little it was employed by women *or* men.

It was a provoking, pointless line of meditation. She took a last look at the sun-spangled palmettos and went into the house. Hester's fire was still smoldering in the yard; Hester herself was washing up the skillet, coffeepot and plates.

"You're tired," Paula said.

Hester's eyes responded.

"There won't be any use—yet—going into Miami to find your daughters and grandchildren. You go to the guest room and sleep."

"In the *guest* room?"

"Where else?" Paula answered. "We haven't any other rooms."

"But the *guest* room! I'm a colored woman, Mrs. Gaunt—"

"You should thank God for it. At least you can still feel things. Leave the door open, Hester, in case the kids cry. I guess you know we have a boarder? Martha?" She saw that Hester knew. "Before you go, though, how are we on butter—bread—bacon—staples?"

"Kind of run down."

Paula put her hand on Hester's shoulder and gently turned her toward the door; Hester went slowly, uncertainly.

Paula opened the refrigerator, gave its contents an inventorial stare, and winced slightly at the discovery (which she felt she should have made sooner) that, with power off, the box had defrosted. She looked quickly into various cupboards.

"'Old Mother Hubbard,'" she murmured.

She hurried outdoors, slid into one of her two cars and drove toward Coconut Grove. The morning smelled of smoke; a few columns of smoke still rose along the horizon. But these, even if they flared up, could be contained. They had daylight, now, in which to experiment with the fire engines, find dynamite and figure out how to blast. As she drove, her glance dropped to the dashboard and stopped at the gasoline gauge. She frowned: *another thing*.

It was still early. But cars were moving. Quite a few women were in their yards, talking to each other. And soon Paula encountered a milk truck. It was driven by a woman who wore a plaid cap. Paula honked hard, slowed, and tried to head off the truck. But the driver cut onto somebody's lawn, yelling about "regular customers." Her own milk hadn't come, and Paula also realized that the morning paper hadn't been lying, folded, in the car porte either. "Damn and damn!" she said.

In the business center of Coconut Grove many cars had already arrived and more were arriving—moving slowly, hunting for convenient parking spots. Drivers exhibited their usual Coconut Grove lethargy and, as usual, honored traffic regulations in their flagrant breach. Paula was obliged to go clear through the village; the good parking places were taken. As she drove she realized the other women were doing exactly what she had planned to do: waiting for stores to open.

They're going to *hoard*, she thought—even while she confessed that her own intentions had been no different.

The filling station she regularly patronized was still closed. A few women in cars waited there, beside the pumps; some of them now and again touched their horn-buttons with the impatience of regular customers used to quick service.

Paula remembered, then, an obscure side-street station—two battered pumps—which was generally tended by a middle-aged woman with a pasty face and a grumpy expression. So she drove on, not quite certain where she had seen the place; but presently she found it. A block-long line of cars had already formed. Paula joined the line. After a while she noticed a pudgy girl with dark curls and a dirty face going from car to car. The child's visitation irked some of the waiting women for, after she had spoken to them, they pulled out of line with angrily spinning wheels and drove away.

The girl reached Paula and leaned in, smirking:

"There isn't any power to pump gas," she said with relish, "and Maw has put on a hand crank. You gotta pump your own—Maw's too tired. And besides, if you want it, it's a dollar a gallon."

"That's profiteering!" Paula exploded. "Your mother will be put in jail for doing a thing like that at a time like this!"

"Go call a cop," the child said derisively. "Just go an' try it!"

Paula bit back her vexation and crept forward with the line. She needed fifteen or sixteen gallons to fill her near-empty tank.

When her turn came, she was enraged to be told by the pallid woman, "It's two dollars a gallon now. 'Most gone. I made up my mind to get it while the gettin's good! Lord only knows when there'll be another truck delivery."

Paula said nothing.

She had seen, in past years, young men quickly and easily crank a tankful of gasoline. But either they had been stronger than she by a remarkable degree, or this pump was inefficient. Panting, sweating and disheveled, she finally got her gasoline and bitterly handed thirty-three dollars to the woman. It was more than half of the cash she had put in her pocketbook.

She parked in the nearly filled drugstore lot and crossed the street. Nothing—absolutely nothing—seemed open yet. The biggest crowd—perhaps fifty or sixty women—stood in front of Sam's Market. She joined that group.

She recognized Mrs. Ed Bantley and the very important Mrs. Treddon-Stokes. She nodded to Mrs. Clinton Brown and to Ella Evers—who looked dreadful, as usual, in cerise pedal-pushers. The untouchable, stately Myra McCantley was there too, with others Paula knew. The enterprising ones, mainly.

Now, for the first time, Paula had the opportunity to listen to the reactions of comparatively calmed-down, ordinarily normal house-wives, the steady patrons of Sam's rather expensive market. These were women not easily distracted or upset. In their twenties and thir-ties they had borne children; then and later they had participated in their husbands' stressful campaigns for success; they had sent sons off to war; they had made for themselves and their families very comfortable, and in some cases palatial homes. Thus, through experi-ence, they had grown inured to life's rugged episodes, however pam-pered they made themselves appear.

Most of these women had been crying recently. Their eyes showed it and their voices contained the memory of it. All of them were frightened—and frightened in many different ways at once. All of them tried to hide their fears.

As Paula came up, Mrs. Treddon-Stokes was saying in a high, stilted tone and with an unprecedented effusiveness, "I spent the night with my Master! When I was sure that Walter had been taken —along with the others—I threw myself in my chaise. I must have spent hours there! Darkness came. I knew prayer was the only thing but I didn't dare call dear Reverend Connauth for fear of contacting" —her eyes, hollow but still penetrating, beaconed over the listening ladies—"that perfectly impossible woman he had the misfortune to be married by! At last I undressed slowly, prepared a bite for myself from the little upstairs pantry in Walter's den, and simply cast myself upon the Lord! I felt very near to Him, at first. But as the night passed, and as I perhaps had a little fitful sleep, I seemed to drift farther and farther away. This is a *most* somber punishment! I hardly feel that all of us deserve it, though the Scriptures make it plain how the innocent must suffer with the guilty. *Think* of it! Half of them taken straight to hell, I feel most certain, in just agony for their low, immoral ways!"

Someone in the little audience made a rude sound.

Mrs. Treddon-Stokes did not turn her high-carried head but she said, almost as if she had eyes hidden under her tight back hair, "What did *you* do, Ella?"

Since it was Ella who had greeted the religiosity with what she would frankly have called a Bronx cheer, it might have been expected that Ella would have been embarrassed. But anyone who knew her, or any stranger who had closely noted the damn-you-all clothes she wore, could have foreseen a different result.

She gave her medium bob a toss. "A hill," she said in a theatrical voice. "As soon as I *knew*, I found myself longing for a hill. A hill to throw myself down on, to let the wind feel over me, to get a perspective from, to watch the blue mystery of the sky, to sense the awe and the wonderment!" It was, Paula knew, satirical.

"I just cried," said a little woman quietly. "Cried all night! And I'm not through. Oh! *What is it?*"

Mrs. Treddon-Stokes, who towered like a parsimonious steeple over most of the others, gave Ella an acid look. She then noticed, above the general level of clustered heads, the classic part and ashen Psyche knot that, along with her height, distinguished Myra. "And *you*, my dear! Where were you? What helpful community task occupied you when the Visitation took place?"

Paula was sure that Myra gave the lank old snob a startled glance. The banker's wife didn't speak immediately, either; she licked her lips and formed a smile which it took a second to make acceptable.

I wonder, Paula thought, where Myra actually *was*. Some place, evidently, that she'd just as soon nobody knew about. The idea connected with another: recently Paula had listened to a lengthy and detailed rave about Myra by Teddy Barker. Paula gasped at the possibility and then stared thoughtfully at Myra, wanting to laugh and at the same time feeling indignant.

"In the Gables at the Salon," Myra was saying. "Having innumerable things done."

The old Trojan horse, Paula thought. That's Myra's story and she's going to stick to it, even if not another living woman ever again has a chance to flirt, let alone commit adultery. You go in the front door and you take a soundproof booth and you get fixed in a hurry and you go out the back door and then between the cedars, and you've stepped right out of this world for the afternoon—but literally!

"Don't you *want* to talk about it?" Mrs. Treddon-Stokes asked.

"Why should I?" Myra seemed bitter and edgy, which, Paula thought, was not the expectable or appropriate mood. "Talking doesn't seem to change anything!"

"That's right," said a woman Paula did not know. "I've stood here listening to personal history for nearly an hour! Does anybody in the crowd *know* that Sam's is going to be opened?"

"He has a wife," Mrs. Treddon-Stokes said with vigor. "After all, with Sam gone, it's her *duty* to take up things—"

"My husband," Myra said in a cool voice that possibly showed enjoyment at the chance to return one baiting for another, "is a director of the bank down the block. And I assure you, Mrs. T., it hasn't entered my head to find out how to *open* the bank—let alone start cashing checks for people or taking deposits!"

"It *ought* to have!" the spirelike woman retorted. "It ought to have, indeed! Isn't it perfectly obvious that all of us women will simply *have* to take up where our husbands left off? Otherwise, things will go to *pieces?*"

"And the women," said Ella Evers, "whose husbands did absolutely nothing—will have to do the things left over. Like driving garbage trucks."

Mrs. Treddon-Stokes said, "Really!" and flushed.

"What *is* obvious"—Myra's voice was now steady—"is that just marrying a man doesn't teach you his business. I'm sure I'd be utterly helpless in a bank. I wouldn't know how to deduct a cashed check from the assets, or how to add on a deposit. Would anybody here?"

No one, it appeared, would know.

"But what are we going to *do*?" one of the women wailed.

"All I've got," said another hysterically, "is eighty-five cents. Sam would have let me charge. But will—somebody else?"

Paula called, "Ladies!" They turned toward her. "Let's not get excited. After all, the things you're worrying about are trifles compared with the things we're soon going to have to worry about. It isn't just getting checks cashed and getting into grocery stores. It's— for instance—how to refill the stores when we've bought them bare."

"We'll go to the wholesale places, direct," someone said brightly.

Paula snorted. "There is probably enough food, in Miami, to keep all of us alive for a few weeks. When it's gone—"

"Don't be panicky, Mrs. Gaunt," another woman said. "After all, we live in the middle of America's winter truck gardens. And there are cattle ranches simply everywhere—"

"Will you pick the vegetables?" Paula answered sharply. "Can you drive a truck to bring them in? Can you rope cattle? Can you butcher? Can you run refrigerator trains? And if you can do that, can you breed more cattle and plant more crops to keep us going?"

A woman who had just arrived, as several had, during the discussion, shoved herself forward. She was an unknown—heavy-shouldered, with large breasts and thick ankles. She wore men's trousers. She had not combed her iron-gray hair that morning or powdered her thick-lipped, snub-nosed face. But she had, apparently, met the crisis with the aid of spirituous liquors. She was drunk but not uncomprehendingly drunk. She was energetically drunk—drunk to the point where her obviously meager ethics were impaired.

She pushed rudely forward and said in a slattern's half-shout, "Maybe all you fancy ———s,"—the word made some ladies gasp and left others unaffected, since they had never heard it—"are going to stand around here all day snapping your traps about what to do! I, personally, drove into town just to get some grub and grub I mean to get!"

What surprised Paula was not that no one interfered with her— few of the women would have reasonably dared to, alone—but that they made way for her and watched her with what seemed, in the case of many, virtual approval.

The woman walked up to the locked glass double doors of Sam's. She rattled them. She shielded her face from the sun with her arm and peered in. She backed away and surveyed the two streets that formed a corner behind the crowd. Across one of them was a cottage with a white board fence. The woman strode to the fence and took hold of a board. She ripped it loose. With this she came back. Way was made for her again. She turned her side toward the door and brought down the board. It took several blows to break the glass and several more to knock out the jagged edges.

Reaching through, the woman found the knob and swung back the door. "Come on!" she bawled over her shoulder. "Let's get it while it's here!"

For a few moments the crowd merely watched, some through the door and some through the plate-glass windows. The woman inside grabbed a handcart and began to hurry among the shelves and piles of foodstuffs, helping herself.

"It's the only thing to do!" a voice murmured tentatively.

"It is not! It's criminal!"

Paula recognized Bella. She hadn't seen her arrive—but Bella Elliot was a tiny woman.

"We've got to eat!" another voice protested.

And a woman watching at the door shouted, "She's taking *ten packages of butter!*"

Bella pushed her way to the place where the glass was broken. "We just simply can't start acting like this!" She wore her affectionate smile and her bobbed brown hair shone in the bright sun. She had spoken loudly but much as a mother would speak to a panicky child.

"And," another watcher shouted, "*fifty pounds of sugar*—and she doesn't even *shop* here! *I* never saw her in *my life!*"

Still, Bella might have prevailed. Bella, with help. For Paula and Ella Evers now reached the door. Paula shouted, "She's right! We've got to wait till Mrs. Vilmak gets here—"

"Who is Mrs. Vilmak?" Myra called.

"You ought to know! You've shopped here years longer than I have. It's Sam's wife! That's their name—Vilmak." Paula stood shoulder to shoulder with Bella. "Either that, or until some form of rationing is set up."

"*Rationing!*" another woman cried in a loud, sneering voice. "Will we have to put up with *that* forever?"

The ladies were frightened. They were worried about food. But they were not lawless, at least not in such categories of lawlessness as include breaking and entering, barefaced robbery, or other forms of public violence. They might not have assaulted Sam's store but for a new factor.

Up the street, with horns blowing, came a small cavalcade of disreputable cars filled with women who matched the vehicles. The noisy procession presently slowed and stopped about a block away, in the middle of the street. Women—dozens of them—poured out of the cars. They raced up on the sidewalk. There was a sound of shattering glass and a surge as the women followed their fusillade into a small jewelry store.

"Let's go!"

"That settles it!" someone said sharply. "If we don't get it— others will!"

"We ought to go and stop *them!*" Bella wasn't smiling any more.

Mrs. Treddon-Stokes caused the stampede. "What we *can* do, since *we're* all *thoroughly* responsible people, is to leave signed lists of what we take—so Mrs. Sam can collect!"

That suggestion salved consciences. It had, furthermore, the loftiest social sanction.

Paula and Bella were pushed aside and the women streamed into the big market.

Bella had tears in her eyes. Paula put an arm around her. "Maybe the only thing left to do now is to go in ourselves."

"You go," Bella said wretchedly.

"How will you feed Sarah?"

The other woman shook her head. "I don't know."

"Come on! They'll strip the place!"

"It's a crime!"

"Sure," Paula said, "it's a crime. Or *is* it? When only the fittest survive—who's fit?"

"I'd rather die—!"

"And I'd rather not!"

Already some of the women who had entered the store were coming out with laden arms; a few pushed loaded wire carts. They hurried to their cars. Some drove off. Others returned for a second load. And now Paula saw a woman whom she did now know commence to load her sedan, not from the store, but from groceries deposited in other cars. The ladies of Coconut Grove were not yet accustomed to all the aspects of thieving.

Paula murmured to Bella, "Watch that creature with the frizzy blonde hair! See what she's doing?" She waited for Bella's nod. "Then *think!* Nobody's going to get out of here with groceries enough for more than a couple of days! If a person is really going to help himself, he ought to be smart about it. You and I could stock up—if you'd help. And then, if rationing gets organized, we could turn in what we'd hoarded."

Bella shrugged hopelessly. "If you say so—"

"I not only say so, but I say we've got to hurry or there won't be anything worth taking! Now, look—!"

A moment later Paula entered the store, where the women swarmed. She went through to the storeroom. She opened the rear door a crack. Bella was already there. Behind her was a high stucco wall; between the wall and the back of the store was a mountain of empty cartons.

"Okay?" Paula asked.

Bella looked furtively down the alley between the building and the wall. "I guess so. I closed the gate. I *hope* nobody saw me come in."

The women in the store proper were concerned with their own wants; to that concern was added an extreme nervousness about what they were doing. They paid little heed to each other and none at all to the fact that, fast as Bella and Paula loaded carts they wheeled them not out into the street but into the storeroom. From the storeroom they conveyed the groceries to empty cartons outdoors. And from the storeroom they also took cases of canned goods and sacks of flour, carrying them together and tossing them on the pile. Empty cartons were used to cover the loot.

The work soaked them in perspiration and set them gasping, but they went on furiously, not stopping until the shelves in the store began to grow bare, the aisled mounds of food had melted to the floor and until other women began to enter the dark storeroom in search of more goods. Then, furtively, they closed the rear door and carefully locked it.

Paula brought her car first. She entered the driveway while Bella held the gate. They loaded the car to its top. After that, Bella brought hers and it was filled in the same manner. They crammed the luggage compartments. And they drove away.

Since they had chosen staples rather than the fancy preserves, meat spreads, chocolate creams, caviar, anchovies, stuffed olives and other items which many of the women had first assailed, they carried home, in the two carloads, a very considerable food supply.

Bella's frightened colored maid had come to work from Coconut Grove, on foot, because there was nothing to eat in her house and she did not know what else to do. She had been left with Sarah. Now she and the two women unloaded. Paula and Bella then went back to the store. The streets were bedlam; it was plain that, in an hour or two, nothing of value would be left anywhere on the village main street. They succeeded once again in driving unobtrusively through the gate and up the alley and in claiming second loads from their camouflaged stockpile.

The third time they were unable to repeat the maneuver: their cache in the carton pile had been discovered. The alley was jammed with cars and brawling women threw the empty boxes about. Bella and Paula went back to Bella's house and divided the plunder.

Bella wept. "We shouldn't have done it! We *shouldn't!*"

Her sister-in-crime was more sanguine. "We'll see! I *wouldn't* have done it if there had been a chance of stopping that mob. Since there wasn't—I thought I'd just as soon have something to eat in the next few months as anybody else. If you're going to steal, Bella, you might as well do a job of it. Besides, we'll inventory it and send Sam's wife a check. Which probably won't be cashable for ages! What else *was* there to do? And look! We've got to hide it!"

"*Hide* it?" Bella stopped sobbing and stared at the full cartons and heavy cases. "Hide it, for heaven's sake? Where? And why?"

"Because, from now on, when you happen not to be at home, there will probably be people going through your premises—looking! And not merely window-shopping either!"

"Oh, *dear!* It's *so* awful!"

"It certainly is! See here! Both your place and my place are built high, and on slabs, and have ventilators. We've got three feet under our house—and places to crawl in. You've got a good two feet and a half—"

"Crawl *under* the house—with all the snakes and scorpions and black widow spiders—!" The little woman shuddered.

"We can bug-bomb first. And be damned to snakes! If we put the cases in there—it's dry and fairly cool. Besides, not many women will feel any more like crawling under houses than we do. They won't look there."

It was noon before they completed a job in which Edwinna and Hester were wakened to assist.

When they had finished, they were hungry. "We'll go over to your barbecue pit," Paula said, "and cook steaks. I've got a lot of them; some in the refrigerator and the rest in the deep freeze."

"Steaks?" Bella was shocked. "For *lunch?*"

"You bet! The power's off and things in the deep freeze will spoil if they don't get it on, soon. The steaks in my refrigerator won't last through the day."

Near the Elliot barbecue pit was a long wooden table, with benches. There, under the shade of red-splashed spathodeas, tamarinds and orchid trees, they had their meal; three white women, two colored women, little Sarah, Alicia—who was about the same age—and the girl Edwinna had brought from the wreck.

Her name was Martha and she was still afraid. Dark eyes stared worriedly from beneath her dark, level bangs and she said almost nothing. She had only curtsied when she had met Paula. Now, with heartbreaking difficulty, she swallowed each mouthful. She was nine, she told them, when asked. She hadn't said a word about her mother —or her daddy. She understood the futility of that.

While they were eating, Kate West came up the street, cut through the hibiscus hedge, and stepped into the back yard. She was wearing a fresh cotton print—white, with blue figures that matched her eyes and black lines that were like her long, braided hair.

She addressed Paula, speaking much as a child would: "I don't suppose you want callers. But I was all alone last night. Nobody came at all. I tried to sleep but I couldn't sleep much. And there wasn't a thing left to eat in the house—after I'd had supper. I don't buy much at a time. This morning I turned on the battery radio. One station is broadcasting and I listened to it for a long time. It's the university station. Telling people what to do and where to go. Just like in hurricanes. But finally I simply had to go out. I took Teddy Barker's car—the keys were in it and Higgie left ours downtown, of course. But I came back—no restaurants are open—" She looked at the steaks and the sliced bread and bricks of ice cream taken from the deep freeze and set out to melt enough to eat.

"Sit," Paula said.

"If you don't care. I was mighty lonesome—"

So young, Paula thought. So attractive. A baby, really. She cut a piece of steak, put it between two slices of bread, set the big sandwich on a paper plate and handed it to the young woman.

"Oh, I couldn't *eat*," Kate said nervously. "Nobody's got enough for other people—now!"

"Eat, you dope," Paula answered. "It'll just spoil if we don't eat it up."

"*Really?*"

"Really, Kate." Paula watched the first big bite and turned her head away. She caught the sympathetic glimmer in Bella's hazel eyes.

Alicia began yelling for ice cream.

"I think, Kate," Paula said, "that you better move in with us."

"I wouldn't dream of that!" And by the way she spoke they knew it was, from Kate's point of view, just what she did dream of. And just what she was too proud and too game to let herself do, unless they meant it and urged her.

"It isn't safe—alone—in your bungalow," Paula said.

"Why not? There are only women left. The burglars are all—gone." Like everyone, she carefully avoided saying "dead." "I'm not afraid of women."

"You may be—in time," Paula answered grimly. "And I won't

argue. We need you. I've got outside work to do. Bella will have, soon. Edwinna too. You can hold the fort when we're away—with Hester and Bella's Medora."

"Could I—really? *Help*—I mean?"

You wanted, Paula thought, to hug her. Husband and little boy gone, bewildered, alone, she'd put on that pretty dress and refused at first to eat—accepted solitude and hunger as her lot. Innocence, courage. . . .

After the meal was finished, Paula said, "I'm turning in. Edwinna, wake me at six o'clock. You and I will both go up to the campus and relieve people. Bella, you better plan to stay home tonight. At my place, if you want, though it'll probably be a good idea for someone to be here, in case people are starting to hunt through abandoned houses." Paula was on her feet. "It'll be worst, in a way, for the next few days."

"Why?" Edwinna asked.

"Till they run out of gasoline." Paula started toward the hedge.

She was asleep in her bedroom—the upstairs, yellow-and-powder-blue bedroom—when Edwinna shook her. "Get up, Mum! It's six!"

Paula stared, stretched—remembered. "Anything happen?"

"It was as quiet out here in the country as a grave—as a church! I went scrounging around for a while—left the kids with Hester. I kind of thought I ought to do something to equalize that grand larceny you and Bella pulled." The younger woman grinned.

"Did you?"

"I sure as hell did! One of my recent boy friends is a bachelor who lives near here. House in the jungle, on a little canal that runs into the Bay. He has a motorboat—*and* a gas pump. I didn't expect any of his other gal pals would think of it this soon. I scared up a bunch of five- and ten-gallon cans from the back yards of garages and paint stores and a hardware place. And I filled 'em all—maybe sixty gallons—from the pump."

"Wonderful!"

Edwinna laughed lightly. "I also fixed the guy's pump so it won't work any more. There ought to be a thousand gallons in his tank and now nobody can get it. I busted the gauge too. So, if we can locate a new pump someday and get it into the tank, we can have quite a private supply."

"Right under the very top layer of skin," Paula said, "this family is strictly larcenous."

"You mean—self-sustaining and resourceful."

"I don't know *what* I mean! But we've got to work. I'll take a shower—"

Edwinna shook her smoothly waved blonde hair. "No, you won't. The water pressure failed this afternoon. I sterilized the tubs and filled them. After we use that, we'll have to depend on the hand pump on the well. Thank God for the hurricanes! You set up your place so as to get along without electricity, anyway!"

"What else is happening?" Paula went into the bathroom, slipped off her pajamas, dipped water from the tub into the wash-bowl, and began a sponge bath.

"Plenty. Kate's been keeping a radio vigil all afternoon. Most of the stores not burned in Miami have been absolutely sacked. The re-tail stores. The university squads were smart enough to realize they couldn't hold everything, so they concentrated on guarding whole-sale places and warehouses and docks. Tourists and winter visitors on Miami Beach have got up soup kitchens. They've also formed an organization to demand passage back to their homes—only they don't know who to protest to. Not a thing useful has come from Washing-ton, of course. There just isn't any government. Some state capitals are trying to get organized. A lot of cities are burning to cinders—a mess too horrible to think about. On the other hand, country people aren't so badly off and they're taking in refugees as fast as they can. In some places, money and goods have been ordered frozen. Which will do zero good. Because we dames everywhere are resorting to the old-fashioned ustom of helping ourselves. A good many banks have been broken into and cash is floating around but it doesn't buy much. Like that."

"Bad."

"A shambles," Edwinna agreed. "But organization is at least starting."

"If the men reappeared as suddenly as they went—"

"—which, please God, they will do!"

"—they sure would think," Paula continued, drying her face on a yellow towel, "we'd made a hideous botch of things."

8

OF SIEGE AND A QUEST.

Three days had passed since the "declaration" made by the Soviet government and the beginning of atomic war. In those three days seventeen Russian cities, including Moscow and Leningrad, had been attacked and either partly destroyed or wholly obliterated. Eight manufacturing centers behind the Ural Mountains had been wrecked and left radioactive.

Nine members of the Politburo were dead. They had taken refuge in a subterranean labyrinth prepared for atomic blitz ninety miles outside Moscow—immense chambers furnished with generators, fuel supplies, communications, provisions, and even special tunneling apparatus for use in drilling to the surface in the event that a bomb should entomb the gigantic nerve center.

American Intelligence had long since learned the nature and location of the headquarters. Five special bombs had been designed for its attack. These bombs, flown in separate planes, at different times, had been launched upon the troglodyte citadel on the second day of the conflict. One plane had won through the convulsive defenses and scored a direct hit above the area.

Its "bomb," instead of exploding, converted itself into an atomic furnace of a sufficient intensity to melt and liquefy the hundred-foot rock formation above the fortress. Its defenders, including the government heads, had been baked to death even before thousands upon thousands of tons of radioactive lava had cascaded into the miles of corridors and acres of chambers.

The hydrogen bomb secreted in Pittsburgh had been discovered in time to save that American city. However, a plutonium mine had exploded in the outer harbor of New York City. Apparently owing to some technical error on the part of Soviet engineers, its tritium-lithium envelope had not been fusively activated. The city had therefore been spared all but the relatively minor damage of a blast, which, at the long distance from the mine, merely smashed a few thousand sleazy buildings, mostly of brick and brownstone, and sent avalanches of window glass into the streets at the bases of some skyscrapers. A radioactive cloud of steam, salt water, and atomic debris had blown across Long Island, killing hundreds and probably inflicting ultimately fatal burns and injuries on thousands; but it had lifted before reaching the Connecticut coast and dissipated.

Oakland and Berkeley had disappeared in the whelming holocaust that had wrapped San Francisco Bay in atomic fire. Chicago was gone, as was San Francisco. The radius of severe devastation at Chicago extended beyond Gary, Indiana, on the east, Joliet on the south, and Aurora to the west. This was the flash that Gaunt had seen in the predawn hours of the sixteenth.

In the "total" area of destruction, a region roughly forty miles in radius, little indeed remained of man or his works. The bomb used to cause the ruin was on the order of five hundred thousand times as powerful as the most potent plutonium bomb they manufactured and involved principles both unknown and regarded as unfeasible by American experts. It was dropped at 5.40 A.M., Central Time. Approximately twenty-eight hundred square miles of city, suburb and farm had been flattened and driven from twenty to two hundred feet below their former level. The hammered urban pancake had instantly melted. Planes flying high over the resultant immensely radioactive area immediately after the blast saw it as a majestic saucer, here cherry-red, there white-hot, everywhere incandescent.

At the same time, approximately twenty-two hundred square miles of the waters of Lake Michigan had been dealt with, in two fashions, by the astronomical blast. Surface water had been converted to steam. The violence of the explosion had driven the balance of the quasi-incompressible fluid out into the body of the lake, setting up a tidal wave which had, in the ensuing minutes and hours, inundated all lakeshore communities. In due course a thunderous water wall had poured back upon the gleaming "dent" where Chicago and its environs had been. The heated surface had boiled the awesome ram into steam clouds, also radioactive although in a lesser degree. These, for the next hours, shrouded the dreadful landscape in vapors which were seen to rise, with the light of morning, to an altitude of eighty thousand feet.

It was estimated that in this holocaust some two million six hundred thousand males had been exterminated by one factor or another; and the death list was rising as the radioactive fogs, mists, rains and clouds dispersed over the states to the south and east on the then prevailing winds. Such was the "superbomb."

When Gaunt returned to his hotel on the morning of the third day of atomic warfare, he had reached that pitch of fatigue and shock at which the steadiest nerves and the most resolved minds are unreliable instruments. It was not that, in spite of all conceivable precautions, the annihilation of Washington was momentarily expected by its inhabitants: death had become almost an invalid source of anxiety to the individual. What unnerved Gaunt was universal. A collective part of the spirits of surviving men found itself in a kind of autonomous extremity, a generic, perhaps animal agony over the likelihood of the ending of the entire species. It was the waking of an instinct, the innermost and the ultimate instinct of living things.

After three days and nights of all but incessant conference, of snatched sleep and food consumed without conscious thought, of crisis piling upon catastrophe as the news rolled in, Gaunt felt the frightful drive of that instinct to save, not himself, but somebody, something, anybody, anything.

During the past forty-eight hours he had seen happenings bizarre enough to shatter an ordinary mind. He had read reports that left even the most capacious and prepared imagination utterly aghast. He had seen a lieutenant general of the United States Army calmly repeat what he knew of the San Francisco situation, walk to a velvet-draped window, put a pistol to his head and pull the trigger. He had seen the director of a great industrial laboratory, during a review of the Soviet assault (a review which had involved a wall map and colored pins) burst into uncontrollable laughter, fight off with the utmost violence all who tried to check his shouts of hilarity, and succumb at last to drugs and hospital attendants. He had seen a roomful of haggard scientists, waiting for another conference with the President—silent, bowed, weeping.

Now, entering the hysterical lobby of the hotel as dawn broke, he walked dazedly to the desk. The clerk looked at him with frightened eyes. "Yes, Dr. Gaunt?"

"Is there a piano anywhere around that I could use?"

"Dr. Gaunt!"

A faint smile broke the face which a winter's sun tan had turned a sickly yellow. "I'm all right, Mr. Jenkins. It's just that I'm not ready to sleep again, quite. And it's always been my custom, when I'm particularly disturbed, to play to myself. It helps me think."

"Oh." The answering smile was wan. "God knows, if it will

help anybody like you to *think*—! Let me see. Would you mind the ballroom?"

"Why should I?"

The tremendous portières were drawn. Slipcases covered what seemed acres of furniture around the dully shining dance floor. Here and there light pierced the draperies. Lances of sunshine, not bright enough to illuminate the room, struck prismatic pendants on the chandeliers and so flecked ceiling, walls and floor with tiny rainbows. On the bandstand stood a covered grand piano; beside it, chairs and music racks.

Gaunt had been let in through double doors fifteen feet high, unlocked by a shaky-fingered bellboy. Gaunt closed them and sauntered to the piano, first throwing back its cover and then sitting on the stool. For a minute, he opened and shut his hands. Presently, in the prism-lit chamber, he played "Chopsticks." It was an elaborate arrangement and he did not play very well: his rhythm was good but he occasionally missed notes.

As he played, his face became softer.

He was remembering . . .

Remembering, he began:

> *Say it with music*
> *Beautiful music!*
> *Somehow they'd rather be kissed*
> *To the strains of Chopin or Liszt . . .**

Long ago.

Edwin and Edwinna hadn't been born, then.

Paula and he had gone to Paris that summer.

He could hear foreign fiddles playing the old tune.

Saxophones playing it again at one of the college proms.

He could see people dancing. In a room something like this. The gymnasium.

*Copyright, 1921, Irving Berlin.

He grinned. His right foot chonked on the pedals and his left beat time to "Dardanella."

Memory . . .

It was the 6th of August and 1945 and he and Paula were at their summer place—at Sunset Point, on Lake George. He had known about it all along and expected it: he had been at Alamogordo that fateful night. But this was different. *Hiroshima.* He'd kept thinking: that's the name of the first city—Hiroshima—I wonder what it means in Japanese? And he had asked Paula but she hadn't been able to tell him. So he had thrown away the newspaper with the violent black headlines and gone into the living room and seated himself at the upright and played "Dardanella."

Paula had called, after a while, "How in the world can you just sit there drumming that trash?"

And he'd answered, "Oh, maybe because music is good for savage beasts—like us Americans. Maybe because it gives me perspective to play tunes from the dear old days when I aspired to be a jazz pianist and the world was innocent. Or, maybe, because I'm a vulgarian at heart. Isn't the lake beautiful this afternoon?"

And she'd come in and kissed his head and they had looked at the blue lake, the green mountains, the farther mountains that were olive and mauve where shadows fell in the valleys. Kissing his head—kissing his face—and, presently, since they were alone in the house that afternoon, forgetting altogether that this was Day One of the Atomic Age. Treating it like any other good day.

I—got rhythm . . .

And that newer, asinine thing. How did it go?
The ballroom echoed to the banged-out chords of "Mule Train."

Clickety-clack!

Gaunt felt, in the cold, dismembered portions of his soul, the beginning surge of little forces that added themselves together, perfused and suffused within him, and bit by bit restored his sense of humanity, his strength.

He played on.

By and by one of the great doors opened again but he did not hear it. A white-haired old man entered the ballroom, stared, and stopped short. For a moment his sensitive face was stricken. But soon, as his eyes grew more used to the light, he grinned.

"I suppose," he called, when Gaunt stopped to consider what to play next, "there's a drop of Nero even in a philosopher's blood!"

Gaunt turned and chuckled. "Fiddling while Rome burns? Hello, Tateley! Come in! I was trying to relax."

"You're not absolutely the worst pianist I ever heard!"

"A vulgar taste, I'll admit to. But as for my technique—"

"It's enthusiastic, I'll say that!" The old man stepped up on the stage with nimbleness and sat down on the stool beside Gaunt, who asked, "Can you play 'Chopsticks'?"

"It's been a long time—" The astronomer put his index fingers together. They began.

"Keep going," Gaunt shouted. "I'll do the variations—you hold the main theme. You've got the beat, old boy! The *feeling!*"

They went through the musical rigmarole to the end of Gaunt's variations.

Then the philosopher turned. "You were hunting me up?"

"Of course."

"Something—else?"

"Something." Tateley drew a breath. He rubbed his hands together, then pressed them between old knees that showed thin and gnarled through his gray trousers. "We've all been called back again. How are you for sleep?"

"How is anybody?"

"This is the last gambit," Tateley said, after a while. He peered off into the dusky room.

Gaunt said, "Hunh!" He looked at the astronomer, turned back to the keyboard, and began to play softly, "We're headin' for the last roundup."

The obviousness of the tune, which the astronomer recognized, the *silliness* of Gaunt's piano playing, gave the old man one more moment of anxious doubt. But as he studied Gaunt's face he understood a second time and more deeply than before.

To such a man, Tateley thought, to a man who has spent his life amidst the reflections, the dreams, the hopes humanity has for itself—to a man who has bent himself to learn and to teach what is true and what the world ought to do in relation to truth—these light tunes are a final *yang and yin* of it. They are his ironic commentary on his fellows and also on his kinship with the tawdriness of his fellows. They are, just as much, a kind of *appeal* to that dim intuition which makes necessary for every man, however ignorant and dull, to have his private art. Apology and defiance—abnegation and common prayer—escape and identification.

Tateley shut his eyes for a moment, squeezed them together. Who am I, he thought, to criticize a lack of magnitude? I, who have devoted all my self-important hours to the remotest of the paradoxes: hot stars in cold space? *This is a human being!*

He put his arm across Gaunt's shoulders. "You kind of know, Bill, what I mean by—'last gambit'?"

"I kind of think I do." Gaunt smiled.

There was a pause. Tateley said, "Do you happen to know a song called, 'Any Little Girl That's a Nice Little Girl'?"

Now, that absurd lilt filled the great chamber, as frivolous and pointless as the miniature rainbows that bespattered the bronze gloom.

"I used to sing it," Tateley said, "when I courted Emma. I played the mandolin a little in those days. You know, I'd *completely* forgetten that?"

Gaunt nodded without a smile.

> *Any lttle girl that's a nice little girl*
> *Is the right little girl for me!*
> *She don't have to look like a girl in a book*
> *With a straight front X-Y-Z. . . .*

The old man's eyes were burned by held-back tears. There's another thing about this damned ritual, he thought. It's recapitulation. It's more potent than a calendar, than a list of the presidents and the wars. It's memory in the raw. It's America down the years. It reminds him of the good things, the happy times, the jokes, the sentiment. He doesn't have to think—just play this drivel and it turns into some sort of emotional history.

Gaunt stopped abruptly. He dropped his arms and sighed. "Well? Let's get it done, if that's how things are. They want us back again?"

"God knows what for," the astronomer replied. "They've already made the decisions and sent out the word."

"What was it?" Gaunt played an arpeggio. "They threaten to shoot the works? Blow up the planet? We surrender—or else nobody survives? Something of that sort?"

"You're a shrewd man, Bill!" Tateley shrugged. "An ultimatum came from Borovgrad this morning. It was signed by Karlodtskov. They said they had an oxygen bomb and would use it in twenty-four hours if we did not surrender unconditionally. Said the bomb had not been tested and the People's Republic could not be held accountable for the effect, which might include stripping the earth's atmosphere."

"Borovgrad," Gaunt repeated. "I wonder if that's the last one?"

"I beg your pardon?"

"You ever read *A Connecticut Yankee in King Arthur's Court?*"

The astronomer shrugged. "I imagine I did."

"There's a point at which the hero is about to be burned at the stake. But he's prepared a lot of fireworks. An eclipse of the sun is also about to take place. Just before they apply the torch, and just as the sun starts to show the moon's profile, the Yankee touches off some of his skyrockets, with a hell of an incantation. It consists, as I remember it, of the names of cities. 'Constantinople,' and so on. King Arthur and his minions were greatly impressed, and called off the burning."

Tateley looked at the other man mildly. "I'm afraid the connection still eludes me."

"One of my superstitions," Gaunt answered. "Everybody brought up as we were has superstitions, no matter how he tries to shed them. Culture's lousy with compulsives and taboos. Shed the old ones; new ones appear. And since the atom's beginning, I've collected those weird names—the cadences, and wondered against all common sense what name would put a period to the list. *You* know. Alamogordo-Hiroshima-Nagasaki-Bikini-Eniwetok. Doesn't that sound like a medieval formula for summoning a djinn? One more word, I kept thinking, and the demon will be out of the bottle. So I merely wondered if Borovgrad would top it off and do the trick. Sounds demoniac enough."

"Oh." The astronomer nodded to himself and finally said, "You seem very calm about all this."

"Anything but! Still, since you've said the decision has been made, I take it that our summoning is perfunctory. We're going to be told what's what—and no choice for us. Why, then, should I exert my faculties?"

"We had our chance," Tateley said in a tone of agreement. "And all we did was—"

"Convene, confer, form committees, elect chairmen, fret and stew, confide in each other, brace each other up, tear each other down—in short, behave like a bunch of women delegates trying to decide whether to have the next flower show in the summer or the fall."

"Still, when a matter involving such difficult scientific knowledge is at the center of things, it's too bad the final decision was made, not by scientists, but by one politician and three or four military men."

"Science? I don't know," Gaunt answered. "When the end of the world is threatened, I doubt if science is much involved. People, rather. It's a human problem then. Since the President refused to surrender—"

Tateley interrupted. "How the devil do you know that?"

"Why—if he'd surrendered, you've have come wobbling down here looking for me and when you found me you'd have said in a tottering voice, 'It's the end!' or words to that effect. The possibility of the end of our world, to you, Tat, is less sinister than the ending of human liberty would have been. Dignity versus the ape."

The other man nodded grudgingly. "I suppose you're right. What the President did was to radio back that, unless the Soviet surrendered in twelve hours, we would use *our* untested bomb on them."

"Damn! Great! The untested bomb we don't have."

"And doubt they have."

"Well, well, *well!*" Gaunt murmured. He played a few bars. "I guess we better go back to the White House. I'm tired of that place. But we shouldn't have to spend much more time there. You know, Tat, we're going to learn soon now just how much value there is in poker, as contradistinguished from nuclear physics!"

The astronomer sighed.

After the four quietest and most frightful hours through which Gaunt had ever passed, he, and the hundreds of persons in the White House and the thousands then waiting in the streets, were informed that the Soviet had capitulated. A new government was being formed. Emissaries would be at the disposal of the American government on the day following. All attack had been countermanded and no further atomic explosions would occur in the United States or elsewhere. The American forces were begged to hold their fire. The war was ended.

But it was not an occasion for rejoicing.

Blake said, when the President had made the announcement, "Now we will have time to face *the* problem!"

Gaunt was assigned to attend a conference in New York. He would have gone there in any case, at the first opportunity: Edwin was missing. The efforts he had been able to make by wire, by phone, by letters scribbled to friends of his son after each day's discussion and conference had produced no satisfactory reply. So Gaunt left Washington in haste. And at Edwin's apartment, on the upper East Side of Manhattan, the philosopher found as much of an answer as he was to have for a long time.

It was again cold and lowering when he arrived, such weather as indicates by a frigid atmosphere, a scudding gray sky and the premature beginnings of winter dusk that New York is a northern metropolis set near a chilly sea. The building in which his son, his son's wife, Frances, and their children lived, had a deserted seeming. There was no doorman. The ferns in the lobby were withering. It was probably the superintendent's wife, Gaunt absently thought, who had always watered them.

He rang for the elevator and waited a long while.

"No," said the cross old man who operated the car, "I don't know where he is! Five—six of the tenants are missing—away—someplace. All day long, I gotta tell jerks I don't know where they are. I run an elevator, mister, not an information bureau!" His tobacco-colored eyes squinted at the anxious face of the tall passenger and their expression changed slightly. "Hell! Don't mean to be rude! I had six granddaughters, mister."

"Tough," Gaunt said. "I'm sorry."

He was let into the familiar apartment. The elevator man followed him. "Around six, the night 'it' happened—I went through all the rooms where nobody was. In here, she left a roast going. Just ready to eat. Took it out. Woulda burned. That was the sort of thing I was checking for. Put it in the icebox. Suppose it's still there.

Forgot it." A faint buzz came from the hall. "Gotta go. Help yourself."

Gaunt scrutinized a growing heap of mail behind the door, on the floor. Nothing.

He walked to the desk in the living room and sat down, going through it slowly. A lump came in his throat. Frances was a conventional girl. Ambitious for Edwin, but sweet. The notes she had left unmailed were stiff and schoolgirlish; they were also dutiful and kindly. The neat shopping lists were full of items for the youngsters —new vitamins, special foods. Frances spent most of her time thinking about her children, planning for them and reading conscientiously in magazines for women, for parents, so that her two young daughters would have the latest benefits.

Nothing there about Edwin.

The children's beds were neatly made. Toys lay on the nursery floor.

In the master bedroom, the twin spreads were smooth and the twin blue puffs folded. Gaunt hurried through, unaware of the wetness of his eyes until, in the bedroom alcove, he sat down at Edwin's typewriter desk and found it was hard to read the mail heaped there.

Edwin was a brilliant chemist and an excellent businessman but Edwin, in definite contrast to his pretty wife, was not orderly.

Gaunt came upon carbons of recent letters written by his son. The topmost was addressed to him. He read it with trembling hands.

Dear Dad:

In a hell of a hurry! (He usually was.) So this will be terse. Forgive. Tried to phone you a dozen times. Circuits jammed, service rotten, missed. There is no use trying to say anything here about this hellish phantasmagoria. I can't believe it's *real*, in a sense, can you? In another way, I believe it's all too real! But this is no place, no time, to go into it—from that standpoint.

A report came in yesterday—Air Force channels—that a

whole tribe of native women had survived, in New Guinea, of all places! My old colonel is heading up a fast mission, to find out. It's important, to my way of figuring. If some women *did* survive, it means something real has happened and the rest are—what? Gone forever? Guess so. If the report is phony we can go back to thinking the whole thing is—again, what? Nightmare? Mass hallucination? Something universal, therefore different. Anyhow, I'm going on the junket. Might take a week. Month. Depends. My colonel, I suppose, could order me to, anyhow; point is, I want to go and *know*. First stop, when I get back, will be wherever you are. Love, Dad, sympathy.

EDWIN

P.S. See Blake and the Prexy have appointed you to head up an evaluation commission. Congrats! They picked a good man. Stay on the ball and if you need an assistant, save the spot for me! I was about to add—love to Mother. Appalling, isn't it all? E.G.

A tear splashed the page. Gaunt noticed then that the typewriter paper was wrinkled in two small, circular spots where other tears, those of his son, had fallen and dried, probably when he had read over the carbon copy.

There was no date.

The original might be waiting for him in Miami—although Jim Elliot was supposed to forward his important mail.

The original might be lost, as many letters had been in the first days.

Gaunt got to his feet heavily and walked from the apartment, locking its door. He rang for the elevator. He would not need to seek out men in the building who might have talked to his son, or to hunt up his son's friends. He pushed the button again. His mind named the lost members of his family, listing them swiftly, as it frequently did of its own accord. Edwin, though, would come back from New Guinea. *Edwin remained.*

The philosopher, unlike his ardent son, had no hope—if it was hope—in a rumor about women surviving in New Guinea. Edwin could search the wide world over. He would find no woman, no girl, no female baby.

Gaunt walked slowly in the wintry twilight.

PART III

The Unloved

9

Morning and May. The sun—insistent focus of attention in South Florida, winter pride and summer anathema—rose out of the eastern sea. It burned redly through a cloud bank and thrust soon-white rays among the houses of Miami, the skyscrapers, the beige buildings and buff, cream, eggshell, jade, lavender, mauve, tan, turquoise and pink. On the way, it touched the Gulf Stream, lighting up the blue fires there. Beyond the pastel city it flared on the sawgrass of the Everglades, glittering amongst green shoots; it threw down the rectilinear shadows of tree trunks in the pine forests, penetrated the jungle hammocks, turned the gray canals to azure, hunted out otters at their den mouths and shone in their fur, flashed on the iridescent backs of ducks, set tens of thousands of alabastrine birds winging from rookeries and routed testy moccasins. So it came to the Gulf of Mexico, with Yucatan and Texas dark beyond, and the Pacific, China—the shade of a next night behind, forever following.

Gaunt stirred in his sleep and yawned and made sounds and opened his eyes. The clock said six. He went slowly to the bathroom. His bearded face looked back from the mirror, like a goat's, he thought. He washed. Still in pajamas that needed mending and lacked a button, he moved down the stairs. Rufus jumped from a soiled divan, wagged his tail, hurried to the door and escaped in the scented, dulcet morning.

Gaunt yawned again, pushed through a swinging door that whipped back and forth in a sucking oscillation behind him, and leaned on the stainless-steel kitchen counters to see the thermometer. It was seventy-eight. Be a warm day.

A Chemex, a coffeemaker shaped like an hourglass, stood half full on the back burner of the stove with an asbestos pad beneath it. Gaunt turned a switch, watching for the tiny light but it did not go on.

"Hell and damnation," he muttered.

Electric power was undependable now.

The Sterno had given out too, it proved.

He returned to his living room. For a moment, with an expression of sadness in his eyes, he gazed at the brilliantly colored furnishings—the purple draperies with the Chinese print, the purple and blue striped chairs, the chartreuse sofa where the dog had slept, the black bamboo valances and the free-form chartreuse rug, dirty now. Dirty from the tracked mud of rainy days in March and April. He heaved a sigh and went to the fireplace.

On the white terrazzo beside it was a stack of split wood and a pile of newspapers. The papers displayed black headlines telling of excursions, alarms, rumors and victories in such unremitting capitals that the mind was unmoved. Gaunt wadded up a front page that said: RUSS MISSION ARRIVES and, below that, WILL CEMENT PERMANENT PEACE. Women First on Agenda.

He laid kindling on the paper, lit his fire, returned to the kitchen, dumped the contents of the Chemex into a pan and set it on the andirons over the blaze.

Then he pressed the switch of a battery radio. Nothing but dance music. He smirked his ragged whiskers. There was a movement on foot, backed by churchmen, to stop the playing of dance music, on the grounds that it brought women to mind and gave rise to "unnecessary sex stimulations." There were countermovements, dozens of them, to keep alive by every possible means the memory of women and the sense of their presence—somewhere. Connauth was coming to see him about it, later that day.

His coffee boiled up suddenly filling the room with aroma; he snatched the pan and took a cup—an expensive, thin China cup—from the built-in sideboard. He poured, put in a spoonful of brown sugar, stirred, and sipped. He said, "Ah!"

With the cup in one hand and the hot pan in the other, he went through glass doors to the porch. He sat down. The annuals were still beautiful. Byron had seen to that, watering when the pressure was high enough, fertilizing with compost, weeding. Phlox —a tapestry of many reds, cynoglossum, perfumed edge of alyssum (blue now, and not the plain white he had known as a boy) and waist-high snapdragons.

If they came back suddenly, he thought, at least they couldn't complain about the annuals.

He drank two cups of coffee, went back to the kitchen, fixed three slices of stale bread in a hand grill, and returned to the fireplace. There, squatting, he half toasted and half smoked the bread. From the defrosting refrigerator he took a lump of butter and a jar of jam. On the porch again, he spread his toast and chewed it slowly.

A car passed on the distant boulevard. He heard Gordon Elliot shouting at Rufus and he heard Gordon's father tell the boy not to wake the whole neighborhood. He saw Teddy Barker leave his garage for his new job at the bank; Teddy was one of the government men, now, assisting in the restoration of credit.

Gaunt finished his breakfast. He looked at the miscellany on the long porch—a coat dropped in a chair weeks before, a tie taken off when the temperature had risen or guests had departed, a plate scraped clean and all but hidden under a newspaper, grit and black muck on the marble-chip floor. *Odd.* He had always imagined himself a neat man and thought Jim Elliot (for instance) casual about appearance. But Jim kept his premises immaculate; it was the Gaunt home that suffered from neglect.

Thinking now of the fact—of the myriad procrastinations, the innumerable little jobs postponed—he could see why they said of women's work that it was never done and why Paula, Hester and even Edwinna had always seemed to have something in their hands. A cup or plate, a magazine or book, an article of clothing, a whisk-broom.

Seized, now, with feelings of shame, and mindful of his expected visitor, Gaunt took off the tops of his pajamas, for comfort, and began to collect strewn items. Clothing he piled at the foot of the stairs. Dishes he took to the sink. Papers and debris he carried to the fireplace where it burned with unwanted heat. In due course he fetched a broom and swept such dust and small odds and ends as he could out through the many doors and off various small, brick porches.

Sweating, still dissatisfied, he meditated over the stained white marble and presently nodded to himself. He went out on the lawn, tested the pressure at a faucet, and attached a garden hose. Paula, he supposed, would be horrified. But after he had rolled and lifted the rugs he discovered that it worked, worked so well—with the aid of a mop and a squeegee—he wondered why women scrubbed terrazzo, why they didn't simply hose it down. What he failed to observe was the spotting of various fabrics where the hose splashed them and the soaking of veneers and of the leg joints of several chairs—damage which, if it occurred frequently enough, would dissolve glue and start warping and loosening. He was unaware, too, that the marble floor had been waxed. He shoved out the last puddle with the squee-gee, cranked every window wide open and propped back every door to let the May breeze dry out rooms which, in his view, were pristine. Bugs entered, unnoticed.

When Byron arrived, Gaunt asked diffidently if he would mind washing up "a few" dishes. Byron, who had endured the days in a stoic world of his own, smiled for once: "I been thinking some time of suggesting it."

He was not disturbed by the fact that a "few" dishes constituted nearly all those in the house. And Gaunt noticed later in the day that the grizzled old gardener was hanging fresh-laundered shirts and underwear on the back-yard line. . . .

With this work done, the philosopher climbed upstairs and peered again at his mirrored face. The barbershops were open again, he knew—and he had no shaving cream. But going to one meant gasoline—and gas was rationed. He soaped his beard, finally, put a new blade in his razor, and attacked; the ordeal was not so painful as he had expected. Afterward, he put on slacks and a shirt picked from a pile of worn clothes Paula had long ago set aside to "donate." It was a clean shirt, at any rate. Sandals—no socks—and he was dressed.

His study, which he had cautioned Byron not to disturb, was a shambles. Books lay everywhere. Letters, telegrams, printed scientific papers, unopened second-class mail, magazines and newspapers littered the floor in what seemed at first absolute disorder and only on close inspection revealed a vague method. His wastepaper basket had disappeared under a pyramid of twisted and balled typewriter paper. This heap Gaunt considered for a moment; his eyes traveled to the fireplace in the room; but he decided not to burn the trash now. It would make the place too hot. And he might someday want something in the discarded pile. He might remember that, somewhere in it, he had set down a line, an idea, a hint of possible value to the summation he had for many weeks been preparing, the summation of all relevant material on the inexplicable disappearance of womankind.

That was his task, as chairman of the Committee for Evaluation.

Most of the matter on the floor had to do with the work in hand—letters and reports from his committeemen and from scientists, bulletins, abstracts, technical papers and journals.

He had been invited—even urged—to remain in Washington and work there. But he had refused, pointing out that his own home, with the solitude it afforded, would better enable him to think, collate and write. Actually, two different factors had motivated his decision to return to Florida. Postvanishment, postwar Washington was having its customary raw spring; the city was drab and uninviting; two men had crowded into it for every missing female, so it was more thronged and uncomfortable than ever. In additon to that, Gaunt had felt an indefinable need to return to the spot where he last had seen Paula and to remain near to it as much as possible.

He sat down now in the familiar swivel chair and stared at the pine-and-palmetto vista outside his window. Soon he put on his spectacles. He reread the last sentence on the half-typed page in the roller of his typewriter:

"The most profitable line of inquiry, therefore, may lie in the psychological, rather than the physical sciences; and a brief résumé of the state of that branch of knowledge at this time may be of use to those who are somewhat unfamiliar with the subject."

After reading, he locked his long hands behind his long head and creaked back his chair, smiling sardonically. It was not surprising that he had quit work on the day before at that point. The next promised step was an outline of psychology, an intelligible outline which would wedge its way into the minds of men who took no stock in it—physicists, chemists and biologists galore, doctors of medicine and businessmen too—all sorts of persons who sneered at Freud (still!) even while they adopted crazed notions for present "guidance" and who (in many cases) would not have the imagination or the logic or the freedom from traditional bias to listen to a Jungian hypothesis.

"Jerks!" he said aloud.

He could begin with James, where most of those who considered themselves well educated had left off. James was academically acceptable. In the universities, everything beyond James was generally called "abnormal psychology" if it was mentioned at all. Well, damn it, they should know by now how abnormal their psychology was! People nationalistic enough to threaten each other with the death of life ought by now to be able to discern nonnormal processes in their sluggard wits! And if *that* did not shake them, there was still more material. *Women* . . .

He wrote—beginning with James.

Anger drove him on. Anger that men who called themselves scientists could develop the physical branches of knowledge without paying the slightest heed to the parallel developments in psychic truth. He allowed that wrath to show a little in the text—used sarcasm— lectured his erudite readership for its oversight, and his peroration was finished by the time Connauth arrived.

The minister was not a large man—five feet six, possibly—and a hundred and fifty pounds. The black robes he wore in the pulpit merely produced an illusion of size. There was a further cause for the illusion. St. Paul's had been constructed under Connauth's aegis; he had seen to it that every appointment of the pulpit had been scaled down to give him a greater seeming. And there was his voice, the bland basso which Gaunt had imagined would be expected of God Himself by the faithful. That also suggested size.

Entering Gaunt's screen porch, in a white suit, not very clean, a black dickey and a clerical collar, the pastor seemed ordinary-sized enough—diminished, even, by nervousness. A frown marred the standard benignity of the brow above his sumptuous nose. His meek gray eyes were anxious. His fingers flurried the handkerchief that mopped his face. "Hot," he said.

"Pretty warm. Glad to see you, John. Sit ye doon."

The Bishop glanced admiringly at the flower bed. "Nice! Since they went—we've had almost no altar flowers."

"Send somebody out next Sunday," Gaunt answered, "and they can pick these."

The Bishop's eyes brightened. "That's most generous of you!"

Gaunt stuffed a pipe—he was conserving cigarettes, now, since they, too, were rationed. "What's on your mind?"

"I phoned for the appointment"—the clergyman hesitated—"well! We've known each other for some while. We're friends. You aren't—of my persuasion; I despaired, long ago, of ever convincing either you or Paula of the inner values of our Christian symbolism—"

The philosopher shook his head in a friendly way. He blew pipe smoke and watched it drift into a sunbeam with the mild grief of a habitual user of cigarettes. He looked at the pipe, then, and put it in an ashtray. "That's not quite the way I'd like it put. I think I understand your symbolism, John. I'm interested in them all—which prevents me from adopting any single set."

"Do you consider yourself a Christian?"

Gaunt thought that over. "It would depend who asked me."

The minister smiled. "Man, that's a fine reply! Splendid! Would in my case, too, as a matter of fact! If one of those stiff-necked Baptists inquired—by Jove!—I'd have to say no! *Why* would I? Simply because, from *his* viewpoint, what I believe wouldn't make me a Christian at all!"

"Exactly."

The minister's brows contracted again. He stared off into the woods and at the houses beyond the woods. "I came over, Bill, for two reasons. One—ever since you and Paula used to live next door to Berthene and me—I've liked you."

"Ever since you took that chaplainship and went off to the wars, John, I've not only liked you, but greatly admired you."

Connauth flushed faintly and beamed, not faintly. "*That* war. Seems far off. Great heaven—what years! What cataclysms! And what an apocalyptic situation we still are in—despite our belated peace on earth! Well—let's not swap flattery. One—I like you. Two—you're the most knowledgeable man I'm acquainted with. I came to pick your brains. Frankly, I need guidance. I'm supposed to supply it but find the road is full of hazards I'm ill equipped to estimate."

"And not just you!"

"I know." The clergyman paused again and again pondered. "There's a great schism rising amongst the people—the men. It's tragic. One breach healed, burned out in blood and fire, and another yawns."

"Natural law."

"Perhaps. Your 'opposites.' Though I don't believe in that heathen thesis. Not exactly. Yet—"

"Read the Parables."

Connauth nodded. "I know. I try. See here. On the one hand, we have a rising mass tendency to deal physically, corporeally, *lewdly* with women. Their memory. Have you noticed?"

Gaunt gestured. "Sure."

"I mean—take the movies. Every sexy film ever made is being revived. Theaters mobbed at night. And plays. Men doing the women's parts—overdoing them. Ribald throngs whistling and cheering. Cafés—with every sort of obscene presentation of the impersonated female. I understand, from one of my trustees"—the clergyman leaned forward and whispered in a shocked, confidential tone—"there is a growing underground market, a black market, in *actually vile* motion pictures! Shown in clubs—at smokers—private homes—that sort of thing."

"Bound to be."

"Tremendously obscene. Tremendously—stimulating. Tremendously—ah—frustrating."

"Ever see one?" Gaunt asked.

"Heaven forbid!"

Gaunt chuckled. "You wouldn't find it stimulating, I suspect. I'm not sure. Childish, and maybe rather—sad. See here, John, didn't you *anticipate* this sort of thing?"

"I must say, I didn't—in the first few weeks."

"What *did* you think would happen? That—sex would be put away in lavender?"

"I presume I did—if I thought about it at all."

"Then—you *didn't* think."

"But—what's going on! *Monstrous!*"

The philosopher shook his head. "Not unless you thought sex was monstrous before the women vanished. After all, it's still the same thing—but just without them."

The minister meditated over that and said, "Don't you feel, Bill, that it would be sensible to try to outlaw all this rot and rubbish and travesty?"

"I don't believe you could. Not *enforce* such laws."

"But isn't this a golden opportunity, always granted the women are restored to us someday—and what's the use of thinking otherwise —to suppress, to erase the vulgarism? To reconstruct the male attitude toward women. Destroy the films! Tear down the signboards with their flagrant bathing beauties! You've heard, of course, that many of them *have already* been smashed—burned—?"

"I've seen some, despoiled by bitter men."

"Bitter? Why not *pure*, Bill?"

"It's hard to explain," Gaunt answered. "Where experience is absent. The sensations. The values. I mean to say, you've been brought up strictly. Except for the squeamish little self-sins of adolescence, you've lived the good life. Onanism and its needless guilt and then you married. Berthene is the only woman you ever knew. So how can I go about telling you other men feel differently, have the *right* to their different feelings?"

That question silenced the clergyman. A slow flush came in his cheeks; it deepened and spread until his face and neck were rosy. He made several abortive manual gestures and once or twice opened his wide, mobile lips to speak—only to purse them again. But at last, in a strained, feeble voice, far from his usual register, he began, "Bill, I never expected I would say to a living, breathing soul what I am about to trust you with at this moment." He stopped there.

Gaunt took care to hide his surprise. "You don't need to go any further, John. I understand."

"*You don't!*" It was a hoarse retort. "You take life at a different tempo, without hard, high standards like mine! You could *never* understand! Berthene—!" He broke off, glanced at the shining sky of midmorning and repeated the name. "Berthene was the choice of my parents. She possessed everything *they* regarded as suitable and desirable. A pious disposition and an excellent knowledge of the Lord's Way and His Words. Forcefulness. A good, sturdy body and abundant health, for bearing and rearing children. A determination to marry into the ministry or the missions; a life prepared for that. Even money; a really decent sum! She was the constant delight of my mother and father, the constant companion arranged for me by them. We plighted our troth when I was twenty and the happiness of my family seemed brighter to me than my own feelings, which partook of dubiety. We were married soon after and I went on through divinity school. I obtained a small parish. Just outside of Yonkers."

Just outside of Yonkers, Gaunt thought. Anywhere else, the phrase might seem ridiculous. Here it was charged with wistfulness.

Connauth went on, reaching out a supplicatory hand, putting it on Gaunt's big, bony knee. "You have no idea how difficult this is to discuss, old man! There was a contralto in my choir, beautiful woman with long, golden hair, married to an utter no-account. Genial, fervent person, left alone in her small house most of the time, while her husband went on his traveling-salesman way, drinking and carousing. She called on me, for comfort. Berthene, I needn't say, was above suspicion; such things never entered her head—then, or since. She was busy with church organizational work, busy with what, in all honesty, amounts to the politics of the church. Busy, that is to say, with my advancement, or the hope and intent of advancing me. Naturally, I gave the woman what comfort I could, of a spiritual nature. But there was an earthy streak in her that, I must confess, had a sinister appeal to me. Fed on my mind. Invaded my meditations. Interfered with my abstractions. She was casual, for example, about dress. She would make a pastoral appointment and neglect to finish her household duties so I would find her, like as not, in a silken kimono—"

"Negligee," Gaunt murmured.

"What? Yes. I needn't carry the thing into an excess of detail. Though, once started, momentum does sweep you along. There came an evening when she phoned and left word with Berthene that she was ill. Indeed, she seemed to be. I found her in bed with a hot toddy for her disturbance. Nothing would do but I had one—it was an icy night. How and when it happened to me—how I found myself with her, casting every modesty aside, all shame, all caution—saying things I did not know I knew to say—I cannot explain. My life since then has been a lasting expiation." Connauth was flushed scarlet now, perspiring, breathing sibilantly.

His auditor could imagine the unhappy conclusion of this episode: some parishioner's discovery, perhaps; possibly, the husband. And a lifetime (Connauth was sixty-two) was a formidable "expiation." He murmured, "A long penance, John."

The man of God nodded, or rather bowed his head an inch at a time with pauses between, a motion of assent and contrition.

"For one night, one *moment* of mere error—" Gaunt added musingly. "A *lifetime* of repayment! Surely, a harsh—!"

But Connauth's head had come up and his face was startled. "One night! I said no such thing, man! I tell you, I was young. Vigorous. Berthene was with child most of the time. We had six, you know; five in eight years. For *seven* of those years—!" His flush became purplish—the shocking hue heightened by his white hair.

Gaunt was astonished and then hilarity welled in him. He turned his face, struggled with the corners of his mouth, breathed hard and checked its torrent. When he spoke, it was gravely. "You mean—you had an affair with this blonde contralto for *seven years?*"

"I'm afraid I did." Guilt as if for all human devilment quavered from the constricted throat."

"And *no one* found out?"

"No one."

"That's not sin," Gaunt said. "It's genius!"

The other man's eyes were harried. "I never took it, then or since, with levity, Bill."

"No. Still—"

"Carnal sin. Mortal sin. A commandment broken. One of the Seven Deadlies and, by the clearest inferences, other sins compounded! My life—a lie. A masquerade. A poisoned hypocrisy." He sighed hoarsely. "Berthene's manip—her tact and effort—won me, in three years, a new and larger pastorate. Another town, some hundred miles away. I thought—cheaply, snidely—that circumstance had come to the rescue of my enslaved soul. But the woman moved—her husband did not care much where she lived. And not only that, she took a dwelling a block from my new church, with a wooded yard, so that any idle errand, any anonymous call, served to conceal my actual whereabouts. *Seven years.* Then, quite abruptly, she divorced her husband and married a man I'd never heard her mention. The most horrible part of it all is that for months—no, years—I felt *myself* the one divorced! Yet all the while I knew, and at long last admitted, that this other man, whom ultimately she married, must *also* have walked the selfsame short cut through her willows when neither her rightful spouse nor I was there! Did you ever hear a tale shabbier or more *sordid?*"

Gaunt leaned back in the reed settee and lighted his pipe again. "Frankly, yes. Many. John, let me ask you something. You came over here to get my opinion as to the advisability of passing—or advocating—a new set of blue laws to meet these insane times. Didn't it enter your head there was a touch of hypocrisy in *that* mission?"

The clergyman thought awhile, composing himself. "I think not. I feel I have in a measure atoned—that I have, in a way, a *greater* reason to eliminate temptation, since I have been its most merciless victim and know the strength of it."

"Did you ever look at the matter from the angle of the woman?"

"Virginia's angle?" Having given away the name, the Bishop flushed with fresh humiliation. His eyes darted at those of his friend in a kind of fevered hope that Gaunt had not heard. Seeing he had, Connauth said, "I trust you! Heaven knows why, sometimes! The name's a trifle in the face of the rest of it. Certainly, I thought of what you call her 'angle.' At bottom, she must have been a lustful creature, vain and fickle, who took a secret pleasure in trying to destroy me."

Gaunt gazed again at his pipe. It is, he thought, the one good thing about pipes: they serve better for punctuation than cigarettes; they require looking after. "Really? How did she behave toward you in those seven years? As a friend? Maternally? Was she sisterly?"

"None of those," said the Bishop. "We knew together the carnal abysses."

"Well, I'll be damned."

"Sorry," said the other. "Sorry I ever told you. It came bursting out of me, as things do these days."

"Usually," Gaunt continued as if to himself, "it's sopranos. Parsons and sopranos. Contraltos seem to be the exception. I've known of half a dozen cases, personally. Read of hundreds. Scores, anyhow," he corrected. "*Why*, I wonder? Are those high notes an indication of taut nerves? Instability? Lust? Livelier tissue? Or do newspaper reporters merely know the word 'soprano' and forget about contralto? Alto?"

"It's easy for you," the Bishop cut in, "to make sport of the tragedy of my life!"

"Not sport, John. I'm trying to make *sense* of it. Maybe the woman loved you—"

"That—is not love!"

"Well, it's quite a step in the direction of love, I'd say. Seven years is a good while. Obviously, her first marriage was as empty as your own."

"My life with Berthene has been rich and full and rewarding!"

"But you've just said it's been poor and empty and disappointing."

The eyes of the other man were abruptly angry and without trace of their usual mild aspect. "*There's* the difference between your religious man and your vacuous, truth-torturing 'philosopher'!"

"Is it? Come, come, John! We've argued too often and too long to get peevish now! And it would be Freud, not myself, who'd say sex could throw a man like you—logic, faith, and all. Not any other kind of misbehavior."

"Freud!" The Bishop uttered the name with a derisiveness that was his custom; he rattled the "r" and gave the vowels an umlaut sound.

" 'Rich and full and rewarding,' " Gaunt quoted. "That's what marriage is supposed to be; that's what, in consequence, you say yours was. How childish! How devout! How many people, like you, first read your Good Book and ever afterward lay claim to all the virtues and noble experiences mentioned in it! Since Berthene's gone—to God knows what limbo—you might have had the simple dignity to confess, for once, the truth! Your marriage was not 'rich' or you could not have spent seven years in the bed of a handsomer woman. It was 'full,' full of children; but not of love, which you have only just finished complaining of. As to its 'rewards'—didn't you find the most and best of them beyond the connubial couch?"

Connauth's anger ebbed. He sat limp and his eyes accumulated tears. "Must you be so harsh? Have you never—yourself—?"

Gaunt nodded. And now he gave up the forensic tone. "Paula," he said meditatively, "must have loved me a great deal. So much, I felt ashamed sometimes. Perhaps it was a cultural shame—the guilty sense men have, because, it may be, they are quite different in their sexual feelings from women. Who knows? Who knows how much a

man is woman and therefore able to accept a woman's selfish patterns
for his own? Who knows how much, in two thousand years and more,
women have managed to infiltrate society with the notion that their
egotistical desires are right—and man's wrong? Who knows the
truth?"

"I don't understand you, Bill."

"I don't understand myself! It was *you* who made the confession.
I'd have a few, on my part, if I felt urged to talk—the way you've
felt urged. Twenty-seven years is a long time to be married. Often
we've been apart for months. Would you expect a philosopher to
neglect experience, avoid profound urges, turn aside from what only
the moralistical call sin but nevertheless commit, and live like an
anchorite always?"

"And what stabs of conscience did you have? What amends
did you feel compelled to make?"

Gaunt shrugged. "Conscience? None, unless it was a sensation
of inequality. Injustice. I'm sure Paula never had the feelings that
were sometimes mine. She was devoted. She was faithful. A two-
faced standard seemed contemptible to me. I told her so, as a young
man. When I grew older, I desisted. She had the private right to
choose; she chose fidelity. If I had compunctions, they lay there. As
for amends—what amends are necessary? You owed your Virginia
nothing, I dare say. Quid pro quo. And Berthene nothing, for what
she was too prudish to learn and to be. Your debt to God is therefore
in your imagination."

"You mean to say," the Bishop inquired after a moment, "that
you actually suggested to Paula, your wife, that she be unfaithful?"

"That's a bit twisted, isn't it? I never pandered for her, the way
I've seen other husbands do, often enough. Husbands, perhaps, who
feel subservient to their wives or who have guilty consciences, like
you."

"Under the guidance of men such as you, Bill, the world would
become a wallow! A sexual quagmire—!"

"It would, if people reared in *your* beliefs were given the power of determination. Sure! People reared otherwise—say, the Samoans—"

"Who never learned the Word of God! Who were never Christianized! Civilized—!"

"Do you *still* feel," Gaunt asked quietly, "that humanity is in *any* way civilized? Do you *still* believe, when two continents can respond to common disaster by hurling atomic bombs at each other, that education, or culture, or the Holy Writ has *really* had a prodigious good influence?"

It was noon, now, and the shadows of the pines lay beneath the trees, slanting but slightly toward the north. The summertime smell of Florida came to the porch on hot, damp occasional stirrings of the air, a smell of mold, musty earth, baking pine needles, far-off flowers, and the salty sea—a combination of odors and fragrances which permeated bedding and even clothes, so that a trunkful, packed in Miami and opened months later in some northern region, exuded the nostalgic blend, and the man or woman who had lifted the lid would be transported to that sunlit place where great birds sailed in the sky and the sea was like fire and jungles had their only foothold on American land.

The clergyman snapped a watch case and read the time. "I must go! I gather you'll have nothing to do with my program, Bill?"

"On the grounds, John, that only the innocent should throw the first stone. A precedent from your own sources. And one I recommend you to consider gravely, unless your conscience can stand an even bigger load."

Connauth was able now to answer with a smile—wan, deprecatory, but significant. "Just one more question. Can you countenance the rising tide, the flagrant spread of homosexuality?"

"Have you any alternative in mind?"

"Is *that* the best answer you can supply from all your wisdom?"

"You were an Army chaplain, John. You've seen men penned

with men and without women, before now. The whole world's in
that camp. Even the most austere clerics have had to admit the fact
of libido, although they try to take full charge of it through the
churches and their codes. But sex is permitted a certain feeble sanc-
tification, isn't it? A dirty thing that men do which is made somewhat acceptable by words at the altar and purged with later rites.
Well. What brides can the church offer now?"

Connauth rose. "That's my answer, then! You condone every
sort of vicious perversion—"

"I condone nothing of the sort! Infantile business, homosexuality. Immature, and unfortunate. I simply say, it's bound to be, in a
society of men alone. If you want to stop it, learn what it is and
where its causes lie in your so-called moral codes and in the way we
raise children and in that sex secrecy which is a lot like the late
'secrecy' of our admirals and generals—mythological measures attempting an impossible 'security.' *Nature, not man's ideas, controls
man.* Every boy discovers the secrets kept from him. Every man in-
terprets them according to his compulsions and his fears."

"What a hypocrite you are to pose as a good man!"

"John, John, John! How can you judge me when you do not
even try to learn what I know? I could give you a half dozen books
and if you read them with detachment—as honest works—instead of
in a passion to discern where every sentence deviated from your pre-
convictions, your whole attitude would change. But you don't know
how to read any more! When you open a book, you do it in the faith
and assurance that you are already master of what it contains and that
the author has written only so *you* may prove him wrong!"

"That's pretty cruel."

"Faith's the agreement to *abandon detachment*, John! To sup-
plant a packaged security for open integrity. To agree *not to learn
anything more.* It is the acceptance of a *channel,* by a man who was
previously able to move on the whole terrain. I've done an essay on
the subject—'Conviction.' Well—you have your conversion, and I

will not try to reconvert you, or to deconvert you. Maybe the seman-
tic's wrong. You were never converted from anything to begin with
but only more deeply 'versioned' every day, in the images of your
father and mother."

"Why not give me the books?"

"Because you wouldn't read them."

"Suppose I promised to?"

"Then, as I said—because you'd read them only to show yourself how mistaken they were."

"Suppose you give it a try. After all, I am troubled in my mind."

Gaunt smiled and went into his study. He came back carrying
the volumes, popular discussions of modern psychology.

With these, the Bishop drove away.

Gaunt returned to his labors.

The earth spun away the afternoon.

Toward dusk, he tried a light and found the power on again. He
was hungry. In the kitchen, which Byron had cleaned, he fried six
eggs and heated a can of tomatoes, sugaring it and putting in it
chunks from his stale loaf. This, with two oranges, constituted his
second meal of the day. He ate from the skillet and the saucepan.

Afterward he thought of going over to see Jim Elliot. Gaunt
was lonesome and enervated. But Jim, he knew, would want to while
the evening away in metaphysical discussion. Jim had rekindled a
former interest in mandalas. He was deep in a contemplation of the
thesis that all life is the manifestation of *pattern*, that the unconscious
mind, when wholly integrated, presents to the conscious self (and
presents in dreams) mandala formations—many-colored designs, pentagons (like stars), hexagons (like snowflakes), which are (Jim would
interminably assert) instinct's clues to the nature of consciousness and
the purpose of mankind. They represent (Jim would say) thought-
value pictograms. They are the psychic parallel (or reflection) of the
crystalline structure that underlies all matter. "Find your own mandala—in a dream—by automatic drawing," Jim would say, "and

you will have become One with the heart of Reality, Truth, Nature, God and Peace."

Gaunt did not want to hunt, that evening, for his mandala. His expectations of the night were therefore meager and in no way anticipated its ironic shock.

He had been reading Gestalt psychology, a branch of speculation which required inclusion in his digest. He intended to give his time to it until sleep finally overtook him. It might be morning then. He might have eaten again in the night. What matter? There was no reason to come or go, start or stop, do or refrain. His wife, his family, the basic unit of humanity, was lost. In a world without women, only the fathers of young boys had, any longer, connection with a Plan.

But now, as Gaunt went upstairs to his bed and the stacked books beside it, as he switched on lights, relieved not to have to read by the inadequate flame of candles, he felt suddenly disinclined to continue his intellectual efforts. He stood awhile, as he always did, in front of Paula's portrait, which he had moved from the living room. It was a good likeness, painted some years before by Lescompte, in Paris. Paula in a blue-green evening dress, low cut, with a full skirt. Paula on a chaise longue. She had refused to stand or sit for the painting.

He addressed the picture, as he often did. "Come back!"

He thought he heard, and this was new to his experience, not words but the murmur of her voice in the distance—downstairs or possibly in the garden. He seemed to hear also a few footsteps that were hers. On the impulse, he ran down the steps, crying, "Paula!" But there was nothing in the lower rooms save a sleepy spaniel and the gray glow of the moon; nothing on the lawn but a brighter grayness.

A little shaken, he went back. Another time, he would resist such impulse. It would not do to get hallucinations. He had worked too hard, pondered too much. It occurred to him that Connauth's recital had touched several long-buried recollections. These, even though they referred to other women, referred also to Paula. Somehow. How? He cast aside the question.

He needed a change of chores, something to do rather than something to read or to consider or to write. His haphazard cleaning of the house came to mind. He looked, now, at the single, large upstairs room where he slept and Paula had. This room, also, needed attention. Both bedside tables were stacked with books, magazines and scribbled notes. Both wastebaskets were overheaped. In the corner, on Paula's desk, was a cascade of letters opened and unopened, of bills, receipts, canceled checks, invitations, telegrams and other things which needed sorting. The untidy pigeonholes above them invited arrangement.

So he set to work, first picking up the litter, then emptying the baskets, and finally seating himself to execute the almost superstitiously postponed task of straightening Paula's desk. The bills required classification: when the New Economic System was put in effect, and that would be soon, old accounts would be payable and there would again be credits to pay them.

For an hour he sorted the paper heaps. Then he began to read the letters and messages. To do so gave him a sense, at once painful and pleasurable, of Paula's personality. Here were thanks for donations she had made; here, requests. Here were notes she had written and not yet mailed: a tart, humorous missive to a furrier; a forthright letter to a charitable organization which, in Paula's opinion, had abused its privileges; here was a shopping list; a neatly kept appointment book, a letter to Edwin and several letters from their son, tied together.

Gaunt went on to investigate the pigeonholes and then the drawers. One, the upper right drawer under the desk lid, was locked. Since Gaunt had never investigated his wife's papers, he assumed the drawer was locked against the prying of servants, or children. He thought, too, that it might contain Paula's cashbox. And, partly owing to the fact that cash was still restricted (but not wholly denying his curiosity) he decided to force the drawer. He went down to the tool rack in the car porte and returned with hammer and chisel. It took only a moment to break the small lock.

Inside was the cashbox, as he had suspected, and it required some while to rend the metal. The box contained twenty-five one-dollar bills, a good deal of silver (for making petty cash payments at the door, he thought) and five one hundred dollar bills: Paula's emergency fund. He'd often heard her refer to it. The "hurricane money," she called it. "In case the banks blow over or get flooded."

Beside the cashbox were several bundles of letters, tied together with ribbons. Of the ribbons, some were mildewed and faded. Gaunt supposed, owing to this earlier finding of Edwin's bundled correspondence, that these were more communications from the children. Letters Edwinna had written from boarding school, perhaps, or little Theodora's notes, or V mail from Edwin when he was overseas. But he soon saw that the handwriting was not familiar and that each bundle was addressed by a different person. Letters, then, from strangers, or strangers to him; letters, at any rate, not from the family.

He undid one bundle and idly withdrew the topmost note from its envelope. There were several pages and he turned to the last. "Always," it was signed, "Your Ed."

Ed, he thought. Who the devil would that be? Some old beau? He turned to the salutation:"Darling Paula." But there was a date: "May 19, 1944." During the war—when he'd been working for the government. He began to read.

"Darling Paula—The look, the touch, the every recollection of you seems nearly as exciting as the fact of night before last."

Gaunt put the letter back in the envelope. For a long while he sat without moving. At last he opened another bundle. These were from a "Bill" but not Bill, her husband. "Hello, redheaded magic," the first began. Gaunt winced and looked through the all-too-expressive rest of it. One line was particularly significant: "I think it's pure damned foolishness to write this sort of thing in a letter. But if you want something to remember me by in your old age, why, you already know, your caprice is my law."

"Hello, What-a-woman!" another by this "Bill" began.

I have been married, without knowing it, Gaunt mused, to "redheaded magic," and to "what-a-woman!"

(Or is that fair? What terms have I employed which are acceptable only because they were never written down?)

The time has come, he thought, for the philosopher to prove he is a philosophical man.

(But damn it all. Damn them. Damn what? Who? And what about your advice to Connauth? The first stone. You explained you had long since told Paula you deplored a society with separate standards for the two sexes. And, besides, any violation of woman's precepts involves not just a man but a woman also.)

(What a masquerade! How perfectly she carried it off! I was four times cuckold—he had counted the bundles—by the record! And I never guessed of one!)

(Yet before calling her a hypocrite, he had to try the term on himself. He'd confided once or twice with Paula, obliquely, and probably to salve his conscience.)

Then—why be angry?

(He wondered what she had written back.)

And, most of all, he seethed over one particular author of these foolish and fatuous missives. (She could have spared me that!) *Teddy Barker.*

Athletic Teddy with his shoulders and his hair-oil smell and his absurd innocence of everything. Teddy, who was (he thought) nothing more than a large male ornament to the phallus.

(What about the secretary in Washington? Was she bright—? Heaven knew she was not! An ornamental extension of the procreative organs and their accessories. Nothing else.)

He began to check dates, now, with a fevered fascination.

And in so doing he felt only the more committed. These excursions of Paula's had taken place invariably when he was far from home and lasted an afternoon or an evening; one, for a week.

(Out of twenty-six years, he could not keep his mind from reckoning, she gave you every minute and hour and day but something like a hundred hours which, evidently, she bestowed enthusiastically on others. A Samoan would assent; an Eskimo would encourage her. What am I? Lesser?)

A Scotch Covenanter, his mind ran on, with the concept of the Scarlet Letter stuck in every scarlet cell of my blood and manufactured anew each day, with the enzyme of its bitter prejudice.

He went downstairs and pulled a chair out onto his lawn where the moon would bathe him. He was sweated from head to foot.

(If she were only here and I could talk to her!)

It was that thought which, after a long while, brought easement to the hurtling alternation of his emotions.

He came abruptly face to face with what many, nowadays, were calling "The Absence" and some "The Curse" and others "The Famine." He saw himself as multitudes were seeing themselves, in a new light, brighter and contrite. He felt purer sources of sensation than those corroded by the past times, customs, habits, dead traditions, and obsolete moralities.

What in hell did it matter?

Would he, tonight, reject a returning Paula because she had deceived him?

No.

Had he not assented to deceit itself, long ago?

Yes.

Would he upbraid her for what she had done, what he had?

No.

And if he knew, his mind went on, that Paula returned would be a Paula who would conduct herself in the future as she had in the past, would he object?

He endeavored to be honest. What had he so recently felt? Rage? Jealousy?

No.

Hurt ego; that was the fact entire. *His* wife could do no wrong in any man's eyes; but she had done what was wrong in the eyes of many, which made him ridiculous and shamed, in many eyes. His wife had listened to his credo and followed it; but she had not told him. And *that* was painful. She had, moreover, selected for her evanescent loves one man, at least, whom he had regarded with amiable disdain and condescension.

Who, Gaunt thought, would *he* have chosen for her?

Barker, as he had already admitted to himself, was no more or less than the male equivalent of countless young women he, and most men, found alluring.

He was not satisfied he had guessed the true causes of her behavior; that might take time.

But this much he did know: what she had done, when compared to the whole woman, to love and marriage, to life, was of scant importance now.

With the woman gone, with the species staring at extermination and passing time itself the executioner of humanity, a man could feel in his heart that to love and to make love was more important than any particular *system* of mating.

Gaunt walked tiredly into his house and up the stairs again, determined to read all the letters, so there would never be in his mind a further wondering. So that, when he grew familiar with what had really happened, he would not feel he had balked at truth or refrained from digesting it through some false chivalry disguised as rejected curiosity.

He was very glad he did that, whether or not he had rightly analyzed his motive.

At the bottom of the last bundle of letters was an envelope addressed in Paula's hand *to him*.

My darling:

You probably will never see this. There are so *many* reasons why you may never see it! I may live longer than you. I may decide to burn these letters when I am older. And if I am the first to go [his breath caught] you may—characteristically—file and forget, unread, this little collection of billets-doux. But if you ever, for any reason, do come upon them and do read them, I would like you to read this, too; I wouldn't want you to learn these small truths without hearing more about them, from me.

What's love? It's what I've felt for you, I think. The tides, at first, of physical passion, of possession and of being possessed. Security and sanctuary and a program; the beginning of special design; the leaving behind of formless search. I was a young woman when we married but I do not believe I have wasted a minute of the years, since, regretting that it was you who married me, and I, you.

Love is home, and the place home gives you in society. Love is the opportunity to work with (and on!) a man, as a woman. For me, at least, love was quite a bit *giving up* things —the prospect of what was then called a "bachelor girl" existence, freedom, career, a chance to know many men in every way. And that last desire, at least for me, was strong and seemed to be valid. I mean by that, natural.

Love's a family, of course. The effort and the anxiety are measures of love; the successes, measures of love rewarded. The failures—like Edwinna—I imagine to be in some obscure way the proof of imperfect love. But whether imperfect because we are selfish, or ignorant, or because of our customs, I'm not certain.

I loved you, Bill, truly and tremendously. I loved you, I mean, as *bigly* as I was able. Sometimes it maybe wasn't very big. But, nearly always, you were my whole existence.

You filled me and fulfilled me to such a degree that there was very little "me" which did not constantly participate in our joint life. But there was some. These letters prove that, don't they?

What were the elements that made up the leftover fraction? I know several. I don't know all.

One was, of course, you and your attitudes. The first time you were unfaithful to me, I was horribly hurt and shocked; shocked even more because I *did* suffer over it. I was able to be annoyed with you about it long afterward—even after I'd caught myself having the same momentary urge toward other men. I don't believe you ever fooled me, Bill; you always had a little look of mystery, a shade of guiltiness, and a cover-up of faint pompousness that made me realize you'd strayed. It wasn't often or intensely, I know. And then, you believed so firmly, in your head, that what you did was innocent!

I never quite could copy your ideology. But I had the feelings, occasionally. So I decided, long, long ago, that if I ever gave in to them, I'd keep the indiscretion to myself. I did —as you see. And why? Why? I tormented myself with it— why? Because I am a woman, Bill, and because I think no woman is that impossible character she is supposed to be, in our society. Not by miles! A woman's world is *fascist*, Bill! She lives under a tyrant called Respectability and that is a horrid way of life, of marriage. I rebelled.

You were away. There was a man, a very gentle, sweet guy, who confessed he'd never made love to a woman. He was too timid and inhibited. You away, the opportunity came along, I couldn't resist and I seduced him. Another, I was curious about—plain, physically curious! There is such a thing as being hungry for a man, also. For any man, pretty nearly, for the being-together with a male. Mischief, spite, maternalism in disguise, vanity, a desire to see if I still could be *that* alluring, such things! But I honestly believe, Bill, that most of all, I felt *myself* and life *itself* to be so real and valuable that I could not quite face death with the thought that I, Paula, owing to sheer *social intimidation* had been *born* and *lived* and *died* and *never known* anything more about men than the loving touch of *one!*

That probably is neurotic, or something. But that's as near as I can come to explaining.

So here are *my* sins. In some deep fashion, I must not want them to pass unknown to you. I feel it would be less honorable than the rest of our life together. It has been many years since the latest of these so-called indiscretions. I am not likely to commit any others, though I would never make a promise. Who knows what she will do or think, feel or believe, even one year away? I don't want you to forgive me because I never felt there was much to be forgiven. If you are angry at any of the writers of these notes—I mean, *when you stop being angry at me,* if you are—I have misjudged you.

I think you won't mind, too much. I wish I could have told you directly. But with our upbringing, there's no good way. It's stronger than we are, that dictatorial background! I have, in my mind's eye, a little vision of you. I kept the letters —asked for them, in fact—partly for my own sake but partly because of that vision. I see you, an old, old man, going through my effects and thinking, at that age, it was a fine life we'd led. I see you loving me so much you'd also think, a little sadly, it was a pity *my* life had been confined—when compared to your life. Then, *if* you had felt like that about me, which I believe you would have, these letters could be one more thing to love me by. They represent a kind of being true to *myself.* Good, bad, or immaterial, they are part of me. And that, darling, if I have estimated rightly what really makes you tick, is the sort of thing you cherish most: truth.

If you come upon this accidentally, if it estranges us, then I have made a bad guess indeed concerning you, me, and life—and I'll have to take the consequences of that, whatever they are. But I am not very afraid.

Your
PAULA

10

IN WHICH THE DAUGHTERS OF TWO REVOLUTIONS MEET ON
THE HUDSON RIVER.

In May, the surviving American women made their first attempt
to re-establish a central government. By that time the great fires in
the cities had burned out or had been put out. Millions of urban
women had found housing of some sort in the country. Most of
them, though ill qualified for farm work and resentful of being
bossed by farmers' wives, were making efforts to plant crops and tend
stock. Other millions had returned to the devastated metropolises and
set up sleazy, communal forms of living in the ruins. Trucks, and even
a few trains, were beginning to serve such areas. Some radio stations
operated and a random mail service had been initiated, although no
attempt had yet been made to restore telephone and telegraph
service. A few, single-page newspapers were being printed.

Canned goods had been rapidly exhausted, usually owing to
looting. But even where food had been commandeered in quantity
and carefully rationed, it had not lasted long. Some power plants were
in operation but in May no refineries had yet commenced to produce
gasoline or kerosene. No coal was being mined. Here and there,
natural gas was available. The stocks of petroleum and petroleum
products had largely burned; the remaining supply was jealously doled
out. Household hardware was unobtainable save by weary searching
through masses of charred debris.

The instinct of self-preservation had yielded somewhat, however,
to other urges and moods. Life in May was not so dangerous as it
had been in February and early March. Organized bands of armed
women less frequently assailed houses or communities better off than
the average. Such bands, "raiding," or driving out those in possession
to seize their places, had been common in the first weeks. But by May
the average woman and her daughters, whether they lived in the

country, the gritty residue of a city, or some relatively untouched suburban area, were not in imminent peril of fire, blast, wreck, dispossession or murder.

Central government offered the one logical way of dealing with grotesquely unbalanced local circumstances. Several states had a measure of self-rule. In other areas women had organized for maintenance and defense without regard to state boundaries. Trade among such groups was difficult. Here, money was pegged; yonder, prices found their own level; elsewhere, the dollar was ignored and all business was conducted by barter. This region had beef; another, vegetables; between them, there might be no transport. In some sections, the rare trains ran intermittently and at times empty, or carrying nonessential goods.

Thus, into Omaha, a freight with a proud blonde in the cab of its locomotive—the first train to reach that city from the outside world, brought three carloads of kapok, a car of upright pianos, two cars of circus animals (cats for the most part and hence inedible) a half-car of hat trimmings (the other half was empty), and eight carloads of baled wool. The press of hopeful, hungry women who greeted that train had become a furious mob; the cars were burned on the tracks. The blonde engineer luckily escaped that show of public wrath. She had simply brought, from a nearby town, such cars as happened to be coupled to an engine which she and two friends had contrived to fire, start, and run on a stretch of track that chanced to be clear.

But the infinite multiplication of such witless episodes—added to the daily ordeals—set up a nation-wide cry for "order."

Its institution was first undertaken by an assembly of the wives of congressmen. This Congress of Wives (it was dubbed COWS within a day) met early in May.

Unfortunately, the American people had usually selected their Congressional representatives with the view toward gaining local or even private advantage. A lawyer, a "neighborly" fellow, who promised that he would use his office to obtain every possible dollar and benefit not just for Oklahoma, but for certain Oklahoma counties, was the sort who won most of the seats in the House. Senate seats went as a rule to shrewder samples of the same species. Both frequently made promises to the people they had no intention of keeping and secret promises to the heads of various large industries, which were kept, to the public detriment.

Hence America had long been represented by men who did not have the nation as a whole in mind when they considered legislation. Moreover, vast problems of agriculture, taxation, welfare and the like were beyond their average competence. Few had broad education. Foreign relations were foreign, indeed, to such: they were as ignorant of England or France as of ancient Chaldea. The history and traditions of their own nation were closed books to many. Others had no understanding of the philosophy of liberty, which was the core of their nation; they traded freedom for mortgages on the future and for every imbecilic kind of "military security." Scientifically, of course, a full nine-tenths of them were ignoramuses—although nine-tenths of the problems and the laws with which they were supposed to concern themselves were rooted in matters of a scientific nature or matters upon which science had shed a great light they had never learned of.

The cosmic ignorance of America's representatives, though grossly and horribly displayed in every Congressional session held during the twentieth century, did not impress itself upon the American public because these men reflected and personified the stupidity, greed and ignorance of the electorate.

As the will to defend liberty ebbed, and then as liberty itself diminished, the sick condition of the Republic remained invisible to all but a few individuals. Chicanery and bribery increased as they do when confusion is every day augmented. Cow hands, mill hands, farm hands and other oafs who had "made good" financially or politically or both (but learned nothing in the process) came to be "spokesmen" —in a world of intricate psychological conflict, or nucleonics, of complex biological discovery and every sort of applied technology. They understood none of it. The astonishing feature of the unsteady shambles democracy had unnecessarily made of itself was not that it came to be before the Disappearance, a society doomed either to change or to collapse, but that it lurched along with the outer semblance of sanity for so many years, under so many incompetents.

Such men—there were, of course, exceptions—could not be expected to have chosen for wives women more knowledgeable than themselves. And since, in the pre-Disappearance era, women were regarded as inferior persons (and had so been regarded for thousands of years), the men could not have chosen superior wives even if they had wished to do so; there were too few. No desire was further from their minuscule personalities, in any case.

Their wives had been selected, as a rule, for one of two reasons: youthful physical appeal or wealth, with the former predominating. The selection was made, customarily, during or soon after adolescence; but the congressmen were, on the average, middle-aged. Hence their wives—again, with some exceptions—comprised a miscellaneous and inept group who generally spent such time as they did not devote to their children in a passionate attempt to elevate themselves in the pecking orders of Washington society.

These were the women summoned in May. Slightly fewer than three hundred could be found in Washington, or elsewhere. They convened in the hall of a club of which, as the wives of congressmen, they were automatically members. Thence, in buses, they moved to the Capitol with pomp and tittering. The most able among them had prepared agenda for the conference and, after its opening, tried to present their policies and aims. That soon proved impossible.

A "president pro tem" was easily elected, a Mrs. De Wyss Altbee, the wife (or former wife) of Senator Altbee and, of course, a woman very high in social circles. Mrs. Altbee chose a cabinet—and the ensuing four days were spent in ratifying her selections. She was forced to change all but one to gain the ratification. On the fifth day the convention was thrown open to a general discussion from which, Mrs. Altbee stated, she expected "the main lines of immediate action to emerge."

Unfortunately, her secretary of state (whose husband once had held that office) made the first proposal. Her suggestion was that, in view of the general confusion, the need of leadership and the appalling shortages of everything, the initial step of the "congress" should be to design a suitable uniform for the members. Such a uniform, she said, ought to be chic, to keep up morale. But it ought to be practical, to provide a good example. And its adoption should be their first business so that, wherever they went, the ladies would be marked as persons of authority.

The women of sense in the assembly tried to postpone consideration of that suggestion. They were overridden by a majority of four to one.

The secretary of state, twice listed amongst America's ten best-dressed women, had had the forethought to invite to the congress her world-famed couturier. That designer, Elsie Bazzmalk, had already "created" a number of sample uniforms. She dressed several Powers models in them. Scarcely a woman in the convention but had yearned to wear a Bazzmalk frock; as a result, the desperate business of the nation was set aside while the mannequins, flown from New York by a famed woman pilot, paraded incessantly.

Some of the responsible members tried anew to quash the matter. But others argued that, since the ladies were so urgently concerned with it, the best thing to do would be to hurry the selection and get on to real problems.

However, there was no hurrying the ladies' choice. Almost every point of the sample uniforms became the subject of vehement discussion. The width of revers, the most practical color or colors, the suitability of peaked caps as opposed to brimmed hats, the matter of skirt length, and a hundred other details carried the opening debate well past midnight and took up the whole of the following three days. On the fourth day a woman from Atlanta, who had staunchly held out for a less "mannish" and "dressier" costume than any offered, and who had gained considerable support, hit upon the notion of filibuster. An exhausted and enraged congress adjourned five days after that—without having accomplished anything save the selection of temporary officers.

Later in the month the officers were forced to act.

The circumstances surrounding that emergency were typical of the period.

Certain radio stations and a few amateur radio operators had irregularly communicated with various European countries. Many sets in America were able to pick up the gradually increasing broadcasts from overseas. The women of America knew, in general, that their sisters everywhere had shared their fate. Western Europe was in no different condition from the United States. The women and girls of China and India were gripped by starvation and pestilence. The Soviet was silent.

It was, therefore, a shock to Mrs. Altbee to learn by way of such broadcasts that the women of Russia were about to dispatch to the United States an "Armada of Liberation."

This armada, increasingly frequent broadcasts made plain, would be escorted by naval vessels bearing atomic weapons and well able to fend for itself. A hostile reception would be met by the vengeance of the "free, women Soviet workers." A friendly reception was hoped for and expected, on the grounds of "our common destitution," and the further grounds that "the Soviet women come in friendship and with love, bearing only liberation, peace and culture for the capitalist-enslaved masses of their American sisters."

Mrs. Altbee was frightened.

She was even more frightened when a report reached her of the passage, through the English Channel, of an aircraft carrier, a heavy cruiser, three destroyers and two submarines, all Russian and all headed in the direction of the United States.

She was not acquainted with the fact that, since the Revolution, Soviet women had participated in men's affairs—attending engineering schools, fighting cheek by jowl with the army, serving in the merchant marine, running locomotives, superintending the erection of steel buildings, doing a fair share of laboratory experiment at all levels and holding executive posts. So, at first, she tried to allay her panic by the wild hope that some men must have survived in Russia.

That was the idea she finally presented to her secretary of state, who scotched it instantly: "My husband and I spent three dreadful weeks in the Soviet, dear! Those women are capable of anything! They pave the streets. They repair airplane engines. I've seen them! They run factories!"

The cabinet was therefore duly summoned to Mrs. Altbee's country home, "Oak Manor," situated in the center of some two hundred undamaged acres near Kensington, Maryland. The ladies who arrived were aware that they had been virtually commanded to attend, but they thought the principal purpose of the convocation was social —tea and bridge. Mrs. Altbee had used the stratagem to prevent, as long as possible, news of the actual sailing from spreading through the land.

In a plum-colored tailored suit which, as several ladies agreed, "did things" for her iron-gray hair—in a wide-brimmed hat of matching hue, with a dark fitch stole thrown over one shoulder—Mrs. Altbee informed the assembled ladies of the situation.

Their shock was of such proportions that initial reactions were not of a very useful sort.

"Our Navy," said Mrs. Weller, the secretary of the interior, "will have to steam out immediately and destroy them!"

"Who'll steam it?" asked Mrs. Dwight, the secretary of agriculture.

There was, at that time, no secretary of defense to reply. An appointment for that office had not been deemed necessary.

"We have plenty of women fliers," Mrs. Leete, the secretary of the treasury, said heatedly. "Let them carry atom bombs to sea!"

"Do we know where the atom bombs are?" Mrs. Guegresson, secretary of commerce, asked.

"They're at that place—that Lost Almost, I call it," said Mrs. Weller.

"And do we have anybody," Mrs. Altbee put in, "who understands just how to use atomic bombs? I mean to say, I feel they have to be fiddled with, to shoot them off. They're terribly on the gadgety side."

"Some of the girls must have worked on the project," said Mrs. Clatley, of labor.

"I don't believe," Mrs. Dwight responded, "that women got very high up in that secrecy business. I mean to say, the men were horribly careful about it all. You know how they feel about women's wagging tongues. I very much doubt if many women were given information classified as top secret. Perhaps a few. Secretaries and such. But I doubt if any of them would violate security—with the men away. They'd be loyal types, I'm sure."

"Idiots!" snapped Mrs. Guegresson.

"Poor, poor dears," Mrs. Weller murmured, taking out her handkerchief and dabbing her eyes.

Mrs. Dwight stuck to her position. "Of course, it turned out the men blabbed all over the place—and I, for one, don't blame them! How would you like to be a nuclear physicist—and refused permission to talk by a lot of brass that hadn't the faintest conception of what you wanted to talk *about?* They should have known they could never keep their little secrets! After all, the Russians *are* clever; and the secrets really *weren't* anything but plain facts our men had found out. Besides, when hundreds of people know anything, everybody knows it. When even a dozen do, everybody does, more or less. That's rudimentary!"

"Maybe," said Mrs. Leete cheerfully, "there'll be a storm, or something, and the Russian ships will sink. After all, remember the *Spanish* Armada—"

Very few of those present did clearly remember the Spanish Armada; but all of them gave Mrs. Leete unencouraging looks.

"We might try to radio them," Mrs. Dwight suggested, "that the United States is being simply devastated by epidemics. Smallpox and things. Maybe they'd turn back."

"Oh, no!" cried the secretary of state. "You don't know the Russian women! Things like epidemics don't bother them in the *slightest!* They would either come right ashore and start vaccinating us, probably for the wrong diseases, or they'd ignore it. After all, people in Russia die like flies and nobody turns a hair!"

"Couldn't we just surrender?" Mrs. Weller asked. "I, for one, don't particularly care *what* happens—with the men gone."

"Apparently," Mrs. Altbee reminded them, "we aren't being asked to surrender, exactly. We're to be liberated." She gave her purple hat a push. "The effrontery of it! The gall! The presumption!"

"Well," said Mrs. Dwight, "we could pretend to be liberated and see what happened. After all, a few shiploads of women can hardly take over the country—not when we can't seem to set up any management of it ourselves. I think we should agree to *parley.* Let them land. Give them a banquet, or something. Then, if we don't care for the look of things, we could simply arrest the ones on shore! After all, the Greek women did something like that, once. I saw a play about it. Or maybe it was one of those Balkan countries, in the last war."

"What if they shoot off their atom things, then?" Mrs. Weller asked.

Mrs. Altbee was evidently in favor of Mrs. Dwight's line of

thought. "A few of them could hardly make such difference, the way conditions are. I believe we should get in touch with them immediately—"

"Who speaks Russian?" Mrs. Clatley asked. "We'll have to find somebody to interpret."

There was a pause. Mrs. Guegresson suddenly said, "I know a perfectly darling woman that does!"

The ladies looked at her with suspicion and doubt. Mrs. Weller gave a nervous laugh. "Why, Ada! Surely you don't know anybody who speaks *Russian!*"

"But I do, though! She majored in languages and has a Ph.D. She's terribly bright—"

"We'd have to be extremely careful," Mrs. Altbee murmured judicially, "in the matter of anybody who *actually spoke the language!*"

"Not in the case of the woman I know!" Mrs. Guegresson snapped. "She is an alumna of my university. She comes from quite an old American family. Very respectable, too. She told me, once, she had eight claims to D.A.R. membership, though she never would join—"

"There you are!" said the secretary of state, gesturing with a petit four. "Traitor to her class! Communist at heart! To have eight Revolutionary ancestors and to refuse to belong to the D.A.R. is the same thing as being a member of subversive organizations."

"Rubbish!" Mrs. Guegresson replied. "Ridiculous! Her husband is one of the most famous men in the country. He had a very hush-hush job in the war. He was quite close to Roosevelt—"

"And you call *that* a recommendation—!" the secretary of state half shouted.

"Ladies!" Mrs. Altbee said firmly. "Ada! Who is it?"

"Mrs. William Percival Gaunt. Paula Gaunt. They've built, recently, somewhere near Miami."

The secretary of state said, "Oh."

"At the time she studied the Russian language," Mrs. Guegresson continued, "people didn't feel the way they do now. They were *interested* in Russia. Anyway, Paula was a language phenom. She knows French and German and Latin and Greek and Italian and Spanish and I forget what others." She pressed an advantage indicated by a momentary cessation of protests. "We've got to have *some-body* who can talk to them, after all, and she's *our sort.*"

"Maybe they talk English," Mrs. Clatley suggested.

"You wanted an interpreter. I remembered one—an ideal one! If you aren't interested—go ahead! Radio them in English."

The secretary of state spoke. "The Gaunts are somewhat unconventional from what I've seen and heard of them. His books were *quite* extreme. But there can be no question of loyalty in that direction. After all, my husband had a tremendous *respect* for Dr. Gaunt."

That settled the problem.

It settled the problem because it delegated the responsibility.

Perhaps, in their way, these women, through their contacts and the employment of their instincts, through the interaction of their very penchants and prejudices, had arrived, however indirectly and by whatever irresponsible means, at a solution which the most able and highly educated of their sex would have reached more logically. For what better step could have been taken than to put in charge of the "welcoming committee" (which was soon organized) a knowledgeable, sophisticated woman who knew something of Washington and politics, a great deal about life, and who also knew Russia and the Russian language?

The ladies of the cabinet, at that time, were still in the grip of intense shock, the shock not only of the instantaneous loss of all males but of the appalling disasters that had ensued. If their practice of clinging to the frivolities and vanities of their previous lives was absurd, it was also pitiful: they knew nothing else. Even the fact that they were able to quarrel over a costume for themselves when the whole of America cried out for aid and direction and organization was, in a way, evidence of a certain kind of character. They had the strength, in the face of everything, to sustain what they did know and feel. It was not their fault that they were hopelessly unprepared in mind and personality for the burden they accepted. Their husbands had been little better equipped. And some peoples believe, notably the English, that not mere democracy but the destiny of man rises from and securely stands upon an inherent capacity of the veriest fool, if he be free, to do the right thing under extreme pressures.

On the 22nd of May, Paula left her home in Edwinna's charge and emplaned for New York, where the Russian flotilla was to arrive. Two girl pilots flew her, in a DC-3. Both the Miami airport and LaGuardia Field had long since been cleared of wrecked planes and put back in occasional use. Nevertheless, the arrangements for the flights had been elaborate. The acting President of the United States had been obliged to intervene to obtain the necessary supplies of aviation gasoline. And the journey was not without danger, owing to the lack of advance weather information, the absence of dependable emergency landing fields en route, and the uncertain mechanical condition of the ships then being flown.

Mrs. Altbee, who was head of the welcoming committee, rejected the opportunity to fly from Washington to New York in the plane that conveyed Paula. She made the trip by automobile—a hard journey owing to the insufficiently cleared state of some stretches of road and to the now rare but still real peril of encountering women bandits at hastily erected road blocks. Her journey, however, was uneventful.

Paula's trip, too, was without mishap. It gave her an opportunity, as she winged north, to see for the first time the plight of the great seaboard. Cities over which they passed looked bombed-out. Three or four had been spared, by rains, as in the case of Miami, or by luck, or by the concerted action of women survivors. Small towns, also, were often burned, showing acres of standing chimneys and the empty wall-rims of buildings. Open country everywhere seemed more thickly populated than it had been. But little traffic moved. A truck was an encouraging sight and a convoy of trucks brought one of the pilots back to point it out.

In all the long way Paula saw only six steam locomotives in motion and perhaps twice that number of Diesels. Many women were at work in the fields. But they labored without the aid of much machinery. The problem of farm equipment seemed to Paula the most pressing; machines would be even more needed out on the prairies where the grain crops were raised.

From time to time, as she flew, Paula studied a book that showed signs of much recent leafing, a Russian dictionary. She had once been fairly proficient in the language but that had been long ago. Since word of her "appointment" had arrived, she had been brushing up.

From time to time, too, she considered courses of action which might be pursued after contact was made with the Soviet women. It was difficult to foresee what their attitude would be. She had some ideas; she had formed certain plans that had already been carried out. But she was extremely uncertain about the feasibility of those plans. Who could guess how the Russian women would feel?

New York shocked her.

They came in from the west and flew across Manhattan at about Seventieth Street. Areas she had remembered as a repetitive geometry of brownstone houses were now black wreckage. The skyscrapers were still standing but many of them were scorched and stained, their windows jagged, their interiors obviously gutted. Some of the cross streets were clogged with toppled buildings and impassable. But the avenues seemed to be open: thin streams of traffic moved along them. She could see that the downtown slums were destroyed too; and the distant view of Brooklyn and Queens conveyed an impression of similar ruin. Only certain of the New Jersey suburbs had looked untouched, their houses tidy and their trees pretty in the light shades of spring.

The Triboro Bridge was unchanged. East River Drive was

usable in spite of the wreckage piled alongside it. And the Park Plaza hotel was exactly as she remembered it, except that the doorman was a doorwoman, the bellboys were bellgirls and the manager was a Mrs. Moore. Central Park, viewed from her eighteenth-floor room, had a border of dead trees even though blocks of park-facing buildings, like that which contained her hotel, had escaped the general holocaust.

New York was quiet, too. No cacophony of horns and whistles and tires and abrupt brakes rose to the high room. And there were no pigeons anywhere. That was the kind of thing Paula noticed.

When the sun set, the great metropolis did not spell out its modernistic poem of light, which had always enthralled her. Manhattan became, instead, a gloomy, ghostly place, with isolated wan lights in the buildings. Passing cars threw discrete beams and cast particular shadows now. It did not smell like New York any more, either—like wet bricks and the sea's salt, tar and coffee and women's perfumes; it smelled of dank ashes and stale smoke.

On the morning after her arrival, Paula woke with the sensation of fear. For an instant she was unable to recall its exact cause or even to remember the meaning of the hotel room in which she found herself. The feeling passed as her brain recovered memory: she was in the Park Plaza and the hotel was just the same, although New York was appallingly different—at the Park Plaza, where she and Bill had often . . . *Skip it,* she told herself. At nine o'clock a flotilla of Russian naval vessels was expected to anchor in the bay and she and a committee were to go out to meet it.

With factual recollection came a sickening sense of incompetence. They had sent all the way to Miami for her because she could speak the language and because the ladies in the "cabinet" had felt she, among all persons they regarded as suitable, alone could be trusted in the event about to occur.

Six-thirty, Paula saw by her watch. A bright, sunny day, if the slit of sky visible beyond the drawn blind was an honest sample.

A warm day in May.

And she was going down to meet a woman-manned Soviet mission, on naval vessels, bearing one or more atomic bombs and bent on the "liberation" of America's women, who needed aid, heaven knew, but who reviled the Soviet concept of "freedom."

She.

Paula.

She thought of the committee. She had spent the previous evening in session with it, considering plans and settling, at last, on alternatives.

Mrs. De Wyss Altbee had the most money, the big, Victorian house in Kensington she'd inherited from her mother, the oldest family line and the most firmly entrenched social position, so the wives of the congressmen, faithful to their long, climbing pursuit of Mrs. A., had continued the game by "electing" her "President" of the United States. Until the menacing news about the Russians was received, the administration had been an expectably preposterous joke: one filibuster and nothing else. America's women had learned, laughed grimly, and gone on with desperate local endeavors.

Poor Mrs. A.! The trouble was that her useful knowledge extended no further than household goods and games and clothes; her executive experience was limited to the management of clubs, balls and cocktail parties; her diplomatic training was only in regulating social status; and she hadn't a brain in her head. A good, busty figure of a woman, Paula meditated—something of a battle-ax, well dressed and well heeled and ruthless in her fashion. Perhaps even well intentioned when her own interests weren't involved. Paula decided she would have made Warren Gamaliel Harding look like a fifty-fifty mixture of Jefferson and Lincoln.

She called for Room Service and was surprised when it answered. She ordered orange juice, toast and a big pot of coffee. She was told there was only grape juice. She assented to that and went on thinking.

Her friend Mrs. Guegresson had traveled a good deal and possessed some sense, as evidently did Mrs. Dwight. The three other ladies on the committee were presidents of women's universities. After listening to them for several hours, Paula had realized that a knowledge of truth and a "higher education" were two matters as different as feathers on a hat and a flock of vultures. She had forgotten, in the years with Bill, that he was not a typical professor—forgotten what yeasty, impractical mythology passed for common sense among the flat-hatted Phi Beta Kappas.

A knock came on Paula's door; she thought that Room Service, under female aegis, was a great improvement on its male-conducted counterpart. But it was Mrs. Altbee. She wore a negligee of pale-rose silk; but she was personally white to the lips.

"They're *here!*"

"Here? Who?" Paula sat up in bed.

"The Russians! They said they'd anchor at nine in the harbor! Actually, at daybreak, they steamed straight into the Hudson River and anchored in a line right off Manhattan and *trained their guns!*" She gasped the last phrase and leaned against the wall.

Paula had an impulse to laugh. "We never catch onto them, do we?"

"Catch onto them! Do you realize—?"

"Did they shoot?"

"They haven't—yet—or we wouldn't be here!"

"That's typical Russian bravura. Getting the jump. Pushing us. The smart thing to do now is to—"

"That's what I'm here for! You'll have to send somebody out to implore them to hold their fire at least until we can *talk!*"

Paula yawned. "The thing to do is to let them sit there till noon, when we had an appointment—"

"Suppose they fire? Set off an atomic bomb—!"

"And blow themselves up? We went over that last night."

"They're capable of *anything. Anything!* And so barbarically quick-tempered!"

"Funny. In all they've done, I've noticed plenty of barbarism. We have our share too. But not one scintilla of quick temper. They are as patient as oysters making pearls—"

Mrs. Altbee relaxed somewhat and took a chair. Paula's tray arrived. She drank the grape juice, made a face, and tried the toast.

The pro-tem President said, "Don't you feel it's dreadfully risky to let them sit out there for five hours without doing a *thing?*"

"Sure." Paula chewed. "But the males are gone. It looks as if the human race had come to a slow stop. Half the cities in our country are half ash heaps. So what the hell is a little *more* risk, nowadays?"

"I would hate to feel I'd failed to do my duty."

Paula found the opening irresistible. She asked, "Why?"

"I beg your pardon?"

"I mean—" Paula poured coffee. It steamed and the room smelled of it and the smell was heartening. "Why are *you* afraid to fail to do your duty? The whole country is a mess. You were elected President, after a fashion. And your duty was to accomplish something for the tragic condition of the people, not to preside over a finish fight on pleats."

Tears came into Mrs. Altbee's eyes and she shook her head sadly.

Paula again felt sorry for her. "I know, and I apologize. Nobody's normal. The superficial things were once the most important things we had to deal with. *Women.* What a predicament we've *all* been in! Maybe, just by sticking to trifles, you showed character and courage. Who knows?"

"We haven't any character," Mrs. Altbee said unevenly, "and not very much courage."

"Nonsense!" Paula's inner sentiments half agreed. "Let the Russian women sit! At noon—"

At noon, aboard the *Bessie,* the committee put out on the river. For all her plebeian name, the *Bessie* was a prepossessing vessel, a private yacht, one hundred and twelve feet long, equipped with every luxury that could be stowed away on and built into a seagoing ship of

her size. She belonged to a Mrs. Trafalgar, a personal and dear friend
of Mrs. Altbee. The yacht had cost upward of a million.

Mrs. Trafalgar, unlike her eminent Washington colleague, was a
woman of some practical enterprise. She knew how to handle and
navigate the *Bessie,* how to start her engines, and how to dock her
smartly. When asked to prepare to meet the Russians she had trained a
crew of college girls sufficiently for the purpose. The *Bessie's* crew
wore blue skirts and white blouses; they had been chosen as much
for good looks as for know-how from amongst the semiseafaring
debutantes of such maritime regions as Larchmont and Southampton.

The white yacht, elaborate goldwork glittering in the hot sun,
moved slowly up the Hudson River past the submarines, the destroyer
and the heavy cruiser, to the aircraft carrier. On all these vessels female
crews stood at silent attention while the *Bessie* passed. A landing
stage had been let down the carrier's side and Paula translated the
name of that ship as the panicky committee prepared to be transferred
by launch.

"It's called the *October Revolution.*"

"What an absurd name!" said Mrs. Guegresson, checking her
hair and lipstick.

"Not really. It's like the *Independence*—in Americanese."

Mrs. Dwight was gazing at the lined-up crews through binoculars
"They're kind of little—you know it? Short. And they keep looking
toward New York."

"They're probably thinking of firing," said Dr. Joan Clemment,
one of the university presidents. Her face was clay-white.

"They're probably comparing the skyline," Paula answered, "not
only with Moscow, but with all the garbage they've been taught. It
may be quite a shock to them. Well—the launch is ready!"

Stony-faced women in uniform helped them onto the landing
stage. Women with rifles at attention lined the way as the committee
climbed up the forbidding steel side of the carrier. On deck, they
were confronted by what seemed regiments of uniformed women-

sailors. In the center of a human square, facing the landing stage, stood seven or eight women who wore gold braid.

Above their heads four huge guns pointed in bleak significance at Manhattan. Paula estimated them to be eight-inchers. Behind the dressed-up naval officers, or political officials, or whatever they were, was a band. It now struck up, to Paula's surprise, "The Star-Spangled Banner." Paula came to a halt. She was in the lead, so the pale and shaking women behind her followed the example.

Paula was wearing a green hat that matched a green tailored suit. Mrs. Dwight and Mrs. Guegresson also wore suits. Mrs. Altbee and the college presidents wore silk prints. We must look like hell, Paula thought.

After the "Star-Spangled Banner," another song began. Paula felt motion behind her and murmured, "Attention! It's 'The Internationale'!" None of the ladies had ever before stood at attention for that piece. None even knew what it was. But they stood now.

When "The Internationale" was finished, the officers moved forward. At their head was a powerfully built, rather handsome woman with short, muddy-blonde hair, slaty eyes set far apart, high cheekbones, and a big, very firm mouth. She had not changed expression during the music. She approached the committee and suddenly, stiffly, held out her hand. She spoke in throaty, noncommittal Russian:

"Welcome. I am Ilnya Basrov, special commissar for foreign affairs and commander of the American Liberation Expedition."

Another woman stepped forward and opened her mouth, evidently to interpret.

Paula glanced once at the interpreter and back quickly at Ilnya Basrov. She said, in swift Russian, "I am Paula Gaunt, American citizen. You are welcome to our country. I would like to introduce the President of the United States and the members of the official welcoming committee."

Ilnya Basrov was startled; it showed for an instant. Then she smiled in the way an acute woman will smile when her mind has solved a small puzzle. "Ah! You are one of *us*, then? You speak the language quite well! I knew we had many, among the Americans—"

"I am *not* one of you," Paula answered firmly. "I think communism is foolish. Madame Basrov, I have offered to introduce our President!"

The Russian leader flushed slightly and handshaking began.

"You offended that woman! Be careful!" Mrs. Dwight whispered to Paula.

What Paula was noticing, at close range, was the stupefaction in the eyes of the crew, eyes that failed to stay "front" and strayed continually to the Manhattan skyline. The handshaking ended and the formal smiles that went with it also vanished.

Ilnya Basrov and her associates stepped back a little. A camerawoman commenced to take motion pictures. The Russian leader looked at the committee and then gazed off into the distances. She was, plainly, about to make a speech.

"We come in peace," she began "We—"

"We come in peace also," Paula interrupted.

Mrs. Dwight said nervously, "Shhhh—!"

"We are nevertheless," the Russian went on, "prepared for all eventualities. In the holds of our ships we carry atomic bombs. We are prepared to withdraw and to hurl these upon you and your—spectacular—City of New York—"

Again Paula broke in. Her voice was amiable, clear, and loud. She wondered, as she spoke, if atomic bombs *would* be in the hold, at this point, granted they had been brought along. She half suspected not: they would be out on deck, in view, if there were any. Paula said, "We are also, of course, ready for eventualities. This river under your ships is mined. So is the harbor. Any hostile act on your part, or the appearance of such an act, would result in your instant dissolution. You were in great danger this morning when you trained these small cannon on our city."

Ilnya's flush was now quite evident and it was followed by a slight pallor. Her upper lip, on which was a peach-down mustache of pale hairs, showed sweat beads. The crew and the officers said nothing; but they surged minutely as if they were made of paper and a faint breeze had blown amongst them.

Nevertheless, in spite of Paula's ominous, wholly untrue assertion, the Russian leader thrust out her broad, hard jaw and smiled. "We were prepared to run such a risk. We are familiar with the technical abilities of the American people. For the last day's steaming, we have been on the alert, half expecting that you might attack at any time—"

"Look—" Paula cut in.

"I have prepared an address for the occasion. It is necessary for me to explain why we Soviet women have come this long way to liberate the American women slaves of capitalism. I—"

Paula turned her back and rapidly, rudely translated what had been said. Then she pivoted again and smiled charmingly at Ilnya Basrov. "Look. We, the women of America, know all about your Soviet ideas of our need for liberation. We don't happen to agree we require the effort. We're glad you came across. We don't care much for long speeches. I realize what I say is neither diplomatic nor proper protocol and I don't give a button on Stalin's pants. Besides, it's hot on this damned steel deck. If you have any liquor on board, we'd enjoy a cocktail. Afterward, we want you to come ashore—as many of you as dare leave the shadow of your little guns. We want you to see our city, our country. We've arranged a banquet for you tonight. The whole gang of you. If you want to make speeches, you'll get a chance then. As far as we're concerned, politics have shrunk down to something mighty small. Our men and boys are gone. That's what interests and worries us. If you have any ideas on that, we'll be only too glad to listen."

Ilnya Basrov and her colleagues exhibited changing emotions as Paula spoke. It angered them to have their leader interrupted. It obviously infuriated them to be told that the women of America had no interest in their mission. The statement about not liking long speeches was a simple insult; yet it was uttered so candidly and with such a friendly smile that they did not know how to take it. Besides, they had thoroughly digested the thought that the Hudson River was full of mines. The American woman had not even bothered to say whether or not they were atomic mines. The Americans, of course, were a formidably technical people even though the samples before them looked like the cartoons of typical capitalist wasters and exploiters. But their curiously redheaded spokesman sounded as if she meant what she said—she seemed good-tempered—and she showed common sense. No one had looked forward to long speeches in the full sun on the steel deck. This American had also asked about a drink, which was flattering, since an enormous buffet had been prepared in the officers' mess and there was vodka for all the toasts that any woman could stand and drink.

The invitation to go ashore—and the sight of New York had filled the women with a desire to do so—was perhaps a trap. Still, some could be sent ashore while the majority remained on the alert. The fleet might even be withdrawn to the high seas during negotiations.

Ilnya Basrov had such thoughts. She decided that temporizing was advisable. She swallowed her indignation. She even smiled. While Paula translated what she had said to the horrified committee, the Russians conferred. At the end of the parley, Ilnya beamed. "Come," she cried. "Let us have the drink, then!"

In the dining salon, where damask all but disappeared under a load of delicacies, Paula raised a glass and made the first toast. It pleased her hosts; it pleased Paula also: "To Stalin, wherever he is!"

In emulating the toasting tactics of their male diplomats, the Russians had failed to reckon with one factor. For, while they were solid and rugged women, they were not accustomed to the rapid imbibation of one glass of vodka after another. Vodka, like everything else, had been short in Russia since 1917; and the comrades were not encouraged to use it freely, in any case. The American ladies, however, were graduates of a long schooling in the cocktail hour. Mrs. Altbee in particular had a competence in that respect: she had been seen to drink, by actual count, fourteen stingers in an hour and a half and to leave the cocktail lounge where she had done it with a steady tread—with not so much as the flicker of an eye.

It was true that, after the fifth toast, caviar was served along with several kinds of smoked fish, the pickled eggs of Siberian ducks, fancy breads, rare cheeses and other victuals which the American delegation fell upon with appreciation. But it was also the fact that Mrs. Altbee took Ilnya Basrov and two of the other Russian plenipotentiaries to a corner and engaged in a series of private toasts, not without malice aforethought. It soon became evident that the Russian leader, although she kept her balance and her look of great physical strength, grew flushed, began talking rapidly and laughed with almost every sentence she uttered.

When, acting as translator, Paula noticed that Ilnya had taken an interest in the material of Mrs. Altbee's dress, and when the latter woman gave a furtive wink, Paula felt that the situation was ripe for further action. She tapped on a tumbler with a knife and brought silence. She said buoyantly, in Russian, "I suggest that you ladies, having shown us such extreme hospitality, come ashore now and permit us to begin a return of the kindness."

There was consultation and some bickering. But presently a delegation of fifty-five women, under Ilnya, began to be ferried, ten at a time, to the *Bessie.* The Soviet women wanted desperately to see what lay beneath the skyscrapers.

Paula's recollections of the remainder of the afternoon and evening were somewhat hazy owing not to the vodka but to the number and variety of scenes in which she participated and of interrogations for which she acted as interpreter. In the last she was aided by some of the guests who, it proved, spoke English quite well.

Fifth Avenue buses were waiting at the dock for just such an opportunity as the shore party furnished. The Soviet women insisted on examining the buses before they rode in them—not for fear of infernal machines but, simply, to see what the engines were like. They next demanded to be let out at the base of the first real skyscraper they encountered. Its interior had been badly damaged by fire. But the fact only pleased the Russians because it allowed them to see more of the structural members of the building.

At a subway kiosk the procession made another stop and they descended to the dark, now-unused platforms. The women who came from Moscow were smug concerning the superiority of their handsome subway stations. Shown around with flashlights, they asked to board a train stalled there. They said that their subway cars were better planned. When Paula's torch fell upon the map of the subway system which every car contained, Ilnya asked immediately, "How many miles per inch?"

She was told.

"How much is built—how much proposed?"

"It's all built."

Ilnya scowled; she thought she was being told a lie. "How much does it cost to make the longest ride?"

Paula told her that too.

Ilnya translated it to kopeks. She scowled again.

The buses reached the Greenwich Village area of Manhattan.

Not all of this region had been burned. There were women on the street, young girls and babies in the parks, women running stores, women driving cars and trucks.

"Rather nice houses," said one Soviet woman.

"These right here happen to be where working people live," Paula said. "Would you like to see inside them?"

The Russians picked a block of identical houses. The nature of the visit was swiftly explained to its women tenants.

What they then saw had an astonishing effect upon the women from the USSR.

"Imagine!" one chattered afterward. "The husband merely drove a truck. The wife is not employed at anything but the raising of babies. And they have beds with springs! Irons which electricity heats! A stove of gas, without coal or wood to carry! An electrical machine to clean the rugs! Two kinds of water in pipes, the hot and the cold. And many things the use of which I do not know and cannot imagine, but all very complex! Eight different dresses for the woman! Nine pants and eight coats, the man! Clothes for twenty babies and children, where they have three! A radio, even, and she says, unless the interpreter lies, they were soon to buy television, radio pictures! It is *fantastic!*"

Paula hid a capitalistic grin. . . .

It went on until the early hours of morning.

The Park Plaza did not greatly impress the visitors. They assumed it to be the lair of plutocrats. However, when they were shown scores of hotels equally luxurious, one woman asked, "How many capitalists do you have?"

Most stores, of course, had been burned or looted. What was left, what nobody wanted or had stolen, still enormously impressed the women. They began to believe accounts given them of what the stores had once contained, the quantities, the quality, and the prices.

Toward evening, Ilnya confided to Paula, "We have much to learn. And in some things we have been misinformed."

"What you ought to see," Paula answered, "is how it looked before the catastrophe. You ought to see, also, how our farmers live, and our miners, and the rest. There is poverty—sure—"

"In the Soviet," Ilnya sighed, "*all* are poor."

"I know. Except the Politburo. Artists and writers. Politicians. Commissars. The bosses. All are poor. Here—well—if you will stay—"

"I will stay," Ilnya answered, "until I am satisfied we have the facts. After all, the NDVK has vanished. So who will punish us for staying? We Russian women felt we should carry out what we could of the Plan. The police we have not yet reshaped. Perhaps it is just as well. I would like a dress such as the one you wear."

"Nothing," Paula said, not truthfully, "could be easier!"

The Russian women were even more astonished, almost embarrassed, to be assigned individual rooms. Paula had a feeling that they would feel lonesome—a feeling verified by the fact that the shore party spent more time grouped in the corridors than in their private quarters.

While she changed for dinner, Paula had another visit from Mrs. Altbee, who entered looking triumphant and made a circle with her thumb and forefinger. "When I think how scared I was this morning—!"

"Me, too."

The President was amazed. "*You* were?"

"Poor things! Sure, I was scared. Everybody is—of Russians. But they're just women, kind of nice women, with a few nutty ideas."

"They show an aptitude for conversion."

"We'll try to keep 'em ashore overnight. The longer they stay, the more they'll see. The more they see the more ground Lenin loses. It would be a good idea to scare up clothes for them. It would be another good idea to get together all the hairdressers we can find and open all the beauty parlors around here that are intact and treat the officials and officers and the crew to a complete going-over. We should find more and better presents for the banquet—"

Mrs. Altbee nodded. "What about jewelry? I could collect quite a lot of that before the evening is over. Sending around to women I know."

Paula shook her head. "I doubt if they'd be much interested in jewels. Plans for a bulldozer would be more like it, or one dozen traveling cranes, or perhaps just a nice assortment of vacuum cleaners. I don't know for sure, but apparently they haven't got a single one of them over there. Did you notice the way the naval officers ran them—cleaned that truck driver's carpets?"

"I did," Mrs. Altbee replied. "And I also gathered there are plenty of Russian women who can do lots of the things we can't. Like run city water chlorination units and inspect sewers and service power plants and pour concrete. What would you think of my making a proposal tonight to exchange goods and *people?*"

"I think it would be fine." Paula gave her hair a last touch. . . .

It was three in the morning. . . .

With Ilnya, after an exhausting and scary climb by flashlight, Paula stood at the top of the Empire State Building. The night was clear and there was moon enough to give some concept of the size of the wrecked metropolis at their feet. They talked, their words ignored by the half dozen women who had accompanied them on the climb.

"It will be difficult," Ilnya sighed, "to explain at home the real facts."

"Not very. For one thing, we'll send you back with a shipload of books and magazines and movie reels."

"And machines?"

"And machines," Paula nodded. "And you'll send us technical experts—"

"—who will be ordered to learn English as of the day they are ordered to duty."

"Why *order* them? Why not ask for volunteers?"

A grim, faint smile was visible on the Russian's face. "Because they would *all* volunteer."

There was a pause. Ilnya stared into the night and shook her head.

"Then," Paula said, "call for volunteers and pick from them. After all, it's *fairer.*"

"A funny word you use so often! 'Fairer'! What is fair? To lose all the men until we can learn to fertilize the female artificially?"

"You think you can?"

"Why not? Soviet science can do anything!"

"American science, though it hasn't tried much yet to crack that problem, thinks the chances of synthetic human fertilization are pretty slim. And might produce only girls."

Ilnya shrugged. "To us, what matter? My husband was a general of the Red Army. I had three sons. Two daughters. Fifteen lovers, maybe twenty, who knows? Soldiers are away a lot. You had lovers?"

Paula didn't answer.

"Yes?" The Russian insisted. "Oh—no? No, I see. You are timid in strange ways, you Americans."

"I had them," Paula replied quietly.

Impetuously, then, in the gloom, on the forbidding tower, Ilnya leaned and kissed Paula. "I like you," she said. "I *trust* you. You tell the truth. It is sad, yes? We shall have no more lovers and no more husbands. Nothing." Her deep voice fell lower still and abruptly she began to sing a love song which, like most Russian songs, was melancholy. The Russians among the women behind her joined in and the notes swept across the great, destitute city. The American city.

We've found peace, Paula thought, and sisterhood, too late for brotherhood.

What's happened?

Where is this turning planet taking us?

What are *we* still here for? Was there any *reason* behind the vanishing of our men?

She joined falteringly in the song. She felt Ilnya's muscular arm come lightly to rest on her shoulders. She put an arm around the Russian woman.

If we can get the world going again, Paula thought . . . *if* the women can create a really effective government . . . *if* they can learn all that they were not allowed to know and neglected even to wonder about . . . and *if* friendship of all the women on earth can be made real . . . then perhaps some laboratory worker will find a way to start babies in us and even to produce boy babies, and by the time we are old and *they* are mature . . . humanity may be *worthy* of two sexes.

With that thought, fierce and impellent, came homesickness.

It was as if home had bells and she could hear them ringing, calling . . . had its own particular perfume and above the harsh odor of ashes she could sense that distant sweetness . . . or as if Bill was walking in the house and on the lawn but she, a deserter, was not there to join him.

"I am nostalgic," said Ilnya.

"Me too."

"But you will soon be at home. I will stay here, I think. So much to learn! To do! Your mission is finished. Mine begins."

II

IN WHICH CERTAIN FURTHER CHANGES ARE ENCOUNTERED.

G aunt drove into Miami. It had rained in the early morning. His tires churned through puddles and marred their surfaces. Behind him the water stirred, settled and again mirrored green palm fronds, scarlet and yellow flowers, the blue sky. It was hot. Vines draped the empty lots on Brickell Avenue, vines which sagged from tree to tree like camouflage nets. Clusters of heavy blossoms hung on long stems in the dark shade of the vines.

To his surprise, the drawbridge was lifted. He stopped. After a time another car stopped also. The man in it looked at Gaunt and Gaunt looked at the man. They did not know each other. They watched the ship, a small one, putting out to sea. It was the kind of vessel that had traded in the Bahamas and Gaunt wondered idly about conditions in those nearby islands. The ship clanked into the channel; the bridge closed with a series of unsure, quivering descents. Gaunt drove over it and into an untended parking yard where, months before, boys had hustled the myriad cars away and an hourly charge had been made. It was free now, and no boys worked in the sunshine. Perhaps fifty cars stood haphazardly where there was room for a thousand.

Some stores were open. Above most of them, newly painted signs indicated what sort of credit numbers and ration ticket colors were required of patrons. Men walked on the street. Men and boys leaned in shady places against trees or sat on lawns and curbs; a frustrated and desultory look showed in every eye.

On the corner of Flagler Street, a newsman, hard faced, bull lunged, yelled his version of the afternoon's headlines:

"Woman rumored found in Cape Town, South Africa! Willowy blonde discovered, report says! Alive and in good health! Read all about it!" His voice throbbed and echoed in the quiet streets. Between his shouts, the twitter of birds sounded clearly.

A few men bought papers but in the expression of none was any sign of such excitement or hope as might have been expected. The men of the world had first wearied and finally despaired of "rumors" of a woman found. Usually they were inventions of bored journalists in far places. Sometimes they were the beginning of sordid tales, tales about quacks and liars who claimed to have a woman on display and charged admission and who, perhaps, were later lynched by an investigating, disillusioned mob. On occasion the "discoveries" had concerned hermaphrodites; but it had been found, long ago, that all such had spontaneously reverted to masculinity at the instant of the Vanishing.

Gaunt bought a paper—but not to read about the rumored woman. That headline but made him think with a dreary hopelessness of Edwin and his quest; the hard effort to get news and the ultimate, resigned acceptance of his son's loss, long ago, in New Guinea.

He found a place in the shade and he, like the others, leaned against a building. The front page was largely concerned with government orders, new bureaucratic laws and plans for the resumption of some service or other. Foreign news, on an inside page, told of a revolt in Hungary and of the burning of public buildings by an "Anti-Sex Party" which resented the lowering of general morality. The insurrection had been put down with machine guns.

He heard a murmur in the distance. A half dozen homosexuals, or "G-boys" as they were called, came chattering and laughing up the street. The "Girl-Boys" traveled in little bands. Alone, they were liable to different kinds of assault: assault by men made lustful by the sight of lipstick, powder, dresses and the synthetic female shape, or by men enraged at such a spectacle. The G-boys minced past Gaunt, who gazed at them with eyes at once somber and repelled. Whistles and catcalls showered from the shady places along the thoroughfare.

A lone cop, walking his tiresome beat in the damp warmth, stared stonily at the G-boys. He was not allowed to arrest them, any more, except for flagrant exhibitionism. They were too numerous. Amongst them were men who had been important citizens, rich citizens, men with position and power, men of all ages. Besides, many who didn't dress as girls, many who ignored all such human travesty, "decent," "normal" men in pre-Disappearance days, had changed their attitudes, their behavior.

Conscious of the universal attention paid them, the G-boys went on, smirking and smiling, rolling their eyes, winking, flirting, waving handkerchiefs. Two or three bystanders accosted them. The girlish group stopped and giggled. From it rose the sound of tenor and baritone voices with female accents and intonations. Presently the whole group went into an open bar. Someone had offered to buy them a drink—picked them up—and the masquerade of femininity departed from the thoroughfare.

Miami steeped in high noon. A little wind stirred papers and rubbish on the dirty sidewalks. Sun sluiced hazily down thousands of unwashed windows and myriad pastel walls from which, already, faded paint was peeling.

Gaunt folded his newspaper, took a pencil from his pocket, and began to check a list, using the paper for backing. Perhaps, he thought, that was why he had bought it.

Trips to the city from his house involved sixteen to twenty miles of driving and consumed a good deal of gasoline. It was necessary to make every mile count. The list said:

Haircut
Gas and oil
Meat
Aspirin
Tooth paste, powder, etc.
Shoes?
Watch repaired?
Typewriter ribbons
Send telegram WH
Call on anybody? Connauth? Ableson? Weaver?

He compared the list with his undependable recollection of items needed and items running short. Then, heaving a sigh, he reexamined his ration tickets, credit number cards, travel blanks, special permits, identity certificate and other papers currently associated with shopping. They seemed to be in order.

Briskly now, compared with the general pace, he started up Flagler Street. First, he showed his communications permit and sent the wire which informed the White House that his report of the investigative projects was about three-quarters finished. In the telegram he used no clearly comprehensible key words.

Thus Tateley's inquiry into solar, planetary, spatial and cosmic conditions prevailing at the moment of Disappearance was known as PROJECT ETHER.

Steadman's biological inquiries into the possibility that the Disappearance might have been implicit in cells and tissue (an instantaneous, gasifying cancer, someone had suggested in a lengthy paper) and into the possibility of growing human embryos in mammalian uteri, flasks or test tubes (though where and how to find or create the starting ovum was an apparently hopeless problem) went under the respective names of OPERATION PROTOPLASM and OPERATION PROTOPROTOPLASM.

Bob Blake's teams, investigating at every atomic and subatomic level, were engaged in what was known (among the knowing) as PROJECT X.

The young clerk at Western Union was awed by the address on Gaunt's wire and careful to check every word and letter: people were arrested quickly for carelessness, these days, where official matters were concerned. . . .

The typewriter ribbons proved easy, to Gaunt's relief. Little things of that sort were in uncertain supply and to be without them was sometimes to cease functioning altogether.

There was no meat.

His watch was not yet ready. It had been promised, but the repair man said he was behind schedule. Gaunt felt undue wrath— he often did, these days—and found himself "pulling rank" on the bent, mustached, unhappy watchmaker. "Look here! I'm on the NTS Board, that's the National Technical Survey Board, in case you don't know, and I need my watch to carry out my duties!"

"I'll sit up tonight! Deliver it? I have a bicycle!"

Gaunt's irritation vanished as it had come, quickly, and was replaced by another emotion: "Oh, hell! We all feel the same way! Take your time! I'll stop by again in a week or so. Sorry to be mean about it!"

Small, grateful blue eyes looked up at him. "Thank you, sir."

Tooth paste, but not his customary brand. Aspirin. "Anything else, Dr. Gaunt?" the druggist asked. "Barbiturates? Hard times for sleep! Codeine? A few quarter grains of morphine? Dangerous days."

Gaunt's surprise was evident.

The druggist leaned over his counter so the other customers would not hear. "New ruling. With the doctors having to do nursing as well as medicine and surgery, with transportation so poor, we've been instructed on the q. t. to make drugs available to responsible people. Naturally, we don't intend to supply addicts. But for men like yourself who are capable of caring for their neighbors, giving first aid, treating minor things, it saves sending for a doctor, who probably wouldn't get there anyhow."

"I see," Gaunt replied.

"Sulfas, penicillin, aureomycin, and so on. I've fixed up at least twenty customers who have good judgment with outfits that can handle anything from an acute appendix—with the molds—to a fracture."

"How much?"

It was an expected question. The druggist shrugged. "A simple kit—ten dollars. A complete kit in a suitcase, seventy-five dollars."

"I'll pick up a suitcase on my way back to my car. It wouldn't be a bad idea. God knows *what* a man will want in the days ahead!"

Gaunt did not need shoes—yet. But he had neglected, for the past two years, to keep his stock of footgear at its usual level. His brown brogues were badly worn. His "best" black shoes were cracking across the instep. Since May he had been intermittently visiting shoe stores. Immediately after the Disappearance, shoes had been looted; they were for a time nearly as scarce as women. Shoes were coming back now; but Gaunt was waiting for their quality to improve.

At Bosterman's he found nothing but cloth and suède.

At Kallan's, cordovan shoes, not well made.

At Bloom's Shoe Mart he was offered, for fifty dollars, brogues manufactured before the catastrophe, near-duplicates of his worn-out pair. They were black market. He wrestled with his conscience and decided he could wait.

He had his hair cut.

The barbershop floor was unswept, the bib used on Gaunt was soiled, no tissue or towel protected him from its greasy folds, and the barber's instruments were unsterilized. Gaunt sat finickily in the chair and listened to dirty jokes and uproarious laughter. Nowadays, many men went to barbershops simply to hear and to participate in such talk. Gaunt listened indignantly. Jim Elliot, revolted by the salacity of barbershops, had already taken to cutting Gordon's hair and his own —with two mirrors. Gaunt thought that, the next time, he would emulate his lawyer friend.

When he left the barbershop, the sight of a crowd of men in front of the windows of a department store caused him to turn his head to the right, with the result that a man approaching him from the left collided with him.

"Sorry," said Gaunt.

The voice that came to his ears shook with rage. "You're damned rooting-tooting you're sorry! Why don't you look where you're going?"

Gaunt wheeled. The man was middle-aged, big-bellied, thick-armed and trembling with exaggerated response: the collision had done him no damage but his fury kindled, in the philosopher, an equally abnormal anger. "It takes two people not looking where they're going, to collide."

"Oh. A wise guy!"

Gaunt calmed quickly. "Skip it."

"I skip *nothing!*" said the man childishly—and he swung at the philosopher.

The blow caught Gaunt on the shoulder. Before he knew what he was doing, he swung in return and felt his fist push into the gristle of the man's nose. It was a rewarding sensation.

The nose began to bleed, its owner, to weep. He stood there, trickling crimson, sobbing. "It hurts," he moaned.

Gaunt was overcome by contrition. He took a clean handkerchief from his pocket and handed it over. "I'm sorry. *Sorry.* . . !"

The man shrugged and walked back in the direction from which he had come.

Temper that rose from an absolute and insatiate hunger, an utter frustration, and an inner loneliness . . . temper which made the presence of men, and of only men, a constant source of bursts of violence. The papers hardly bothered, any more, to run the police court reports of blows, grapplings, stabbings, even meaningless shootings. Every man knew why such things happened because nearly every man had the same sensations.

Gaunt stood awhile on the sunny side of the street wondering if he ought to follow the fat man—grieving—making up his mind to prepare a discipline of himself, henceforward, so that whenever he walked in public he would be restrained *before* any provocation. He would be able to say, no matter what happened, *It's just the temper of these days. Forget it.*

He decided to see what held the interest of the crowd. It could be anything. A man with a monkey. A man playing a violin. A fight. A vendor of lewd photographs. Anything.

Even on its fringes, the crowd smelled sweaty.

It was an old, unwashed sweatiness, a stagnant smell, with underodors of rancidity and sickly sweet putrescences.

Where was the incentive to wash? And soap was short.

He pushed among the men, the dirty T-shirts, the smudged, bare arms, the soiled linen and occasional seedy jackets. They faced a row of department store show windows and in these Gaunt saw a number of mannequins. Female mannequins. His thought at the moment was concentrated wryly on the fact that his own jacket had a torn pocket, his trousers bore coffee stains, and he, too, beyond doubt, exuded the smell of a hot day even though he had bathed in the morning.

There was nothing new about the display of mannequins in store windows. If even remotely lifelike, they invariably drew an audience of desultory males. These, however, were not leftovers from pre-Disappearance days. They were new and different and it was no wonder the men ogled, stirred restlessly, talked in excited tones.

Along the top of the windows was a large sign:

THE NEW MISS AMERICA DOLLS—COME IN FOR A
DEMONSTRATION

Amongst the "dolls," on metal rests, were other signs.

The dolls were life size. They had realistic hair—perhaps some had real hair. They were molded and painted to resemble nature as accurately as possible. Some were nude and some were dressed. The nude ones revealed, at a glance, that no detail of female structure had been overlooked. Their substance, Gaunt saw, was some sort of foam plastic which, he did not doubt, had a texture as similar to that of flesh as technologists could make it. From the heels of these huge dolls, electric cords ran to outlets.

For a moment, Gaunt was puzzled. Then a clerk stepped into one of the show windows and snapped switches. Several of the dolls began to dance and gyrate like hula maidens. From a loudspeaker outside the window came a throaty, voluptuous voice that sounded female.

"I love you very much, darling," it said. "Don't be afraid of me. Put your arms around me . . . there! . . . that's better—!"

Gaunt read the placards:

"These Miss America Dolls are a complete, mechanical simulation of living womanhood. Any perfume selected by the purchaser may be atomizer permeated into the material of the dolls. A variety of love-languorous, talking-doll records are available to simulate speech. The dolls are electrically warmed with a thermostatic adjustment to maintain normal body temperature or even simulate an exciting fever. They are light, supple and pliable. Motorized dolls capable of reproducing a wide variety of dance (!) steps are now on sale. The dolls come in three sizes, large, medium and small. Hair coloring and other details to suit the purchaser's choice. Prices range from three hundred dollars up."

Another said:

"Why be alone? A Miss America Doll is the next best thing to a real sweetheart! Take one home with you now! She will end the sleeplessness of your nights. She will divert, entertain and satisfy you, keeping alive your memory through the Famine Period. She will talk to you as women talk—and she won't talk back!"

Another:

"Price too high? Form a syndicate with your friends. A Miss America Doll is "wife enough" for a dozen! *Think of it!*"

Gaunt thought of it.

With many emotions—revulsion, disgust, enraged mirth, a sense that this was truly obscene. He thought of Connauth and thought that perhaps Connauth's planned crusade should have been carried out, after all. "Motorized rubber women!" he said to himself.

And at the same time, because he was an honest man, he realized these undulating, lush-talking dummies had a fascination too, in all they so completely brought back to the memory. He wondered what Paula would have said about such articles, such a display. Probably that the dolls would make better wives than a lot of women. Paula would say that, not exactly meaning it, but implying the inadequacies of so many of her sex.

His accurate perception of the wry manner in which his wife would probably respond gave rise to further thoughts which were soon substantiated by the emergence from the store of a man carrying one of the dolls. The crowd made jubilant way for him, sniggering, cheering—half sardonically but half as primitives might have cheered that other brave person who ate the first oyster and proved it was good food.

The pioneer purchaser was short and thick at the waist. He had big, bland eyes and a motile, mucilaginous mouth which he kept licking as he lugged his burden, a doll taller than himself in a yellow semitransparent evening dress, beneath which black underwear could be seen. He squeezed his doll significantly. The crowd laughed. He put a nubile doll arm around his neck. The laughter increased. He made certain further explicit gestures and winked and went on to a parked car where he tenderly seated the "woman" in the place next to the one he would occupy. He walked around the car, stepped into it, patted the doll, and drove away.

What Gaunt considered then was related to Paula's imagined comment: not that the dolls were "better" wives than some once-living counterparts but that, to many men, a wife was *little more* than such an object as these dolls.

Men of that sort were allured by the externals. Their response to the opposite sex was limited to physical sensations. They chose a mate according to criteria of eye and ear and nose and touch. They married not a personality—a mind, a cultural entity, a bundle of genes, ideas or a soul—but a blue-eyed blonde with a good figure and a low voice who used a perfume called Détroyez-moi. They took her home and dressed her up as seductively as purse and taboo allowed. Their "love" was confined to using her as an erotic toy. Quite often, the better she complied the more likely the spouses were to extend the range of their erotic toying. Often, too, such a wife's not unnatural opinion that she was more than mechanical lust-putty led her to resentment. Again, and most often of all, when the girlish rectitude of her upbringing prevented a woman from joining even in the rudiments of a good bedfellowship, both she and her miserable husband became embodiments of a general resentment—against each other, life, and the wide world. In this last, both spouses were self-cheated even of such stimuli as dolls furnished, dolls with perfused scent, recorded love-patter, and motorized pelvises.

Indeed, Gaunt went on thinking, as he walked back toward the parking yard, to get a live woman who could, among other attainments, approximate the values and advantages of the dolls was more than most Americans could hope for.

And even when they were successful, another element soon supravened: excepting for the physical differences of size and color and smell (and, possibly, motorization), the dolls and the doll-like women were interchangeable; they could not be told apart; hence they were monotonous as individuals and monotonous as a group. A man seeking to escape he knew not what insatiety (since he would hardly recognize his own limitations as the cause of his tedium) could clasp a hundred such ert bodies without surcease—and would likely try to do so.

Meantime, his chosen mate would age, age while neither he nor she matured. The lowly ideal, what Huxley had called the "pneumatic" ideal, would go on dancing before his mind's eye while childbearing, child rearing, domestic duties and perhaps a job (along with the years) would gradually destroy in his mate every vestige of the reason he had once discovered for marrying her. So he would turn to prostitutes, younger women, or consort with high-school girls as Gaunt had seen so many middle-aged men do. He would get a doll a generation behind himself. He would pervert an instinct to be the suitable father-image for his daughters, into a quasi-incestuous relationship with their contemporaries.

It was not surprising, therefore, that the young American woman called her old beau "daddy," or that he called her "baby," or that a universal American term for woman was "doll."

The national psyche was that infantile, exactly.

Gaunt stopped at the drugstore, picked up the kit he had been sold, went to the paved lot for his car, and drove through the hot afternoon toward home.

The source of American sex confusion, he thought, had lain in the near-total concentration of the American mind on objectivity. Excepting where psychology examined the subjective aspect of life and sex (and excepting for the precepts of religions—unreviewed and grown stale in millenniums of lopsided "progress"), there was no good counsel, no awareness anywhere, of inward human experience. Even the most modern literature on marriage concerned itself with just such qualities as had been built into the dolls. And the nation was (or had been before the Disappearance) a litter of psychological wreckage caused by the headlong efforts of almost everybody to retain the doll-aspect in matrimony without regard to the subjective wear and tear of such behavior.

Marriage was, consequently, a secret fear and an anathema. Its American premises and requisites usually doomed it to eclipse, since time doomed all Cinderellas to become old women and all old women, by American standards, were witches.

None was wise or wondrous, learned or loving; for the "wisdom" of the current American era insisted love and learning and wonder were exclusively *young*. Grandma delighted no one unless she was still a flapper. She did not even live at home any longer. The grandchildren had to grow up without the association of age. The young married people, horrified by the isolation of the old, which they had themselves arranged, sought pensions and old-age security against the sure time when, dolls no longer, they too would be cast aside. The very idea that Grandma might be ardent, or amorous, was regarded as disgusting. And nobody thought any more, in America, that love and wisdom might be related or that it might take time to perfect both. Starvation of the spirit and a loss of life's meaning were the penalty for the pneumatic ideal. It was no wonder women spent billions in beauty parlors to prolong the apparent nubility of the flesh; old age was more feared than death itself. And rightly, as things had been.

If further evidence were needed, Gaunt thought, one had only to consider the general term for the figurines: Miss America Dolls. *Miss.* He felt sure that, were the dolls renamed Mrs., sales graphs would soon decline. The American male did not truly want a Mrs. for his companion, but a Miss. Mrs. implied responsibility, authority, claims, duties—and *age.* But Miss was perpetually *young.* Miss had the look, sound, feel and odor of youth, the be-all and end-all of American libido. A smart widow, Gaunt thought, would have been well advised to change her name back hurriedly to Miss. It was a Miss the male yearned to possess even on the connubial couch; so, in the mere act of marrying, he had—in millions of cases—devaluated his bride in his own estimation.

What woman, he asked himself—what woman in all the earth— required to perform the principal function for which she is designed in body and spirit, could gracefully or happily take up the endeavor when, consciously or not, she was aware the very acceptance of marriage had classified her downward in the minds of her own spouse as well as of millions of other men?

The cruelty of the predicament burned in the philosopher's mind brighter and fiercer even than the clear recognition of its cause. To be mere materialists concerning women was to be traitors to the brain—and the soul of whoever believed he had one. It was to be the opposite of all that humanity had recognized as human, a mere beast sniffing about another beast, eying, dancing ritualistically, paw-ing the fur. It was to omit from the relationship of the sexes every-thing but brute mating, the purpose of which the brute knew not and the man (or woman) permanently avoided, often enough. No doubt frogs and worms had the same sensations of allure; hence for men to have none other was infamous. It was also the American Ideal. Its cost was the ruin of the brain, which would not accept sex in its infinite provinces. For there was no *human sexuality*; it had been denied, evaded, tabooed, overthrown.

And perhaps, he thought heavily as he followed the curves of his driveway, *that is why they left us.* They could not be other than human but we refused to accord their humanity. So they ceased to exist.

The back door of his house hung open.

He was perplexed; he had left it locked. A long edge of splintered frame set his heart beating faster.

He hurried through the jimmied door.

The place had been ransacked.

Drawers had been pulled out and dumped on the floor, rugs lifted and tossed aside. His butter and the last cans of corned beef were gone. The refrigerator door and the deep-freeze lid had been left open. Mattresses had been slid from the beds.

As he hurried from room to room he could see that money and food had been the objects of the raid. But the looters had, evidently, found too little of either to satisfy their expectations. Or perhaps no amount of booty would have done so. For, when Gaunt came to his study, he saw his books and journals, his papers and the long manuscript upon which he had been working piled in a mound; over this, the contents of a dozen pails of variously colored paint had been wantonly poured so that there seemed at first to be no way to extricate and reclaim the fruits of his months of effort.

He stood in the doorway, stunned and sickened. His bony hand, extended to support his tall frame, rattled against the wall. He went, after a while, to the edge of the mess and picked up here and there a paint-blotched sheet of paper. He could not read what was there.

He rubbed at the enamel, which was the Tyrian purple Paula had used in certain places in the living room. The words came clear. His lips quivered, set. If he could get assistance before the paint dried, perhaps the pages could be sufficiently cleaned so that they could be copied. If Jim Elliot and Gordon would come over—Teddy Barker—

Teddy?

Teddy Barker, his mind went on, and other neighbors . . .

He rushed out to seek them.

It was after one in the morning when the Elliots prepared to go home. The job was done; the bulk of Gaunt's work had been salvaged, and was spread now on the floors of the bedrooms and the living room, each page wiped by hand and weighted with nails or bolts.

"I'll brew coffee," the philosopher said with some cheer, "and we can have crackers and sardines. They didn't find *every* cache I've got, damn them!"

The lawyer and the boy were tired.

But Teddy, after his hours of sticky work, assented. "Coffee? Boy! I could use some! Anything to eat! I'm hungry."

So Gaunt brought food he had hidden in the tool shed and he made coffee. He and Barker carried it to the porch, which was heavy with the sting of fresh paint and the perfume of night-blooming jasmine. They sat together without saying anything for some minutes. Enough light came from the lamps indoors to silhouette Barker's profile and broad shoulders above the back of his chair.

Gaunt looked at him, thinking of Paula's letters, of his own hesitation to ask any favor of Teddy, even in this wretched emergency. The younger man seemed at ease and that very composure irritated his host. At the same time, Gaunt found himself provoked at his irritation. He was trying, he realized, to see Teddy with Paula's eyes; but that was extremely difficult, perhaps impossible.

"What you been doing?" Gaunt finally asked.

"Mighty little. For a while, during the spring, I got in a lot of fishing. Rounded up a couple of pals. We tore down to the Keys together like schoolkids playing hooky." Teddy chuckled. "*Married* pals," he added.

Gaunt remembered that Teddy Barker, on the night of the catastrophe, had said he would do just that. But he was surprised to find Teddy had meant what he had said. A fishing trip, under such circumstances, seemed asinine.

"I was down there," Teddy went on, "when the hydrogen bombs fell. War was all over when we came back to Miami and we didn't know there'd been a war! Funny."

"It must have been a shock."

"Shock? Hell! Nothing the commies could do would shock me! But it's peculiar to have to remember there isn't any San Francisco any more. Or any Chicago. I keep sending bank mail there, out of habit. I *was* shocked, I must say, when I found out the old Stock Exchange was going to be nailed up, sine die. But the banks needed extra personnel, so I just rustled up a job helping launch the New Economic System."

Gaunt found himself wanting to eradicate the hostile feelings he had concerning the younger man. But how to go about it? "Darn nice of you," he said presently, "to come over and help with this dirty job."

"Glad to do it!" Teddy spoke heartily. "Not much *to* do nights. I bowl Wednesdays and Fridays. I generally sit around at the club Saturdays, watching guys drink themselves out cold. Taking 'em home, pretty often. Somebody has to. Tuesdays I work at the bank late. Thursdays I go to the fights. But that still leaves me with a lot of spare time."

"A man like you must *especially*—miss them." Gaunt said it tentatively, almost hoping his guest wouldn't pick up the thread.

"Who doesn't?"

Gaunt was silent.

Teddy went on: "I can see now, of course, that I was making a big mistake. There's plenty of men—men like you—who can look back, at least, on a long, damned happy life with one dame. What do I look back at? At a lot of horsing around. At nobody who ever gave a damn for me personally. To the girls, I was something they wanted, for a minute or two—not *somebody*. And look at Jim Elliot, now. He's got Gordon. What have I got? Empty rooms. If I'd had a couple of sons, I could be teaching them to fish and shoot and row and paddle and sail and hit a golf ball and a tennis ball and how to block a fast left and a million more things."

Gaunt smiled.

"You realize how it is, Bill. You're alone too. Where *is* Edwin, incidentally?"

"I don't know," Gaunt answered sadly. "I never heard from him. I tried to trace him but the closest I got was that his expedition piled up somehow."

"Tough."

"Tough." Gaunt sipped coffee, leaned back and nervously recrossed his stretched legs. Stooping all evening had made him stiff. He tried another approach to the barrier between them. "Maybe you're hard on yourself, Teddy. Maybe you meant a good deal to a good many women."

The silhouetted head shook and the athletic chest collapsed in a sigh. "Sure! I meant a lot as a *sample* of something! But nothing as *me*! Maybe you don't understand."

"Maybe not. Sample of what?"

Teddy thought that over. "Let me ask you a question. You told me, once, you hadn't stuck to the strait and narrow. Well. Were the other women, so called, young and good looking? Or were they—?"

Gaunt grinned. "Check!"

"We do it to the women. You do. Can you be annoyed at them for getting a yen to imitate us?"

"Logically, no. On the other hand, if you were an average married man with the normal belief in your wife's fidelity, and found your belief was mistaken, you would also find, Teddy, that the knowledge was vexatious."

"Shouldn't be."

"No?" There was rancor in the syllable.

"I said 'shouldn't,' old-timer! Husbands don't seem to appreciate the little woman is just as much a person as they are. She has feelings. Ideas. Gets curious. Wants to know. Has a streak of adventure in her. Romance." Teddy pondered. "Don't you learned boys write about it all the time? I mean, the standard's cultural. Isn't that the word? You get 'vexed' purely because of how you were brought up. Other people don't, brought up other ways. Anthropology, isn't that?"

"I dare say. But how would you go about changing the pattern?"

"I've thought that over, too. I wouldn't change it, so darn much, I guess. Just take the 'private property—do not touch' label off homo sapiens."

"Wouldn't that put the final touches on what used to be the shaky institution known as the American home?"

"Did Repeal make more drunks? Or was it Prohibition that turned us into a nation of guzzlers?"

"It's a point."

Teddy yawned. "Yeah. People ought to be allowed to get all the puppy stuff and the deprived feeling out of their systems while they are growing up, not after age thirty, or forty, or fifty."

"Would you say," Gaunt asked, "that a woman like Paula, for instance, suffered from 'deprivation'?"

Teddy answered with the utmost aplomb, with friendliness and warmth. "So you know about that? I was beginning to wonder. What ho? Find the letters I wrote?"

Gaunt answered, "Yes."

"Darned foolish of her to get me to write 'em! You know, I felt like an ass. Never did write letters to dames before."

"Your letters—" Gaunt began coldly.

"Look here, doc." Teddy used the word "doc" derisively. "I like you. I like you one hell of a lot. I respect you and that's something I do to few. I'm actually proud of being your neighbor and being allowed to come over and sit on your veranda and chew the fat. That's how I feel. Now. Do you want me to kid you or do you want to stop talking about this, or what?"

Gaunt suddenly found in himself an urge to laugh. "Good Lord," he said, "that's some rebuke—to a self-styled philosopher."

"You asked for it! I begin to feel that I misjudged you and that I'm not really welcome."

"Maybe," the older man said after a pause, "I'm just trying to understand things I don't understand."

Teddy pondered again; it was hard work. "God Almighty, what a problem it must be to have brains! Here's how it went. And if you want to toss me into the night, go ahead." He took a long breath. "One afternoon, downtown in Miami, quite a lot of years ago, I was coasting along Second Avenue in my convertible. It was pouring as hard as it did this morning and I spotted Paula in a striped dress trying to keep out of the splash from a folded-up awning that was the best shelter she could find."

Gaunt nodded.

"So, okay. I stopped and she hopped in. Wet as a hen. My place was close and yours was over on the Beach then. And you were in Boston at a scientific meeting. You'd been gone three weeks, so she said when, in the normal course of being the old chivalrous Barker, I took her into my apartment, got her a highball, and lit the gas logs to dry her out. Because it wasn't warm like today. It was a lousy, cold winter afternoon or I'd probably not have made the emergency stop. She was chilled through."

"I see."

"You sound like you see absolutely nothing! I had no more design on your wife than I ever had on Berthene Connauth, though Paula is about as handsome as they come. Nor she, on me. I gave her a dressing gown and I hung her things in front of the fire and I got her a drink and she began kidding me about my reputation. She said if anybody had seen her come in with me her name would be mud. And she teased me about what it was I had that made all the girls so tiddly about me. It was all just kidding."

"It sounds," Gaunt said, "like the classical gambit. Rain. The fire. The highball."

"Go ahead and take that line," Teddy answered, with heat. "I'm telling you, for my own good. So all right. It got dark and we had several highballs and neither one of us was talking from the sober book, quite."

"Try," Gaunt said, tensely still, "to imagine a wife of your own, on a rainy afternoon—"

"Damn it, what *else* have I been thinking about since they went? I think, if I'd married and if I *really* cared about the dame, I'd give her twenty-four hours a month off, and no questions asked, and she could even save up the days and take two weeks at the end of the year if she liked it better that way. What in hell *is* a woman but a part of the whole person?"

"I don't understand that."

"Maybe you will someday," Teddy replied. He went on, grinning stubbornly: "So, we continued—whether you faint, bawl or start throwing furniture, Bill. She asked me."

"And you were amazed."

"I was about as surprised as you are happy right now. I said no."

"But she persisted?"

"She was *there*—and she probably thought she'd never be in such a situation or such a mood again. She cried. So I knew exactly how desperate she felt—and for a woman like Paula it was plenty desperate. I made love to her." Teddy shook his head meditatively. "It's funny. Whole books, thousands of movies, all based on the build-up to about the simplest thing people can do."

Gaunt shook his head slowly again and again. He wadded up an empty cigarette package. He went into the living room to find another. He came back and paced his porch a time or two, trailing smoke. "Pathetic," he finally murmured.

"I thought so."

"Not revenge. Not rebellion. Not even lust, in a way."

"You might say," Teddy nodded, "that some damned fine women seem to feel as if they had to have a 'past' to be complete. Part of living. So—they make a past for themselves—"

Gaunt paced. "I'm glad you told me, Teddy."

For the first time, the younger man relaxed. "I was staking a lot—a lot, to me—on hoping you would be, in the end."

Gaunt looked at the younger man. "I know."

"I better skip soon. It's getting right seriously late. I'll tell you something else, Bill. You're not the first husband—since they went—to talk things over with me. And not the first one to realize that, no matter how much a dame loves her man, she, also, loves feeling of freedom even more."

"You seem to know several things," Gaunt answered, "that I'm just beginning to catch onto. A little late!"

Teddy rose; it occurred to Gaunt that he had sat there, quiet, with his back turned, when Gaunt had left the room. If an aggrieved husband had wanted to drive, say a poker, through his skull—well, Teddy had taken that risk with tranquillity. It was another facet of the younger man's code; he had exhibited a sense of values Gaunt would not before have attributed to him. Now, as the philosopher held out his hand, he did not think: this man stole the affections of my wife, or, this man has shared my wife, or, here is a man by whom I have been made cuckold. He thought: This is our friend.

He walked halfway home with Teddy.

It was just before dawn that Gaunt had the first dream.

The dream began with the sensation of flying through a dense, enveloping radiance and was accompanied by a feeling of nearness to Paula.

The mist broke. Gaunt found himself disembodied and seeing through eyes that looked down from a sky. Below was familiar landscape: the flat Everglades and their green pox of puddles, the islands

in Biscayne Bay, Miami and Miami Beach, their suburbs and the in
digo sea. Over this he circled.

He noticed differences in the scene. Where "colored town"
sprawled was ruin; large buildings and residences nearby had been
burned; weeds and vines grew amidst the charred shambles. There
were notches in the Miami Beach skyline, also, as if occasional hotels
and apartment houses had collapsed. Elsewhere, only the windowless
walls of certain familiar structures remained standing. The devastation was widespread although he soon saw that the university, the
Riviera section, and the area around his own home appeared untouched. Very little traffic moved on the streets of this strange-looking
Miami—much less than the actual volume even of these days.

He approached the airport, still as if in a plane, and landed.
People descended from the dreamed ship. People waited at the barrier
for the arrivals. People hurried out to service the airplane. *And
they were all women.*

One was Paula, Paula carrying a heavy suitcase, Paula wearing
her beige traveling suit and a beige hat that sat prettily on her lus-
trous hair. But Paula with a strange, haunted expression, though
she smiled and waved.

Now, a crowd gathered around her. Flashlights exploded in silent brilliance. Women, there were only women, asked questions.

Gaunt realized they were reporters.

"What were they like?"

Paula seemed to be amused. "All kinds."

"Can we trust them?"

"What's left to do, but trust one another?" Paula seemed un-
satisfied with that, and corrected herself. "I'm sure we can."

"Is it true that they had no atomic bombs?"

The smile, still; but, still, the haunted look. And Gaunt could
not imagine who "they" were. "It's true. In fact, they didn't know
how to fire the naval guns or launch the torpedoes they brought. Just
how to run the ships."

"When do you think, Mrs. Gaunt, the new government will be formed?"

"This summer. Probably this next month. A conference will be held—thousands have been invited—

A younger woman asked, while she kept scribbling, "Is it a fact that the Russian women think they can lick the problem of nonfertility?"

"They have a lot of hope."

"Have you? Have we?"

"It's not my line," Paula answered quietly.

Now the interview faded and Gaunt seemed to be riding on the streets of Coral Gables and down Sunset Boulevard and drawing into his own drive. Edwinna and Alicia, Hester and a dark-haired child he did not recognize rushed out to welcome Paula.

"God!" said Edwinna. "It's good to have you back! You going to· stay?"

"I am, yes."

"I was afraid they'd hook you for something."

Paula's head shook. "I did my part. And I feel as if I ought to stay here."

It was a reunion that brought a lump in the throat of Gaunt's dreaming sensibilities.

He followed them indoors. The house seemed just as it had been before he was left alone in it. Paula dropped down on the chartreuse divan. "What's new?" She set Alicia in her lap.

"Plenty!" Edwinna smiled in a way Gaunt did not recognize, a way that showed courage and compassion. "The worst news is, just about all that food we swiped, and paid for, and stashed away—I divvied up for an orphanage. The poor girls were starving!"

"If that's the worst news," Paula smiled, "the news is good."

"Not bad," their daughter agreed. "But tell us about your trip! *Everything*! How was New York? Was the first cabinet as asinine as it sounded? Are they really going to get an effective government started?"

There was a sound of a car stopping. Of footsteps. Now, in his dream, Gaunt had a sense of the scene withdrawing, of a shadow eclipsing it, and an inner sensation of loss, or frustration, or disappointment, or even danger. The last of what he saw furnished no explanation for his anxiousness. Kate West, her black braids shining, bundles in her arms, came through the kitchen door and looked delightedly at Paula. "You're back. Oh, how *wonderful!*"

The dream ended.

Gaunt woke, shaken. His unkempt sheets were dank with the perspiration of a hot night's sleep. The room was different from the way he somehow knew it would have been, in his dream; how, he could not tell. He had the formidable sensation that the world upon which he opened his eyes was no more real than the dream. *Maybe,* he thought, *the same thing has happened to them.*

But the idea seemed senseless to his conscious mind. There was no way to explain it in the space-time framework of reason. Objects, whole cities, could not coexist in two different forms. He brushed the fantasy aside and rose and washed his face in tepid water. It was a wishful dream, a dream born out of the undying hope that the women were not "gone" altogether and forever.

Still, as he prepared to get a breakfast for himself he could not quite throw off the forceful realism of his dream and with that the even stranger sense of its conclusion on a note of alarm, a note for which there seemed no reason, taking the thing at its face value. Kate West had joyously entered the scene—and it had been as if bells of warning sounded.

Even by noon, even in the hard sunlight, he could not entirely banish the memory of his vision, at once so hopeful and so inexplicably ominous.

That night he told Jim Elliot about it. The lawyer listened

with the odd glitter of eye that was reflected by his most occult thoughts. But, in the end, Jim shook his head:

"I'd *like* to believe your dream was a mirror of truth. But doubtless what created the dream was your wishing. As to Kate, she's a sweet, innocent, forthright child. The very fact that her appearance was coupled with your anxious sensation proves, to my mind, you invented the dream. That it *was* a dream—and not second sight. Your guilty conscience, maybe." Jim smiled. "You never—lusted for our handsome young neighbor, did you, Bill?"

And Gaunt said, "How can I answer that? I have only begun to know that I *do not know!*"

"Ah!"

Night sheltered them together in the world-wide loneliness.

12

A WORLD OF WOMEN—O TEMPORA! O MORES!

The approach of Christmas brought to Paula her first sensations of absolute despair.

Christmas had been the children's season. But it had also been Bill's special day—and week and month. He had conspicuously connived over surprises, chuckling when he'd let big packages be seen by the youngsters and then archly refusing to discuss them or claiming they were wheelbarrows, dictographs or other bulky items of no interest to youth inflamed by Santa Claus.

He'd been an inspired stocking filler. Pillow stuffed and cotton bearded, overplaying the role, he had made a stupefying Santa Claus. Every year, with stepladder, hammer, wires and nails, he'd decorate not just a room but the whole house. That custom had started in their first little flat near the campus and continued through all the houses of their happy marriage—the big house across from the University Chapel, the house in Princeton, the apartment in Paris (on their first sabbatical), the Lake George summer house (when they'd winterproofed it and spent several skating, skiing Christmases there with the twins), and the Miami Beach house (where Bill had hung colored balls and lights and tinsel on palms in the yard). Of course, the previous Yuletide in the new house had been the most exuberant of all.

So it was impossible for Paula to think about Christmas without thinking of hammers pounding and Band-Aids on Bill's fingers, of miracles of glitter, red ribbon and green festoons, of delivery vans driving up with "Do Not Open Until" packages, of hubbub, excitement, gaiety and such smells as mince pies and plum puddings add to an atmosphere already aromatic with the breath of a big spruce tree.

If she had told the truth to herself Paula would have admitted that at times and in certain ways the absence of Bill had compensations. Appalled by the whole, she had taken certain pleasures in parts of the bereaved present. She enjoyed *management* free of criticism and safe from arbitrary change, change without adequate reason (from her viewpoint) and without notice. She appreciated being given, even by universal tragedy, her own way in every personal matter. She had put to good use the good brain she owned; she was, in every possible respect, her family's head, as a result. Besides, in a moment of national crisis, she had been valuable. Such conditions and facts were satisfying to a hitherto frustrated element of her nature.

But the approach of Christmas brought her face to face not just with physical limitations but with a lack of certain *emotions* which Bill had buoyantly provided. She had saved from their strictly rationed food the makings of a comparative banquet. At night, when the children were in bed, she and Edwinna and Kate had refurbished and painted old toys and dolls exchanged with other women to furnish Christmas with surprise, at least; newness was out of the question. And she had helped Edwinna with the decoration of the house.

There were gifts for Alicia and Martha and also for four other little girls who had recently been assigned to the Gaunt house, in lieu of two adults. These solemn, sometimes fretful school-age youngsters were subject to fits of weeping, to colds and chickenpox, to measles and "nerves." They were the Gaunt family's white "quota"— girls who, with their books and their sandwiches, each morning walked the quarter mile to school.

There were gifts, also, for the six Negro families who lived in tents pitched in a cleared area on the Gaunt acres between Paula's house and the cottage that had been Teddy Barker's. Their voices, so often raised in laughter, and their music nowadays came constantly to the big, modernistic house just as the chlorinated reek of their outdoor latrine came also, on every southwest wind. Paula had organized, arranged, managed that. Her "quota kids" and her colored colony were as "happy" as any in the county.

Paula served on many committees now, and served ably, as was attested by the constant increase of electric lights in the area, the steady gain in trucks running, the restoration of water pressure and other such triumphs. The women were "organization minded." Once they overcame the initial months of shock—once they realized that, of the many hundred trades, businesses, professions, techniques and jobs in America, at least a few of their sex were skilled in all but six or seven—they set out to teach and to learn so as to restore what they could of "civilization."

In the direction of all such activity Paula had been a local Trojan. Still Christmas stumped her.

Standing in Sam's Market with a wire cart one day, at the end of a line, waiting for five pounds of potatoes, Paula was suddenly overcome by such a feeling of fatigue and misery that her eyes filled.

She turned away from the chilly gray light outdoors toward the dismal interior of the storeroom, so no one would see.

Such tears were not unusual. Women, anywhere, anytime, would thus burst into silent weeping. And no one would appear to notice, usually. At most, a firm hand would squeeze a weary arm. That was what happened to Paula, surprising her because she hadn't realized anyone had come up behind her. She turned, forcing a smile.

The bulk and the bovine countenance of Berthene Connauth blocked out a wan section of the half-denuded store. There was no one, Paula thought, whom she would less like to see at that instant.

"I know how it is!" the clergyman's wife whispered hoarsely.

Paula jerked her head in assent and turned again, hoping to engage the woman in front of her in talk, so as to escape Berthene. But that woman was busily discussing Christmas plans with others in front of her.

"Buck up!" said Berthene.

Paula thought acidly, Now she'll quote Psalms!

The clot of yellowish-white hair leaned closer, the wrinkled features, sagging putty nose, lamblike, glasses-enlarged brown eyes, mustache and bristled moles. She was as ugly as a sea elephant. "I had a dreadful sinking spell, myself, this very morning, my dear!"

Paula nodded and shrugged.

The woman's heavy sigh was scented with violet "breath pills" which had been consumed to sweeten exhalation in Paula's mother's day. "You look so *pretty*, my dear!"

Damn it, Paula thought, *the worst thing in an ass is sincerity!* She *is* sincere. "Thanks. I feel stinking."

"One's troubles bow one down. I know. But you should be proud of yourself, my dear. *Proud!* I don't know *what* our community would have done without you! And you've been of such *immense* assistance to the whole *country!* I tell you, just *knowing* there are women like you positively makes my skin prickle with pride!"

Paula's own flesh crawled a little at this obvious attempt of the self-righteous old futz to cheer her up. "Thanks."

"I'd misjudged you, my dear. *Misjudged* you!" The sweet violet sigh came again. "I'd thought of you as such a frivolous person. Such an atheist."

"By your standards, I suppose I am," Paula said coldly.

"*My* standards? They're *changing*! Yes, changing! Very often, as I read the Good Book these evenings, whole passages seem to have a different meaning from the one I'd accepted. Often, indeed, the very opposite meaning! And I find myself inclined, amongst the paradoxes, to accept the side I had formerly rejected!"

The queue was moving as tiresomely, Paula thought, as queues would move in Purgatory. "A lot of us have undergone changes." Paula felt it was wrong to be mean to the old frump because she felt low.

The bland, appallingly large eyes now had a twinkle. "You know, Paula, if things ever went back to their former state—I'd *never* be the same! *Never*! I've missed all the fun in life because I was so set against it in my youth. I honestly no longer ever deplore my husband's—sins."

"I wasn't aware he had committed any," Paula answered, more politely. It was better to hear about sin than to continue in the sin of self-pity.

"Few were. He drank a drop now and then, of course. Our denomination is broad-minded in that matter. Though not *my* parents! You know, Paula"—the harsh voice dropped to a sotto voce rumble—"for a month, now, beginning at Thanksgiving, *I've* had a glass of port every single night! The Thanksgiving sup was my first. And, I must say, I've greatly enjoyed it. I actually quivered with horror when I decided to see what the evil was! And now I'm quite the toper!"

Paula could not repress a grin: the old crocodile had a *jolly* streak in her! A shame it had emerged at this too-late date.

"And I've utterly forgiven John even his great *youthful* sin."

"The *youthful* one?"

"You'll never tell a *soul*, Paula?"

"Not a soul!"

Mrs. Connauth either believed her or had reached that state of grace and insouciance in which she secretly hoped the tale would get about, in a discreet way. Such was Paula's thought. The news that came with it flabbergasted her:

"For seven years, wholly unaware that I knew of it, John had the most *lurid* sex affair with a blonde woman in the choir!"

"No!"

Berthene was nodding calmly. Paula had never said a rhetorical "no" with more emphasis. For a moment she thought that deprivation had cracked the old woman's mind. But nothing about Berthene supported that idea. She was placid; her eyes were even a little more human than usual; and her big frame was firmly planted on her large, flat feet.

"It's *quite* true! Someday I'd like to tell you all about it, how I discovered it, my sensations, how it embittered me! Now, with John gone, I have come to realize it was no one's fault and, from the standpoint of evil, a *lesser* thing than I had imagined! The Seventh Commandment, my dear, is softened by the admonition to the by-standers. You remember?"

Paula was still astonished. "About the man who is innocent throwing the first stone?"

"You show an *admirable* knowledge of the Scriptures, my dear! Of *course!* The Saviour knew! To Him, it was *not* a grave sin. A *human* thing. To be *forgiven!* But I did *not* forgive for thirty-three wasted years! *Think* of that! Think of being guilty of such an excess of *wickedness*, disguised as virtue!"

"Berthene," Paula said impulsively, "if I were a man, right now, I'd take off my hat to you!"

"Bless you!" The old woman patted Paula's back in a motherly way and kept smiling. "You see, my dear, we all have burdens."

The line moved on.

It was only when Paula was driving home, and only after a wild hoot of laughter at the remarkable confidence, that she went over the sequence of the conversation and realized that Mrs. Connauth had had a reason, a subtle and generous reason, for making the confession. She had done it all deliberately—playing the role of her old self at first. She had told Paula the scandalous news just to shake Paula from her depression. It was, so to speak, Berthene's humble and humbling contribution to morale.

New tears came into Paula's eyes but they were not tears of defeat. If that old horse of God can change so much, Paula thought, then women are *really* wonderful. *All* women!

The atmosphere at home seemed different after that. Edwinna, on a stepladder, was singing carols to a bunch of the kids while she tacked more branches from the Caribbean pines on the beams overhead. The children joined the choruses in their woodwind voices.

Upstairs, Paula found Kate West mending doll clothes and humming with the singers below, while her new-washed black hair dried on her bare back.

Paula hugged her affectionately, fingered the long locks, and said, "I'll comb it for you, child."

"It is kind of hard to do yourself. Paula, you look all bright!"

"It's Christmas," Paula answered as she hung up her coat. "The old Yule spirit has just got to me!"

Kate's pretty face lighted up. "Then I guess *everybody* will feel Christmasy! I'm so glad!"

Paula stayed in the closet for a moment to overcome an inexplicable sense of joyousness, of strength restored and command regained, which seemed, somehow, out of proportion to reality. Then, almost as if to punish both of them for unwarranted happiness, she took a heavy comb and attacked the young girl's black hair with hurtful energy. But Kate didn't appear to mind; she kept on smiling and singing the carols, softly.

When Christmas was over, the household settled down to what Edwinna called "grimy-scrimy grin-and-bear-it." The winter was an unusually cold one, with an excessive amount of rain. Three of the quota children were in bed at once with measles. In downtown Miami, smallpox broke out. The entire population was vaccinated. Edwinna got the flu and a bronchial complication which kept her in bed with a fever for many days. These same infections, and others, appeared in the colored colony, where Hester's daughters and her female grandchildren camped out, with other families.

And, of course, there were no doctors to attend them.

As Edwinna said, one night when her temperature was high and her head was light, "According to the regulations, I've figured out that you couldn't call a doctor even if you broke both legs. 'Splints—and take her to the hospital,' for that. If you were giving birth to a child at the same time—which anybody would break both legs to do—you probably would *still* get no doctor, unless it turned out to be a breech presentation. If you also had double pneumonia —or thought you did—you would be 'entitled to a prescription for penicillin.' But no doctor. If, in addition to pneumonia childbirth and double fracture, you had an infected blister from hoeing with the Farm Crews in the potato fields—as I have been doing—you *could* get medical attention for the blister! 'It is vital that our land girls be kept in good physical condition'—so infected blisters probably *are* on the list of ailments entitling you at least to a nurse's squint!"

Paula agreed it was almost that difficult.

"Mother," said Edwinna, later that night, "did you ever know I detested you when I was a little girl? And thought you were ridiculous and hateful when I went to boarding school? And decided, in college, to ignore you as much as possible the rest of my life?"

Paula began mending stockings. "I knew you always felt—hostile—to me."

"Did you ever know *you* felt hostile to *me*?"

Paula flushed. "I don't believe I did, dear. Why don't you rest? You're pretty feverish."

Edwinna laughed, but not nastily. "It's like three Martinis. Makes you babble. You always *were* hostile—"

Paula found herself at once annoyed and trying hard to seem anything but annoyed. "You were an extremely difficult kid to raise, Edwinna. Perverse and stubborn and—destructive. Wanton."

"Did you ever think you might have been jealous of me?"

"Jealous?" Paula murmured. "Of course not! What a crazy idea!"

"You were, though. I can remember, even when I was little and Daddy used to play with me—take me horseback on his shoulders—you'd get a *look*. And I'd know you didn't approve. I'd—"

The older woman frowned. "You shouldn't carry into maturity a lot of feelings you had in your childhood, Edwinna. Bill *spoiled* you, right from the start!"

"Daddy was crazy about me," Edwinna answered. "And you knew it. He didn't 'give me up'—the way you did—until I was grown and married and he didn't like my second husband, or anything about me, any more."

"Bill never 'gave you up,'" Paula said quietly. "Nor I. We both—simply never figured you out—"

"Or else—yourself. I don't think"—her tone was detached, musing—"you were jealous of the *attention* I got. What I think you didn't like was the fact that, when I was very small, I'd do *anything* for Dad. And dispute *you*. I'm not trying to rankle you, Mum. Or pick a fight. Just to think out loud. You know, darling, you have got a grade A managerial complex. It always irritated you when I wasn't being managed to suit your ideas of child rearing. What I suspect you were jealous about was Bill's *authority*. Anything in that, do you think?"

"I hope not," Paula answered. "It would mean I was a pretty poor sort of parent."

"We all are," Edwinna replied. "Why don't we admit it? I got thinking about these things when I was watching Alicia try to make time with the older girls yesterday. There she was, four years old, and a greedy, stuckup little bitch, if I ever saw one. And my fault —and why is that? No father? Fatherless girls aren't all so touchy. Do you know what I realized?"

"What you ought to realize is that you should rest." Paula walked from the divan, which was made up as a bed, to the fireplace. She put on a log. The living room was the warmest room in the house, so Edwinna had been moved there.

Now she ignored the admonition to rest. "What I realized was that all parents are frustrated all their lives in umpteen ways. They never really know what they are, or think, or feel, or should become. They just know the *system* is cockeyed in relation to their inner urges. And so they try to raise kids in such a way that the kids will adapt better than they did to a system they really have no faith in or respect for."

"Isn't that a shade cynical, Edwinna?"

"In view of what's happened to *us*, how can *anybody* say that a dim attitude toward our past is cynical? We've got a tigerish yen for power. All of us. Maybe women *especially*, because they've been so limited for so long. Anything that clips our little prerogatives is un-bearable. Dad could command me, and you couldn't, when I was a nipper. You *hated* that. I hated *you* for hating that. So I married a gentle guy, thinking it would be fun to pull his wires. But it was *too* easy; and besides, whenever I pulled too hard, he got drunk. So then I married a so-called he-man and he didn't have any wires to pull. I tried pushing and when I pushed he just socked me. *That* was *very* no-good. Meantime, Alicia had got into the act. So I concentrated all my beat-up desire to run the show on her. In addition, I felt stuck with her. It's damned hard to be the bride of a jerk who thinks a woman is something to go whistling down cold hills in ski pants with, when you're due in twenty minutes to sterilize the next bottle and mix the formula. Never take a baby on a honeymoon. People should be drilled in that." Edwinna chuckled. "Well, Alicia's an emotional orphan—the way I was finally. *My* fault. *I was jealous of her.* I loathed her sometimes. I hated the cinch her two popsies had, making her coo and giggle. They got all the laughs and I got the diaper end. The whole psychology is loused up—was. And I've only begun to see the answers. We should have had *a lot more love."*

Paula didn't reply.

Soon a reply was unnecessary: Edwinna was sleeping and the firelight revealed that sweat had broken out on her forehead.

In the morning she was better.

During that winter and in the ensuing spring, the "crazes" commenced.

The world's women, inadequately housed, hungry, in many regions starving, working long hours at jobs to which only war veterans were accustomed, nevertheless found the energy and the leisure to begin to seek entertainmnt.

Where electric power was sufficiently restored, movies had huge audiences. Romantic films were revived. Rudolph Valentino became more of a household name in that era than he had been during his lifetime. Discussions of the "romantic approach," the "technique," the "appeal" and the putative erotic habits of male movie stars were soon conducted at a level of candor that would have horrified nine-tenths of the ladies who now most ardently took part in them. With the need for "modesty" absent they showed a frankness about their sex sensations and fantasies that Western men, under similar circumstances, probably would have been incapable of displaying.

"Bees" and "socials" for the purpose of companionship while useful work was accomplished became a fad. Women foregathered, as in the time of their great-grandmothers, to quilt, sew, mend, knit, make clothes, weave, cook, and perform other tasks which could be enjoined communally.

Just after New Year's, a song writer named Margaret McKee produced the first post-Disappearance hit. Called "Remember Them," it had a rhythm and a sentimentality that set America singing and sighing at the same time. With that song, dancing was revived. Some women had always danced together and enjoyed it. Now bands were organized, parties were given, and women of all sorts and ages began to learn dance steps.

Edwinna, Kate and Paula took avidly to the vogue. At night, although they were always tired, they set the phonograph going and, while the old records tortured them with nostalgia, they practiced tangos, rumbas and fox trots. They felt less tired for the fun; and eventually Paula, a natural "leader," grew so skillful that she and Kate gave exhibitions for other dance enthusiasts.

"Bar parties" became a rage at about the same time. Women who could prove they had contributed their stint to the common weal pooled their drink tickets and entertained in reopened cocktail lounges. Since the women were lawfully restricted to a maximum of three drinks each, these festivities provided a good deal of relaxation without occasioning much drunkenness. But a special fad developed in the bars and lounges, one supposedly originated by Midwesterners. In each cocktail room appeared a life-size wax or plaster figure of a man, the image of a real person, such as a movie star, or a mere idealization. These "men" sat as "hosts" in the drinking places, in cowboy costumes, dinner jackets or even swimming trunks. They were toasted by their loyal women "guests," each of whom felt a mirthful (or sorrowful, or sardonic) "attachment" for the "man" at "whose" bar she whiled away an occasional evening. The bars, not surprisingly, took their names from the images: *Gary Cooper's, Clark Gable's, Cowboy Dave's.*

Another craze was the wearing of a large medallion containing the photograph of a husband, a sweetheart, a lover. That fad embraced at first pictures only of real persons associated with the women who wore the medallions. But it changed to the wearing of pictures of handsomer, if unknown, gentlemen. Amongst girls of high-school age it became a fashion to adorn the pictures with the large, crimson stains of lipstick kisses.

"Pants parties" were still another fad. For such occasions, women drew lots and half appeared, on the night of the party, dressed as elegantly and accurately as possible in men's clothes. The temporary transvestites provoked mirth and relish by aping and caricaturing the behavior of the vanished males. They flirted clownishly, courted grotesquely and chased genuine girls, screaming, through the diverted onlookers. It was fun. And sometimes these impersonations were good enough to make hearts sick—or to make them skip beats.

"Crushes" became, expectably, a pattern of behavior that gained social acceptance. Women found it socially permissible to pair off, exchange infatuated looks, share secret laughter, accompany each other everywhere, hold hands and act generally like doting schoolgirls. A song called "She's My Crush" in turn became the most popular tune of that benighted spring.

In the first issue of the *Journal-Companion*, a joint publishing effort of the staffs of five women's magazines and a new triumph of "Recovery," three noted women psychiatrists collaborated on an article dealing with the subject of "crushes." One favored the practice as an "obviously necessary and currently harmless emotional outlet"; one seemed to believe it was a matter for individual discretion; and the third opposed it as "inherently homosexual and regressive."

The magazine, printed without advertising in an edition of a million copies, was read until every one had been shredded. It contained fifty pages of counsel on what to do, how to do it, where aid was needed for the national program, how to apply and what was required of drafted workers. Women, accustomed to guidance in such a form, found the appearance of the first issue of that magazine among the most reassuring events of the period.

The second issue was even more heartening. It featured a discussion of parthenogenesis—the development of a viable fetus from an artificially fertilized egg.

"There is reason to hope," the article began, "that the problem of artificial reproduction, like that of artificial insemination, may eventually be solved in the case of human beings, so that the species will not die out and women may again bear children. There is even some reason to believe that ways may be found to assure offspring of *both* sexes. Female frogs and even rabbits have for years been produced by artificial stimulation of ova. Though the human problem is more complex, the existing facts and experiments make its solution expectable.

"Russian biologists have apparently already made some remarkable advances in the field. The day may not be far off when, by surgical means, any normal, healthy woman *may* have a pregnancy 'planted' within her. The day may not be much farther off when such pregnancies will produce *boy* babies! So, however tragic and terrifying the situation of today's woman may be, it is not necessarily shadowed with that blackest prospect of all—the slow, certain extermination of humanity. A female world may be the human world for some while; but a world there will doubtless be!"

A national glow followed that summation of what had thitherto been no more than speculation, scattered fact and rumors in the newspapers and on the radio. Reflective women had long since observed that the greatest hazard of the period was spiritual: the absolute despair accompanying the idea that, without males, life had lost its purpose.

Indeed, thousands of women, arguing *What's the use of any-thing?* had turned even from good homes, from lofty precepts and restrained habits, to every sort of violence, viciousness and evil. But now the prospect held out hope. Self-sacrifice was necessary; perhaps one human generation would be "lost." Yet the generation beyond might witness the restoration of the two sexes, wherefore the re-creation of humanity and the return of life's purpose. The deepest instinct of mankind, of the host of other animals, the instinct to preserve its own species at whatever cost, was given fresh outlet and expression.

Millions of women were exalted by the thought that they might yet bear offspring, even sons, though denied husbands.

Some took a special view of the possibility, pointing out that not only would women perhaps be self-sufficient without men but that they might *create mankind without men,* thus reversing the story of Eve's fabrication from Adam's rib, along with all the inferior, even insane connotations of the legend. . . .

It was in such an atmosphere of sordid struggle for survival on the sordid continents, of moments of perfervid play and of endless hardship matched by elements of hope, that Paula's personal di-lemma had its beginning. The stage had been set long before; but the fact that she was in dilemma could not be made evident to Paula.

Edwinna once tried to warn her. . . .

It was the evening of a typical day. Martha and the four quota children had come home from school, hungry and restless. They had played hide-and-seek in the yard, trampling the untended flower beds.

·One of them, a nervous girl named Doris whose mother had been crushed under a collapsing hotel in Miami, stepped on a rake and badly lacerated her foot. Kate, in charge of the house that day, as usual, called on Bella Elliot for assistance. The two women held the screaming, wildly fighting child and managed to clean out the wound, disinfect it, and put on a bandage. Then Kate, using precious gasoline, drove Doris to Miami and spent an hour and a half in a line of mothers and children. After filling out three forms she had managed to have a tetanus shot given Doris.

When Kate returned she was both weary and shaken. Bella had gone home. Kate was obliged to hurry to get dinner ready for the six children and three adults who constituted that household, or "food group" as the ration blanks now called it.

Nothing unusual had happened to Edwinna. It was one of her days in the field. She had spent its ten work hours under a broad-brimmed hat, setting out tomato plants in flat shimmering acres near Homestead. She had thereafter come back to within a half mile of her house in a truck crammed with women, both black and white, who rode as inertly as zombies: they were not yet accustomed to such labor.

Edwinna walked the stretch to her home and did not even bother to ask Kate why she hadn't heated the water tub on the outdoor fireplace; she bathed tiredly in cold water and lay down afterward for a nap.

Paula was therefore the freshest of the three. Her day had been active but it was a kind of activity to which she was better adjusted. She had met with three committees. The first was the State Liaison Board which, through channels in Tallahassee, kept up with Washington's orders, plans, projects and procedures. The second was the County Health and Medical Committee, a layman-nurse-doctor organization designed to deal with the endless shortages, with catastrophic, chronic and trivial sicknesses, with epidemics, and with the appalling difficulties of sanitation, of proper food handling, of milk pasteurization and the like. This was an Augean task in a region with only half the necessary housing, few sewers, novice inspectors who were often unable to enforce the simplest edicts and, of course, one doctor where a hundred were desperately needed.

The third committee was the Crime Commission, a group in control of some eight hundred young women volunteer police. As these girls had been recruited to strength, instructed and drilled, the sound of plate glass breaking at night had grown rarer, robberies fewer, and women had commenced to feel fairly safe even at night and even, if they were bold and self-reliant, alone.

For lunch, during the incessant discussions, Paula had eaten two peanut butter sandwiches and drunk a glass of milk. So she was hungry, rather than exhausted, when she came home. She found the children racing noisily around the house, a huge pot of stew steaming on the stove, and Kate sitting in the living room with her eyes closed. Kate recited the events of the day and added that she had a headache. Paula then visited Doris, who had been put to bed and was reasonably comfortable. She opened the door of Edwinna's room and found her asleep.

"You're just tense," she said to Kate when she had finished making rounds. "That's why you have a headache, poor lamb! You often get the rough end of our assignments, staying home. Nobody knows better than I what it means! Come over here to me."

Obediently, Kate stretched out on the divan while Paula massaged her neck and shoulders.

To do so gave Paula deep satisfaction, a feeling of the direct outpouring of herself and a pride in her protective capacity. The act also gave her an experience of possession and control. Watching Kate relax made Paula happy through a sense of aggrandizement. After a moment of hesitation, she undid the back buttons of Kate's dress, loosened her brassière and took the pins from her long, black hair, letting it fall loose. Then she rubbed the scalp from which it grew so thickly.

The young woman accepted those attentions with an occasional, grateful murmur. At length, Paula was roused from a long bemusement by Edwinna's voice.

"Where's supper?" She called the question loudly as she approached. "I'm starved! And the kids must be, too!"

She came into the dimmed living room and saw Kate lying there. For a moment, her face showed with its old rancor. Her lips became hard and hateful. "If you're running a massage parlor, Mother, how about *me*? I've got a case of stiff muscles that would paralyze an acrobat! After all, Kate hasn't been farming the whole damned day!"

Paula said confusedly, "Why, of course, dear. Kate! Get the kids in and the table set. Edwinna, stretch out here and I'll do you."

Sitting up, buttoning herself, Kate gave Paula a low-lashed, long look. Then she smiled, rose and went to work.

Edwinna lay in her place, grunting. After a while she said, without further resentment, "Mom, you're getting a crush on our good-looking guest."

"Ridiculous!"

"Ouch! Take it easy! Nothing ridiculous about it, excepting maybe the way you're kidding yourself. And don't mind *me*! I wouldn't blame *anybody*—!"

"*Edwinna!*"

"Sometimes, especially at night, when Alicia's asleep and I'm lying awake, I wish I *could* get crushes *myself*! Golly! It's a terrible thing for a woman not ever to—!"

"See here, Edwinna! I want one thing understood. Kate is a great help and a friend in need. She's a good, sweet, innocent child who never had much of a home or much mothering—"

"Take another look at her, darling," Edwinna said dryly but amiably. "Kate's all growed up. Adult. She's been married. She's had a child of her own—and doesn't talk about her Georgie, though the poor kid must feel a lot. I don't know much about her background. But I will say this: If she's as naïve as she acts, I have a date tonight with the King of England! She went through high school, and high school isn't the playpen it was in your dear old East Orange days.

She has a couple of older sisters who really get around. Kate's here on good behavior and she likes it here, so she intends to behave. That means, behave any way *you* want. Which is all right with me, only don't try to pull that Mother Superior line, darling!'"

This, Paula thought furiously, is too much! This is more than can be borne! I believed Edwinna was changing; but she isn't! Underneath is the same sadistic, perverse streak! What she accuses me of feeling comes out of her mind, not my mind! It's how *she'd* like to feel and doesn't dare! *Yet,* anyhow! God knows *what* people will feel or do years from now!

With the last reflection, her anger inexplicably ebbed. At the same time, tension must have left her fingers. For Edwinna sighed softly and turned her head to one side in such a way that her mother could see the elegance of her profile.

"I'm sorry," Edwinna murmured. "We all get tired as hell and cranky as hell's population! I didn't mean to shock you or to hurt you, Paula. But I guess I've run around with some pretty amoral people, so I've quit thinking how decent, normal women actually feel."

"What's decent?" Paula asked quietly, after a pause. "What's normal? What's moral? What's amoral? I was tired too, Edwinna. Nervously tired. There are so many things to think about, so many problems, so many tragedies to listen to! I suppose, sooner or later, the problem of what to do about sex when there's only one sex will become the uppermost problem in the whole world. Maybe I was being narrow-minded."

"You were just being my mother," Edwinna answered. "Get that place behind my shoulder blade. It's as sore as a bruise! Being my mother—not wanting a soul to get the jump on you. Honestly, Mum, what *earthly difference* do such things make? *Now?*"

"There's Bill," Paula answered slowly: "I loved him."

It was the first time she had used the past tense since the Disappearance.

13

AN ESSAY ON THE PHILOSOPHY OF SEX, OR THE LACK THEREOF,
EXTRANEOUS TO THE NARRATIVE AND YET ITS THEME, WHICH
THE IMPATIENT MAY SKIP AND THE REFLECTIVE MIGHT ENJOY.

Gaunt sat at his study window and read the Conclusion of his "Preliminary Survey." It followed his analysis of the lines of research which scientists everywhere were pressing and represented the philosopher's effort to add to the whole something original. Something new enough and broad enough to suggest different lines of inquiry and novel states of awareness that might lead to fresh formulations. As he read, he looked up from time to time, not really seeing the landscape beyond.

The windows had grown opaque with greasy salt blown from the near sea by summer wind, with summer's sticky humidity and the dust of months. Spiders had nested in outside corners; the debris of their prey, chitinous carapaces of beetles, miscellaneous wings, legs and antennae, was strewn on the sills. Webs stretched across the dirty panes.

Below the window, a large croton grew rank and untrimmed. Paula's gardenia at the corner of the house was perishing for want of water, want of aluminum sulphate to acidify the soil, want of fertilizer to enrich the peat moss in which it grew. The lawn was knee high in weeds, unmowed and going to seed. A fire in August had burned the palmettos; now they were reappearing, light green shoots ascending amongst the blackened trunks and the gray ashes. Only one or two of the fire-resistant Caribbean pines were dying but their brown needles came spinning intermittently from the crowns to the charred earth. The annuals were all dead.

He read thoughtfully through the chapter upon which he had spent weeks of work:

Disorientation

Two dichotomies have characterized Western twentieth-century society: a scientific objectivity that had no equal subjective logic, and the schism of the sexes. "Modern" man was never in any complete sense scientific. To objects he applied the honest scrutiny of his mind and so developed his technologies. To every instrument with which he examined and measured objects, *save one*, he gave the most critical analysis. The one was himself. For *the scientist* is the final, supreme and absolute instrument of his "sciences." Not to understand the doer is to have no certain knowledge of what has been done, or why it was undertaken.

Soon after the nuclear physicists delivered to the world an atomic bomb they asserted that "man" must develop a "moral science" as effective as his objective sciences or perish from an imbalance of objective power and subjective imbecility.

How pitiful, how pretentious, how ludicrous! Yet neither the physicists nor any other "scientists" of their ilk seemed to be embarrassed. They were saying in effect that they had carried the pursuit of the knowledge of *things* far beyond the intellectual capacity of average men; with the same breath, they demanded of average men—or at least of others, not themselves—the development of a new "science" of ideas to bridge the gap their one-sided enterprise had created, a "science" whereof *they* had no clue.

These same gentlemen would scarcely have fired a boiler without first checking its gauge. For some centuries, however, they had stoked the flames of objective learning without troubling themselves to check rising pressures within the species or even to discern whether the assumed pressure levels were correct. Thus the search for "pure" knowledge was conducted by the methodology of pure ignorance: the man sawing off the limb on which he perches is every whit as "scientific" as most of the great men in the lexicon of the pioneers of "learning."

The fact that when they cried out for a "new" science (to save the lives of their species, countrymen, colleagues, children and selves) such a science *had been* developed in their presence for half a century, but revealed one more blurred facet of their minds: like most of their scientific predecessors, they lacked the energy, the detachment, the acumen and the *integrity* to investigate knowledge outside their own narrow spheres.

At the turn of the century the science of psychology concerned itself with such phenomena as sense perceptions, reason and logic, reflexes and their conditioning, the relationship to these of heredity and environment, and the like. Most *academic* "psychologists" today are still ignorant of discoveries in their own field outside such exceedingly *objective* regions. A few concede that, through medicine, Freud and others have made certain contributions to what they term "abnormal psychology." But it is a subject neglected or regarded with suspicion by most institutions of so-called higher learning. Unfortunately for the wisdom of modern men, fealty to the tradition, along with neglect of the new findings of psychology has rendered most of them, in Cousins' word, obsolete.

What has been learned reveals that the best educated persons seldom accurately identify the *motives* of their acts. Men do not know what they are doing because they do not know *why* they do it. Obviously, the gathering of objective information for the subjectively naïve is not a sensible procedure: the man in the street and the researcher into physical phenomena *ought* to know something of human motives. So the idea of "knowledge for its own sake" is the alibi of a long and tiresome retinue of men, clever but not wise, who refused to face *themselves* scientifically. It is a lame and sorry defense of weak men who wondered about stars, and weighed them. Wondering itself, they never weighed. . . .

Personality is shaped in infancy and early childhood. The conflict between the raw cravings of the infant and the efforts of its elders to mold it to some particular cultural pattern is the tense matrix that sets the "style" of every adult. The infant's cravings (id) were identified as *instinctual*. What happened in the cradle (or failed to happen there) may be repeated, in endless forms, by the adolescent, the college student, the man as he marries and the same man as the bad-tempered, ill-adjusted, prejudiced, child-adult who presides as chairman of the board of a great corporation. That is the essence of Freud's discoveries. He showed how early the conditioning of human reflex begins.

Other psychologists have demonstrated that instinct is not merely a vestigial phenomenon in the young child but that, in man as in all creatures, instinct unfolds a series of compulsions and taboos which parallel biological development. Jung revealed *collective* aspects of instinct: man, the maker of symbols, images, words and myths—and religions of these, and from religions, cultures—thereby expresses *versions* of the basic pattern of his instincts. That theory stands as the only complete and plausible explanation of human history, in this essayist's opinion. It defines the religious and/or cultural imperative in man; at the same time, it shows how cultural diversity came about—just as Freud's concepts show how culture is imbued in each generation. Jung presents, also, the only satisfactory accounting for what *happened* to instinct (which so largely controls the behavior of all creatures) when one of them at last evolved a measure of consciousness and reason. It is coherent, "general field theory" of the psyche, seen finely in each man, and broadly in the record of man's ascent from apehood.

These findings have been arrived at by scientific investigations not always of what man *thinks* and *believes* about himself, but very often of what takes place in his subconscious or unconscious mind. It is here that instinct (repressed through ages by a creature attempting to seem "superior" to the rest of instinctual nature) works autonomously. Efforts to perceive instinctual compulsion, whereby men are able to cling to the shameful chaos of their present innumerable "convictions" or (with equal and equally insensate vigor) to their conscious *lacks* of conviction, *have succeeded!*

Psychology, in revealing that much of the inner nature of humanity, has also disclosed *why* and *how* its own overwhelmingly important findings are still almost universally rejected: the ego of man, the one subjective entity he has thus far come to recognize, sees that what the psychologists have found—if analyzed, ingested and digested —will change ego itself. And man's greatest fear then summons instinct to defend ego: the animal dread of *any* change in his personal identity. Only those courageous enough to master that primordial fear have been able to understand, or to benefit by, psychology. They are as yet very few, even amongst the brave physical scientists, who often regard themselves as the repositories of all erudition.

Persons of prior conviction, whether in Roman Catholicism, Presbyterianism, atheism, dialectical materialism, spiritualism, or Mohammedanism—as may be seen—have thus forged unconsciously such bonds between ego and instinct that the penetration of the complex whole is well-nigh impossible. Here instinct rules them, not reason; here instinct identifies the "light" of their convinced egos as the sum of enlightenment. Such is the mechanism of faith and belief; such, the iron curtain confronting the modern psychologist.

The problem is not unprecedented. Even physical "scientists" have never taken an open-minded attitude toward truly new ideas, in spite of their pretensions. The learned of his era did not examine Galileo's hypotheses; they put him to Inquisition. Darwin is today disputed: the bones of a hundred "missing links" stand assembled in museums, yet many scientists still assert the parent betwixt themselves and apes has not been dug up and never will be. Medical doctors allowed generations to die of infection after Lister and Pasteur; they rejected the "germ theory." It needed a martyr to abate childbed fever. What Einstein announced early in this era was regarded as ludicrous by many mathematicians—who smile at the postulates no longer.

Strides in new knowledge are taken slowly, usually against the will of the currently knowledgeable; and "education" is designed far more to freeze learning than to advance it. For education caters to the cultural pattern, and promulgates it. Education slams the door of every tabooed vista in the face of all youthful interest. It meticulously blunts imagination and stultifies criticism. It but *conveys* a culture; in that task, the errors of the culture and its unchallenged prohibitions are handed down. It discourages the rebel and the innovator; it sedulously abets the conformer.

No society yet has evolved a technique for *progressive change* in its cultural ideas, because religions, on which cultures are founded, would be avowedly tentative in such a process. But as long as religions remain *unconscious* efforts to patternize instinct they will partake automatically of instinct's compulsiveness. That is, absolute *doctrine* will characterize them and *tentativeness* will seem heretical and will be abhorred.

To incorporate a new advance of fundamental awareness, mankind has therefore always found it necessary to build a new culture on the wreck of some older one. The nearest approach to a resolution of this wasteful habit is found in the idea of freedom. Freedom supplies the theoretical room, at least, for subjective advances. But freedom in practice has generally deteriorated, under the pressure of new ideas to which it always gives rise, to a status where "liberty" is transferred from the innovators to the traditionalists so that, once again, it finally surrenders its franchise to tyranny.

Men have only now looked at themselves with the intellectual techniques the objective sciences have developed. And only a very few have so far summoned up nerve enough for that. The spectacle —like each spectacle of fresh discovery—is so *different* from contemporary belief that most persons summarily reject the whole finding. Indeed, the essayist has heard it said repeatedly in the past decade that Freud has gone "out of date." Disturbed myriads said Newton was out of date too, and Copernicus, and a hundred more; but all such efforts of the willfully ignorant did not, in the end, prevail against the simple facts that Newton, Copernicus and the rest had turned up. Since Freud and Jung similarly discovered new truth (and empirical, clinical evidence proves that they did), the willfully ignorant of this age, however highly placed or many-degreed, cannot prevail against those findings in the end, either.

Quackeries have flourished in every science, especially at its beginnings when the public had no sure basis for evaluation. Quackeries abound today in psychology. Also, the early accolytes of every science made blunders; psychologists are making them today. But each new branch of science has gradually established itself and its principles. Psychology has (or had, until the Disappearance) the same prospect.

Meanwhile, such pseudo sciences as economics, sociology and political "science" will continue to thrive anomalously because there can be no *science* in any of these fields until psychology has been incorporated by them. Man's economics, politics and society rise from currently unconscious motives; hence contemporary economists, political scientists, and sociologists merely document events without knowledge of or concern for motives. They have developed sets of tables but no instructions, directions or sensible interpretations. They deal in man and his motives without referring, as a rule, to what is known of human nature and its motivation; thus these "social sciences" are the alchemies and astrologies of the twentieth century and the "science of education" heads the claptrap retinue.

Here, of course, is the commonest, saddest and most ludicrous posture of our species: where we think we have knowledge (a "science") even our learned men relax, and even though the "knowledge" may be but some higher form of superstition. (In the "social sciences" the superstition is partly a credulity about statistics.)

The belief that we know what we don't know is another handicap of the new science of psychology. It may be set beside the damage done it by quacks, the inertia toward new learning our species has always exhibited, the fixational function of education, the diehard behavior of vested interests (in this case, of vested ideas and beliefs), and the situation of faith itself, which renders the individual impermeable to greater wisdom and especially to greater wisdom about instinct, simply because it blindly incorporates all it can of instinct. Psychology today faces a further disadvantage:

Because it is a new science its most accomplished proponents and interpreters rarely apply to it that apparatus of extrapolation which would disclose something of its probable destiny—granted, of course, that man still has a destiny. The reason for that is partly the modest tradition of scholarship and partly the limitation even of good minds. Many psychologists and psychiatrists still think of their subject only in therapeutic terms and few truly glimpse its potentialities. Old Leeuwenhoek, peering through his early microscope, hardly foresaw what changes would be made by way of the field he observed in medicine and surgery, health, sanitation, engineering, food transportation and storage, and so forth. Faraday, watching his laboratory toy revolve, did not conjure up Bonneville Dam. With our ingrained objective attitude, we Americans have been even less inclined to foresee what a new science of the mind could mean and do to our then-smug way of life.

Such is the first dichotomy. Western society, concentrating its integrity on objects, has lost touch with the subject. Eastern societies made the opposite blunder, dwelling upon subjectivity and ignoring obvious facts and laws in the external world. Their "orientation" was too much inward; the Western, too much outward. It might be called "occidentation," a style of personality able to harness atomic energy but one which has so little learning of the energies of instinct that it greets its greatest day with the cry, "We are doomed! Somebody save us!" "Orientation" and "occidentation" are both schizoid.

The second dichotomy concerns sex.

In nature, sex is an instinct served with felicitous collaboration by paired individuals for procreative purposes. It is the chain of life; it is the trunk from which life's variegations, its evolutions, have branched ever outward toward enhanced consciousness. Sex is almost as old as life. From the cosmic standpoint, sex is measurelessly more important than humanity. Without man, sex might again produce an aware animal. Without sex, nature could but manufacture amoebas and slimes till the sun went cold and time ran out.

It is expectable, in a species that has unconsciously perverted its instincts for its immediate vanity (as religions, faiths, dogmas, dialectics, "sciences," and so on), that strong cultural compulsions and taboos would everywhere surround the ancient, potent instincts of sex. Such, of course, is the case. Western man's religions (and hence his culture) are *rooted in sex management and sustained by inculcated sex fears.* Disobedience of the "sacred" rules or of the "common" law is "sin" or "crime." Sex hunger has here been made *shameful* so as to elevate the vanity of man in relation to other animals and so as to enhance the controlling power of cultural tradition and its agencies—the churches, courts, and so on. The inescapable result is anxiety and tension in society—hypocrisy, confusion, neurosis and madness along with vast "safety valves" of vulgar activities in which libido is expended in "acceptable" forms.

Half this nation's sick have suffered not from physical disease but from psychic. Half its hospital beds were occupied by the mentally ill or mad. The figure has doubtless risen since the Disappearance and will doubtless continue to rise. Sex is *innate and essential.* But since it is regarded here as shameful, since this particular nation has indeed tried to establish *perfect shame* by the abolition of such sexual customs as older societies tolerated, at least sub rosa, the American people lived to the very hour of the Disappearance in *perfect guilt.* There were individual exceptions. But a national neurosis was everywhere discernible and it resulted, here even more than elsewhere, in a hostility of each sex toward the other. That rancor could have been predicted by any wise, impartial mind analyzing *a discipline of shame and guilt as the social means toward enforcing sex patterns designed not for the sake of sex, or to enhance its expression, but merely to exalt egos by a lustful identification with an arbitrary "god," a varied set of "righteousnesses."*

This second dichotomy lies entirely in the subjective realm and has lain there uninvestigated through ages and until recently. A consideration of it here may shed some illumination on the broad splitting of personality—even amongst "convinced" persons. And that, in turn, *may* give rise to new and different formulations for considering the present awful predicament in which men find themselves. Such, at least, is the essayist's reason for the undertaking.

Such—say rather—is my personal hope, and it is but a hope. . . .

The half of a world that now survives is, in many senses, a whole world. It is a whole world owing to the fact that nearly all of humanity, in nearly all of its recorded or known existence, has consisted of *two* worlds: the world of women and the world of men. In primitive societies, in barbaric nations, and in our civilization, the training of the two sexes has been different, the freedoms permitted them have been different, and the powers delegated to them or taken from them have been different. Man's greater stature, his considerably greater strength, his apparently greater penchant for the hunt, for aggression, warfare, and the construction of useful apparatus, his emancipation from the reproductive functions of child carrying, childbearing and suckling, and his recently touted larger skull capacity have caused man to regard himself as the "dominant" or "superior" sex.

For thousands of years he has exploited the role. A human tribe in which the males think of themselves as substantially inferior to the females is a rarity, although there are a few in which childbearing is deemed the supreme human function and males consider themselves of secondary importance owing to their incapacity to give birth.

But generally, in marked degree, woman has been accorded a secondary place. She had been regarded as a slave in countless societies. She has a property status in numerous areas today. She has been denied many social, economic and political privileges accorded to men. Before the law, she is seldom equal.

Where sexuality is concerned—and in this discussion the concern is nothing other—woman also has been grossly *denigrated*. In both the Old and the New Testament (on which Western "culture" so largely rests) woman's biological functions have been repetitiously and remorselessly associated with filth. According to the legendary attitudes, a woman during menses is "unclean"—even though this period corresponds in certain other mammals to "heat," i.e., to the time of "desirability." Conception itself, in such frames of reference, is regarded as vile; so is parturition. The female who has borne a child is often supposed to be in an "unclean" condition that demands certain rituals for the restitution of her decency.

The etiology of those callow notions is obvious. A woman bleeds and desquamates at intervals; she bleeds again when her offspring is born; and she expels its placenta. To the naïve savage those processes may have seemed repugnant, especially since, owing to her structure and to such functions, a woman is liable to infections and parisitisms of a noxious nature during such occasions or following them.

Furthermore, until very recently her childbearing was an ordeal whereof she became the apparent victim. Upon her, savages reasoned, an *affliction* rested; ergo, it was a sign of her inferiority, a punishment of the gods for what manifestly must have been implicit evil, or a visitation imposed on that weaker sex which somehow must have deserved it.

On every hand, these old stigmata have survived. "Bloody" is foul to an Englishman because the bleeding of woman was presumed foul. To American womanhood, the menstrual period was "the curse."

The woman giving suck must do so many times each day; the necessity in primitive societies compelled her to feed her child openly; in so doing, she was spontaneously likened to the "lesser" beasts —and, again, unfavorably compared with man, whose sexual activities are more often concealed in the hut. Owing to man's millenniums-long attempt to dissociate himself from other animals for the advantage of his ego, the mere biological means of infant nurture have been taken as one more evidence of woman's beastlier estate!

Setting aside all concern for the justness or the reasonableness of such opinion, the fact must be recognized. No male Protestant exists, no Roman Catholic (in spite of the adoration of Mary, who is, fortunately for the Church's ends, the result of a "virgin" birth), and no person subject to such "Christian" traditions (or any other religious doctrine) but holds in his mind an array of the ugly, repulsive and biologically preposterous woman-concepts set forth and implied in the Holy Bible or its equivalent. That venerable Anthology contains most of the wisdom of the ages—and most of the blunders and prejudices. So for two thousand and more years parts of it have conveyed to every Believer the far, far older association of inferiority, of uncleanliness, with woman!

Indeed, a Gallup Poll conducted amongst surviving men would doubtless show that the overwhelming majority still holds these special attitudes of shame and guilt and filthiness toward woman's biologically most lofty functions. Perhaps not one in ten has availed himself of knowledge enough to dispute the slanderous delusion and not one in a hundred, on psychological examination, would prove free of derivative, *unconscious* impressions.

With such views, engraved for such periods of time on all but a small fraction of the species, and with the apparently supportive physical criteria, it is not possible to consider that men and women in the modern age lived in the same world or (from both physical and psychological standpoints) even in a similar world!

The two sexes dress differently and are differently trained. Such elaborations of different manners toward each and between each exist amongst them that hardly a word is uttered or a course of action taken that does not contain and reflect a special attitude or group of attitudes toward sexuality. In addition, while the social and outward manifestations of sex differences are given universal and incessant attention, the *true biological aspects of sex are everywhere repressed and suppressed!* Hence, beginning at birth with the pink or blue raiment that is the first mark, and continuing in each category of behavior to the grave, the externals of sex are forced into every cranny of consciousness while the truth and nature of it are left in a darkness as near-absolute as "righteous" traditionalists can keep it. In Jung's terminology, the *persona* is given every emphasis, the *anima, subjective* sexuality, is kept at an infantile (primitive) level.

So the sexes were set in inferior-superior relationships and so they have stood immobile for aeons. So, in recent centuries, a further terrible division has been artificially made between the sexually known and unknown. It is a rare society indeed in which male and female consider each other as equivalents or complements, evenly share work, play, counsels and society and take no magical affront, on either hand, from any aspect of the biological necessities.

The recent efforts of women in Western society to achieve "equality" with men and "emancipation" from their ageless subservience (and their successes in obtaining certain social, economic and political opportunities and enfranchisements) indubitably sprang from the gross and deep insult women have borne since long before the time of Christ. But these enterprises *merely obscured the real nature of the problem.* They tended to create the impression that the sexual schism lay in the *objective* realm; and, of course, the orientation of

Western man was a fecund soil for that sort of superficial, deluded concept.

The "liberated" women found themselves (until we lost them) more restless and dissatisfied then ever before, precisely when they had achieved the "objectives" of their gallant crusades! For they had *not* removed or even *sought* to remove the *subjective stigmas* that have for so long militated against them. The attempt would have been futile, beyond doubt, since, though women suffered and even accepted the mental sickness of the species, the *cure* could have been effected only in the minds of the principal carriers: *males*. And, as in the case of every psychological blunder, the blunderer must heal himself—with whatever guidance or help.

Here is the classic circumstance of psychological oppression: it is not (for example) the Jew who can heal anti-Semitism but the Gentile alone, whose intellectual sickness anti-Semitism is. *Only the brain can change its brain and only by first recovering the emotional sensations with which inappropriate concepts were instilled and by next replacing them with realer values in the logical expectation that new and deeper emotions will then sustain a more honest and better integrated personality.*

Woman could not change her status by donning the clothes of the free male citizen and going through his motions. In the subjective realm, from which rises all outward behavior and in which reposes all inner opinion and sensation, "emancipated" woman was still as much prisoner of the sexual prejudice as ever. And she was unhappier; for when she thought of herself as "free" she made the walls of humanity's most colossal bigotry *invisible* and so lost even the cold comforts of enslavement. She could no longer discern a boundary she still encountered. She no longer had any idea when the guards might assail her, or for what reason or under what conditions she might run headlong into barricade, or who among men might suddenly prove to be an implacable warden, or a sadistic jailer, or a male immured amongst the women in their impalpable penitentiary.

If there is an instinct toward *realizing a pattern* in man (as certain uniquely informed and acutely discerning philosophers now hold), a negative evidence of it is found in this tragedy of the woman who thought she had "advanced." For *any* subservient role, be it that of a slave, of a Victorian paragon and housewife, of a man-sharer in a harem, will be seen to satisfy *in some degree* a putative instinct for order and arrangement. But the woman who caused the conscious mind of her society to agree that no pattern could compel her, and who was nevertheless obliged to live within the frames of old phobias, compulsions, taboos, rites, formulae, fears and repugnances, was a woman damned to be unable to discover *any* design for herself——and her anguish in the void is evidence of what was lost.

She was (as women sadly, if unintelligently, observed before the Vanishment) *emotionally worse off* even than that slave who knew she was obliged to conduct herself in accordance with the rules or die. A slave might hope for an appreciative master and a biologically effective life from which psychological satisfactions could be derived. But the modern free woman showed by her suffering the want in her ways. She walked in the dark amidst set traps, pits, steel points, poisons, and infernal machines, where she had been led to anticipate a safer and easier passage. Consciously "free," she was unconsciously everywhere ensnarled; and *no* pattern, either visible or invisible, was any longer available to her.

The average male survivor of this age will probably reject the idea that woman's dilemma has for ages been far greater than even she imagined, that it was not ameliorated in modern times, and that venerable, largely male attitudes have been the occasion of it all. But some readers will at least appreciate that, psychologically speaking, the man and the woman of the "West" have inhabited two ut-

terly discrete worlds. The current absence of women and the powerful longings that consequently prevail may give rise to a degree of
fresh perspective in the matter.

I can but wish forlornly that I had the power to convey this
truth as I have at last come to see it. For in the demeaning of woman
man has demeaned himself. His chivalry, his mother reverence,
are but sickly pretenses to hide his ageless, vile convictions. What
would we say of any other beast that held its mate in secret revulsion? What do we feel of the spider that copulates and then devours
its mate? Let *that* be said of humanity!

The *actual* differences between the sexes of genus homo are not
very great. Some woman are larger than most men; some have bigger
brains than most men; some are stronger. It is quite possible that by
the use of genetics mankind could have reversed all conventional
tendencies. And had females remained on earth instead of the males,
had they found a mechanism for parthenogenesis and sex determination (which they would have had a better opportunity to do than
ourselves), it is likely that in a few generations they would have
accomplished precisely such reversals.

Indeed, it may be that in some remote, unrecorded period the
mere *ego of the male* of a species possessing powers of choice not
given to the lower orders became the *sole* determining factor—rather
than any "natural" element. Men may have unconsciously commenced to keep the weaker sex weaker by electing its weaker ex-
amples for mates. That is an idle and perhaps trivial speculation. But
it suggests the arbitrary fashion in which genus homo often ap-
plies choice to certain functions and rejects choice in the matter of
the *results* of many of his elected acts—which is still another dichotomy I shall touch on.

Mankind has everywhere emphasized the sex *differences*. He has
only recently known much of the *identities and parallels*.

In the human embryo, until the fifth or sixth week (a period
corresponding with geological ages of evolution), the genital ridge

of both sexes is much the same. But as "ontogeny recapitulates phylogeny" (in *that* great, pregnant pattern of all nature!) each sex produces the *same* cell groups, which only gradually take on separate shapes.

The epithelial cords form the seminiferous tubes—or the mesenchyme. The graafian follicle comes into being in one sex; in the other, from the same tissue, a transitory network in the mesovarium. The mesovarium in the female is, in the male fetus, the mesorchium. Paroöphoron and organ of Giraldes; common Wolffian duct—and Müllerian duct, becoming Fallopian tubes, uterus, and perhaps vagina in the female, uterus masculinus in the male. So, endlessly, the anatomical parallel continues. And while each emergent body of protoplasm takes up its appointed form and situation, neither male nor female lacks in embryo the same entities, or their rudiments or vestiges. Our outward organs appear greatly different only to the mind that does not intimately know how alike they are and of what identical tissues they have been composed. How superficial, then, how *ignorant* it is to postulate an important differentness of spermatozoa or ova, clitorises or penes or any other aspect or characteristic of the sexes!

But, again, the blunder is ageless. Again, humanity has done its utmost to enhance the final apparent differences. Once, long ago, we may have had the sensations of equality and complement which are, alone, implicit in the protoplasmic truth; we have lost them, traded them for sham and vanity, for illusion and delusion.

Modern insight into these objective identities has not been employed by us to influence the mistaken concepts. It is forbidden to discuss such matters! The object rules; the truths about it, and all suitable fresh inferences, are repressed. The parallels of the embryo are ignored; so are the likeness of girls and boys. The small differences of adults are exaggerated to crowd and color every nook of consciousness and natural empathies are thereby pushed into the limbo of the subconscious. We see a man, a woman; we have made ourselves unable to see two *alikes* in all but minor ways and even there, in *process,* similar.

Lately we have discovered "sex" hormones: male, female. To the disquietude of some, we have also learned that each sex possesses both and that no more than a slight preponderance of one over the other exists in either sex. With pragmatic zeal we have caused cockscombs to grow on hens and found that female hormones relieve to some degree cancerous conditions of the prostate. We have even somewhat changed personality by injection, and disoriented libido. We might have done better. We might, for instance, have wondered more what such facts *mean.*

It could plausibly be inferred (for instance) that the psychological nature of men and of women is not, intrinsically, as different as the average person thinks—and all biology might be turned to evidence. It could be imagined that nature had no intention of causing the two sexes to take such opposed attitudes toward each other—that two very similar physiologies with one common end in view were not designed to sustain ideas of inferiority and superiority, of uncleanliness and hence of comparative cleanliness, of strength and weakness, modesty and valor, and the rest. Even though a division of the social responsibilities is implied by the *ultimate* differences, the *common aim* suggests that the duties of neither sex are lesser or greater and should be conjoined.

It must be assumed in consequence that all our inequities are the product of gross, calamitous, long-standing *error.* The motivative basis for such assumption is plain. When burgeoning "reason" ranged itself against the "blind" instinct of prior apes, and vanity was sired by success, the product (calling himself man and stripped of such automatic "divine" guidance as was available through instinct to a billion years of man's progenitors) became so entranced with himself that he never found enough objects of odious comparison to satisfy the greed of his inner conceit. He went to war with other men exactly like himself, always on the grounds of their "inferiority." Not satisfied even by that, he declared another war on the still-more-similar half of his own tribe: woman. She was necessary to him, so he could not exterminate her; but he put her in her place to give his own a more exalted seeming.

It is a hypothesis worthy of intense reflection—nowadays.

And woman's new place, essentially "inferior," was not in any way the place nature had created her to fill. For her, the game of life then perhaps became a game of wits and of revenge and mankind has not known any happiness since that hideous day.

The legend of Adam and Eve and their expulsion from "Eden" is an excellent allegory for what thus may truly have happened in the dawn ages. (Those psychologists who find legends to be the allegories of instinct, accounts of its evolution in man, will see that story in such a light—see it with depth and clarity.)

Note, first, that, since it was Adam who got the upper hand over Eve, the legend attributed the "original sin" to woman! In "Christian" civilization that pagan fable has been used to short the psychological circuit and slam the book. The old, universal "sin" *is* certainly man's and certainly *was* man's; its fearful consequences obtain everywhere without regard to the particular religion underlying any major culture. In that sense, it is fitting that that Saviour who is presumed to have died for our sins was a *man*—for the women were *innocent*. (What shall we say of them now?) And although women have abetted the ignominy—the blasphemy of the species by itself—they have done so with the pitiful motive of regaining some favor amongst the men they had to love no matter what men imagined of them or did to them!

The atmosphere of such argument may seem rarefied. Let readers endeavor, in that case, to bear in mind they have never before come in contact with it, in all likelihood. The poisonous notions that pervade their minds are *all* they have known.

Doubting readers will not deny the *rage* that has characterized humanity in all its known periods. The fact that the males of the world, stricken by what is likely to prove a mortal blow, should, in the very moment of catastrophe, turn to hurling hydrogen bombs on one another is a proper criterion of that state. *Hatred* is man's principal characteristic; hostility and aggression are the chief manifestations of it in the objective realm; ideas of superiority and inferiority are the constant subjective shapes of the condition; and his history is the story of war. The urge to *love*—the real message of every sincere, sane messiah—is always ignored, save briefly or locally. By man, the greater appeal has *always* been found in the instrument of his own destruction: hate.

It was this deadly wishing that the Greek tragedians took for granted. It was the evidence of this that made a man of such insight as Freud pessimistic about his species. Two thousand years ago —and yesterday—able minds have accepted the massive illusion as *inevitable*—taken it, even, for a "natural law"!

And the hatred cannot be denied. But a question can be asked:

If their sexes so revile each other, *how can a species love?* How, if one sex regards itself as superior, can it refrain from detesting the "inferior" sex? And how in the name of nature and of God can beings regarded as inferior by their mates bear toward those mates a whole affection? Creativeness, that ineffable First Principle of life, is not possible where the creators are at such odds, and have been for hundreds of generations. A hate of life is inevitable.

We were reared in that madness of our forefathers, and they in the insane evaluations of theirs, and thus it has gone, back to the caves and back to the forest fringe, until we have come so to adore our hateful composition that we found our religions upon it, incorporate it in all our virtues, make our laws from it, declare wars because of it, practice it by the wayside and in the seats of the mighty, and we cannot see behind it, or beyond it, or know what to do about it, because *we do not truly know any longer that we hate*, and most of us would rather perish than be reinformed of the Truth.

From that one illusion may stem all our sorrow; it may be, in solemn fact, the original sin.

We—male and female—are the same flesh and the flesh is beautiful. We have all the same organs, differing only in specialty. The same chemicals course in us both. When we love each other it is the same love. When we lie together we are in solemn truth that One. And until men made it so, in prestigious excesses of egotism, no such thing existed as a woman and no such thing existed as a man. The fact ought to be exceedingly plain today, since, without females, we males are in a lingering death. We do not exist—alone. We cannot.

A "person" is a-man-plus-a-woman; with one or the other absent, there is no person. Hate is still possible but not love. Destruction is still easy but creativity is done for. In the world we so recently inhabited, where woman existed and the pride of man has sullied all, we had reached the very edge of that circumstance in which we now find ourselves! The soul of woman had long ago been slaughtered; our women were spiritually dead—so we were dead also. We were both dead sexually; the mind of man had grown as morbidly demented as it was gigantic; the long paroxysms of instinct that our harsh history exhibits were approaching some final masochism; life to nearly all of us was inner anathema.

In a mystical sense it might be said that, since the women vanished, they were probably spared (owing to their innocence of original blame) from the dreary spectacle of slow death that now confronts the cruel and idiot descendants of the cruel and idiot sponsors of the blight: ourselves.

The sin was shame, as the legend implies. But not the hateful shame we bear today. The sin was to convert sexuality itself to a shame and, in the dire doing, to shame women especially. We have (inevitably) taken the very opposite of the true position in defining the "original" sin. Our common sexuality, which was intended to be the ecstasy of our species, as a flower is the sexual organ and the ecstasy of a plant, was turned to shame—in order that we would appear (to our conceited human selves) loftier than other beasts, better even than nature, superior to law, even to God as men, so far, have invented Him.

Those advanced psychologists and psychologically informed philosophers who deal with the relationship of mythology to instinct will find—as I said—in the fundamental idealogy of that "Old Testament religion" which underlies this civilization a clear "statement" of a dawn-age double error which has never been corrected. To some of these thinkers, the "Garden of Eden" is an archetypal memory of man's "peace of mind" in the days when pure instinct guided him. His effort to "sanctify" himself by shaming instinct, and the sexual instincts especially, has left him with a second archetypal memory; it appears in his legend of being driven from the Garden. What that "means" is, merely, that there exists in man an indelible, *protoplasmic* recollection of a happier estate, of a blunder (sin), and of the stemming of all subsequent woe from that first error. What it "means," again, is that the back-brain of man—perhaps the very spinal column—recalls *and turns into legend* the fact that he has cut off his consciousness of the instinctuality of all life and now suffers for the unwarranted, arrogant deed.

The story of Genesis is reflected not only in other old legends but also in the universal hope of "hereafters" which will restore the estate that is man's "due." The ubiquity and vehemence of human beliefs in humanesque hereafters becomes, by such logic, a measure of the strength of instinct still at work in genus homo!

Freud was able to penetrate the ageless layers of credulity laid upon the error, to the degree that he saw, appraised and proved the *sexual* basis of Western, Christian neurosis. He did not see the still-broader frame of reference from which the situation rose—the development of ego-repressed instincts into myths, legends, and at length into formal regions. That was Jung's vision. Freud, however penetrated a curtain of *time* when he showed that most of modern man's neuroses and psychoses derive from misinterpretations of the relation of id to ego and to the "superego." It was the first great clue to the "wherefore" of the Toynbeean rise-and-fall of civilization. With Jung's formulation of the Freudian discovery into a timeless whole, the means for a renaissance like that of the awakening of the physical sciences become available. It has not much been used, or even studied, as I have said.

Why not?

It took man centuries to learn to apply honesty to objects; even today only certain men, called scientists, are honest altogether, and then only where certain objects are concerned. But by such means we have found out *what things are*! Is it inconceivable that men (had they yet the chance) might someday apply the identical honesty to the subject? Is the definition of man this: he is an everlasting liar to himself about himself? Or would he someday learn—painfully, as he learned the "scientific method"—also to be honest with himself? And would such honesty begin to unlock the greater mystery, the mystery of *Why*? I believe it would. I believe it is our "sin" that prevents our sciences from asking "Why?" There is no *reason* we should not ask—none to expect the answer is inexplicably denied to those who seek. And the field for the inquiry doubtless lies not amongst comets or bacteria or flying mesons—but *within ourselves*.

Such is the substance of my effort to conclude this report with a personal "contribution." I realize that what I have offered is at best but ground for speculation. It is my hope that the ground will be examined, the speculation attempted. For we can be assured that the physical scientists are doing the utmost of which man is capable to resolve the shocking riddle of our days. We can be sure that those psychological scientists who are able are also investing their energies and their best thought in the same effort. But they are very few.

Perhaps all I have expressed is the wish that more men of imagination, courage and logic would apply their minds in the subjective field.

I do not intend to suggest, by recommending psychological research, that the disappearance of females is illusion. I do not mean to imply that the sad scenery of our times is the result of some collective, hypnogogic fantasy. Such *may* be the case, and if it is, not the "physical" but the "psychological" sciences will offer a better approach to what seems so real now, and so terrible, so tragic. I do not wish it inferred, either, that I regard our wretched status as a "punishment" of Nature or God—the working of some unknown, fabulous cosmic Law. What I wish to leave is an impression that we are disoriented in our minds toward sexuality—toward love—and in other ways. Even such a presentation—a philosopher's poor best—may be regarded as out of place in a "factual" report. To all who so regard it, my apologies. To the rest, let us dwell on the sensation of love, imbuing it with all our new objective knowledge, to see what new forms this act may awaken in the mind.

We have lost everything. With love, with truth, this might not have been.

14

A PASSION OF THE ELEMENTS AND AN ELEMENTAL PASSION.

The women of Florida had no Hurricane Warning Service. Restoration of such technological luxuries was not even on their agenda. Very few ships plied the seas. No planes could be spared to scout low-pressure areas in the distant doldrums. No radio network existed to relay data on humidity, barometric pressure, temperature, and wind velocity. It was a day at the end of October; Florida's old-timers, if they thought of hurricanes at all, felt relieved that the season of menace had passed uneventfully.

The early morning was as bland and bright as three hundred others in every year. A little hot.

Paula attended a meeting where half a hundred women, in workaday clothes now, slacks, blue jeans, men's pants, old riding breeches, endeavored to cope with the increasing multitudes who descended upon the state: women from northern towns and cities, with their daughters, seeking refuge from the coming winter, seeking a little plot of ground where vegetables would grow year round and pigs could be fed. They arrived in thousands now, and it was evident that when the northern fall congealed hundreds of thousands more would forsake their homes and move south. Whether to turn them back, or to establish a quota beyond which entry into Florida would be refused, or to accept all comers and hope they could be fed, were questions upon which opinions varied. So the meeting dragged on.

A rising wind and darkening sky were hardly noticed during the debate. Squalls were expectable at that time of year. . . .

Kate drove back from Coconut Grove with Alicia, a few precious packets of food at her side. She noticed that gusts of wind wrenched the treetops. Noticing, she slowed and watched. It could be, she thought—in which case, someone should get the shutters out of storage; someone meant her. She stepped on the accelerator, regretting that she had not yet, like most of the others, given up the habit of wearing a fresh dress downtown, to shop. It was Hester's day off; Kate regretted that too. . . .

Edwinna's crew was taken from the fields when the downpour began. The superintendent, after some difficulty, got a call through to Key Largo and learned that rain was incessant to the south. "That's all today," she announced. "Pile in the trucks and go home! Gonna rain all the rest of the day, most likely."

Toward midafternoon, Edwinna reached home, soaked to the skin, and found Kate panting and sweating as she dragged the storm shutters from the grimy recesses of the tool shed.

Alicia was staring sulkily from the kitchen window. She had been trying to "help," a nuisance in Kate's path as she staggered out with the heavy shutters, and a spider in the storage shed had bitten the child. There was a splash of Mercurochrome on the bite and Alicia showed it aggrievedly to her mother.

"Yes, dear," Edwinna absently said; and she said to Kate, "Do you *really* think—?"

"I don't *know!* All I do know is, if it keeps building up, we better try to put them on the windows."

Edwinna pitched in.

The children came, running through the wind and the downpour, barefooted, carrying their shoes in old newspapers. They liked it. They began to help too, lifting shutters, moving the stepladder and picking wing nuts from glass jars that had been filled with kerosene to prevent rust.

Paula finally returned—driving fast.

The wind moaned steadily by that time and the trees bent and surged. Rain fell in shivering white veils that swept processionally across the landscape. The copper gutters roared; their spouts erupted loudly. On the lawn large pools of water formed, dimpling and frothing in the deluge. The women and young girls trudged through the heavy weather, trip after trip, bucking the shutters that pushed against them like skaters' sails.

Paula parked in the car porte, checked the car windows and plunged into the rain. "You girls think we're going to have a blow?"

"Kate does," Edwinna said. "Anyway"—she spat water—"anyway—we're boarding up."

"What about the colored people?"

Edwinna shook her head. "We've been too busy to investigate. I heard them pounding more stakes a while ago—"

Paula slogged through the palmettos to the row of tents. The cleared area was not spacious. Its congested tents were tied shut.

Every available rope and bit of wire led from some eye in the canvas to a tree or a rock or a driven peg. Paula yelled outside the tent belonging to Hester's oldest daughter.

"Margot! Oh, Margot?"

A smiling face appeared.

"You all right?"

"Yes, ma'am."

"If it blows too hard—if it starts to damage the tents—get everybody and come to my house."

"Yes, ma'am. We were talkin' about it."

"Any time. Now, if you want to."

"We got some pork an' pigeon peas cookin' here. We want to serve it—"

"All right. Tell everyone."

Paula tramped back. The rain was beginning to hurt. By five o'clock it would probably be as dark as night. Fronds of palmetto slapped and sliced at her; their spined stems raked her. "Damn it," she said, and rain entered her opened mouth. "Double damn it! Something every day—every minute!"

She assisted with the last dozen shutters. It was by then all but impossible to carry them in the wind and rain, to fit them over the bolts on window frames, to climb the ladders, and to turn the nuts until they were battened tight.

The white women and children finally assembled in the living room. Shutters placed across the huge glass doors to the porch had made it dark and Kate lighted a single candle. In its rays, they stood about dripping and exhausted.

"I'm hungry," Martha said.

"I'm shot," Edwinna answered the child.

"It's not suppertime," Paula smiled at them firmly.

"Couldn't we," Kate asked, "break the rule? I mean, we've all got to change, and we could have a snack after that. Couldn't we?"

Paula wrung out her sodden, gray-streakd hair; rain dribbling from it was added to the puddles and the smeared dirt on the floor. "Oke."

Cold baking-powder biscuits, some honey Edwinna had bought near Homestead, and a rarity: coffee. No electricity: wires down already. A single candle's light to permeate faintly the hot, steamy living room. Children, eating ravenously. Outside, the wind and rain.

The hurricane itself arrived in a matter of seconds although most storms increase slowly in violence. Occasionally, as happened that day, the belt between peripheral gales and hurricane winds is narrow. Paula had not counted on that or she would have made the colored people move.

Trees hissed and muttered in a full gale; the earth gurgled in a plunging rain. Then, while a person might have climbed a long flight of stairs or read a page of a book or eaten a biscuit, the thing was upon them.

It came with a far howl and a shudder in the woods. Floors vibrated. What they said was suddenly inaudible and mouths moved incomprehensibly. The children cried out: their eardrums hurt sharply. The house was struck as if by a mallet bigger than a house. What had been a howl became a shriek, the shriek of nature suddenly put to torment—a roar, a bellow, a screaming, uncanny high sounds, rattlings, the tympani of typhoon. It seemed the strong building would fall in the lunging wind. Rain squirted under doorsills in spite of the metal stripping; the metal itself began to buzz weirdly as the tempest fiddled on its edges.

Trees broke. Sounds of their splitting were louder than the wind. The house rejoined with a crash as the bole of a tall pine was hurled upon its eaves. The candle blew out and the children whimpered—unseen, unheard.

Paula struck a match, put the candle on another table and yelled at Edwinna, "My God! *The tents!*"

Edwinna, her amber eyes as steady as ever, looked at the walls, the board-covered windows, the ceiling, nodded her head and shrugged.

She thinks we are going to die, Paula heard her mind saying. *Maybe we are.*

Another crash, and a crack showed in the wall afterward. Like a wound, it bled; rain streamed into the chamber and the children backed away from the place. On the ceiling a dark spot spread quickly and dripped. Plaster began to fall.

The noise was now too formidable for definition.

Paula saw, presently, that the glass doors were jerking. The hurricane was trying to walk into their precarious sanctuary. As she stared in horror through the dim candlelight, the doors separated an inch. She rushed toward them, determined to force them together again, lock them, and shut out the wild fiend.

During that moment her sense of personification was vivid. She reached the door. From the calamitous wet dark beyond, a black human hand grasped at its frame. She screamed—and the scream was lost in the tumult. Then she remembered and opened the door. The candle went out. But a flashlight beam illuminated the women and the children on the porch.

Their clothing was torn from their backs; water dribbled from the remnants and from their gleaming brown flesh—water and crimson stains. Some stood, some sat, some lay on the flooded floor. Paula flinched at the half-drowned, dazed faces, the injuries, the blood, the white end of a broken bone held by a quivering child with her usable hand. She opened the door and let them in, one by one, and the room was filled with dreadfulness.

Edwinna had gone swiftly upstairs. One bathroom alone was accessible: the other parts of the house could be reached only by crossing the wind-struck porch where the trees were falling. She brought down all the bandages and useful drugs she could find.

It was not possible to talk much.

Margot managed to yell into Paula's ear. "The tents just bust!

The trees fell! We crawled on the road! They's two-three kids and women got kilt!"

Edwinna gave a hypo to the child with the broken arm.

Paula set the bone.

The child's brown and white eyes remained fixed upon the crack where a tree had split the roof; in silence, she sat staring.

And so time began to pass.

It was nine o'clock, or thereabouts, when Alicia started to rock and hold her abdomen, abandoning the impromptu games that Martha and the other girls had fearfully, industriously organized. Edwinna picked up her daughter. She put her ear to the child's mouth.

"My tummy hurts. It hurts terrible."

The mother felt the abdomen; it was rigid. She thought with frenzy, *appendicitis*. In that case, sulfa drugs might have stemmed the infection. But they had been used up on the Negroes.

Kate saw what was happening—saw Edwinna with her child, a hand under skimpy dress—saw the mother's pallor and the little girl's sweat of pain. Her face showed a sudden dread. She hurried across the room.

"Sick?" she shouted over the tumult.

"Stomach-ache. It's hard. Might be appendicitis."

"She got bitten by a spider!" Kate yelled in the listening ear. "Could have been a black widow!"

Edwinna, with a frantic look in her eyes, clutched the child. "What do we do?" Her mouth said it in the din.

Kate spread out her hands and shook her head. She went to Paula's side. The child's grandmother rose from attending to a minor cut of her own. With her hair streaming, her eyes glittering in the pounding room, the murk, the heat, Paula looked like a witch.

She made a sign of giving a hypodermic.

Edwinna nodded.

They gave the little girl a quarter grain of morphine.

The storm fell silent.

Women got up. Children began to talk. Alicia's moans became screams of pain as if, assured suddenly of audibility, she could afford to exert the energy that would compel some more effective attention.

"Hush, darling!" Edwinna murmured.

"It hurts! It hurts awful!" Her short legs were contracted; spasms racked her abdomen.

"Stay inside!" Paula called. "Everybody! This is the eye of the storm. It'll come back, instantaneously and from the other direction, in a few minutes!"

She looked at her granddaughter attentively. "It must be—!"

Edwinna, ghost pale, nodded. "I guess so. But what can we *do*?"

Paula exhaled. It seemed unnatural, now, to be able to hear a voice, her own—anybody's. "Nothing. There was some sort of antidote—but we wouldn't have it here. You couldn't get to a drugstore. Or a doctor. We've just got to—"

"I know," the child's mother murmured. "I *know*." She carried Alicia to a divan tenderly, put a pillow under her head, and watched as the child gathered herself to scream again.

The colored women watched too. The colored children watched.

Stars showed for a little while, outdoors. Then, in the distance, they heard the tumult approach. . . .

Alicia died just as the wind blew itself out and the first drab intimations of day had shown those who ventured on the porch a shattered world, dim-seen in an easy rain.

They made a coffin from plywood that afternoon. Edwinna lined it with the silk of an evening dress. They dug out the biggest pothole they could find in the limestone yard and buried Alicia there.

In nearby potholes, dirt-filled funnels dissolved in the limestone by millenniums of rain, the colored women dug also for their dead.

A doctor, with whom Paula chanced to talk some weeks later,

said there was nothing that could have been done under the circumstances. The child, she had said, was undoubtedly particularly sensitive to black widow venom. Some people were—though, generally, adults recovered and children too.

The physician had blinked large, tired eyes at Paula with what was meant for sympathy, pushed her mannish felt hat down on her white hair, and hurried away on the appalling, perpetual schedule of every surviving doctor.

By that time they had chopped away the trees that leaned against the house. They had repaired the crumpled eaves. And by that time the hibiscus they had transplanted to mark Alicia's grave had leafed out and was bearing bright yellow flowers.

She had liked yellow.

Alicia's death was a wanton attack upon the fortitude of Edwinna, Kate and Paula; it seemed so indirect a casualty of the storm. Everywhere in the South Florida area, deaths had been numerous. Owing to the lack of all warning, the community had been victim, as in earlier times, of every hazard of a hurricane which accompanies surprise.

Very few houses or other buildings had been boarded up. The assumption that the danger season had passed, the preoccupation of the women with urgent work, and the normal squalliness of the the month—added to the absence of bulletins and advisories— had brought multiple catastrophe.

Apartment houses, homes, hotels and office buildings spared by the fire had lost their window glass. Interiors had been flooded. Cars and trucks, caught on the streets and especially on the causeways, had been blown into the Bay or rolled like barrels down rain-slick pavement. Women—and children trying to get home from school— had been struck by flying missiles: coconuts, garbage cans, park benches, branches. They had been knocked unconscious and drowned in pools where the tempest had caught them toiling. They had been hurled bodily into canals. Trees had fallen on them and pinned them down. Cars had rolled over them and walls had toppled upon them. The total death list, though never accurately ascertained because of the uncertain knowledge of who had survived the first chaos and who had since moved to the region, amounted to many hundreds. Several thousand women, girls and infants were hurt.

In the days immediately following, when the sun came out again, when the dead had been buried and the injured treated and while Greater Miami was a spectacle of furniture and bedding and clothing set out and hung out to dry, a listlessness came over the people. What they had already suffered was so formidable that this added blow found them without resilience.

Kate blamed herself incessantly: "I should never have let Alicia 'help' me in that tool shed. I was even scared some old scorpion or spider might bite *me*. I'd have bug-bombed, but the bombs are all used up. It's my fault."

Edwinna tried to be stoical. "Nothing is anybody's fault, Kate," she said repeatedly to the repeated self-castigation.

And Paula, over and over, tried to give the tragedy its correct perspective. "Kate, you mustn't! After all, you were one of the few people who did sense what was coming and did get ready. If you hadn't boarded up, not just Alicia but all of us might have been killed. The storm wind would have come through the windows and it could have torn the house down. Things would have crashed into the rooms. We'd all have been hurt and soaked for hours. Alicia might have died of pneumonia. Don't keep reproaching yourself, Kate!"

But whenever any of them looked out at the yellow hibiscus, their eyes filled and work stopped awhile or went on less efficiently.

The work itself constantly increased.

From Washington came one command, cardinal and peremptory: *food*. Raise food. Start gardens. Produce.

Parts of Europe were now starving. Russia claimed to be hold-

ing its own. There was little news from China and India: a cabled
dispatch, now and then, of rout, riot, and epidemic and hunger
everywhere.

The Gaunt acres were changing under these exigencies.

Negro women had cut up into lengths the fallen pine trees,
and chopped down the rest, to build for themselves rude log cabins.
These would be stronger than the tents. And, in any case, there were
no more tents to be had: the Army's stored supplies had been exhausted by the millions driven from cities.

Hour by hour, day by day, the colored women now hacked at
the prostrate tough trunks of palmettos, stacking and burning them
as they were grubbed out. Every afternoon Paula, Kate and Edwinna assisted in this clearing of the land.

Paula had a promise of a bulldozer, but it never came.

As fast as the scrub was removed the ground beneath—here
bare coral ledge, there pothole, and here, again, sand a foot deep—
was planted in crops with the best promise of calories and vitamins:
sweet potatoes, tomatoes, pigeon peas, beans. A cow foraged
for sparse grass on the land and its milk was divided between the
children and six young pigs. Every acorn from the live oaks was re-
trieved by the children and fed to the pigs.

Food. There was no longer quite enough, ever, for anyone.

Even so, Florida had one food source which gave it an advantage: fish and game. In this period, teams of women, taught by the
wives of commercial and charterboat fishermen, put out to sea every
day and brought back groupers, mutton snappers, mackerel, kingfish
and other edible species. Additional teams, in rowboats, equipped
with lanterns and spears, nightly coursed the immense flats of the
Bay of Florida in search of spiny lobsters, crabs and even rays.

At first a good deal of the catch spoiled before it could be dis-
tributed. But by late autumn the housewives were accustomed to
long walks to market and used to queuing up for their portion of
sea booty. Besides, some ice plants were in operation again.

But there was never enough food to satisfy a nation which had constantly overeaten. With ceaseless effort, the women produced, in Greater Miami and its land-sea environs, barely enough to maintain life and energy. If only the migrants had not come pouring over the faraway border of the state, they might eventually have stabilized their food needs. But there were always more mouths, more thousands of mouths, tens of thousands more. And the arrivals, after their formidable journeys, with their heartbreaking destitution, were very seldom able to take a useful place in the community enterprises until they had been rehabilitated and trained. . . .

That autumn Edwinna was transferred to the Hunt Section. Her twin brother Edwin had taught her to shoot and taken her many times into the Everglades in quest of doves, quail, ducks, rabbits and bigger game. Once, Edwinna had bagged a panther. Twice, she had shot at—and missed—bears. Several times, she had brought down a deer. The transfer took her away from home on the long trips arranged by her section.

She and other women would camp out for a week or two while, by day and night, in saw grass, hammock and cypress swamp, by boat and on foot, they sought food for the hungry coastal cities. The chase not only fitted Edwinna's temperament but was infinitely preferable to backsplitting labor on interminable rows of garden truck. Moreover, she did not have to look, every evening, in the exhausted sunset hours, at Alicia's grave. She did not have to watch each daily step of Paula's losing fight to maintain morale. There was danger in the chase, exhilarating danger; and it was not just the formidability of terrain, or the risk of getting lost, or the peril of diamondback rattler, coiled moccasin and night-slinking coral snake, or the jeopardy of a wounded, threshing alligator, a hit panther, a cub-defending bear.

A new hazard lurked in the endless grasslands and the silent, pool-floored forests: the risk of a rifle shot. For some of the Seminole Indian women, dazed by the catastrophe that had taken their males,

decided the event was caused by their old enemies, the near-exter-
minators of their tribe: white people. Furthermore, they had always
regarded the Everglades as their own. The organized invasion of its
deep reaches threatened resources upon which these women and
their men had always depended. So, in a sullen fury, they fought
back. From the center of jungle islands in the saw grass, where their
dugouts had been hidden, or from behind the marching arcades of
cypress trees, they would greet a group of white women and their
dogs with a fusillade. Some of these would die. Some would be
wounded. The unscathed would fall to the ground and shoot
back.

But the Seminoles were never foolish enough to close in: they
would hide until darkness came and paddle away—murderous ghosts,
ghosts with an understandable reason for their hatred of the white
man's white women.

Edwinna became one of the "scouts" of her section, going always ahead, stealthily, to locate concealed assassins and give warning
in time. . . .

All over the world where law had not yet been established, in
cities, in towns, in the country, such small "wars" were raging. Bat-
tles for game, for granaries, for cropland and for the most habitable
quarters left in burned-out cities. . . .

In this same period, another fad developed which was to have
its shattering effect on Paula.

A year before, with hope of the return of the males still vividly
alive, with partial mastery of the original catastrophe as a heartening stimulant, with stores and supplies of goods manufactured before
the Disappearance on hand, the women had beguiled at least some
of their hours by giving parties and bees, by playing games and dancing.

Now, month by month, a grimmer reality asserted itself. The
civilization in which they lived and upon which they depended was
not one they could maintain alone. Here and there a woman under-

stood the operation of a plant or a machine, laboratory technique, an industrial process, even an entire business or a profession. But those who had the knowledge could not train sufficient numbers in time to save key equipment and machinery from ruin.

Thousands upon thousands of plants and factories lay idle because women could not learn fast enough how to run them. Idle, the machines rusted and corroded; idle and untended, belts moldered away, gears and bearings froze in red decay, intricate mazes of electrical equipment lost their glitter and their power of function, insulation rotted, foundations gave way, minor fires chewed at individual installations and were extinguished too late, windows broke and the weather entered, followed slowly by insects and vines.

In addition, the competence of women in heavy industry was small. There was no one to mine coal. Few volunteers could be found even to try, for the dank galleries alarmed the unaccustomed women, uncertain power supply often stranded them at the bottoms of shafts, and unfamiliarity led to mine explosions. The women chopped wood for domestic fuel and concentrated on trying to maintain and expand a remnant of the petroleum industry. Oil wells still pumped in Texas; the Big Inch was made to flow and, in lieu of ocean tankers, trucks carried gasoline from those few refineries in operation.

The making of steel was given up. There was steel in the burned areas to cannibalize. It was chore enough, and more than enough, to rework what metal lay above ground. Other types of mining, except where open pits gave access, were abandoned; and other basic industries perished through default.

What had always been a fact—ignored, unnoticed—now became the most cogent fact: humanity had built its cities largely to lighten the burden of domesticity, which had been woman's burden. The bulk of all civilized activity had directly or indirectly entered the service of woman and her home. Steel was forged for rails and bridges which in turn transferred food and fabrics, small machines and materials that, in the end, went to houses, the buildings serving the houses, and the goods and gadgets that steadily moved from the buildings to the houses. Woman, with her car, her supermarket, her department store, her home and its electrical accessories—and the children of the woman—were the chief consumers. Yet women, by and large, knew very little about the mechanism sustaining them.

The dilemma was simple: their dependence upon civilization was equal to their ignorance. Having employed, consumed and come to count on thousands of "products," the mechanical etiology of which few had even contemplated, women were also cut off from simpler, more primitive techniques.

Even farm women were thus at a loss. Many had never milked cows or churned their own butter. When the milking machines stopped for want of power, when the trucks no longer called for the waiting cans, when the separators broke down, they did not know how to tend the cows or dispose of the milk. The "civilizing" of womankind had proceeded at a very superficial level, a level which had rarely aroused any extensive intellectual curiosity in them. So, with the civilized plant stopped dead, most women had no resources on which to fall back.

After recovering from the initial shock, they had experienced a surge of hope founded on the surprising discovery that some few of their number were competent in most fields, for millions had worked in industries and tens of thousands in professions. But when time passed and it became apparent that "man's world," which had been largely devoted to woman, could not be restored in anyone's lifetime, that hope withered.

A remnant of faith was pinned on the possibility of parthenogenesis—the chance that a means of artificial fertilization might be discovered. But it finally appeared that, even under the best of fortunes, generations would have to be born and live and die—generations in which the putative men were trained by women—before a flow of minerals, metals, timber and industrial vegetable products would furnish the basis for any such luxurious bounty as had obtained in the old civilization.

That fact had widespread psychological repurcussions. Women at first had tried by every means to keep alive romantic images of the male sex. But in the second autumn following the Disappearance, an opposite reaction occurred. Feeling themselves victims of a circumstance both overwhelming and without justice, frustrated by lack of knowledge precisely where their dependence was greatest, many began to *blame* men for their predicament.

That bitter note first appeared in the harangues of instructors and lecturers who fanned out from Washington to "orient" various groups. Paula encountered it in a talk given by a Miss Edna Wentler, who wound up an address on Sanitation Management, at the Coral Gables Town Club, with an extraordinary statement:

"We from the nation's capital are particularly concerned to warn against softness, sentimentality and lowering of morale, at this time. In my own *personal* opinion, the going of the males is a deserved fate. They spoiled us. And they left us without the means to sustain life as we had known it. Our present situation is thus, doubly, the fault of males! At Washington we have every expectation that a way will be found to restore childbirth and so to sustain our kind. It is my own *personal* feeling that we might do well, when we learn to propagate without males, to continue our species *without* males! We were *able*, but they kept us from learning. We were *willing*, but they voted us the lowly chores. We could have been their *equals*—their *superiors!*—but they maintained us in subservience. Now they are gone. This is *our* century! Out of these dark and trying times a new world may be born, a world of and for women, ruled by women alone!"

At the conclusion, it was Paula's first impulse to boo, or to call out, "Phooie!"

Yet she did not. Instead, she found in herself a vague agreement and even some slight pleasure. There was a wisp of truth beneath the silly phrases of this spinster who, Paula thought, had known nothing more about men than she had read and heard. So Paula smiled, but she also nodded. For she had taken on responsibilities far beyond her known capacity. She had done what many men would have funked. She was too compassionate actually to enjoy, as some women did, authority amidst the misfortunes of others; but she felt self-satisfaction in the effective performance of roles which had always been masculine.

Paula did not boo. Yet she was startled when many women applauded—and with violence.

"She's got something!" Ella said after the talk. "I would have loved—just for one day—to have the men *but* under the thumbs of women!"

Bella Elliot demurred. "She's just an old pickle! Nobody ever loved her. She's probably a Lesbian."

"And what," Ella answered, "is wrong with that—in a manless world, darling?"

Bella laughed gently, shook her soft, brown head and answered, "It's ersatz."

"Tell me something nowadays that isn't!" The blonde poetess walked away.

Mrs. Treddon-Stokes took her place. "An excellent lecture! Inspiring! A world of women—forever! A quite new thought!"

It was not so much the argument as the manner of Mrs. Treddon-Stokes that caused Paula to say, "Don't judge everybody by your own lack of loneliness. We weren't all married to your Walter."

The towering woman pursed her lips. "Good breeding has disappeared along with other things!"

"Breeding that interfered with truth was never any good. We've *got* a woman's world. Do we like it?"

"Give us time!" said the tall matron. "*Time!* Personally, as I grow more accustomed to it, I find it increasingly interesting. I have formed new, fascinating friendships! I have found out what an utter wretch my husband was! My secret impressions of him—and of marriage—were far from incorrect!"

"I wonder what Walter's were?" Paula said rudely. . . .

The attitude of hostility toward the memory of men persisted and increased. Most of it was childishly emotional; but some took on the forms of intellectualism.

Thus, "Better-Off-Without-'Em" clubs spread amongst lower-class women while at the same time pretentious discussion groups considered whether or not (providing human breeding again became possible) women should take advantage of the potential "opportunity" and either limit the number of males to a select "breeding stock" trained for that purpose alone or do away with males the moment it was scientifically certain their "service" no longer would be required.

Hostility became a source of resurgent social life. Once again, women dressed up as men; but now their caricaturing was unleavened by sentiment. They acted out vicious roles: the drunk, the bully, the wifebeater, the cheat, the gambler, the criminal, the martinet, the fop, the sadist. Any argument that women had produced comparable types was refuted by attributing the cause of that to males. Women without men commenced proving, everywhere, the depth and the fury of the cruel slight they had endured for so long a time. . . .

One night, several Miami Better-Off-Without-'Em clubs paraded by torchlight. Paula saw them on the way home from a meeting.

The "men" were as repulsive as was customary—the women, as appealing. Pretty girls adorned floats, girls uninhibited by a two-sexed "modesty."

The floats represented community enterprises and service units; but the girls took delight in revealing beauties and charms for which there was no natural demand and which, these days, were generally sullied by labor and concealed by rough clothes.

Alone in her car, parked at a corner, looking over the heads of the crowd, Paula suddenly appreciated what it was men felt about women—as women.

A band played. The lighted, paper-decorated trucks moved slowly. Paula's conscious sense that the new tendency to demean men was wrong diminished as she watched. *What else could they do?* A feeling that this odd attitude was *justified* pervaded her mind and with it came an awareness, at first inadmissible but soon accepted, that ever since the Disappearance she herself had been a "man" amongst these beleaguered women. She had led, organized, fought to maintain her own household, accepted directorships, planned, ordered, and helped to govern. She, she alone—through her knowledge of languages—had even been her country's brief but effective ambassador in dealing with the preposterous "mission" from the Soviet.

If men were gone forever, she was like a man.

She stood up, at that point. A warm breeze blew upon her, a breeze that carried the fragrance of nearby frangipani. The band played with a rare ecstasy, it seemed to Paula. And as the girls went by, dark hair, gold hair, red hair stirring, bare flesh shining, Paula had a diffuse, physical sensation of their desirability. For the instant, she could project upon the flash of every eye, the curve of every shoulder, the shimmer and shade of every lock of hair such desires and such aggressive passions as men have.

A moment later she sat down—collapsed, very nearly, from the intensity of the sensation. She was shaking. Her mind teetered between two emotions—one of yearning for the men to return and the other, an abnormal desire which, she believed, rose from the long assumption of men's duties.

When she drove on toward home, it was with reluctance and regret. She had felt the same way in her childhood when the curtain had been rung down on the first play she had seen and the glamour of theatrical spectacle had abruptly become the getting of hats and coats in a people-smelling, bleak auditorium. The parade, the beautiful girls, the glitter, the frangipani fragrance clung to her—or she to them; it was hard to bear the commonplace night, the dirty streets, the bumps and turns and the occasional glaring trucks.

Kate was at home, quietly sewing by candlelight. The children were asleep.

Paula looked at the dark-haired girl, at the strain and sadness in her eyes as she smiled a welcome. Paula dropped her notebooks and put her long-strapped bag on a table. She thought Kate was like the girls on the floats.

She sat down and talked about the parade.

Kate parted her lips but said nothing while she listened to every uneasy intonation.

"Of course," Paula said at last, with a shrug, "anybody with a psychological background can understand this whole down-with-men business! What women are doing is expressing the frustrations—the hostilities and aggressions frustrations make—that had piled up even before the Disappearance. We were forever being told we were equal—and forever being kept from behaving equally. We were brought up to think of ourselves as independent—and then forced into dependence. Look at us now! We don't even know enough to do more than barely exist!"

"Besides," Kate interrupted, surprising Paula a little, "we haven't anything *better* to do with our emotions *anyhow*. Anything *whatsoever!*"

"There's that." Paula gazed curiously at the girl and returned to her theme. "We couldn't, actually, most of us, *love men completely,* because the whole picture of life was too *un*loving! Follow some of your feelings for one little evening and you were disgraced! Even divorced! Yet they insisted you should have freedom and initiative! Get even a *political* opinion contrary to your husband's and, for most wives, hell moved in! They sent you to school and made you work and told you good marks meant everything. If you were like me, you topped *all* the boys in your class. You went to college. You studied. You earned degrees. You married. And then—*what?* You had to learn a lot of new things about running a house and raising babies and taking care of measles and ordering groceries and then about architecture and interior decoration and plumbing and how to run a waxer. Meanwhile, the years of hard, hard work to get an education went down the sewer! You married a *brighter* man with an even *better* education and your light went right out, no matter how bright *it* was! Is it any *wonder* women feel hostile about men? Aggressive?" Her eyes flashed.

Kate nodded gently and sighed more gently still. She sewed while Paula reflected, not contritely, on her outburst.

Presently Kate said, "You know, I think I'm going to get a job somewhere and go away." She didn't look up.

"Go *away*! *Kate!* You couldn't quit us! You've got a tremendous job right here, running things! And Hester to help you! If you went away, you'd wind up with a flock of odious characters, sleeping in bunks and eating stew twice a day, working in a mill or in the fields!"

Kate nodded in miserable agreement and stopped sewing. A tear, shiny in the candlelight, fell from her eyes onto her wrist.

"Is it still—Alicia?" Paula asked softly.

"Oh, partly." Kate put her handiwork on the divan.

"And partly—what?"

"You wouldn't understand." Kate looked up now, smiled as if forgivingly through more unfallen tears, and said, "I guess I'll go to bed. I'm tired." She began to loosen her long, black braids.

The fact that Kate would be irreplaceable, that she had come as the one boon in a period of endless difficulty, seemed of less consequence to Paula than a sudden-glimpsed loneliness. With a murmur, she crossed to the divan, moved the sewing and put her arm around the girl. "You mustn't go, Kate! You just *mustn't*! Honestly, I'd feel utterly lost! I'd have to stop all the work I'm doing and take over the household. I'd feel"—she laughed—"like an abandoned husband."

"Would you?" Kate's eyes fixed hopefully on Paula's. "I didn't believe any of you—Edwinna or you or Bella—or *any* of *you* had such feelings! You're all so darned cold! You always seem to approach everything with a lot of thoughts, merely, and talk. Talk, talk, *talk!*"

"I know. We do. It's foolish."

"I'm fond of you," the younger girl said urgently. "Very. Maybe too much. You've been good to me. I've felt, since I came here, there wasn't anything you wouldn't do for me."

"But there isn't, dear!" Paula said it quickly.

Kate lowered her head. "I know. I guess, inside I'm just a beast. And not appreciative."

"What do you mean, Kate?" Paula's voice had become flat and tense as a different interpretation of Kate's mood occurred to her.

The girl untwisted her braids and shook out her hair. "I wish," she said in a low tone, "I *was* your wife, in a way. Sort of. I wish— you were—a man. I wish"—her voice rose—"you, or Bella, or Edwinna—but mostly you—weren't so damned *prissy!* That's what I can't stand! I wasn't brought up the way you were. My people may have been no-account, but they wouldn't kill themselves, practically, to keep from admitting they had feelings! And they wouldn't just give you the cold edge of a dirty look for showing the feelings you had, no matter *how* you showed them!"

"I see," Paula said in a dry voice, after a pause. "I'd always thought—you—"

"You always thought I was a grown-up baby!" Kate interrupted. "You knew I came from the wrong side of the tracks. *Everybody* knows that! But you never stopped to figure what *that* meant!"

"What *does* it mean?" Paula felt her heart pound.

The blue eyes were not meek now, and not angered. Kate's mouth was relaxed. Her hair fell darkly all about. She no longer seemed tired or taut but flexible and without resistance. She leaned back, her knees apart, her hands at her sides. What Paula had thought of as helplessness and adorableness had changed; the quality in her now was not merely wantonness, but inviting surrender.

Seeing it with her newly opened eyes, with a surge of sympathy, Paula made a strong effort to weigh her emotions: *That's what men see! When a girl looks like that, they know!*

Kate answered gently, "I'll tell you what it means on my side of the tracks. It means you have older sisters and brothers; younger ones too. It means, in families like mine, your father runs around. And your mother takes her revenge when she can. It means you long for just two things—money and a good time, Paula. Pleasure. To be satisfied. It means your sisters grow up ahead of you and make a pass at getting things any way they can. If they meet a guy with a big car, they go in the big car. If some older woman with dough gets a crush on them and wants to do things for them and 'help' them, they let her. And they tell you all about it, Paula. If you're attractive—like me—when you get to be about fifteen, your sisters·take you along. They know men who like them young, the younger the better; and the more *you* know and the more *you'll* do, the better."

"Oh."

"In a city like this people like that are common. There used to be a big future for party girls here. And the less fussy girls are about what kind of party, the more they get asked places."

"Of course I knew that," Paula said. "In a sense. I just never connected it—"

"—with me. With anybody *you* met. Sure! I understand. And no wonder! I'm smarter than you think. I always was. I realized, by the time I was sixteen and my sisters were dragging me everywhere, that if you played innocent, it paid off. People are so darned stuck on themselves that even when they think they're sinning, they want to think nobody could make you do it with them, but them! A whole lot of what people call 'love' isn't a darned thing but that!"

Such an observation from Kate astonished Paula and it added force to all she was feeling. She nodded and swallowed.

Kate went on: "What finally happened to me, was I fell for a fellow, though. Higgie. And got married. And had Georgie. And I didn't mind it or miss the life I'd been having. Not really. I liked it. Except, once in a while." She frowned, smiled—and did not take her eyes from Paula. "Yes, once in a while, I missed *some* things. If you've been around as much as me—no one man, no *guy*, alone—will leave you always completely satisfied. And there it is!"

She mused a moment, her eyes friendly, unwavering, appealing. "Anyway, when the men vanished, I was scared. It was *too* much of a shock, like it was for almost everybody else. I was also stuck, *plenty!* I knew I'd have to get out of the bungalow. That night I decided I'd have to find a place to live where people had money, and an inside track, and could get things and help me. I always did like you, Paula, even if I hadn't seen you very often. You're smart and you're important and you know how to manage and you're rich and you've got sex appeal. You're the bossy type but I don't mind that. You're the protective type too, and I like that. I knew, though, you'd only care about me if I seemed to be the innocent type. Meek and helpless. So that's how I acted."

"It's funny!" Paula murmured after a quiet moment. "A couple of years ago I'd have been thoroughly outraged. I'd have felt taken in. Now I don't mind. I feel flattered. Maybe even charmed."

The younger woman answered knowingly, "*That's* how it *really is!* Only, we're not allowed to admit it. Even the people who do find out stay scared. Scared of other people. Reputation. Of cops, even. I'm glad you aren't mad at me, Paula."

"No, dear." Paula looked away.

This was the moment of final determination. Her heart still beat heavily. In her memory she saw again the procession of girls and, again, the lascivious throngs of women along the street. In the same memory she saw a group of other women, women who had sometimes held important executive positions in the days before the Disappearance, women who had cropped their hair short and worn mannish suits, man-strong women with men's wills and a yet curious immaturity toward men. In imagination she now could see herself, sleek and dashing in a new, secretive way. And suddenly she could see more: the image of Bill. Her man.

Curiously enough, she could see her lovers too. In that churning sequence of thoughts she discovered what they had meant: reassurance, symbols of emancipation, proof of independence, tangible evidence to her inner self that she was free and equal with men. With all men. They had meant more: compensation, revenge, envy paid back, a woman bitterly justifying her resented womanhood.

The spectacle was no longer exciting or strengthening. All she had attempted was to balance a dishonest scales, to assert the power of certain hidden but genuine impulses. These, in a world without men, had finally bloomed as extravagant emotions and strange perceptions. A great, concealed part of her had unconsciously *identified itself as a man*. At length, under unnatural conditions, it had broken through its own barricade and she was conscious of the truth about herself.

She had become conscious with a fierce pleasure.

But pleasure, like every inordinate tide, ebbed as she sat there. All that she had been forbidden to let herself feel about herself when she was young, to explore, if she had wanted to (and she would have explored it if she had been allowed to)—all she had been ordered to dismiss as unworthy (all that Kate still felt, all that was, indeed, forever embodied in Kate)—had been bottled up intact through the years. It had been socially exploited, to cause her to compete with men. And she had been left without a way of escape or a means of unreserved emotional expression. She had envied men, always. She had come close, at last, to being a charademan. She had reached that place in frustration and want and nervous confusion where she had nearly become, in the real world, all she had hidden inside the woman she had merely believed to be real.

"What are you smiling at?" Kate asked sharply. She had been watching Paula in silence for several minutes.

"The world. Not *us*, darling. *Not* us. You better go to bed,

Kate. I'm shot too. Going, myself, in a few minutes. I'll sleep on the couch in Bill's office tonight. You can have the bedroom."

The girl's eyes filled with tears. "I—thought—"

"I know." Physically, Paula felt exhausted. But she had found a way, or the hope of a way, by which a powerful weakness could be made the source of a humble strength. Her eyes shone.

"I was *right!*" Kate said in a loud ugly voice. "You *are* prissy! You're too good for your *own* good! You don't *really* know anything at all!"

"Kate! Go to bed. I'm sorry for you and I'm fond of you but I'm not a child, thank God! Good night, dear."

15

IN WHICH THE PARALLEL LIMITATIONS OF MAN AND SCIENCE
MEET THIS SIDE OF INFINITY.

Gaunt spent that Christmas at Princeton.

He arrived in the university town too late on Christmas Eve to join a modest party by means of which a group of scientists from the Institute for Advanced Study were trying to forget their failures and their many sorrows. His plane had been ordered to take him to New York, but it had landed in Camden, with engine trouble. By a taxicab, which had also broken down short of Princeton, and thereafter by arduous hitchhiking, the philosopher approached the home of Emerson Mobley, vice-chairman of Gaunt's committee. He walked the dark, familiar streets wearily.

In the days before the Disappearance, Mobley, a noted physical chemist, and his handsome young wife had entertained Paula and Bill Gaunt in a house now unlighted. A house with a decrepitude that could be discerned even in silhouette: the leafless shrubbery was untrimmed and a tree limb, felled by some autumn gale, lay embedded in the lawn. The porch, had, even in the wintry chill, a smell of dust, of old paint, of rust and dry rot that exuded from summer furniture standing wretchedly in the murk. The boards sagged as Gaunt dropped his big bag with a tired "Damn!"

He saw an envelope pinned to a part of the screen door which had not fallen away. After beating his mittened hands together to warm them, he took out a pocket flashlight and read the note:

> Bill—!
>
> There's a party in progress at Blake's place. Come over if you feel in the mood. God knows, it won't be much. A few drinks, some music, and perhaps a wraith of gaiety before we give up the effort. I waited for you till ten o'clock and then left, hoping one of those infernal accidents that are slowly thinning us out hadn't taken our Chairman. If you arrive beat up, there's a leg of lamb, part of one, anyway, in the kitchen window box.
>
> EM

Gaunt opened the door, aware, as he did so, that a night watchman had seen him arrive and was peering from across the street. Evidently the watchman had been forewarned; he didn't accost the philosopher. The flashlight led to a wall switch; there was electric power. Gaunt left his bag in the hall.

He was eating some of the lamb—there seemed to be no other food in the house—when Mobley returned. A short, stocky person with light-brown eyes, large ears, a stamping tread and enough gray hair for three or four men of his age, which, Gaunt thought, was less than fifty. The chemist was quite deaf.

"Welcome!" Emerson Mobley yelled as he slammed the front door. He sounded slightly drunk. "Welcome to my falling-down demesne! A House of Usher in slow motion!" He tramped across the kitchen and gave Gaunt a thump on the back. "Lucky guy! Florida! A sun tan! And we sit in this gelid Gehennah, trying to work on something nobody understands!"

Gaunt grinned. "You should see my place! Hurricane last fall. Piled trees on the house and knocked my pine woods to smithereens. I plugged the roofholes with concrete and left the trees for firewood—if the insects don't get them first." His breath, Gaunt noticed, was visible in the grubby kitchen; he still wore his overcoat.

Mobley picked up a slice of cold meat and bit out a semicircle. "Got a fire laid in my den upstairs. Come on. Hard trip?"

"Nothing unusual. Slow. Couple of delays."

In Mobley's room the fire was presently lighted. He pulled up leather chairs, rummaged in a box of what appeared to be wastepaper and located a bottle of gin, half full. "Care for a dram?"

Gaunt nodded as he took off his coat. In front of the fire he felt warm for the first time since leaving Miami. He accepted the liquor in a none-too-clean tumbler, drank half of what his host had poured, shuddered, and relaxed a little. "How goes it?"

Mobley set his drink aside untasted, took a chair, and eyed the rising flames. "Rotten! God! I wish Marinda was around! It goes lousy, Bill. The university, for instance. Thinking of closing after this next semester. There's no incentive and the students won't work. Just sit in class and glare at the lecturer. Or start horseplay, and mighty rough stuff too. Or cut class altogether. Last week I leaned forward on my desk while I was lecturing"—the chemist shook his head and suddenly sniffled, as if the memory had started tears of self-pity running into his nose—"and the whole thing fell apart! Pitched me over it, off the podium, onto the floor. Sprained my shoulder. The class thought it was hilarious! They'd taken advantage of a habit I have of leaning, and spent the night sawing up the desk and covering the saw marks."

"Shame."

"Sure, it's a shame! Though I don't feel very different, myself.

Then there's mob temper. Any little thing will send the whole campus into a violent brawl. They just pile on each other without asking what the fight's about. A dozen of them have been badly hurt and it's only a matter of time before somebody's killed."

Gaunt nodded again. His host reached for his glass and emptied it at a gulp.

Gaunt said, "How are things at the Institute?"

"Bob Blake can at least keep order there. And he's still full of ideas. Starts some new project every day. The same old limp nonchalance that hides the slick strategist and the steely brain."

"A great man, Em."

The chemist thought that over. "Yes, Bill. A great man. For a long time I wondered what still drove him on. A passion for pure science? Maybe. That damned common motive of wanting to get back your wife? Partly. But it didn't explain enough. Blake's fiddled with Oriental philosophy and I wondered if he had that karma, or Atman-identification, or that Nirvana, Orientals are supposed to achieve. It's rubbish, of course. But I wondered. Then, one day, I hit on it. Remember, after he got through the uranium bomb job, he kept talking about how the scientists had sinned?"

Gaunt smiled wanly. "I remember."

"It's *that*! Our pet genius is driven by a guilt complex. He thinks the women vanished because of what he—and I—and to some extent you—and a few hundred more of us—worked out for the love of dear old Manhattan District!"

Gaunt stared into the fire. "Seems far off."

"Light years!"

Mobley offered Gaunt another drink, saw that he had not finished the first, and poured his own tumbler half full. He swirled the transparent liquid. "Every night now, Bill, this is it. A pint. Some nights a quart. Then, for a while, I sleep. A while. When I wake up, I have about four fingers. Then I can stand beginning another day. Classes, my lab in the afternoon, maybe a conference or two in the evening. Then—home, the bottle and bed. I'm an alcoholic."

The philosopher was moved by regret, by sorrow, by pity, and by anger at this evidence of one more progressive defeat. "Why not lay off, Em? Your brain's among the best. If the world ever needed it, the world needs it now!"

"*What* world?" Mobley rose and stood in front of the fireplace— short, heavy body and big, square head. "A world of residual lepers. A world, you might say, where our very disease has destroyed the frontal tissue that might once have found its cure. It began long ago. Long, *long* ago! Pure science left out man, so it was just pure ego. And that's all that remains nowadays—ego. Right?"

"I know what you mean."

"The ego—and hunger. And death, in the future, somewhere. Marinda gone forever. No substitute. Heavens knows, I've tried to find one. Haven't you?"

"No."

"The more fool you, then! The more prude! Or maybe your glands are second rate, Bill! If you were like me, a shaker of pepper and salt with the emphasis on pepper, you'd have tried to find escape. Some solution for the world as it is. And it would always have left you thinking of—your Paula. As I think of my Marinda."

"That was my starting thesis."

Emerson Mobley shrugged, poured more gin, and, to Gaunt's weary horror, commenced to snivel. "Everything in me is dead, Bill. Dead—dead—dead! I don't *give* a damn! Someday, when I see the students brawling, I'll pitch in, just for release. And I wouldn't be the first professor!"

"Maybe," Gaunt replied with quiet compassion, "we ought to go to bed, Em. I've had a rugged day."

And that, Gaunt thought—grateful for quilts and blankets enough, heedless of the faintly sour smell that showed they had long been used without laundering—*is*—*was the magnificent Emerson Mobley!*

The man who could make molecules of the isotypes, with one hand tied behind his back!

Gaunt sighed morosely in the darkness of the clammy bedroom—and fell asleep.

Bob Blake sat on a table cross-legged. His crewcut was as crisp as ever and his smile as boyish. His perpetual cigarette snowed ash on a floor that showed how often he sat on the same table and how infrequently the lecture hall was cleaned. Gaunt saw Tateley, tired and looking a decade older; Wendley had come down; Ascott and Tretter, two more of his committeemen, also had managed to make the trip. A dozen other scientists were there—young, middle-aged and one very old man with dark-brown eyes and a far-off smile whom they addressed in almost reverential tones. Aside from these few, ranged in wooden seats that faced Blake and the blackboards, the huge room was empty. But it was warm.

Blake opened the conclave. "First, gentlemen, I think we ought to thank Bill Gaunt for his summary of our work. A fine job!"

"Until," said Wendley, "he tacked on that psychological garbage."

Blake's gray eyes twinkled. "I was going to suggest discussing that. I thought it was first rate. But, let's at least have the courtesy to acknowledge the committee's effort. It helped us here at Princeton. Brought up several new points. Stitched a lot of theory together. Bill, it was masterful. Few men alive today could have applied such broad knowledge to so many different fields. The chair would welcome a motion."

"I move," Tateley said, rising tremulously, "that we thank Dr. Gaunt for his report and his committee for the surveys and the research that went into the report."

The motion was seconded and unanimously carried.

"As to Bill's own suggestions—" Blake then began.

Wendley was on his feet. "Perfectly monstrous! To begin with, it is an imposition on Faith that a layman, an intellectual alchemist, should even suggest the Word of God is open to *any* analysis! The idea that the Original Sin is the reverse of what we know it to be, I, as a learned man, a scientist and a devout Christian, regard as pure and perfect diabolism!"

Mobley, who had breakfasted on more cold lamb and his "four fingers" of gin, seemed nonetheless to be his old self. He now jumped thumpingly to his feet. "Doctor," he boomed, facing the physicist, "you'll find yourself alone in that position. I was fascinated by Bill's argument that genus homo had made a basic psychological error 'way back in the dawn age—and stupidly stuck to it. If for no other reason than that man's history ever since he came down from trees has been a constant parade of ambitious starts and flat failures, the thing seems worth considering. Is there"—he turned to the group of men in the way a panoramic camera surveys a crowd—"anybody *else* here, who thinks it's wrong for an abstract thinker to contemplate, critically, the legends in Genesis?"

One or two men laughed.

Mobley nodded. "There you are, Dr. Wendley! My *own* feeling, as I read the paper at the end of Bill's report, was that he had got to the edge of some new foundation of the relation of mass energy to consciousness. But I couldn't go on from there."

"I think," Blake said, "Bill made himself pretty clear."

Gaunt had not expected the meeting to begin with a discussion of his essay. He had not even anticipated his effort would come in for much comment. He said embarrassedly, "It was intended merely to suggest lines for a new orientation. Perhaps we'd do best just to skip it."

"No, no, *no!*" Blake responded cheerfully. "The implications are too important. One of them is what we think incorrectly about man—so that *all* man thinks and does is incorrect. The corollary that most interested me was the notion that as fast as we found anything out, from how to use fire to how to split atoms, we had applied it in the most *immediately expedient* fashion."

"I didn't say that," Gaunt protested. "Not precisely."

The young physicist chuckled and nodded. "Implied it." He dropped a leg over the table edge and began to swing it. "And it's true! Objectivity, you said, was our God. Subjectivity—where our God is—we avoided or treated in some banal stereotype. That was the thesis, Bill. What does it mean in everyday terms? It means that man *never* developed—he never even seriously considered developing a way of evaluating what he learned *before* he applied it. When he hit on fire, who knows what he did first with it? Maybe, for centuries, he used it only in religious ceremony. Maybe only for torturing captives. Maybe only to signal with. Maybe only as a weapon, to burn out an enemy ambush or to hurl on spear points. The artifacts don't go back that far, that lucidly. Maybe he hit on light and warmth and cookery only after *millenniums of misuse!* If so—why? Because he didn't work up a technique for self-evaluation. Because he never bothered to consider, to *discover*, what *he* really was and really *needed.* He made up that part, conceitedly! We still do. He never extrapolated long-range consequences. We don't now. He probably *never* meditated the discovery of fire, as a whole, in relation to his species, as a continuing whole." Blake paused and said, "Yes, Tretter?"

Excited by this line of thought, the New Yorker leaped to his feet. His black eyes shone. His black Vandyke bristled as if its follicles were capable of pointing their separate hairs. Incredibly learned, fabulously energetic, Saul Tretter was a renowned anthropologist. At this time, in an unspotted tweed jacket and unsullied gray slacks, he also happened to be the best-dressed man in the lecture room.

"A very useful analogue!" he began in a shrill voice. "Another way of saying what I have harped on all my life! The twentieth-century procession of discovery and invention has been accompanied by social imbecility. Take electronics. Did anybody ever ask whether we *wanted* the so-called commercial radio? *Needed* it? Would *benefit* by it? Not really, no! Was there a social body to consider whether or not the arts and the sciences—every communicable idea—should be crassly *exploited* for the mere purpose of *selling oatmeal?* No! Were the people *ready?* We didn't ask. Was there serious meditation on the *moral lullaby* effect? The *hypnosis?* Or the spectacle of young children *disturbed* by titillations of a nightmarish sort? Of *students* doing their lessons in the bland, psychological bath of comfortable sales talk? *No!* Or television. Were we asked to ask ourselves what it could do, would do, and therefore *should* do? No! Or what it should never be allowed to do? Not by anybody! Gentlemen, consider! For century after century the Chinese had gunpowder and never used it in a *weapon!* Most laudable! The protective and directive functioning of what Dr. Gaunt would call an instinct has been repressed in Western man. Also the dignifying function and the integrating function." He bowed jerkily toward the philosopher. "Others would call these things common sense."

Gaunt nodded back. The audience chuckled.

Tretter went on: "In short and in sum, to exploit every finding amongst a public not well enough educated, not even bright enough in many cases to understand the exploitative mechanisms, has been insane. Yet it has been going on since the first human brain made the first superanimal finding. What appealed at the moment to the finder—what seemed useful at the moment to the group—that, alone, controlled the future use of the new information. From that, I argue as follows: vanity has been the potent motive: the desire of the little person, or the little people, to do, right now, the most immediately prestigious thing. To *profit*. To become *powerful*. To defeat unexamined *adversaries*. To make garments and ornaments without regard to the extirpation of species. To eat now even though it destroys tomorrow's topsoil. To attract a woman unnaturally. To make women attractive, according to any of a thousand momentary criteria. Hence, to show off. That, above all else! And here is my point, gentlemen. We learned *to use time as a dimension* and it greatly differentiated us from the instinctual world, the merely three-dimensional world. Man had a fourth. But we exploited it, wholly. We never used the time we had to contemplate what we were or what we did. For determining *that*, we merely took a tradition, a religion, a culture—lock, stock and barrel, and went ahead uncritically. It was convenient. And *mad!* The brain that learned, the brain that discovered, the brain that invented, was never brain enough to say, 'I must also think about *results*. *About applications*. *Consequences*. About needs and uses *beyond my own* and those of *my tribe*.' Never! Never! Never!"

"Hear, hear!" someone murmured.

Tretter whirled in apparent rage. "You, gentlemen! With the knowledge of an atomic chain reaction, what did *you* make? A power plant? A still to remove salt from the sea and irrigate deserts? An engine for travel? No! A *bomb*. It was the *expedient* thing, the final and quintessential example of the process. Ah—this vanity! I will not assert that Dr. Gaunt has correctly explained its etiology. But I *do* insist that the *fact of human vanity*—the *failure* to use our new human dimension of time—not just to discover and exploit the new discovery but equally to think of *how* to use it, or *whether* to spread it everywhere instantly—is the *curse* of the species. In that, Dr. Gaunt is eminently correct! We *are mad*. We have *been* mad since we decided to use our frontal lobes consistently, but only in half a fashion. In the present tense alone, and the future—posterity—be damned!

"It is not surprising that so many older societies were repelled by America! They felt instinctively the lack of balance here. Most of us were devoted most of the time to accelerating appetite. To creating enlarged and abnormal appetite. To setting up hungers even in areas where we were already stuffed and overstuffed. Then, to satisfying these induced excesses. We called the process 'creating new and broader markets.' We called the result our 'high living standard.' Like banqueting Romans, we built short life and obsolescence into our products, or we soon made them obsolete with new things and arranged to junk the old, to market them secondhand or to export them. We feasted on objects and vomited them up, to gorge anew—around the clock and through the year and down the decades.

"In the face of such gluttony the God of our forebears became a depraved symbol. Churches were able to abet the farce only by degrading God. In any case, we hadn't had the courage and the initiative to revaluate God to match, at least, what we did know. And that, gentlemen, is a historical necessity, for whenever human images of God and human learning diverge—when God stands still and man progresses—it is God who must evolve, not learning that must be erased.

"We didn't bother with God. We raised the living standard and left untouched the standard of *being*. It declined, perforce. I'm an anthropologist, not a psychologist; certainly not a theologian, which is something I have hooted at all my life not so much for theology's lack of reason as for its cowardly failure to learn what's known. But I believe, gentlemen, that we, sitting here, right now, are in a state of schizophrenia. As Bill Gaunt said, the sexes were intended to add up to make one personality. Through the process he described, we have become split personalities. The women are here. It is *we* who are absent, absent because we have lost our minds, by default, by discord!"

He sat down abruptly and, for some time, no one spoke.

At last Blake, who had listened with half-smiling lips and occasional nods, said easily, "Well, Saul, supposing you and Bill *are* right?" He chuckled at his copying of Tretter's emphatic way of talking. "Supposing we have been crazed for ages, which any detached reading of our history would tend to confirm? Supposing we, sitting here, are lunatics? But, supposing, now—by some lucky stroke —we learned what happened to our females and got them back? How would you proceed to *restore* sanity?"

Tretter, it seemed, had not actually been angered at any time. His bright, black eyes flashed with amusement and his body shook with unvoiced laughter. "How shall the inmates of an asylum deliver themselves? you ask. Why, gentlemen, if I have put the *right* question—if Dr. Gaunt has done so—isn't it part of your scientific faith that you can then find the answer?"

Blake grinned ruefully. "We've boasted it was, yes."

Tretter got up again. "If—*if* we should hit upon one more miracle and undo the sinister condition in which we have spent nearly two hideous years, I would earnestly suggest that we at once assemble to consider what applications of science in our culture are dangerous, foolish, wasteful, or of no immediate great value. Abolish them. Continue research, of course. But concentrate, for a century or two, on human nature and *its* needs! Shape environment to those findings, but only after a long and judicious evaluation of humanity. Perhaps reduce the population by controlling birth; we breed with the immoral violence of *fish!* It is obscene, such a nonuse of the brain! Abandon cities! Who can live sanely in such places? Teach a good clean sex desire to the young: so taught, they might be prepared for more eugenical matings and they'd cease to be hundred per cent neurotics. Improve the stock. Great *Heaven!* We've applied the knowledge to cattle and *superstitiously* denied we could apply it to men—denied, even, we have the 'right' to try! What is the brain for, but to study *rights* and learn *the* right? Here's the dismal phenomenon I have often outlined, again at work, making us think in some obsolete moral pattern that we have the compulsive duty to save all life, prolong it, maintain hordes of the senile, but that we *must not* use the same brain to guide, control or delimit such repellent results of its activities! You understand? Suspend the old ecologies that have kept down our numbers and determined what sort of 'the strong' shall survive—as we've done—and man *must* then arrange a *deliberate* ecology! *Moral*—yes! But what is morality if it does not embody *all the truth we know?* It is rubbish! Superstition! Obscenity! Crime on racial scale—on planetary scale! Death!"

Wendley again said, "Diabolism!"

Ascott rose tremblingly and tremblingly said, "I agree with Tretter." He sat down, nodding, perhaps involuntarily.

Tateley, who had listened to the anthropologist with his head tilted back, his fingers raking through his white hair, now said, without getting up, "It would be a hell of a blow to what we used to call 'business enterprise'—until of course, men of affairs caught up with the new conditions. I agree, also."

"Does anybody," asked the hugely fat Miersner, of Harvard, "care to argue with these gentlemen? I mean to say, will any one defend man's ways and works of, say, 1950?"

Wendley responded, "We deviated from God's will!"

To which Tateley answered kindly, "Perhaps we did, Wen. The trouble with your viewpoint is, you won't find a man here who regards *your* personal capacity to *know,* to *accept on faith,* to discover by *revelation*—or otherwise singlehanded to infer and assert 'God's will' is in any way superior to *his* capacity. Why *should* anyone knuckle to your faith? And isn't that the trouble with religion in general? Gaunt says it's merely instinct. Lord knows, men cling to whatever they happen to have been taught in childhood, or whatever they have accepted since, with all the *tenacity* of the most instinctual insects. I'm no biologist. But the present behavior of religious men, and the whole past history of their behavior, looks entirely compulsive to me. Inflexible, unadaptive in the individual, reasonless. It sures does seem like instinct, like tropisms blown up to nth degrees by creatures capable of turning their sensations into images—who then *deny* they invented the images in order to worship and serve them. 'Faith,' seen that way, is wholly a *denial.* Another description of 'Original Sin' which I give Bill Gaunt free of charge. Religions explain what is autonomous in man and then are used to escape man's responsibility for servicing the creeds with reason and integrity. Compulsion and taboo is the process at the root of every living thing *but* man, and probably at *man's* roots, though he hasn't yet more than glimpsed the fact."

Wendley sighed without responding.

Blake said presently, "As we indicated some while ago, Bill Gaunt's summary might lead somewhere in our present situation. We physical scientists have hit on nothing suggestive. Nothing a tenth so suggestive, at any rate. However, bearing Bill's thesis in mind, I think this meeting should now review the main lines of current inquiry."

It was raining when Gaunt stepped outdoors. Raining in the cold, late afternoon. His colleagues moved, alone or in pairs, down a long walk under skeletal trees. Gaunt turned up the collar of his worn overcoat. Blake locked up the building and ran a little to overtake the philosopher.

"Pretty dim prospect."

Gaunt nodded.

"Where's your next stop?"

"Urbana."

"Good." They walked slowly in the sodden leaves. "Then?"

"Cal Tech. Maybe a stop or two en route."

"It's rugged—traveling, these days! But we need you, Bill. We need you—especially—to try to build up morale, and a co-operative sense, in the research teams. A lot of men have quit. Some are dead."

"I know."

"Branleigh committed suicide the other day."

Gaunt made no comment.

The young physicist went on: "Good man. He'd been working on the neoplasm end. Under Steady. Too bad."

"Too bad."

"Incidentally," Blake said, after several silent steps, "don't drop off at Portland. Trouble there."

"Riots?"

"Nothing so easy. Rain. Radioactive. Nobody knows how badly the area was poisoned—how many have been fatally injured. Place is being evacuated until the counterstudies come in."

"Russians?"

Blake sighed. "Yeah. Thank God, at least, we know what happened! They are still working on the power angle. But they let go a particularly potent hydrogen blast on the edge of the Yellow Sea. Bigger effect than anticipated—trust the muzhiks to make some damned grandiose mistake! They radioed instantly. Apologized mightily. Nothing we could do but watch. And traces began to show on our side of the Pacific in early December. Must have been a concentration—intact—that moved over Portland. And came down in the rain."

Gaunt shook his head sadly. They reached the corner. Blake grasped his arm. "I've got a little gas, Bill. Give you a lift anywhere?"

"No, thanks. Only going to the station from Em Mobley's house. Not far. There's supposed to be a train around eight."

"Em," the physicist mused, "is cracking up too. Liquor, for one thing. Notice?"

"Yes."

The younger man sighed heavily; his breath eddied visibly in front of his sharp features and rain drizzled through the, vapor. "Seems as if the brighter they are the faster they go, when the crack appears! You won't mind, Bill, if I replace him on your committee—?"

"He seemed all right today—"

"It's at night that he's anything but fine. In an emergency—"

"Of course, Bob. If you have to, then replace him. He's a friend. Good brain. I'd hate to lose him. But—"

Bob squeezed the philosopher's arm.

For a moment they looked into each other's eyes with friendship, with understanding, with the utmost compassion. Rain trickled down Gaunt's neck. Rain dribbled from the brim of Blake's flat felt hat. They shook hands.

"So long," Blake said, and swallowed.

Gaunt threw his arm over the other's shoulders and hugged him. "Stay on the job, Bobbie, God bless you!"

They parted.

In a shadowless glare at once too bright and not bright enough, the hard, mean illumination of railroad stations, Gaunt put his suitcase where he could watch it and queued up to buy a ticket. A few undergraduates were in line, boys who had not gone home for Christmas because they had no homes to go to and were on their way to Trenton, perhaps, or Philadelphia, in search of such squalid diversion as these cities afforded. A few plain citizens of Princeton, going God knew where.

The queue moved up and waited, moved up and waited, in the accustomed pace.

Gaunt found himself looking at the ticket seller with a realization that the man's face was familiar. He couldn't place it. But the conundrum was preferable to his dismal thoughts, to a vacuous observation of countenances pinched by the unkind illumination, to the chill and the enduring of the burnt tobacco smell.

A man with brown hair—clean shaven, a high, important-sounding voice, and a row of pencils in the pocket of a time-buffed, faded corduroy waistcoat that once had been green. Gaunt had it: *Averyson!*

On the semi-Gothic campus that sprawled and towered in the night beyond the station, Averyson had once been a great economist. At the White House during the atomic war, this same man had cracked up. Apparently they had brought him home and Averyson had recovered enough to become a station agent! He was adding, with the pompousness of a man calculating billions owed by governments to governments, a few pennies of tax to the cost of a round-trip Trenton ticket.

Gaunt worried when his turn came. Averyson looked him in the eye and did not recognize him at all. He firmed his lips in a bureaucrat's smile and gave his voice the inflection of vast significance: "Where to, my good man? Don't stand there ogling! You're holding up Progress!

A week later, Gaunt left Urbana by plane. He had arranged to cross the Chicago area, although such flights were ordinarily forbidden. To himself, he admitted mere curiosity motivated his wish to see the devastated area from the air. That was the only way by which it could safely be observed. In requesting the flight to be set up, however, he had stated that he believed a personal inspection of the results of atomic warfare might be of use in his evaluation program.

A special plane, its underbelly sheathed with lead and its observation ports made of resistant glass, had been dispatched from Washington by the now almost nonexistent Air Force. It carried Gaunt over the site on a clear and frigid noonday after a light, fresh snowfall.

Everything, of course, was now known concerning the annihilation of Chicago by Gaunt and by all others who cared to read. On the night of death, a Soviet jet bomber had left an arctic base (not then known to American Intelligence) across the Pole. It landed (on skids) on a snowfield prepared by the crews of five submarines. These subs (type and capabilities also then unknown in the United States) had traveled in secrecy from Krondstadt to Greenland, whence, proceeding under the ice, they had entered Hudson Bay in January.

(Here, again, a thitherto unknown fact was revealed. The ultimatum and onslaught with which the Short War began had been planned long before the Disappearance. That unanticipated event had not, however, interfered with the Kremlin's scheme to assault America at many points and without warning. On the contrary, the violent shock following the disappearance of the women had caused the Soviet government to set ahead its schedule, partly to take advantage of a presumed equal chaos in America and partly to enable the Communists to impose the harshest disciplines of war on an awed and frantic male population.)

The specialized submarines, long rehearsed in their particular duties, baked their way through the ice to the surface of Hudson Bay during a blizzard, broaching at a point ninety miles off the nearest shore. Their crews, using bull dozers, cleared an airstrip on the ice. The huge jet bomber thus was able to land, take on its single immense bomb, refuel, and head for Chicago at its battle speed of six hundred and eighty miles an hour. It reached the target early in the morning.

The scientific monstrosity in its bomb bay was a plutonium-tritium-lithium missile of a type similar to the one luckily discovered, before its detonation, in Pittsburgh. It was officially known as an XFR 17, and familiarly, amongst Soviet scientists and military men, as a "Lenin." Most of its weight was casing, designed to act as a millionth-of-a-second "tamper." The casing, radiation absorptive, was of a sort unknown to American scientists; after the blast it was deposited in a thin sheet so radioactive as to heat up the elements upon which it "rained." The plutonium detonation mechanism was remarkably light. A water hammer, involving tritium and the liquefied second isotope of hydrogen, aided in obtaining the "tamping" effect. The weight of the whole bomb (which was actually more like a physics laboratory combined with a machine shop) was eighty-nine tons. The fact that the distance from the submarine rendezvous point in Hudson Bay to Chicago was small enabled the six-jet plane to carry the large bomb to its target.

The flight was made shortly after the destruction of San Francisco by a suicide submarine, the ineffective effort to wreck New York City, and the unsuccessful attempt to detonate a bomb smuggled piecemeal to the U.S.A. and assembled and hidden in Pittsburgh. It took place in the predawn period when fighter defense in Canada could be expected to be handicapped by darkness. The great, swift plane was heard by many but seen, apparently, by no one. Chicago officials, in spite of being "alerted" by Washington, presumed the only immediate threat would be to coastal cities. (No city, at that time, had been advised of the finding of an H bomb in Pittsburgh, as it was certain that such news would create national urban panic with side effects probably more disastrous than the total loss of half a dozen major cities.)

The Soviet jet plane arrived according to schedule. Its bomb fell, as planned, toward the coastal rim of Lake Michigan, near the Steel Pier and "exploded" six thousand feet in the air. The plane that had carried it had been ordered to put back to Hudson Bay where (the crew had been told) submarines would return all hands to Russia—and they would live out their days with pensions and extra privileges, as Heroes of the Soviet. The jet plane had fuel enough for the short return, but, although it aimed its bomb by radar from an altitude of sixty-two thousand feet, the blast instantly destroyed it—an inevitability known only to the superiors in the crew.

Such were the principal facts which, at the conclusion of the Short War, had been shared with the American government, just as data on other secret and surprise missiles had been exchanged upon the signing of the Co-operative Peace.

When his plane swung in toward Hobart, Indiana, Gaunt could see Lake Michigan, blue and partly frozen, on his right. Ahead on his left were towns, villages and farms such as he had crossed all the way from Urbana to this point. Snow lay whitely on them. Horses and cattle could be discerned. Here the stubble of a cornfield showed mathematically; there a black rectangle revealed a hogpen. Smoke rose from chimneys. Trucks, cars and occasional sleighs could be seen, along with several working snowplows. It was the familiar landscape that any traveler on commercial airlines would see all the way across the Middle West in wintertime.

But just beyond Hobart a change became noticeable. People and livestock vanished. Presently, Gaunt saw a little church with its steeple cleanly broken off. Then a farm that had been flattened.

White walls of a clapboard house, red walls of barns and outbuildings, and even the chimneys lay spattered on the earth, identifiable only because wind had cleared away the new snow.

The plane began to climb. Its pilot, a major in a winter uniform, waved a gloved hand toward the area ahead.

"The 'rim' begins soon. Still hot. Got to have altitude. In this area, the blast effect was freaky. Took a farm here, left a town yonder. Took a village. Left the farms in front and behind."

The copilot, a lieutenant, pointed toward the earth directly below. "That was New Chicago, that pile of junk under the snow."

Gaunt nodded. He had seen much of bombed-out Europe; this did not seem new to him. But as the plane, still climbing, approached Gary, he stiffened. For here the lake came inland. Where once there had been a city, a bay spread out beneath them, a shallow bay, evidently, for its frozen surface was dotted with "islands."

Again, the major pointed—to one of the snowpowdered islets. "That's all that's left of the Bragerton Iron and Steel Works. About fifty acres of buildings including seven blast furnaces. Nobody's been up there, personally. Robot boats were sent through to take pictures. It just looks like slag. All these islands you see are either hilltops or the remains of buildings. The land around here was hammered down below water level and Lake Michigan poured in."

There wasn't any Chicago.

Just an estuary that ranged out toward Oak Park and included Evanston on the north. Where a "shore" emerged, the land, for miles upon many miles, was slick. Wind had bared great patches of it. In the bright sunlight, it glittered.

"Silicates?" Gaunt asked.

The major jerked his head in confirmation. "Melted. Ran like hot wax. Tidal wave cooled it off when it roared back, afterward. The bomb's hammer effect depressed the shoreline, all along. Threw aside the water. Then the lake rushed back to its level—set up a hell of a steam cloud—and that was it. You have to go about fifty miles from the old Loop district to find any body living, these days. Place is mostly too hot to explore. We did a lot of telephoto work last summer for the Department of Agriculture. Some green stuff is springing up in the hot areas. Botanists were anxious to look it over. From the pictures, it seemed like new species—genetical morphosis, I think they called it. Radiation result. Our pictures created a lot of excitement and discussion—but nothing satisfactory. Next year, they hope to drag the place with hooks on ropes, pull up some of the vegetation—find out what it is. And was. The plants themselves will be hot, I'm told."

Gaunt had seen enough. More than enough. Here, beneath the pale-blue ice and the bluer water, here where the glassy shores glittered in the January sunshine, had once been a mighty metropolis. A city he had loved. A university where he had held a chair for three contented years. Laboratories in which he had been a distinguished visitor. Stores he had shopped in. Schools his children had attended. People, young and old: brilliant professors, genial neighbors. Everything that had meant security, prosperity, civilization and home, to millions. All of it gone. Melted, vaporized and partly covered by a silent lake.

Was the mere inclination to perform an act of such a sort the force which, in some inscrutable and "unscientific" fashion, had denuded earth of women before the awesome inhumanity could begin?

Who could say?

He heard about it from a survivor. . . .

At Waukegan, where the plane came down, Gaunt. presented his Federal Food Ration Card at a lunch counter. Its sole factotum, a redheaded, pimply young man in a battered chef's cap, whose neck bore the purplish-red scar mass of a radiation burn, talked readily. Indeed, he talked incessantly, mechanically, with a puzzled, faraway look in his pale eyes and a voice that spoke from rote, so it was evident he had told the same tale over and over to hundreds of diners at the airport.

"See you came in on a lead plane," he began. "Musta been taking a squint. What'll it be?" The young man chuckled. "We got eggs. What eggs'll it be?"

"Fried—poached—boiled—anything," Gaunt said.

"I was in it." The man pointed at his neck. "Radiation. Doing okay, too. No cancer—so far, anyhow. Just scar tissue. You know how I got it?"

"No." Gaunt wasn't eager to hear. He'd read accounts enough. Still, the man wanted to talk—seemed to need to talk. So Gaunt raised his eyebrows and gave the eyes beneath an attentive look.

The young man nodded in agreement with himself; he had decided evidently, where to begin and what to say. "I'm a poker player." He turned his back and spilled vegetable oil on a hot griddle. "That night I was at it, with a bunch of pals, in the back room of the Elks Building in Mellodilla—that's a suburb—thirty-six miles as the crow flies from the Loop. As the crow used to fly." He laughed at his own, old joke. "My wife, she was twenty-two, used to give me this night off, once a month, and we boys made the most of it. Poker till daylight—that was us. The dames go." He paused. "But we play, anyhow."

Gaunt grinned, as a fellow poker player might.

"I'm about eighteen bucks ahead and holding three queens when the whole world lights up, bright orange, I say it was. Some said reddish. Some said yellow. Some, white. But I'm facing the west, away from Chi, and I see the reflection and it's orange. 'What in hell?' asks somebody. Jev Connors, he's a mortician—was, yells, 'Bomb! The goddamn Rooshians have hit Mellodilla by mistake!' And he nose dives under the poker table, taking his hand along. A couple of other guys do, among 'em yours truly. What the hell! Bombs I have seen before, at Guadal and other spots. Now, a little time passes. That orange light dies down but she don't entirely go out. Through the windows, from under the table, while the bunch is telling us to come out and it was only a trolley or a frozen wire, I see a glimmer of all sorts of colors that keep fizzling up and down and I say to myself, 'Will, that's an atom bomb! That's Chi!' "

Eggs broke and sizzled. The redheaded man went on. "Somewhere along in there, real soon after the flash, the Elks' hall rocks like an earthquake and slowly falls apart. The lights go out. The cinder blocks grind and wallow around. The boys begin to scream where they're hurt. There's a concussion that saps out your wind. And the Elks' roof goes for a sail. You can feel the cold rush in, and now it's dark. It sounds like the town is coming apart in a Cecil B. De Mille spectacle. The yells increase and the old poker table takes a rafter across the middle that splits it and I'm knocked out. Sunny side up?"

"Please," Gaunt said.

"I wake up. It's daylight. I get loose from the debris. I'd of been frozen stiff, but four-five guys were on top of me. The top ones *are* froze. I check. I'm not hurt, just scratched up and beat up and aching inside, but not bad. I get loose and walk around. Between Mellodilla and Chi, there's big hills, otherwise I wouldn't be telling you this. So I stumble out and the town's a wreck. People ambling here and there like zombies. I head for my place, which is five blocks, and I ain't got no place—no home, no two boys, no uncle lookin' after 'em while I'm out that night. Just a mess, with frozen flesh in it. I steal a coat off a corpse and some other extra duds—and I trek.

"That day I make about three miles. It's like walking through where there was an avalanche. I meet folks. We don't speak much. I don't eat. It doesn't enter my head to. That night I hole up in what's left of a factory. Can't tell for sure, even, what kind it was. Metalwork of some type. Place partly burned and it's warm. I sleep with my damned neck next to a big metal plate." He touched the scar. "Thing must have been hotter'n radium; that's where I picked up this burn. Well, I go on the day after. Trying to get far away from Chi. Hearing the news, seein' the sights. *You* know. Like all

the blind people. And the crazies. Like men dragging the frozen
corpses of their pals along on kids' sleds. Such stuff."

"Yes."

"And finally I'm picked up and taken care of for shock—that's
eight days afterward—and all I eat in the whole time is about a case
of condensed milk I snitched out of a groceriteria that I haul along
on a sled I foraged. I don't even care much for that, since I seen
two-three of the crazies, somewhere on the way, sittin' around outdoor fires in the snow, eating what looked damned like roasted human parts, to me. And seen a lot of spattered human parts too, like
at Guadal, so I'm kind of an expert on the subject. The bread's
lousy here at Waukegan. Want bread?"

"Thanks," Gaunt answered, "I guess not. Just the eggs."

He had hoped it would be warm in California.

That February, it was not. Every morning a gray fog rolled in
from the sea. Nearly every afternoon the fog lifted enough to become clouds. From the clouds a chilly rain descended.

Los Angeles seemed without liveliness although it teemed with
life—with people, unoccupied for the most part, hungry, and ap-
prehensive, now, about the rains. They knew the Portland story.
They feared that somewhere, out over the Pacific, another "undissi-
pated air mass" was drifting eastward from the site of the unfortunate
Soviet experiment and that it would reach rainy California in a
sufficient concentration to duplicate the "Oregon effect."

The retired aged, the war workers now without work, and the
numberless citizens whose trades, businesses and professions could not
be conducted owing to shortages, or to the lack of market in a listless
world, or to government order, were preoccupied with somber
chores.

They searched for extra food; they scoured their environs for
fuel in a land where fuel was scarce; and they still made efforts, by

letter and through the "interview centers," to get in touch with loved ones missing now for two years.

It was difficult to arrange transportation to Pasadena and Gaunt's encounter with Amos Steadman was like the rest of his Hadean journey.

He could not at first believe the huge man could have lost so much weight. "Steady" was sitting behind his paper-heaped desk and its racks of cotton-stoppered tubes. The monel-metal tables and the glass labryinth of his laboratory were visible through an open door. He saw Gaunt come in, rose halfway and spoke in his always melancholy voice:

"I got word you'd arrive around now. I'm glad to see you, Bill. I hope you've got good news of some sort."

Gaunt sat down and smiled and shook his head. "That's what I hoped you might have."

Amos Steadman's lugubriousness had once concealed a merry disposition. Long ago, Gaunt had said of him, "I know a lot of biologists, but only one the subject has made humaner, though you'd think it ought to. Steady learned how to be a better, happier person by studying protoplasm."

But now, looking at the man, he felt that melancholy had sunk into the bony frame, extinguishing the fun, the whimsy and the humanness of the man. He looked such a figure of despair as John Bunyan might have dreamed. His skin hung upon him like a man's robe on a small boy. His eyes were bloodshot and evasive.

"We're nowhere," he said. His head shook. "Nowhere!"

"I'd heard—last spring—"

"That was last spring." Steadman leaned back; his swivel chair creaked as if it soon would break. "We had a somewhat promising line then. We had raised heaven only knows how many fertile ova of mammals in the uteruses of different hosts. So we felt we had the medium, if we could get the first fertile cell. And there was where we had an idea. A certain rare, cancerous affliction of the testes occasionally sets the spermatozoa dividing in a way that resembles the early mitosis of the fertile ova. Under the microscope, it looked as if multiple pregnancy had begun in the testis."

"I've seen pictures," Gaunt said. He hadn't been asked to sit or to take off his coat. He did both. "Somewhere. Years ago. The New York Academy, probably."

Steadman stared at him for a moment and grinned a little. "Damn! Bob Blake told a bunch of us you knew everything. Maybe it's true!"

"I wish it were," Gaunt said ruefully.

"Well. About these quasi-embryonic cells. We thought, if we could get them in a live state—the poor devil afflicted with the thing has to undergo orchidotomy, anyway—we could implant them in other-than-human hosts, naturally, since no human ones exist—and perhaps rear something that began to have a human look."

"They didn't 'take'?"

"Our little effort to find the means to continue the species without females came a rather remarkable cropper." Steadman raised his voice, "Oh, Jenkins! Bring my exhibits!"

A pasty-faced young man in a white coat soon appeared with three glass specimen jars. They were filled with alcohol. In it floated what looked like fetuses. The assistant hurried away after setting the bottles on the desk in front of Gaunt.

Steadman tapped them with a pencil, one by one. "These three most clearly exhibit the invariable phenomenon. Take a look. They seem human. All are in the fifth month. Notice the well-formed body—heads—sensory organs—and so on. These are the standard results of biological science we've pushed ahead—ten years? Fifty? Maybe a hundred! In the last two. They *look* promising, Bill. But not one has internal organs. Not one has a brain. Not one is viable except in utero. These were reared in cattle. The host doesn't matter.

And we've found out enough in the past four months to realize the dividing spermatozoa *never will* give rise to a whole human being!"

"I see."

A full minute passed while Steadman stared at his glass jars. He shrugged. "It was my only really hopeful concept. One of my men killed himself. You know, I see. Flat failure. Blind alley. Only thing left is to wait a few million years and see if the monkeys are fools enough to try again."

Gaunt stirred uneasily. "Surely, Steady, you intend to turn now to some new line of investigation!"

"I *don't!* I'm through, Bill. I wish you hadn't come out. I hate to have you see me in this shape. I feel we're up against something so much *bigger* than we are—intellectually so much *beyond* us—that I have decided research is a waste of time."

"Stead, what else is there to do?"

The once-huge man leaned back and grinned with an expression like malice. "How do you like L.A.?"

"Don't."

"Nervous. Hungry. Jobless. Someday it's going to pop."

"Pop?"

"Wide open. Men can't stand the idleness, the inanity, the pressures. Every kind of cockeyed cult has been initiated here. Nothing makes any real difference to anybody. Someday, in a blaze of pure bestial rebellion, this city is going to tear itself apart. I'm quitting Pasadena next week. I know a little village in Mexico where I used to go to fish. I'm sneaking down there and I'm going to fish and drink pulque and sing, with a bunch of Mexicanos I like."

"A damned good idea," Gaunt immediately agreed. "Rest up! Forget biology awhile. When you come back—"

"I'm never coming back, Bill." Silence returned between them. Gaunt considered whether to ask his friend for lunch or to wait to be asked. He was heartsick—and used enough to that to realize he was hungry as well. But the geneticist merely stood up and held out his hand. "Appreciate the call, Bill—"

"But—I'll be around awhile. Other men to see—"

"Don't advise it. Nothing else going on here worthy of the name of science. If I were you, I'd beat it while I could. You are going back to Florida, I presume?"

Gaunt said eagerly, "Why not go with me? Wonderful weather now! No end of room in my house! I'm alone. Food's plentiful there too, compared to California. Got a man to take care of me —colored fellow. You could fish all you wanted in Florida—"

The flicker in Steadman's eyes had already expired. "Thanks, Bill. But—no. I've done too much. I don't want even to hear about work any more. And you're still steamed up. Someday you'll quit. Like our crowd. Thanks. But definitely, absolutely, no."

Three days later, Gaunt began the tedious trip back to Florida. He made a stop in Texas and another in New Orleans. He wished he had not taken the trouble.

When the slow day coaches at last rolled into Miami, into the level land where the vegetation was jungle lush even in late March, where the sea sparkled and the sun was warm, Gaunt did not know whether he was glad to be home again or not.

PART IV

Dream and Dimension

16

IN WHICH PRACTICAL MEN FOUNDER AND A MYSTIC TRIES AN
IMPRACTICAL APPROACH TO THE COMMON PROBLEM.

Time passed like time in a sinister dream: who would run in such nightmares finds his feet glued; who longs to stay is propelled toward his dread. The dramatis personae are similarly turned about: the virtuous seem foul and the meek ferocious.

Gaunt, who was alone except for Byron (and for occasional visits from Rufus), found that the summer days and then the winter days were either interminable or shockingly brief. A morning spent with the reports that crammed his mailbox seemed like a week and he would discover that he was waiting with an inexplicable impatience for the call, ceremonial and often short, of Edwinna's spaniel, which now made its home with the Elliots. Then a week would pass as if it had been an afternoon while he cooked food and did his errands, pondered and conjectured, wrote and rewrote.

In the period, those men he knew best and saw oftenest showed odd reversals of character. Jim Elliot, from whose house came the frequent sound of hammering, had grown as taciturn as his Yankee forebears and would not say what project engaged him. The extroverted Teddy Barker was as glum as the lawyer. Young Gordon Elliot, so quiet and sensitive in his earlier years, had taken to the company of rowdy boys and was forever shooting things off in the yard or whizzing about the unkempt back lanes on scooters, using stolen gasoline. Even Connauth, who had agonizedly confessed adultery, these days brought up the matter whenever he could, as if, with the women gone, it was more important to have known another woman than to have had intimate knowledge of the Holy Ghost.

It was grotesque.

Grotesque, yet, to the philosopher, predictable.

When frustrated in one means of realizing its purpose, instinct spontaneously attempts the opposite method. Thus, the good man, whose virtue balks his inner necessities, often turns to evil; thus the conscious sinner compensates with deeds of charity or heroism. And only the arrogant Western person, white and Christian, dedicated to "reason" however mad his social scene may be, presumes his species can be made to follow his special description of right and wrong, and does follow it; he winds up deluded, reasonless, and wrong about nearly everything.

Gaunt, among a handful of his compatriots, understood the schizoid process and was not surprised (but only bemused) to see how a unique adversity threw character into uncharacteristic behavior.

What surprised him, what had always surprised him, was not the collapses and alterations in his country but the momentum of his culture: not decay, but the slowness of decay.

The people of the so-called Christian nations had long been appallingly vulnerable to psychological assault. Hitler had proved that with his many aggressions and the lies that covered each; half of America had been deceived by the trick. Russia had gone ahead with it and the "free" world had not even then caught on.

The recent cold war had been, in Gaunt's opinion, the same theatrical for which Nazism had provided a dress rehearsal but Americans had not discovered the ways and degrees in which their "sacred" beliefs and commercial wishes duped them. Turned hot, become shooting at the parallels, military difficulties, fighting without declaration, war itself, the ideological aggressions had not been met by that better ideology of liberty but only with hasty arms and hastier emotions. Even the final effort, the mining of a nation and its assault by air and sea with fusing atoms, had not in any way shown the surviving American men how they had betrayed liberty through half a century by a refusal to resist the oppression of others. So long as they thought what they did was reasonable, so long would the laws of instinct remain obscure to them.

Hence, in this third winter of the Disappearance, Gaunt was not surprised to hear that those nations which had endured tyranny and peonage were turning toward freedom or to discover day by day how dictatorial his own land was becoming. All his adult life he had resisted the process because he had understood the psychology and the biology of it; he resisted still, in his writing. There was no other way or place to resist.

A man who thinks ahead of his era and who knows beyond its common knowledge must only write or be written about. His sole opportunity is to advise the future. *Action* along his lines of thought is impossible; the lag in the evolution of awareness prohibits action. It would have been as foolish to try to compel all twentieth-century men to act according to the hard-earned knowledge of a few as to try to force amphibians to open schools and elect senators on the grounds that amphibians eventually would evolve into mammals and those mammals into men.

Gaunt often thought that even the truth which Jesus knew and uttered fell so far ahead of its possible enactment in the human calendar that nearly everything done in Jesus' name would have outraged Him. What He said that was enlightened and important went ignored. The word for Him, affixed to every sort of cult, merely supported further millenniums of pagans—of animals who had neither the desire nor the intention, yet, to behave as men.

Action would have resulted in martyrdom. And martyrdom,

Gaunt felt, was the mistake too many had already made. The beastly aspect of it produced neither decency nor forbearance but only collective blood lusts. Thus, the Bhuddists were peaceable men; but the Christians were forever alight with devilment, carrying their Cross and everywhere avenging it by tormenting the innocent with it. Gaunt therefore concentrated upon his thesis of what men ought to become, and could become, but not now. And he watched freedom, that only valuable truth of his age, crumble away at home as inferior social tendencies persisted.

Stern dictates were of course necessary to meet the shock of Disappearance and to deal with its horrendous sequels. But these did not diminish even when no planetary foe remained and even when order was attained—when supply and demand had been adjusted downward to much less than half the previous standards owing to the fact that women had been the greater consumers and that men had consumed many things for the sake of women. Reason for alarm diminished but the government seemed ever more afraid of the people. The government no longer appeared to trust the people. There were causes for that.

Elected men had come to fear above all that they would fail to be re-elected by the people. Bureaucrats, ignorant of their century, its sciences and psychologies, unable to predict what people would do, feared people. And multitudes of men in government, without probity or integrity, attributed the same rotted nature to all with the unastonishing result that they, too, feared everybody.

In addition, the wars (and the threats of wars the Americans had refused to face when they were but threats) had turned the national confidence away from civilian authority and invested it in the military, so that the very basis of liberty was exchanged for myths of secrecy and faiths in weapons. The pure faith in freedom existed almost nowhere in America by the middle of the century; hardly anyone appreciated what such freedom was, and what it had meant, or what was necessary to regain and maintain it. An *idea* opposed the Americans but they had been jockeyed away from the idea that would have destroyed the concept of tyranny. Nothing but brute force remained.

Yet a perverted ghost of liberty still whispered to Americans.

It was the ghost that gave incentive to the General Strike that winter.

The railroads stopped. The telephones went dead. The wheels in factories stood still, greased heavily against rust and idle time, while armed guards and pickets marched outside eying each other with malevolence. The newspapers hurled black ink at labor for adding misery to perpetual dismay. Labor, in turn, defied public opinion and demanded, not shorter hours or higher wages, but a mitigation of restrictions and regulations, rationing, paper work, and the mazes of taxation. In the midst of this dissension, with facilities paralyzed and many beginning to suffer hunger, medical deprivation and other wants, a federal attempt was initiated to help feed Europe and perishing Asia. The effort, noble in itself, was accompanied by a new reduction of farm parities and the withdrawal of certain crop supports, a drain the government could no longer afford. Indignant farmers, accustomed to vote-purchased priorities at the economic teats, rebelled as individuals; their machines also fell silent.

A stasis came, a sullen hush.

Martial law returned.

What Gaunt witnessed on Miami's MacArthur Causeway happened in a thousand places.

A power plant stood on the causeway, a handsome object of tall chimneys, shining metal and soaring cables; it was set along the ship channel so that tankers might be moored hard by—such a technological plaything as a Brobdingnagian's child might build with his box of structural toys.

Here, on a brisk, bright January morning, wind from the northwest and the sun friendly, several hundred strikers held the powerhouse, supplied with food by boats at night and supported by the crews of two tankers. A high wire fence surrounded the grounds. The men behind the fence had kept the plant inoperative for more than five weeks.

Nearby was a Coast Guard station. . . .

Apprised by friends in Washington, Gaunt went as an observer to a position close to the causeway's traffic lanes and somewhat below their level on the appointed day. With him were a dozen city and county officials. They had come in the scant morning traffic, parked their cars and waited about, nervously watching the movement of strikers inside the plant and the pacing of their armed patrols. They were not surprised (and the strikers probably were not) when a column of men, rifles shouldered and bayonets fixed, emerged from the Coast Guard base and began marching down the causeway toward the plant.

That was what Gaunt and the rest had come to observe. It was what was happening at other struck plants and factories.

The marching men followed a band which approached playing "The Star-Spangled Banner." Behind the band was a sound truck and behind that were Coast Guardsmen bearing arms and a company of National Guardsmen.

The column halted at the fence. No further traffic appeared from either direction, the police having closed the causeway.

Gaunt and the officials, most of whom wore threadbare garments and were somewhat unkempt, moved through weedy grass to the place where the land descended into the Bay. The tide had gone out and a mass of algae-covered coral rocks was exposed on the slope, which in an emergency would provide cover. So Gaunt stood amongst the slimy stones with the politicians—at their backs the villa-crowded islands of Biscayne Bay and ahead of them grass, a three-lane road, a narrow parkway planted with oleanders, hibiscus, yuccas and sea grapes, another three-lane road which ordinarily bore traffic in the opposite direction, and last, the fence.

The Anthem came to an end. The patrolling strikers beyond

the fence had not waited it out at attention but, instead, had one by one vanished into the immense building. Now a Coast Guard commander stepped up to the truck, gestured pacifically toward the plant and addressed a hand microphone. His voice boomed immensely:

"All other measures having failed, the President of the United States, acting under emergency powers granted to him by Congress, has ordered the end of all strikes as of today and throughout the nation. New arbitration boards will be set up, but persons refusing to obey the order will be dealt with forcibly. Fifteen minutes are hereby granted for the evacuation of this plant. Strike leaders inside will arrange men in a double file. They will march out with hands raised, carrying no arms, stones or other weapons. Failure to comply with the order will be regarded as *an act of treason*. The plant will then be stormed. There is no wish and no disposition on the part of the government to use such methods. Nevertheless, disobedience will be met by assault. It is now ten twenty-six o'clock. Unless you men begin to emerge as directed at ten forty-one o'clock, firing will commence."

Gaunt thought the arrangements were perilous. He knew that here on the causeway at least, police had not been able to prevent the bringing in of arms as well as food to the strikers; small fast boats had managed that at night. Hence the soldiers and Coast Guardsmen were as exposed as the British before Bunker Hill. No doubt their vulnerability was agreed on—an attempt to show the willingness of law to take risks and an evidence of the government's reluctance to employ force. A foolish display.

Five minutes passed.

The commander picked up the microphone and repeated his speech.

No response came from the plant. No one could now be seen inside it.

The band began "My Country, 'Tis of Thee" and a panickiness was detectable in the music. The leader, a thin man in a red and gold uniform, waved his baton with white-faced urgency; but the horns lagged and the drums rolled uncertainly.

Gaunt found himself both frightened and angry. Suddenly, face tense and fists clenched, he raced across the causeway and up to the cool commander. He gave his name and said that he was a personal friend of the President.

"Mine's Werdlum." The officer held out his hand.

Gaunt talked rapidly. "I doubt if they're coming out! I think they may start shooting any time! I'd like to offer to go in and talk to them—"

Commander Werdlum was a heavy-set man with steady blue eyes and white eyebrows. He smiled. "They damned well may shoot!" he said. "But, unfortunately, Dr. Gaunt, I've got orders. *Exact* orders. This is the way I've been told to do it—this is the way I'm doing it. After all, they've had hundreds of conferences, everywhere, and *not* yielded—"

Gaunt looked down the line of rigid men facing the plant. "If they should fire—"

"Orders." The commander repeated calmly.

"I'd be willing to take full responsibility—"

For perhaps thirty seconds the officer considered, gazing at the building and then at the long line of young, pale faces. "No," he said mildly. "Sorry. But, thanks." He examined his wrist watch. "You better get back with the mayor and the rest—"

Gaunt went.

The fifteen minutes crawled to an end.

Then it seemed that all the windows in the great plant burst outward at once and from every window came the muzzle of a rifle, from every barrel, fire. Gaunt dropped down among the rocks. The air was stung by bullets at a hundred points; steel ricocheted from the pavement, from stones, from the bones of men.

The drawn-up column screamed and roared. Part of it fell to

the ground, streaming blood. Gaunt saw a clarinet shot from a bandsman's hands. He saw the tuba player spit blood upon his golden instrument and look worriedly at the stain and fall with the horn on the hard road. He saw men not immediately hit take cover behind oleanders and other shrubs and he ducked low as machine guns in the plant began to probe the flowers, cutting down branches, so that soon the parkway was cleared of its pretty verdure.

He didn't see more because the man beside him, whose unshaven face he recalled, whose name he did not know, tried to stand in order to observe better and was hit in the shoulder and fell back into the warm, dirty water of the Bay. Crouching, Gaunt waded after him.

From the Base, beyond the plant, came booming sounds; other explosions, mushy but heavy, could be heard as gas shells burst inside the building. The men there were screaming too. Gaunt knew they would not be able to hold their position for long. Not with the plant a haze of gas.

That was the strategy, then: expose a column, play the songs, make an offer and a threat and then—if the volley came—gas them out with the new weapon.

Gaunt made a pad of his handkerchiefs and tied it in place with a necktie and settled the wounded official on a little patch of sand below the line of fire. The other men looked frightened and sick and one of them began to cry. There was clanking on the causeway, now—armor moving. Light tanks, Gaunt imagined, and when they began to shoot Gaunt knew they were picking off strikers who came choking from the untenable building.

The next day the Miami papers had the statistics. So many members of the Coast Guard killed and wounded; so many of the National Guard. Commander Werdlum dead, his body, on the center westbound lane, shot to bits by vengeful strikers. One hundred and three of these dead, two hundred and six injured, a hundred and fifteen unharmed and jailed.

The national story was in the same scale. A White House spokesman said that "civil war had been prevented."

Editorials attacking the useless exposure of troops to assassination were written . . . and filed away unprinted when a directive about such comment was received by every paper.

But the General Strike had ended. Trains ran. Phones rang. Food moved. Planes flew. Factories churned. Men shut their mouths and looked at the ground, worked, ate, and accepted the new orders.

Most men.

A few here, a handful there, a total of many, moved outside the law where marauders had camps in swamps or held remote villages in high mountains.

Gaunt had driven home shakily at noon on the day the strike had been broken.

He felt that he had done what he could.

He felt that he had done nothing.

That was all he could do: nothing. Talk to a commander who was killed minutes later. Tie up a wounded city commissioner. Help lift him into an ambulance. And go.

Work after that on his next report.

Work, in a slow period of time, when his feet seemed dead and horror pursuing. But he was not surprised at what had happened or at what was happening. A free people had thrown aside the meaning of liberty, traded it for goods and rising production, bull markets and a chimera that went by the name of security, for another legend called secrecy, for weapons when the thing they had needed was a thing they might have called character—if they'd had enough character left to name itself.

Now, when iron discipline came down, they tentatively accepted it, having no longer a discipline of themselves. They accepted it, or if not, their rebellion lacked the noble quality of American tradition. It was not an attempt to regain liberty but merely the embrace of crime. They did not even see there was a choice left of self-government and private determination; they saw only the alternatives of mass submission or of outlawry. And most had for so long romanticized thugs that many of these believed the banded criminals were the last representatives of "pioneer" spirit.

Music on the radio grew louder and more martial.

Television shows enjoyed a governmental relaxation and became obscenity feasts.

Bread from Washington; circuses.

Uniforms multiplied.

Men by the tens of thousands were sent to places not called concentration camps.

But the government was referred to as the "regime" openly now; and all good citizens wore red, white and blue badges that said simply "100%" and suppozedly stood for total support of the regime. Support meant subservience.

Gaunt wore one.

So did Jim Elliot.

Not to wear one was to be struck without warning by a hostile fist, or arrested, or even clubbed to death by the rifle butt of a man who was not called a Storm Trooper.

Europe, long used to tyranny, was amazed.

But Europe, trying *its* opposite, was shaking off "regimes" and "orders."

Spring came at last.

From his study windows the miserable philosopher could see a dilapidated neighborhood. Borers, bred in the hurricane-felled timber, were pitting his pines, streaking their boles with the red sawdust of chewed bark, turning their needles brown, killing all of them. A vine grew out of the broken roof of the Wests' bungalow—grew, branched and blossomed claret. Occasional cars and trucks banged on roads that had not been repaired for a long while. But the birds still mated. He watched enviously one day while a cardinal, like a red ball falling from a Christmas tree to a green rug, landed on what was left of his lawn, bounced a foot or two and danced in front of a pink-billed female. Springtime.

Whenever he peered in the mirror in Paula's and his bathroom he could see winter coming to him: the whitening of his thinned hair, the deep creases in his cheeks, the leathern look and the yellow-ness of eyeball that came from age, improper nutrition, anxiety and fear. He had cramps in his belly, often, now, unexplained diarrheas, rheumatism of his sinews. Sometimes he thought of the drugs in the locked suitcase he'd bought long ago and always, when he did so, he told himself, "Not yet." The need would be greater in a time foreseen but merely slow in coming.

It was in April, on a bland evening, that Jim Elliot came by and invited Gaunt to see what he had been building during the winter. Jim's coal-black hair was white-shot nowadays. His hands always shook. But his voice was unchanged.

Gaunt went over, glad that his friend's taciturnity had at last ended and supposing Jim had remodeled his house to while away the days, or perhaps fortified it.

They went through the kitchen and down the hall. The door to the high-ceilinged living room was shut. A dim light revealed on the hall floor a heap of shavings, sawdust and scraps of bright-colored paper. Gaunt was puzzled. He was more puzzled when his friend fumbled for a key: the door was locked.

"Glad the power's on," Jim said. "With candles and kerosene lamps, the effect isn't so good. And, besides, there's a fire hazard—"

Gaunt nodded as if he understood.

Jim unlocked the door. Darkness lay ahead; he reached around the wall and began to snap electric switches.

What Gaunt saw was breath-taking.

Jim Elliot had changed his big living room into a fantastic place. It was no longer oblong, but star shaped. The sides of the star curved up and in, so that the ribs supporting the sides met, like groins, at the center, fifteen feet overhead. The floor was gilded. Each "point" of the star-shaped chamber had been laboriously constructed of wood, plywood and paper. Each was brilliantly painted. And the rising walls were cellular, with colored tissue paper glued on the backs of the "cells." Lights came from behind or outside the "star" itself, so when Jim turned the switches the enormous contraption was like the midst of a rainbow.

Jim stepped forward and beckoned Gaunt to follow.

It was like being inside a gigantic paper Christmas bell of the kind that opens from a folded half-bell into a compartmented tissue-paper whole. Like such a bell, but a star, and hollow within.

Jim walked to the middle. A single chair had been placed there.

"Try it," Jim said.

Gaunt very nearly smiled. But untold work had gone into the structure; it was spectacular, it was pathetic, and it would not do even to show a smile.

"Of course," Jim murmured as his guest seated himself, "I'd like to have been able to project the thing down too. This is just half—an upper half. If I could have got mirrors, I'd have covered the floor to reflect the top half, which would have given the effect."

Gaunt found that the chair was on casters; he could swivel himself around to face any part of the "star." He turned slowly in a circle. The geometrical shapes of the compartments in the walls gave the place depth and dimensionality; the translucent, colored backing of each of the hundreds of recesses—with light flooding from behind in every hue and shade on still other yellow, scarlet, green, purple and blue segments—increased his vivid, yet baffling sense of space built upon space, dimension added to dimension. The eye could fix on no one point, detect no dominant hue; it discerned myriad patterns, yet the beholder remained aware of the spatial star that contained him. The external illumination, furthermore, lent a simultaneous impression of a *containing and outgoing* radiance beyond the walls so that dimensions beyond the familiar three were more than suggested. They seemed here to *exist*.

The desire to smile, which he had first felt, and the sense close to pity, which had quickly followed, changed as he revolved the chair. The "room" was affective. Glowing compartments in its vaulted, five-pointed "corners," childish at first glance, primitive, superstitious seeming, soon conveyed an elusive sense of identification, of half-recognized meaning, and of *awe*.

The philosopher had thought of the new room, immediately, as a three-dimensional "mandala." He was familiar not only with the mandala concept but with his friend's researches into the concept. But it would be difficult even here, he realized, to explain to anybody what *that* was; and he wondered idly if there was even one more person in the state of Florida who, seeing this place, would comprehend it.

"I've brought children in here—Gordon and others," Jim said. "They love it."

"A handsome toy?"

"I don't believe so. What you professors call culture—what Freudians call superego, rubs out of existence so many inklings and intuitions and—maybe—memories that few adults can even remember what went on in their daydreams when they were children. The sense of *knowing* that children have is destroyed. Even the desire to know. How many adults are left even with that? One in a thousand?"

Gaunt shrugged. It might be true.

There might be, implicit, inherent in the center of the imperfectly known phenomenon of personality, a diagram of the basic scheme of things. That pattern might give rise to images of a geometrical sort, pure abstractions of line and color, or balanced designs composed of pictures. The truly introspective person, under certain circumstances, *might* see such pictograms or dream them. They could be hexagons, or pentagons like this new room, or circles or squares and composed of human figures, flowers, trees, landscapes, mere lines, colors, anything. To them the old Sanskrit word "mandala" might apply.

From such a mandala, buried behind man's consciousness, perhaps summing up his unconscious-conscious mind, or his instincts, all men might have received their impulse toward pattern, order, balance, harmony, organization. A mandala *might* be the core of it.

Might, Gaunt thought. Looking at Jim's "room" he gave the thought more attention than he had ever before accorded it. What was the line of reasoning on the mandala? The argument for it?

That every human tribe, however barbaric, had endeavored, automatically, to sum up its notions of the nature of man and cosmos in some geometrical pattern. Thus, even the simplest mandala was a form of shorthand for a "religious statement." The swastika—one such—was not Nazi invented. In fact, the Nazis had got it backwards, making what dead millions of savages would have anxiously called a bad-luck sign. To the savages, a proper swastika would have represented man, man-and-woman, the sun, and therefore, God. They had used it as that symbol for thousands of years. In Christianity, the Sign had become a cross; rather, all the crosses, but always with parallel meaning.

The mandala, the sense of centered design, the illustrated need for harmony and balance, appeared in every Oriental art form. You could see it in old Persian rugs. On Chinese pottery. The Goths had elaborated it in stained glass as rose windows. Their cruciform cathedrals were mandalas. Form of the flower, the snowflake, idealized, it was used to represent the center of Nature, for the Sun and its rays, for God, for the concentrated, attentive soul, reflecting these. It was a symbol whereby a man, one who could not read, might still have a literate communication with the Perfect, the Integrated, and the Infinite.

It was also, Gaunt thought, the basic design of nature known to modern man: the crystal whereof all things are constructed. And it was more: the sun and its planets, the turning nebulae, and the electrons spinning through their orbits about the atom's nucleus. All such "mandalas" described, in periods fantastically long, unbelievably brief, centered patterns both gigantic and minute.

In some almost but not quite comprehensible fashion, Nature seemed to manufacture her every composition from the single thesis of a center surrounded by balancing parts, in circles, in squares, in cubes and spheres, in polygons and polyhedrons. Long-dead authors of the Vedas, who had discussed the phenomenon at length, and certain of the most modern nuclear physicists, had both suggested that, in the Beginning, there was but one entity in cosmos, one supercrystal, which had exploded into the universes.

Could this "source" design therefore be repeated in all its parts, in atoms, in molecules in the crystals of matter in spheres and solar systems, galaxies and island universes? And could the recollection of the original state sometimes become *conscious* when (as in man) enough crystals had been brought together to make awareness possible? Was the pattern nature's own final definition of *itself*? Was it a set of directions, everywhere intrinsic, for the eventual restoration of the original, sublime substance—a feat to be achieved by a universe grown altogether conscious at some remote period in time? Or was it the vision from which visions came, the ultimate revelation of God, the instinct's own instinct of itself, the key to the way of individual being (as all old religions had assumed), and the key, also, to the *purpose* of evolving life?

And artist, on one hand, and a mathematician, on the other (Gaunt thought), would dismiss such tenuous speculation as a waste of time. The artist would say that harmony in pattern is a "natural" or "obvious" fact; the mathematician, that the structure of things demanded equation, and so there was no mystery about it: two does not equal three. Only a very analytical person, dissatisfied with all existing descriptions of nature and man's relation to it, only such a one searching amongst unconventional relationship for fresh clues (amongst old, abandoned theories or amidst new hypotheses seen in a different light) would undertake to think long and soberly about pattern itself and what its significance might be. And a rarer person still would be needed for the deliberate construction, in light and color, of a pure pattern in which to meditate—a three-dimensional mandala—an old thing, yet very new.

"It's beautiful," Gaunt said at last.

Jim sighed, as if he had been holding his breath all the while his friend sat and stared. "Yes. I like to be here. I play music to myself. All kinds. It seems to fit all kinds." He had a look of meekness in his eyes and of determination around his mouth. "You see what it is?"

"Yeah. A mandala."

"A chapel. An abstract chapel. I have thought a great deal about how a good purpose, conducted without much consciousness, generally turns into its opposite; and a great many wiser men have appreciated the same thing. It occurred to me, for instance, that during the past few centuries, when we wanted to worship, we've always gone into some gloomy, tomblike building—a church—and knelt and chanted in the murk like beetles grubbing underground. When we wanted to think, we built cells as bare and colorless as possible, with as little light, and put on sackcloth, and fasted: we became monks. It doesn't make sense."

"It is to prevent distraction."

Jim shook his head. "No! It's because we've got *everything* wrong! We identify serious thought with death—worship with death—ourselves with death. God is death to us all—and has been for ages. Nobody *lives* this life—really; everybody is interested in an afterlife—so this one we know is *ipso facto* a kind of death. If we were really alive, the way we were meant to be, we would not make so much of death, in the way we do. We think, for instance, that the cosmos is mostly cold, dark space. Actually, it's mostly light—and most of the

objects in it are burning suns. Only the planets and gassy clouds
have shadows, and not all the clouds; some glow. The suns are
shadowless. When we cannot see our one sun, we call it the dark of
night, even though we're looking at thousands of suns!"

Gaunt nodded. "A thought."

"A good example of how mistaken and superpersonal our
thinking is. The universe is brilliant. Only man's view is dark. I decided a chapel should be brilliant also. Light is true and natural—
as the Bible tried to say. Life is light. Light is life. *We* are alive. All
the gloomy churches, the dark monks' cells, are places for devil worship. Denial of life, of light. Nobody has a true sense of reality in
such abominable environs. So this little chapel is my effort to make a
suitable cell for *my* kind of meditation. For *communication*. The
black-robed clergy has sung a fearsome, enslaving litany of death to
the living for a thousand years and more. It's time to stop revering
the grave and commence to worship Light again."

"What happened?" Gaunt asked after a moment.,

"That's peculiar too. I couldn't tell you. You'd have to try it."

Gaunt gazed again at the polychromatic walls, gleaming softly,
honeycombed so the senses were confused and yet, as Jim had intended, given a feeling of repose and balance, of integrated relationship. The strange chamber seemed also to possess an immense energy
but energy in peaceful fixation, energy applied nowhere, doing nothing. "In tao," he murmured.

Jim nodded a time or two.

"Autohypnosis is what most of my psychological colleagues
would call it."

"No doubt." Jim almost left it at that. But soon he said, in a
defensive tone, "Actually, *they* wouldn't try to sum up the whole of
human speculation on the nature of Nature, make a room-sized
symbol of that, and sit in it to see what happened."

"No. They'd think that would be like going to a witch doctor.
Or a spiritualist. A medium."

"Funny! And typical of *every* civilization. People always imagine that whatever they believe is *it*. Nobody else, so far as they are concerned, ever knew anything truer or more real than whatever they happen to think. Nobody ever hit on a valid, different idea. Millenniums of reflection *and experiment*—especially in the Orient —are tossed aside with a word, by some Columbia Ph.D. in Behaviorism. 'Mysticism,' he says. Knowledge, in his opinion, is a gathering river; if you're at his contemporary bend in it, you know all. A few selective glances backward and you've mastered the whole flow. He lives now; he is 'educated'; ergo, a smarter man never breathed. *Phooie!* It's entirely possible—even logical, in many ways —to assume that mankind may once have learned, and already has forgotten, the most penetrating and important parts of wisdom. There are other routes to learning than the measurement of objects, which is science. There are other sorts of knowing than the mathematical. We may have *regressed*. We may by now be cerebral dinosaurs, using our brains as those big animals finally used their bodies, merely to deal and ward off terrible blows. The brain *could* have been meant for something else, and it *could* have known what it was meant for, long ago. Not to have one war after another, for hundreds of centuries, as we've done. Not to promulgate ideas of shame and guilt, either, as has been done steadfastly in Jesus' name for two thousand years. Not to scrape up and waste every usable molecule of matter on the planet—which men have done since history shows a record. We *might* have been intended for something different altogether! Anyhow, that's the feeling I got in here. One feeling—amongst many."

Gaunt was no longer inclined to patronize Jim's effort. The more he considered and the more he listened the more he realized that, of all the attempts he had seen in all his trips, all the sweating of the scientists, the thunder of huge machinery, the flash of electron beams and swing of telescopes, this room represented the most original endeavor. And it took nerve. For Jim Elliot was anything but superstitious, anything but credulous; he had engaged on the experiment with the indubitable realization that it was very near the edge of folly.

Because he knew Jim well and knew Jim was satisfied by his reaction to the prismatic chamber, Gaunt said quietly, with a twinkle in his eyes, "And the sixty-four dollar question?"

Jim shook his head. "Nothing. I haven't got the slightest hint. I've got an immense impression of things wrong with humanity. But as to what happened to the women—no."

"I'll try it."

"Will you?"

Gaunt looked at tne curving walls and smiled gently. "Sure. Why not? I'll pray in your chapel, Jim, and see what answer this poor dumb brain hears."

That next night Gaunt sat in the strange place. He had many sensations, many fantasies, many bizarre ideas; of these, some had never before passed through his head. But nothing was explained to him and no new course of behavior suggested itself to him.

When, toward morning, Jim looked in to see what he was doing, he found the philosopher lying on the floor, asleep.

17

A LADY RECOVERS BUT A MULTITUDE FALLS ILL.

Paula Gaunt washed her hair and put on a dress. It was the first time she had worn a dress in months and she enjoyed the feeling it gave her. With Kate gone, she had an afternoon of sewing and mending to do and dinner to prepare. Both were occupations she had evaded in the past. So she was a little surprised to find her mind was planning the work on the children's clothes and the meal with discernible if slight pleasure. It was not aptitude but inclination that she had lacked.

Before she went downstairs she looked at herself in the full-length mirror. Her hair was definitely gray, in spots, now that she no longer dyed it; but she was still attractive. A college boy wouldn't want her if he were a normal college boy. A man of fifty, looking at her smooth skin, her bright eyes, her vigorous body, might see she was desirable, even without beige-copper hair. That, she knew now (as now she knew so many thing about herself), had not been kept dyed primarily to make herself appealing to men. She had maintained its color because, somewhere within herself, she'd felt it gave her a burning, acquisitive look, a look of incomplete satisfaction. It was a challenge and a dare, an appeal and a threat. It was part of the concealed, unknown masculineness of her. But that part of Paula had been assimilated into her aware mind; she had no further need for unconscious expression.

She was satisfied to be a woman.

That was a great achievement. Not many women she'd known were satisfied; yet, of the dissatiate, few had any inkling of the causes of their restlessness. Paula had grown beyond adolescence, not with a psychiatrist's help, but by the harder road of experience, candor and self-analysis.

She would live out her days unable to do more than recognize the sensations of maturity: there were no men. She would in any case have lived them amongst the arrested adolescents who composed the American population. As it was now, she would live in a *regressing* world. That was tragic. But in her uncorruptibility she had a surer power than what is called "strength" by most persons. Such "strength" is masochistic, the willful flagellation of a spirit in perpetual conflict; Paula's new power flowed of its own accord from an inner self where conflict no longer occurred.

She went downstairs and gathered up the school dresses, dresses ripped, worn through, with seams open or alterations needed. She took them out on the porch and sat in the reed divan. Her needle began to dart like a bee and the sun moved down the sky, elongating shadows on the field where Negro women hoed.

When the phone rang, Paula sighed and put down her sewing. "Yes?"

"This is Dorothy Billings, Paula." The voice was urgent.

"Hello, Dot. What's doing?"

"It's cholera."

"What's cholera?"

"I forgot. You skipped the confidential meeting. A lot of people around the waterfront have been getting sick, lately. And dying. The polio was about all the doctors could handle. And this thing was mostly niggers, at first anyhow. Their wells were always filthy. But it's spreading and we got the lab reports this forenoon. Cholera. That means a new organization and I was told to call you right away—"

"What do you do for it?"

"That's the point. We can't get the new drugs now. Not in any quantity." Dorothy Billings's voice rose higher. "It's an epidemic! Or the start of one! But we've got to handle it with old-fashioned medicine! Horrible! There's to be a secret meeting in two hours—"

Paula felt her heart beat faster. Her brain began ticking off names of women who could handle the new castastrophe, forming committees, getting up imaginary substations, seeing herself in command. *In command. Old warhorse. Old firehorse. Old fool!* For part of a minute she wanted to be at the head of things, running them, battling cholera. Paula, the boss and the hero of the plague. *Hero.* Not even *heroine.* The short interval ended and the desire died away.

"I know absolutely nothing about cholera—what to do—or how to organize. The doctors must take charge."

"But—*Paula*—! We're *counting* on you! Lots of women are scared to pieces. Some have already left the city!"

"I've got more to do than I can decently manage, right now."

"You mean you won't come to the meeting?"

"I'm busy."

The woman faltered. "We thought you'd head up the squads—"

"I head up too many already."

"But this is a *plague*, Paula! An *epidemic*—!"

"They're having 'em lots of places. Miami's begged for one, for decades. It hasn't even got sewage disposal! In a couple of years more, it might have had. Too late. *So what?*"

"But we just naturally *assumed* you'd take over—"

"If I'm really needed, I'll do what I can. Right now, I'm doing other things. *They're* important too. You've got plenty of organizers. It's water, isn't it? You boil it. You cook the food. Find out how to protect people. The doctors will know. Then tell everybody."

Paula went back to her sewing.

For a time her hands trembled. But her mind was calm. Cholera was merely one more thing, one in scores. An expectable disaster. Disease was rising everywhere as the drug supply dwindled. Disease spread owing to the paucity of physicians, the crowding, and the dismal living conditions.

After a time Bella Elliot walked up the drive and along the steppingstones beneath the thrinax palms to the porch.

"Hi, Paula!"

"Hello, Bella. Come on in! I'm mending."

Bella smiled as she always smiled. Sun fell on her brown hair, making it opalescent; a breeze from the southeast stirred her curls. She was wearing a white tennis dress, just washed and neatly ironed. She examined the children's clothes, picked up a dress, found thread and needle, and began to sew.

"Long time no see," said Paula.

"Yes." Bella stitched. "You look lovely today."

"So do you. *Every* day."

Bella blushed faintly. "There's cholera downtown. You hear?"

"Just now."

"I've been there for the Red Cross. You know. In the war, I was a Gray Lady."

"I know." Paula bit a thread. "They wanted me to head up a posse of some kind. I refused."

"I should think you would!" Bella exclaimed sympathetically. "With all you have to do!"

"A lot of women won't be so charitable. They'll say I was afraid. Bella, the old jive has gone out of me. The knight-in-armor attitude. Age creeping up, I suppose."

Bella's hazel eyes were intent but affectionate as they studied her friend. "A good thing. There are plenty of people running away into hiding. And plenty left to take charge of the show down there." She made a knot and set a dress aside. "There! That'll be good until whoever wears it plays ducky-on-a-rock. I saw Kate when her sister came for her. She stopped and said good-bye."

It was Paula who flushed now. Flushed, sewed a moment, studied her handiwork, and shrugged. "I sent her away. Kate was a disturbing factor around here. She disturbed me, personally, in a way I didn't know I could be disturbed."

"Yes."

Paula looked up sharply. "You mean, you knew?"

"I guess I always did. You don't mind my saying I was *glad* when I found out she was going to move away and live with her sister?"

"Nope." Paula thought it over and laughed. "Darling, you certainly give out a lot of wrong impressions! In an innocence contest, you'd take first place."

Bella laughed too, then. "The mousy type! If I didn't have

bright eyes and shiny hair, even Jim wouldn't have ever seen me. Poor Jim! But, after all, Paula! I was on a psychoneurotic ward for years during the second war. If there's anything I don't know about what's inside people—men *or* women—it's just because even crazy people haven't discovered it yet. Besides, when I was a freshman in high school, I had a siege of crushes myself. You outgrow it—"

"In some cases," Paula answered dryly, "at a ripe old age."

They smiled at each other.

Before the Disappearance, each had been the "best" friend of the other. For two years they had drifted apart. Now, gazing into each other's eyes, smiling in a certain way, they were what they had been for so long. Paula sighed gently.

But, Bella chuckled. "Let's have a highball. I've got something strange to tell you."

Over the drink, Bella began, "I've been dreaming. About the men."

"Who doesn't?"

"I don't mean *that* kind of dreaming. Something odd. It's been going on for weeks and weeks and weeks! First it wasn't even about the men. I just kept dreaming, every night, of a huge, bright ornament, like a Christmas-tree gadget. A star, all colors, but as big as a house."

"It sounds attractive."

"It was. Then I saw Jim, *inside it*. Then, a few nights later, Gordon. Then Jim *and* Gordon. And, one night, your Bill!"

Paula started. "Bill? Wrapped up in a colored star?"

"Something of that sort. I can't describe it. But it seemed as if they were all trying to talk to me. And then, nights went by. Pretty soon I began to see lots of people. And *places*, Paula! My house and your house and Miami and everything. Only—" she paused and her voice dropped—"it was *different*."

"How?"

"Well, I'll explain. Though I haven't told a soul, because I'm simply terrified of what it may mean. Paula! Both our places were all tangly and overgrown. It looked as if ours had been kept up for a while and then not. But yours was a mess!" She nodded toward the long rows of vegetables where the pines and palmettos had once grown. "Nothing like this. Trees down. Vines. And your gardener was doing work indoors, for Bill."

"For *Bill*? I don't understand."

"Keeping house, a little. Doing the wash. And Bill, in the dreams, was writing all the time. Do you know what on? Reports on the work of all the scientists in the country, trying to get *us* back!"

"Bella!"

"Well—*wouldn't* Bill be doing something like that? I mean if what happened to us also happened to *them*? Miami was *entirely* different, Paula! No fires had burned down the blocks and blocks of buildings. But in every dream it looked dreadfully *tacky*. Not much traffic. Men lounging around. And pansies, going in bunches, dressed up as women. And loads and heaps of new laws and rules and ordinances that my poor Jim keeps studying. You know how neat his offices were? In my dreams, with Miss Keltner and Miss Beelan gone, they're a shambles! And most of the men are bad-tempered, like dogs gone a little wild. They get into fights. A lot of them carry guns. They steal things, in broad daylight. Jim is *so* worn and haggard and frightened all the time! So is your Bill. They've had a lot of strikes and, I guess, rebellions. Because sometimes I see what Jim reads in his newspaper. It's only four pages thick. And it's usually about revolts. Even the National Guard rebelled, somewhere, and shot up a whole town. Gordon still goes to school. He has a man teacher. But they pick up all the schoolboys in a bus now, and the bus driver always has a man next to him with a rifle. Little boys aren't safe any more. *Imagine!*" Bella shuddered.

Paula looked at her thoughtfully. "And you think what you've dreamed is real?"

"Paula, I don't *know*! That's why I decided to tell you—as soon as I realized you were your old self again."

"A new self," Paula replied moodily. "Not that it matters any more." She shrugged. "How could our world also be their world? And different? And separate?"

Bella shook her head. "I just think, most of what I dream is so *logical*. It's what *would* happen if it were them, instead of us. Of course, there are some things I dream about that simply couldn't be." She smiled mischievously. "Like, I dreamed once that Reverend Connauth called on Jim, and you know what he was doing? He was boasting, positively *boasting*, of having had a lurid affair with a blonde, years ago, when he was first married to Berthene! *That* couldn't have been anything but *my* nasty mind—!"

"Yes, it could!" Paula said in a suddenly tense tone. "Because he did have! Berthene told me, one day when I was in the dumps. Told me, to get my mind off myself. It did too. I was dumfounded —and touched. The minister really had that affair, Bella, and *you didn't know about it* or imagine it was *possible*! In a world without women—! Who knows? Even a clergyman might get boasting of a thing like that! Bella, I can hardly dare to think it, but your dreams might be *true*! They may *be* somewhere—even here—alive, separated, like us! Oh, darling!" Paula burst into tears.

"I hoped you'd think that. I was afraid to tell you, though—"

The other woman controlled herself. "What else?" she asked excitedly. "What *else* did you dream?"

"Not much. What I said. And the talk."

"Talk?"

"Oh, sure. Jim and Bill. Nights. They talk."

"About what?"

"Us."

"And what do they say?" Paula's eyes were dilated with emotion.

Bella stared out over the hot fields, her face filled with light, with trust and warmth and sensitivity. "They talk interminably, Paula. About what was wrong. *You* know."

"But I *don't!*"

"About, mostly, what a mess everybody has made of sex. They talk about how sex hungry they were and how ashamed they were of being hungry because they had been taught to be ashamed."

"I was ashamed, myself. We taught Edwin and Edwinna and Theodora, while we had her, to feel ashamed. Every time the children showed appetite for food, we fed them full. And every time they showed a sign of erotic appetite, we slapped them down. Made *sure* they were cowering and scared. That, we called moral training!"

"What *could* we have done? If our kids had been erotic and show-offish they'd have suffered in another way."

"I know. Some people thought they were very modern about their youngsters and sex. So frank and candid, it was painful. But all of them were *still* so self-conscious about it that the kids *knew* it wasn't really frankness and naturalness. Those kids were just balled up in a different way from their parents."

"Like the Eckstrom children at Coral Court School? Remember? The teacher sent them home because all they talked about was how grownups made love and how children were born. They were positively *obsessed* with it, and certainly that's not natural!"

Paula nodded. "You can't change bad ideas ground into everybody by just changing a few children here and there. You can't expect adults, either, to change overnight into honest, normal beings. Reading the facts on top of prejudices and fears you don't even know you've got doesn't made you normal. Practically everybody would have to decide, all together, to shift things."

"Some parents were trying, though—"

"In a half-baked way. But ever since the men went and women have talked freely I've been hysterical with laughter sometimes, and more often just downright furious, to find out how much utter bilge almost everybody believes about sex. And how dreadfully superstitious they are about it. I mean, thinking cancer is caused by venerial disease, or adultery. Things like that! Ye gods!"

Bella sighed. "It is awful."

Paula said resignedly, "*We* didn't do anything, in any case. And now we're whipped. Done for. That's the proper reward, I guess, for being cheats and hypocrites. For trying to lick nature. It can't be done. Whatever a person's real morals are, they have to come from inside that person. Social morals just start underground fires that consume the person. And the people around that person."

"Before the men went I thought all the talk about the importance of sex was silly. Even kind of dirty. Now, being alone, hundreds of nights, thinking without caring where my thoughts go, I know about what *they* felt." Bella looked wistfully at the hot field. "Just to live a day—*really* being the way we *really* are—would be worth a lifetime of most people's lives! The truest feelings we have are some of the ones we called sin. We put thousands of people in jail for doing things everybody would like to do and most people do, sometime or other. It's no *wonder* that we were all so scared and hateful and miserable. We *do* kind of hate our bodies. Hate being people. I guess it doesn't matter that we're destroyed."

"Did you get the feeling, ever, in your dreams, that the men might come back?"

Bella shook her head. "No."

"Did they—have any hope?"

She thought awhile. "No."

"And they thought that our failure to be honest and real about sex—"

"—about love, they called it—"

"—was the cause of the mess?"

"That. Yes."

"Did you think they were dreaming about us?"

"No. Not the way I was."

"That star you described. Did that suggest any kind of beginning point? Any method you and I might try to make them dream the way you were?"

"I don't think so."

Paula lifted her highball, looked at it, and set it down. "Do you suppose there would be any way for us, if they came back, to try to feel and behave the way we think, *now*, that we should? Not to be possessive? Jealous? Envious? Hostile? Not to demand anything? To accept all. To want for them more than for ourselves?"

"I thought I always did," Bella answered, without immodesty. "But I guess where the things I was brought up to believe were concerned, I always really insisted on having my way."

Paula shrugged. "That's *it*! When people believe that what they believe is the immortal truth there's not much you can do. They're born clay with a tendency to become lovely statuary. But some aunt, some mother, a sister, a schoolmate, a church, soon grabs them and bakes them into mean little bricks. And the bricks made a nation. And every brick is faulty and crumbly. And when the pile gets high enough it collapses. Every single nation did; and now, the world."

"That's the sort of thing Jim and Bill say in my dreams!"

"We've got to do something about your dreams, Bella!"

"What?"

"I don't know. Write them down in sequence and detail. Then get people studying what you've written. It could be the beginning of a way back."

"It hardly seems so to me."

"You maybe ought to be hypnotized," Paula went on earnestly, "to see if anything can be found out that way."

"I wouldn't like to be hypnotized."

Paula looked at her compassionately. "I know. Who would? But that's beside the point! We should get your dreams publicized. Find out if other people are having dreams like them. Maybe they are. Couples that have real love between them."

"If that was the case, you'd be dreaming too, Paula."

The older woman was silent; slowly her eyes filled. "No," she answered. "Not me. I was too selfish. Too mixed up to be in love. I liked Bill. I enjoyed him as a man. But love? I didn't know myself well enough, then, to love *anybody*. I missed *my* chance."

The children came soon after that, shouting, hungry, glad to have finished not only school but the afternoon's gardening to which all girls over eight were now assigned.

Bella went home. . . .

That night Paula gave thought to Bella's dreams. They might well be "true" in a sense of truth neither of the women understood.

Men, surviving alone, would undoubtedly grow short-tempered and finally violent. They would allow their yards to become overgrown, their cities tacky. But their cities would not have burned because they would have had the fire-fighting equipment and the firemen to cope with every situation at any moment of disappearance of women. Also, their homosexuals might go about in bands for either (or both) of two reasons Paula could imagine. And the fact that Bella had dreamed of Connauth's love affair, without any prior knowledge, was very persuasive.

The possibility that, through dreams, some contact might be reestablished kept Paula awake until near daylight.

At the same time, however, Bella was having another dream, one that proved to be her last.

She saw her house on fire. She had a feeling that it had been robbed or raided. She thought she glimpsed strangers skulking away in the trees beyond the house. She then located her husband and her son. They were hiding in the thick hibiscus hedge, obviously in terror, watching helplessly as the flames rose.

No one came to fight the fire. At length it burst from the windows of the upstairs bedrooms. Part of the roof fell. She saw, for a few moments, the rear of a huge, incomprehensible framework, in the living room. It was covered with different colors of tissue paper; there were electric wires leading to light bulbs, here and there. It made no sense to Bella and she did not connect the framework with the "star" of which she had originally dreamed. However, as the peculiar structure began to blaze her dream became dimmer. Toward its end she again saw the faces of Jim and Gordon—fading mistily. Her husband and her son were weeping.

She did not dream about them any more, in the same way.

When, some days later, she told Paula, that gallant woman also shed tears.

"I guess," she said, "that ends that! If they are alive and if you did 'see' them, they're having as bad a time as ourselves. Such a bad time that it spoiled any chance of communicating, if that's what you came near doing."

They forgot it, packed it deep in the Pandorean trunk of the events of that summer.

Too much else happened.

August again.

Hot mornings, humid and still.

The light-colored walls of the tropical city hurt the eyes; shadows, intensified by the sun, seemed as black as night; visibility was confined to surfaces. What would have been shade in a less torrid place here was an impenetrable gloom; a few trees or a clump of shrubs had the external glister and the interior murk of a jungle. At midday the sun heated the scalp through any hat or helmet.

In the midafternoon a storm usually curdled over the sea or the glades and bore down on the region in eddies and promontories of gray, white and muddy-blue clouds. Lightning cracked, the rain came in torrents of coarse drops. Then it cleared and the sun set redly, leaving heat to steam on the land in an airless night loud with insects.

On such a day, after the rain had stopped Edwinna came home from the Everglades. She walked slowly with her head bent, from the place where she had been set down by the truck. A woman of angles and sinews, now, with an Indian's skin color; her once-sleek hair was cropped short, disheveled, bleached ashen by the sun. Her eyes had a hunter's squint and she came along the lane silently, not noticing that she avoided stepping on twigs, in puddles that might splash, on bits of coral that might produce a grinding sound. She smelled of wood smoke and laundry soap. A man, an old acquaintance, had there been one, would not merely have failed to identify the lithe figure in the lane with its pre-Disappearance original; he would have sworn they were not the same, on the grounds that such absolute change was impossible.

Yet a man, any man, would have found this Edwinna attractive, as some woman in a Viking's camp might be.

She turned in at the drive. From a shady place amongst the oaks she stared toward the fields where Hester and her relatives and the school children were working patiently, steadily, not stopping any more even to slap at sand flies and mosquitoes.

Then she went on into the house.

From a faucet she drew a glass of water and drank it and another and a third. She savored the last, enjoying the absence of muckiness, bark acridity, and the slightly sulphurous taste of decayed vegetation. She hadn't had water since morning. She was used to that—as used as the Negro women and the children to insects.

She heard a motor, unfamiliar. Footsteps. The kitchen door opened.

Edwinna sprang forward, smiling. "Mother!"

Then she recoiled.

Paula was wearing white, dirty white. Across here nose and mouth was a heavy mask. Gauntlets covered her hands.

"Keep away from me," she said heavily. "Just open the door to the maid's bath."

Edwinna opened the door and Paula pulled it shut with her elbow.

The younger woman sat down. Pretty soon she heard the shower and a sound of scrubbing.

She went to a kitchen window and looked out. The truck her mother had driven was painted black and had red glass in its headlamps. Edwinna shivered slightly and opened the icebox door. There were some frankfurters and she ate them, one by one, uncooked, cold.

Paula at last emerged in a clean cotton dress. She smiled and extended her hands. They kissed.

"What the hell?" Edwinna asked.

"Somebody has to."

"Has to what?"

"Pick up the bodies."

"Ye gods!" Edwinna considered for a moment. "Why you?"

Paula shrugged. "Because it's the one job we can't ever get enough volunteers for."

"Is it all cholera?"

"Guess so. Mostly. Is that why, by any chance—?"

Edwinna nodded. "We had three cases last week. Five, this. So they called off hunting till it dies down. Brought us in."

"I see." Paula sat at the breakfast-nook table. "I'm glad you're here. Mighty glad."

"Can't anything be done to check the damn disease?"

"Not too much. No drugs available yet. Washington just promises. Wells polluted. Rivers. Bay. Always were. Flies carry it. God knows what else. It's awful!"

Edwinna nodded again, silently. She asked, "How many—?"

"I couldn't say. I'm not at the executive end any more. We have fifteen trucks, fifteen teams. City divided up. We took twenty-four bodies today. About average."

"Took 'em where? Cemetery?"

"We used to." Paula walked over to the stove, turned a switch, felt a burner and was evidently relieved to find it working. "We did that in July. Had bulldozers. They broke down. Now—" she shrugged again. "We pumped the water out of one of the rock pits. Keep it pumped dry. Burn the corpses. With what the forage squads can get. Wood. Some kerosene. Used car oil."

"I just ate four hot dogs," Edwinna said.

Paula nodded understandingly. "Okay. Extra food. For sandwiches for the kids in the evening. I've got some stew beef."

"I'll cook."

Her mother shook her head. "You go take a hot bath. There ought to be water. My God, Edwinna, you look shot!"

"Be all right tomorrow." Her eye had moved to one of the windows and focused there. "Hey!" she exclaimed. "A quail!"

"A lot, these days," Paula answered. "And doves. Only, nobody to shoot them—"

"From now on," Edwinna answered, "there will be. My stuff'll be brought by truck in the morning. I'll cadge some ammunition. Also, till we start hunting again out there, I'll get on one of your burial parties."

"Thanks."

Edwinna walked through the living room to her own room and as she went she began to remove her clothes. She was thinking about beef stew and a hot bath, not about epidemic and its charnal chores. . . .

The people of the Miamis—the people who still stayed there, the people who had not yet died and not yet fled—learned that if they came out of their homes and apartments, their shacks and hovels, in the late afternoon, and if they looked toward the northwest section, they could see against the sky a pillar of greasy smoke. This was the smoke that rose from the rock pit, the open-air crematorium. The people came to learn that they could gauge the intensity of the plague by the volume of that swirling, sticky column.

They came to know, also, that in certain weathers the smoke would beat downward and back upon the city. A particular horror would then be added to the febrile moaning of the afflicted, to the fatigue and the universal fear, to the rumble of the black trucks with the red lights, and to the swift visitations of the women in gruesomely soiled white who carried empty stretchers into houses and brought them out sheeted and freighted.

No one knew where the plague had come from or exactly when it had reached Miami. The first dozen dead, or the first score, were buried without diagnosis. A rare traveler from Asia might have brought it, or one of the occasional planes from Latin America.

As the panicky populace fled from it, they fled with it. So cholera burned its way up the east coast of Florida, through the rolling heartland, into Jacksonville, Atlanta, Savannah, Charleston and onward where the women went, with their girl children. Ahead of it a shaky cordon formed, a leaky barricade, that retreated week by week as it found itself infiltrated or by-passed. The radio, and such newspapers as were printed, incessantly advised people to boil water and to take other sanitary measures. But there was no means to cope with the flies in those days; and the small supplies of effective drugs were now hoarded.

September came.

One of the quota girls at the Gaunt house had died of it. Three Negroes had also been trucked to the soot-encrusted inferno and jettisoned by Paula, Edwinna and two helpers—robed, masked unstricken.

In September, Washington took steps.

South Florida was evacuated.

Healthy groups and families were carried as far north as Minnesota, which was where the Gaunts and their people arrived finally.

They were quarantined for a time and then assigned a deserted farmhouse.

There, in the waning autumnal warmth, they took up life again.

They canned and preserved fruits and vegetables. They stored the extra rations supplied by the government. They chopped wood in preparation for Minnesota's winter. They fished and salted down their catch. They gathered nuts. They started their ration of hogs on acorns and garbage.

Nearby was a village where a dozen Russian technologists advised and aided the area in the autumn farm tasks. For these women Paula often acted as interpreter, though most of them had already learned some English.

In October, all the Gaunts' colored people and most of the quota girls had their first glimpse of snow.

In November, Edwinna brought down two deer.

When the lakes had frozen and the drifts began to pile up, they ate sparingly, once a day. They worked then on the repair of the old building and the refurbishing of their clothes. Gradually, they grew used to zero temperatures. And slowly they began to realize that this would be where they would live, always.

There was no way to get back any more, no good reason to go back.

At Christmas, and again at New Year's, Edwinna went to her room and opened a Bible in the center of which was a brown and brittle pressed flower that once had been a yellow hibiscus. She had picked it from Alicia's bush the morning the evacuation buses had come for the Gaunt party. Those two days, she cried.

The remainder of the time she was known, in all that large, scattered community, as a rock among rocklike women. And a mighty hunter, like another whose courage and energy had saved a similarly destitute colony in the winter of its plague and hunger: Captain Miles Standish. He saved the Christians though he was not one of them; Edwinna resembled that man in what she did and how she did it. . . .

The city they had left had been buffeted by another hurricane in October. But there was no one there, or no one legally there, to set the trees upright again, repair the fallen wires, mend the smashed bridges, clear the streets and replace the shrubbery. The windows that had been smashed in thousands remained toothy. The roads to Miami were impassable and nobody wanted to go there, for the reason of dread although the plague had departed with its human company.

Now, only a few Negro women and children who had evaded deportation lurked in the crumbling metropolis. And occasionally a dugout, poled by gaudy Seminoles, moved into the silent city. These women looked at the stores and the vacant streets, the creepers tenting the residences and snakes coiled in the shade of waste bins and fire hydrants. Often they smiled or even laughed a little, as if at Pyrrhic victory. . . .

Where a tree had broached the screening on the Gaunts' porch, a panther found its way and made its residence. It would be a good place to have cubs in the spring and the big cat may have sensed that fact. . . .

In Minnesota, at night, the aurora played and the wind sent flying in the prismatic gloom ghostly devils of luminous snow. But the women slept, in the cold rooms, two in a bed or three. The carcass of a deer hung outdoors, high and frozen, swinging a little.

Dreams here, memory, rest from hard work.

But not hope.

18

THE RETREAT OF MEN OF GOOD WILL.

Gaunt aimed carefully. The fool had showed himself in the bedroom window, knocking out the screen and yelling to the others below. As he aimed, and because it was his nature, Gaunt wondered what it would be like to kill a man. He saw an armload of Paula's clothes dropped with a lewd guffaw, clothes that had remained through the years on their padded hangers.

The range wasn't great and Edwin's rifle had telescopic sights. He moved the barrel on the big pine stump until the crosshairs fell exactly on the temple of the laughing man. He fired.

The gun kicked.

The man sagged over the upstairs window sill, slowly slid out and crashed down.

Gaunt thought, *Now they know!*

Now, the men raiding his house knew that it had a defender. An armed defender ambushed in the palmettos.

When he had heard them drive up, Gaunt had left his typewriter. He had taken the gun standing in the corner by the fireplace, loaded and ready ever since they'd burned Jim's place.

Jim was still in his office, from habit. There wasn't any business any more. But he was not here, thank God.

Gordon was mercifully at school.

Gaunt looked at his watch. Three-twelve.

Hot afternoon.

He moved, keeping out of sight, to a stump some fifty feet away from the place where he had fired.

They were cursing now. Running from the house like ants from a hole. There were ten or twelve of them and they had come in two delivery trucks. There had been no time to phone for police. And the police, in several recent instances, had joined the raiders, when the odds were heavy or the loot was tempting.

Gaunt looked cautiously over the second stump. The men had moved back around the car porte where the brick wall sheltered them, dragging the body as they hurried.

Gaunt began to crawl, keeping his rifle ready. Shooting one sometimes discouraged the rest—drove them off. But these men were not going.

His feeling of rage was his only feeling—consuming, terrible. In a way, acceptable. Even desirable. He had never felt such an emotion before.

A fire lane had been bulldozed through the spiky scrub long since. He followed it now, keeping low. It came out on the three acres of his neighbor's lawn. Along the east end of the grass, on the margin of the Gaunt property, was a low pile of coral rocks, chunks dynamited out to make his neighbor's swimming pool. Now they served as a rampart. He crawled north, behind it. Presently, he could hear the men arguing. Not many words reached his ears but enough so that he gathered they were debating who should go after "the killer."

Gaunt smiled, a smile as mirthless and as steady as a skull's.

He chose a barrel-sized chunk of rock with an oak in front of it and woodbine growing thickly upon it. He raised himself, inch by inch. The men were standing in what they presumed to be the shelter of a thick, brick wall which was covered by solanum in full blue flower. They were passing from hand to hand and hand to lips bottles of liquor taken from his house. They had rifles, a tommy gun, and pistols.

He had a Colt in addition to Edwin's good gun. And he was sober.

He slid the barrel of the rifle cautiously in amongst the vine leaves, on top of the great coral stone. He moved his knees until they were firm and comfortable. One of the men peered around the house, south toward the palmettos that Gaunt had left.

They would take everything they wanted from his house as they, and a hundred other gangs, had robbed a thousand other homes. They would kill anybody they encountered, a child as quickly as a man, in, or near, a house.

He decided he could shoot two: he aimed at one and re-aimed swiftly, for practice. Two. Not three. And not one. There was no great hurry. They were still drinking.

Along the edge of lawn behind him was a cord, weather-beaten and gray, that ran from stake to stake. Gaunt examined it. He relinquished his rifle and pulled up one of the stakes. He crawled and pulled another. Then a third. He broke off a long length of the partly rotted twine. He went a little farther south and tied its end to a young poisonwood tree, carefully not touching its leaves or barks.

The tree, he thought, had come up and grown as tall as a man since the women had vanished.

He crawled back to his rifle, paying out line.

He had about twenty-five feet left. It would do.

Some ways behind his back was the north line of his property; beyond that, a thick pine woods.

He set himself again, knees on the same spots on the crushed turf. Men at that distance, two hundred feet, were big targets.

Who were they? Who were the nearest two, the two his rifle muzzle alternately pointed out? Not hoodlums. Not necessarily. Not delinquent youths. They were *anybody*. All ages, all sorts. Most had once undoubtedly considered themselves respectable. Some might have once had good jobs, responsible positions, property of their own. Not any more. Probably most of them had been married, had children. Not any more.

Life was cheap. Excitement was hard to find unless you made your own excitement. Rations were thin unless you went out and added to your share by force.

Life was cheap.

Gaunt's aim steadied. The rifle cracked sharply. The hit man made two-thirds of a scream. The second shot went unheard in that horrid, flap-jawed, ear-splitting utterance. But the dirty pith helmet worn by the second man jumped into the air and hit the Gaunt lawn and rolled. The front part of his head turned red and slid sideways and gushed clots and blood. He seemed to stand up for a long time.

The tommy gun chattered.

But Gaunt had moved north, paying out line. Bullets pinged in the air, threw a green confetti from slit leaves, tore into the grass beyond the rude wall, spat coral fragments.

The men were all firing now, firing and cursing and kicking each other's heels as they pushed through the back door. Then they were out of sight, except the two dead men.

Windows immediately broke as rifle barrels cleared away the glass. Firing from indoors chipped at the big stones.

Gaunt reached the end of the cord. He jerked it lightly.

Thirty yards to the south, the poisonwood tree quivered as if a crawling man had touched it.

"There he is!"

The submachine gun whittled into the coral. The poisonwood lost its leaves.

Gaunt lay behind the rocks, watching. He allowed the tree to stand still for some time, shook it again, waited through another fusillade, and then pulled up the string slowly so the tree bent a little. He made his taut line fast.

"Fallen against that bush!" a voice bellowed. "Callen! Doyle! Get around the end of that wall! Guy's probably dead!"

Gaunt waited a long while. Then, far down the wall, he saw Callen, or perhaps Doyle, furtively wriggling forward. He aimed at the man's head, fired, and missed.

The man ran.

Gaunt had shot from an angle north of the house where he could not be seen through the windows. Now, swiftly, he backed into the trees, turned, hurried, turned again and looked, saw no one and walked upright, east, through the pine trees.

He came out on a road. From the road his house was invisible. He followed it east a block, then south, walked two more blocks, crossed another lawn, and slunk west again, behind a higher, cemented coral wall completing a circuit of his property.

He knew that he should leave now.

The men didn't have much organization. But they had less sense.

That was how he had killled three of them.

They were in his house, afraid to emerge.

Getting drunk.

Since killing had not driven them off, there was no way to tell what they would do. But they could not fire the house so long as they depended on it for cover. And they did not know where he was, so they did not know which exit would be safe.

The knowledge that he had done what he could, what he had planned to do, what he had somewhat prepared to do—the fact that he was unscathed and could get away, seemed unsatisfying. He wanted to stay. He wanted to kill all of them.

Why?

It was his house.

His house.

Driven from it, bereft of it, watching from a hiding place, like Gordon and Jim while their home burned, was, very simply, a thing some hitherto unknown, inner part of him refused to tolerate.

He was not a deputy. He could have been. Duty did not hold him. It was, rather, outrage.

From behind the wall, he peered at houses and bungalows below his place; they were identifiable as white walls seen through trees and as splashes of tile roof seen over bushes.

Nobody emerged from them. These smaller houses were less liable to attack. But everyone in the neighborhood might be away. More likely, men and boys were cringing in their rooms, listening to the shots and the cries, quaking, impotent.

Gaunt was not very nervous. His hands were cold but steady. His heart was beating hard from hurrying down the street; soon it quieted. He found a place where the palmettos were higher than the wall, and went back into his own property. He threaded his way amongst the clumps, crawling on old pine needles, bare sand, ashes from brush fires, and sooty ledges of the hard, sharp spongelike rock.

In the thickest part of this area, a spot marked by a new, young pine, he had cached another rifle and shells. He made his way slowly, careful not to agitate the palmetto fronds. He found a green hole where he could look through, not over, the tangle. He heard, dimly, the loud talk in his house. Presently he saw a man slide from his upstairs windows onto the flat roof.

He used a crotch in the little pine for a gun rest. There was no sense in taking chances on his own, unbraced aim. He was not a good shot.

The man began moving forward, crouched, peering, his rifle ready.

Gaunt fixed the cross hairs on a point midway between the shoulders. He squeezed the trigger until the gun cracked and kicked. The man rolled off the roof.

Gaunt moved a hundred yards. Bullets sought him at random. Uselessly.

But now, they again knew approximately where he was.

A truck started, rolled along his driveway. Gaunt fired at it without effect and moved again. The other truck remained.

A half hour passed. Flies and mosquitoes found Gaunt.

He brushed the flies away, slapped at the mosquitoes as quietly as he could. A little of the rage in him was distracted by the tormenting insects.

The truck returned, accompanied by two more. Gaunt heard a third vehicle stop on the road south and east of the palmettos. Reinforcements. They had enough esprit de corps for that. Enough to be more furious than afraid, enough to want to pay him back for their losses.

The men in Gaunt's house called, jeered, whistled.

His fingers were sticky with his own blood from the hundreds of fat mosquitoes he had crushed. His trousers were stained where he had kept wiping his hands. He picked up the two rifles reluctantly: he could no longer bear the insects.

He crawled again to the wall and found a covering cabbage palm. He went over.

His house was about three hundred yards away.

He heard another car approach along the overgrown street between his place and the ruins of Jim's. The car turned into his drive. Shots came from the house and from the parking yard where the trucks stood. The car backed furiously, raced its rear wheels and went away. He heard it again, moving down a distant road; then it was silent.

More time passed.

Suddenly the rocks spattered in front of him, near his head, and the sound of a rifle followed the sting of fragments. Gaunt dropped. There were now men behind him, over toward Teddy Barker's. Men, probably, all around the huge square of palmetto and hurricane-broken pine. They would close in.

A second shot did not immediately follow because, by dropping, Gaunt had put himself out of sight behind a clump of weeds. He moved a few yards and lay still: moving made the weeds bob.

But now they had a good idea of his position.

Two men began firing from the ragged shrubbery to the south. Bullets came from the west. Men in the house took up the fire from the corners of windows.

Gaunt did not fire back. To do so would merely hurry the instant when they would hit him.

He rolled on his back, pressed against the wall.

There were white clouds in the sky, white clouds with dark undersides, evenly spaced and very nearly of a size. Caribbean clouds; against them, a curled frond of cabbage palm and the limb of a pine. Here, soon, he would die.

His eyes were speculative. He no longer seemed to mind the haze of mosquitoes around his face, no longer even noticed it. His mouth was smiling. For a few minutes, minutes punctuated by the slap of bullets against the wall, by the downdrift of pine needles and the fall of twigs, he wondered what they would take from the house. Paula's clothes. The "new" money; Gaunt had a few hundred in his desk. The food and the liquor, of course. Maybe a chair or two because his chairs were comfortable and expensive. Some of his clothes because they were good clothes. Fire would destroy everything else.

And he would be dead.

This was the end of the successful philosopher.

Whose philosophy had in no way coped with the events of his life, or encompassed them, or interpreted them.

Whose life had been spent in reflection and in learning and in writing what he had understood of what he had learned.

A man of intelligence, whose last adventure, and most satisfactory in some bizarre fashion, had been the killing of other men.

Why had it satisfied him?

He looked steadily at the clouds and the blue areas between and the answer to his question was as plain as it was primitive. His life had been devoted to thought. He had rarely expressed feelings until he had first considered them. He had not yielded to the push of instinct until he had first defined and clarified impulse and intent, in his mind. But, at the last, because of what he had felt, and without reason—indeed, with an utter lack of sanity—he had remained in a place where death would overtake him, in order to shoot strangers.

He had acted, that one time, from primordial feelings. In so doing he had experienced a primordial satisfaction. It was as if, all his life, he had somewhere doubted that he was truly a man and as if, now that he was going to die, he could do so with the knowledge that in the ultimate crisis he was a man like other men.

He could hear, presently, a clumsy, drunken approach through the palmettos. He did not dare rise to fire again: the men on his side of the wall would see him and shoot. A snapping of dead sticks and a rustle of foliage became grunts and mutters.

Gaunt took the Colt from his pocket. If one of them peered over the wall, he might get one more of them.

Soon there was silence again. A long silence. He wondered about it.

Wondered, and caught sight of what he thought for an instant was a bird. But the "bird" fell within a foot or two of where he lay, spitting fire. He grabbed the wrapped sticks of dynamite and threw them with their burning fuse, back over the wall.

There was a blast. Men yelled and cursed. The wall itself cracked. Mortar sifted on Gaunt.

From the south came a series of shots and more yells. He heard men running.

Then a voice: "Dad! Over this way!"

He lay there. His skin cooled, pimpled. He tried to shout and could not.

"Dad! We're covering you! If you're okay, streak toward Barker's. Cut through the mangoes!" The voice was loud, clear, unmistakable.

Gathering his weapons, Gaunt ran.

As he rounded the bungalow he came upon Teddy Barker and

his son, Edwin. Both held tommy guns. The instant they saw him, they began to run and he ran with them. They leaped into a battered car. Edwin started the engine. He cut west on the coral road, shot past the Wests' place and the row of houses beyond it, turned onto Ponce De Leon Boulevard and turned again, on Sunset.

There was no immediate pursuit.

Below South Miami, on the Dixie Highway, a tire blew out.

Edwin stopped the car with a grim-lipped skill. "Come on!" he yelled.

The three men, carrying their encumbering weapons, hurried from the deserted road in amongst an untrimmed wilderness of hibiscus. Behind it was a house. In what had been a lawn and was now waist-high weeds stood a faded sign: "R. Baxter. Hibiscery."

Gaunt remembered the nurseryman.

Huge, hybrid blossoms glowed everywhere in a thicket of shrubs head high, house high. Red, orange, buff, white, yellow, pink, every combination of those colors, every shade between.

Edwin and Teddy Barker had crept in among the bushes and were staring at the highway, guns ready.

Gaunt squatted beside them.

But no one came.

No trucks hurtled down the road and stopped where the battered car leaned on its flat tire. No armed men swarmed into the grounds, looking.

Far back, to the south of the road, a smoke column rose. It grew in blackness and towered higher. Gaunt caught a glimpse of it and knew what it was and thought fiercely, briefly, of their dead.

At that time, however, his mind was devoted to the other matter. And, again, he was giving his feelings expression without thought: his dusty, dirty, unshaven face was tear streaked.

Yet he didn't speak until the other two abandoned their tense watch and turned to him.

Edwin had a clean-cut profile like Edwinna's and blond hair

like hers, though Edwin's was thinner now: underweight. His eyes
burned too brightly. His hands on his gun were tense and skinny.
He mooched along under the bushes and put his arm around his
father's neck, hugged him. "God love you, you old hoot owl!" he
said. "I turned up just about in the so-called nick of time! And
Teddy, here! He was already stalking those guys south of you when
I showed up in my car!"

"I thought—you were dead."

A truck approached rapidly. They fell silent, hugged the
ground, pointed their guns toward the road. It swept past.

"You knew about me starting for New Guinea, though—"

Gaunt told him—briefly. "And that's all I knew."

Edwin said shakily, "A hell of a long while ago! I went to
New Guinea. Where I once did a little flying, as you'll recall. Our
expedition took to the bush. Never found any women. Found snakes.
Blackwater fever. Other things. The plane left me there with some
Dutchmen, sick. It crashed on the way to Manila, apparently. I
stayed sick for a year and a half and I've been coming back, the rest
of the time, which is another story! Found out, a week ago, in Washington, you were supposed to be down here still. Got a presidential
disposition for gas—a car—and came. Hell of a trip. When I reached
the old plantation I was fired on. Guessed what *that* was! Pulled out
in time and scooted. And ran into Teddy at his place. He had got
out his ammo and squirrel guns to try to rescue you. We could see
you lying there, from his bedroom window. We—"

Teddy came through the bushes; when father and son had first
embraced, he had crept away.

"Look. I don't know where to go in Miami now. Those guys
may hang around our area for a while. Why not change the tire and
get down in the Keys? Not many people there, these days. We can
live. Ed needs rest; you can see that. Up here, unless the government can get things organized again, which doesn't seem so hot a
proposition, we won't live too damned long."

Edwin looked at his father.

Gaunt nodded.

He pushed the dinghy from the mangrove-shrouded fragment of beach where it had lain hidden. Excepting for the absence of wind, it was an ordinary winter day. The sun was well up. White clouds stood against a torquoise sky, reminding him, momentarily, of the days when he'd lain on his back and anticipated death.

Gaunt had a full beard now, reddish, shot with gray. His cheeks and lofty brow were brown, almost as brown as his irises. He wore faded shorts, nothing else.

The shade temperature was in the middle seventies; the sun, much hotter. Gaunt shoved the boat on the sand. Its keel made a mark and he left the boat in the water while he erased that track with bare feet. Then he waded to the dinghy and stepped in. As far as the eye could see was salt water, vanishing along the horizon at the indeterminate pale-blue edge of the sky. Here and there on the motionless surface, low, level keys marked the otherwise indefinable line. The nearest was a mile away, a green eruption some acres in extent with snags of black trees in the jungle. Hurricane remnants. The farthest was a mere pencil line in the formless blue distance.

From the hidden beach the bottom shelved gradually to a depth of three or four feet. The water over it was so limpid, so still, so unrefractive, that he could see a 'cuda waiting in the weeds a quarter of a mile away as clearly as if it had been a hawk on a tree limb. He could see loitering schools of smaller fish and gaudy, nosing angels, orange starfish lying flat, the curious hop of a heavy conch as it moved forward, anemones, eel grass, a ray half buried in the sand, a bonefish "mud" far to the right, and the distant dorsal of a young sand shark, cruising patiently.

The boat had no oars. He picked up a long pole with a wooden cuff and propelled himself, still-standing, out on the bland breast of the sea. It was like movement in the air, a few feet above ground. Presently he came to a large pothole and looked down. On bottom were several rose conchs. He could also see, reaching out from the undercut edges of the hole, the antennae of crawfish. He put down the stob pole, picked up a spear with two prongs, stabbed and lifted. A large spiny lobster flipped and croaked on the tines. He yanked it off against the boat's seat and stabbed again.

When he had taken a third, he exchanged spear for pole, pushed back to the key, and concealed the boat again. He carried his quarry inshore by their antennae.

Under dense mangroves on a small rise of ground stood two shelters, tarpaulins stretched between bamboo poles. Mosquito bars, dyed green, hung around them. Between them was a large, flat chunk of keystone and on that a hand-cut fireplace. Gaunt put a pot of water on the fireplace, lit a can of solidified alcohol under the pot and twisted off the crawfish tails. When the pot boiled, he dropped them in, adding salt. He cooked them for a few minutes, drained them, and, as soon as they had cooled, ate them. After that he lay down on one of the five sleeping places beneath the tarpaulins and closed his eyes.

He was awakened by the return of Jim Elliot and Gordon from a fishing expedition.

The two men and the boy carried several writhing groupers from their skiff, which had been deliberately half filled with water to keep the fish alive, to a small, salt pool in the center of the key. The groupers swam off with others of their kind. In lieu of ice, the pool served to keep fish indefinitely against bad weather or bad catches.

"The big one," Gordon said proudly of the fish, "would go ten pounds."

Gaunt agreed. "Easily."

"And we had one twice as big hooked for a while. We lost it."

"I lost it." Jim smiled. "Got under a rock. What's new?"

"Nothing," Gaunt said. "They're overdue, though."

The eyes of the one-time lawyer were sympathetic. "Don't worry. Plenty of things could delay them. They'll show up."

"Sure."

"Great boy, your Edwin."

"A good lad."

Jim shook his head. "The things he's been through! Gordon, I hope when you grow up you'll be like your uncle Edwin. I hope *you'll* travel halfway around the world to seee your old man."

Gordon looked at the ground. He, like other youngsters, was embarrassed when the men talked to him about growing up. He was embarrassed because the men were embarrassed—or sad. They'd start being excited about what happened when a boy grew up and wind up being silent, or sorry, or even angry. It had something to do with the fact that there were no girls to grow up with the boys. Gordon understood it intellectually. Emotionally, it seemed foolish. Girls were no good, anyway. Growing up like this, like an Indian, on a key, hunting and fishing—what was disappointing about that?

He said he'd be like Edwin and he saw the light die in his father's eyes and he turned away. "Guess I'll go around the key and see can I maybe find me another old turtle, or something."

Jim watched him go, sorrowfully.

Gaunt said nothing.

By and by he began to mix flour and corn meal. "We'll take a look around and I'll make a batch of johnnycake, if the coast's clear. A dry twig fire doesn't make much smoke, anyhow. Teddy and Edwin will probably be hungry when they come back."

Only Gaunt was awake when the third small boat coasted through the night to the remote island. He heard their voices. They were laughing. He hurried to the little draw where they kept the boat with the mast, using his flashlight sparingly.

"Hi, pop!"

The philosopher didn't conceal his relief. "Thank God!"

Teddy was out first. Then Edwin. The boat looked loaded in the moonlight. "We've got news!"

"Big news!" Teddy said, as he made a rope fast on a root. "We went all the way to Key West!"

Gaunt was frightened. "Pretty serious risk—"

"None at all!" The three men followed the path to camp. Jim woke, called a soft greeting, and rose. Gordon slept on.

"I've baked you corn bread—"

Edwin touched his father's back. "We've had plenty to eat. And we've got a boatload more. Dad! The worst's over!"

"*Over?*"

"Yeah. We can light a fire. We can go back to shore. We can do about what we please. You remember, when Teddy and I went on the last forage, there were plenty of rumors around about stopping the hijacking? Restoring order? Well, they're doing it!"

"Who?"

"The United States government, that's who! Things got so bad everywhere that no one could stand it anywhere. Millions took to the woods, the way we did. And the gangs got fighting, of course. Around Thanksgiving, Washington started to clean them out. Militias that could be depended on began forming up, the way they did in colonial times. Men and boys came out of the woods again, and off the farms. And fought. Small armies started shoving into captive cities, by the middle of January. The whole thing faded, everywhere. There are *stores* open again, in Key West! Armed guards on the main streets but the people are *shopping*—carrying things *openly!* From here on in, it ought to be okay."

Teddy said, "I signed up to help, myself. Came back to say so-long. I'm going to be with an outfit that's bulling its way back into Miami."

That, Gaunt thought, was the way it would be: an excess of brutality and barbarism, leading, through excessiveness, to the restoration of law. The pendulum might swing too far that way yet again:

excess of law. Martial law. Stern law. Summary executions for trivial offenses. That was how it had always been with man. Too much of one evil, bringing in its wake a cycle of virtue, and finally such emphasis on the "virtues" that the effect of these, in turn, became evil.

His son had been piling up wood to light their first night campfire. He struck a match. "You don't *want* to go back, do you, Dad?"

Gaunt shrugged. "I don't know. Does it matter? I'm content. I've never been in such physical condition in my grown-up years. And it's *peaceful* here."

Edwin nodded silently. The fire blazed up.

Jim yawned. "Going to hit the hay again. Gordon and I were up at daylight."

"Me too." Teddy Barker accompanied the attorney back toward the tarpaulins. His murmuring voice had the sound of fatigue but a note also of affection.

It was Teddy who had gone back to Miami alone in Edwin's car, not announcing his purpose, and returned to the island with Jim and the boy. The same Teddy, who, in the old days, had once referred to the lawyer in Gaunt's presence as a "woofle-brained old futz."

For some time the philosopher and his son sat looking at the unfamiliar night fire. Their silent attention was a ceremonial in itself a private thanksgiving. And it was also a communion between the two who had been close together spiritually, intellectually, ever since spirit and intellect had appeared in the child.

To both, their reunion was the only joyous event of the sad years; and they reveled in these days of companionship even while both knew how bleak the destiny ahead would be and how likely it was that this blank life was not permanent. Beyond doubt it would end in some savage new assault or else, as now seemed possible, in a resumption of hard tasks which might again separate farther and son.

The fire lighted up the trees; it hollowed out amber holes where paths led to the boats; and it threw latticed, mobile shadows upward from the fronds of giant acrostichum ferns. Edwin stretched a frame as lean as his father's, picked up a bottle of insect repellent, daubed himself and said, "A penny?"

"What do we *always* think about?" Gaunt answered. "What's lost."

Edwin grunted. "I wish I had your first report to read. And all you did on your second. I wish I'd talked to as many scientists as you did. I even wish I'd had a chance to sit in Jim's fancy room."

"Nothing came of any of it—science or magic."

The younger man smiled. "'All the king's horses and all the king's men,'" he quoted mockingly.

"There were times, a few times, when I felt on the verge," the philosopher went on, almost idly. "When *something* seemed about to happen, or to occur to me. And always, Paula was involved. Always, she seemed very close. I've had plenty of opportunities to ponder those moments. But the only common aspect of them was—" he broke off.

"What? Was *what*, dad?"

"Do you imagine a lunatic has instants when his lunacy recedes, is nearly *solved*? When, for minutes as lucid as his habit is deluded, he sees things sensibly, glimpses the truth of his condition?"

Edwin put another log on the fire. "Some loonies. Sure."

"Well, translate that sensation to a general one. A feeling that all of us have been mad for ages. An inkling of the nature of the insanity. And a resulting glimpse of what sanity would be like. I'd get that idea, or sensation, or whatever. And then there'd come that ghostly impression of imminence, of *presence*. As if Paula and Edwinna were in a near room, going about things as always. As if the old world were *there*, only not quite *seeable*."

Edwin nodded. "Me too."

Gaunt was startled. "You?"

"Sleepy?"

"No! You said—?"

"Would you like a cigarette?"

"Good God, son—!"

Edwin left the campfire and soon came back. He tossed a package into Gaunt's lap. The older man turned it in his fingers, opened it, took a stick from the fire and lighted a cigarette with its glowing end. He inhaled deeply, lay back on his elbow and watched the smoke eddy toward the fire. Then he looked at the cigarette itself. "Key West?"

Edwin nodded. "We told you. Things are getting organized."

"I should say so! This is my first in—I can't recall."

"Two things," Edwin began while his father listened eagerly, "occasionally give me that sensation you talk about. One's negative. The other is positive. The first is this: When I ask myself if I'd take the world back the way it was, I usually say yes. But sometimes, no. When it's no, I think why that is. Lots of reasons. Intricate reasons. Let me make 'em as simple as I can. After all, I also have had time, stuck around the Pacific, to ponder. Number one, our whole idea of progress and rising standards and more people was cockeyed."

Gaunt nodded. "No future in it. Strip the resources off the planet. Leave nothing for any posterity—"

"That. The cockeyedness of mass production. A plenty of having things and a total dearth of living a life. You were born, educated, and then what? You tended a machine. You sat in an office. You traveled to and from it. You aged and died. Most of your active self was spent in a long, nasty, unrewarding day. Dumb or bright, poor or rich, that was the schedule for nearly all. *Crazy!*"

"Yet most of the men who retired were miserable."

"And slaves love chains. There were too many people. They exploited their ability to stay alive. Took no responsibility for selecting the stock. For dying. For anything but breeding. And then what? The more there were the harder and harder they had to work!"

"What about shorter hours, bigger pay?"

"What about full employment?" Edwin answered hotly. "Get everybody in the act. Make everybody spend his best hours five days a week doing some idiotic damned thing. And why did we need a hundred and fifty million serfs for that?"

Gaunt grinned. "It's a thing I called the obscenity of purity. The old law of opposites in action. The people who insisted they were virtuous, insisted it was vicious to tinker with nature. With what *they* called nature. So they brought up their kids as chaste as they could, as 'pure,' as far from nature as the mind could get. Then their kids married. And what? 'Go to it,' they were ordered. The hell with *reason* and *responsibility!* The hell with *foresight* and *logic.* Breed like rabbits. Spawn. Throw into jail anybody opposed to *that* order! The effect? The Christian marriage bed was a social orgy that knew no let nor hindrance, no genetics, no restraint, no intellectual decency, whatever. Obscene, for a species with a brain. Truly obscene!"

Edwin nodded to himself. "In my time there was even more to it than that."

"More?" Gaunt sounded dubious.

"Sure. Back before the second World War, when I was a kid, the population experts showed how our birth rate was tapering off. In spite of the holy obscenity you mentioned, people were doing preventive things. Not the right people or the right things. But the birth rate *was* falling. Then—zoom! It shot up tremendously. All calculations off. Not enough schools, teachers, jobs, diapers, meals in sight, for everybody being born. Why was *that?* I've heard fifty reasons and not one was adequate. Not any ten."

Edwin kicked a small branch and watched sparks rise. "Listen. All through history, when nations have been in the grip of epidemic, or faced with conquest and slaughter, people have shown a last-minute tendency to copulate. Sometimes publicly, wildly, frantically. *Why?* Instinct, wouldn't you say, if you saw any other animals than men do it? A fling at preserving the tribe. An attempt to beat the imminent disaster. *Well?*"

"Good Lord," Gaunt murmured.

Edwin nodded. "Nobody could really explain why the young generation of America, before the Disappearance, suddenly changed its habits and took up breeding en masse. But nobody gave it a long-range, statistical squint from the instinctual point of view. You had a bunch of young people, not very bright, not well educated, given to conscious optimism and hope. But every day some graybeard told them that they could and probably would soon be blotted out in millions by atomic bombs, hydrogen bombs, radioactive poisons, bacteriological warfare, nerve gases, all that. Unconsciously they were horribly frightened. How could they help that? So what? First their conscious goal became security, even though there was none in sight. Pensions, idiotic things like that. And, second, they began to breed as fast as they could. Driven by nothing the population experts could understand because those wiseguys did not reckon the terrible and deep forces of animal instinct on their slide rules."

"Never thought of that," Gaunt murmured.

"I did. And when I did, I got that sensation of being near a solution to the mess that you mentioned. Our instincts, back in the old days, were trying to deal in the only way instinct can with forces of fear and with real dangers that our collective, conscious American mind had refused to face and put a stop to. We were trying blindly to get enough A-bomb fodder on hand to make up for the coming casualties! *That* explained the reversal of a trend everybody had thought was firmly established! *That* explained the millions of unexpected babies!"

For a long time Gaunt said nothing. Then he rallied from his thoughts. "The positive experience?"

His son also seemed bemused. He opened his mouth, closed it, murmured, "We wouldn't *face* reality. That was our biggest mistake."

His head shook. "Almost everybody tried to keep everybody even from trying to find out what reality was. Ridicule Einstein, repudiate Freud, suppress Kinsey, let's hear from His Holiness, the Pope. That was the real attitude of everybody, whoever or *whatever* their particular 'pope' happened to be. Yep! Insane!" He hesitated and then continued, "The other? During the war I was stationed on a Pacific island for a while.

"Loka Sorambi?"

"Yeah. Nice place. Polynesians. No shame sense. None of the decayed ideas of Hindus or Chinamen, either. None of that Presbyterian purity-in-talk, obscenity-of-behavior, either. Family ties strong. Marriages entirely happy—not entirely faithful—nobody minded. They all did everything *together*. Men, women, kids. Planted, fished, hunted, laundered, bathed in waterfalls, entertained whole villages, rested up from parties, made clothes, houses, tended babies. All together. Now look. They could have had a certain amount of machinery and medicines and drugs. They could have developed science to any degree and philosophy and art. And *still* lived pretty much as they did, felt *exactly* as they did, behaved socially the way they did. Only *a little* compartmentizing of their society would have been necessary for that. If they'd wanted to know and learn—and remained modest in what they applied and exploited —they probably could even have developed atomic energy without ruining human life, as such."

Gaunt grinned. "Could you sell that bill of goods to Americans?"

"Too late, isn't it?" Edwin grinned also, but differently. "Those were the only happy people I ever knew or saw or heard of. The only *contented* human beings. The only decent ones. The only ones who loved sunrise and sunset, each other, food and air, rain—loved loving, loved kids, loved life. The *only* ones. The only ones on the planet! Now there's nobody."

"What about your family?" Gaunt asked.

"Frances?" Edwin lighted another cigarette while he considered memories of his wife. "Frances had a single principle: it was to maintain the systems and methods recommended by the least unenlightened magazines for bearing and rearing children and keeping a husband what was called happy."

"And that kept her happy?"

"It kept her busy which most people identify as the same thing. That's because when they have nothing to do they're instantly wretched. In other words, they don't like *themselves*. Frances as a matron, a wife and a mother was a social success and a family success. Emotionally, she was a well-adjusted six-year-old. As a wife to me, she was a pretty and perfumed machine. And that was just dandy so long as I didn't have time for anything else, either. Most people never grow up any more than she did. And, God, how I envied them! How convenient it is to go through life as a child!"

"And how inevitable that religion should stress just that!"

The younger man nodded. "Nobody mature *could* stay in a pattern designed for children! Well, Pop, those were the two reflections that put me nearest to a sense of some other, larger reality that existed but that I couldn't see because of the wrongness of all we believed, stood for, did every day, felt, refused to feel, didn't do and so on. If I could do it over—" His voice trailed off.

"You'd what?"

Edwin laughed. "I'm sleepy now."

"*What?*" Gaunt persisted.

His son rose and stretched and kicked a spark-making log. "Lead a rebellion I guess. Against materialism. Against every ism, communism or fascism or pigheaded Americanism, that pretends to be no more than a thing-maker. Start a religion. A cult of learning and expression and enjoying and loving but not of so damned much 'progressing.' A procountry, pronature religion. A cult for reducing the human stock to a tenth of present numbers and bettering the breed a few thousand per cent. A religion that had wiser 'thousand-year' programs than old Hitler. There was nothing wrong with the period. Why *shouldn't* we plan for a mere thirty or forty generations, instead of just our *one?* Rather, why *didn't* we? My cult would be anti-city, also. Did you ever think that, just as I suggested the birth rate went up in response to a threat to the species—at least in America where the threat was dimly appreciated, so, perhaps, people invented atomic bombs because *actually* they hated cities, hated modern civilization, longed of inner *necessity* to smash the whole worthless, foolish mess? Start over?"

Gaunt was standing also, now. He yawned tremendously. "Yeah." His eyes met those of his son with affection but with irony too. "What I've thought about *most* is the difference between what people said they believed and what actually happened. Right *there* is the measure of the unconscious mind of everybody. The yardstick of instinct. The gulf between pretense and fact. It went unheeded in our time and we fell prey to it, finally, because what you refuse to look at is what gets you, always. The rebellion you talk about and the 'religion' belong someplace thousands of years ahead of where we were."

"Why, necessarily?"

The philosopher chuckled. "Because Frances wouldn't like it!"

"If Frances had gone through what we have, Frances might," the younger man replied grimly. *"Even* Frances."

"And where's even Frances?"

They looked at each other in the firelit night and without saying any more they started toward the place where the others slept.
. . .

Toward the end of the afternoon of the day following Gaunt started to the island in the sailboat with Gordon. They had a load of oranges, lemons, limes, taro root and monstera deliciosa, harvested from the remains of a plantation that had been established on one of the keys long ago and long ago abandoned.

There was no breeze, so Gordon was rowing, eagerly. They'd had a fine day.

Looking at the boy, Gaunt had, not his usual sense of tragedy, but a sudden feeling of hope. Here was the future, still. And all his extrapolations of despair did not darken the face or stem the energies of the boy. To this lad, Jim and Edwin and Teddy and he were as father and as mother also. But to this lad the world belonged and all future time. *Not to them.* They had no right to assume that Gordon would fail, as they had, to discover the answer to the Sphinxlike conundrum of the Absence. They had only the right to give him all they could, tell him all, teach him all, make him as honest as they knew how. The rest was his.

It was a new thought to Gaunt, and a comforting one.

He let the sense of it beguile him, stared composedly at the infinite blue of the pale Bay, watched the life on the bottom through the poured-glass water and reflected that spring was on the way. It came very early, always, in South Florida. He wondered about the date. It required some moments of calculation before he remembered: February, it was, the fourteenth.

Anniversary.

He snapped his fingers with surprise.

19

HOMECOMING AND CONCLUSION.

Gaunt snapped his fingers: the light lost its blue luminosity. The vast dimensions contracted. He and the boy were no longer dots in a matchstick sailboat on a pale and vacant sea. His eyes took an instant to reaccommodate. Vista, but where sea had been was a yellow greenness. A less bright sun glittered on a different surface. The one small mast turned into a hundred larger masts, and darker: the boles of trees. It took Gaunt a few seconds to realize this was his own pineland seen from the window of his own office.

Seen absently: he felt he had been staring at it, thinking of other things the nature of which momentarily escaped him.

He detested confusion of the mind, aberration, uncertainty. A scowl came on his high forehead; he moved his head. "Good *God!*" he whispered.

There, in front of him, was his typewriter and part of a page on which he had evidently been writing. His far-focused eyes could not instantly read but soon they made out two lines below the finished paragraph:

Prolix.

The dopes won't get to first base with it.

The words had the sense of something forgotten but familiar, something written a long while ago. Years ago. And soon he remembered.

He shut his eyes, for an instant utterly appalled; his ears took up the shocked function. A woman was singing. *A woman.* High notes trilled; it was the "Italian Street Song": *Edwinna.*

He knew what he had to do now; he did it with agony.

He moved his head. *Paula was there.*

But by now she had ceased digging in the peat moss. He remembered that also, remembered particularly because, in the attempt to solve the riddle, he had often recalled and pondered every detail of the instant of Vanishment.

Paula was there. In the same dress. With the same immaculate coiffure a copper-pink blaze in the sunshine. But her face had turned white as chalk, as the coral roads, as powdered shells. She clung to the rim of the wooden tub that contained the gardenia. Her hands were blanched like the flowers. And she, too, was trying to look.

A half inch at a time, as if her head were a great stone that could be moved only by extreme effort, in fractions of an arc, she faced toward his office. Her eyes, dilated, at length met his. Her lips parted a little, then widely: she would have screamed if she could have found the strength.

Edwinna's song died away in mid-trill.

Upstairs, for another second, the waxer hummed. Then it was shut off and Hester cried out incomprehensibly. Byron, the gardener, made two or three desultory cuts at the roots and then stopped. Alicia gave a sudden wild cry in the living room: *"Mummie!"*

Paula lurched as if a wrestling ghost were trying to loosen her hold on the tub.

He thought, *We have come back.* Those were the words that said what his senses recorded.

He maneuvered his feet under his body, braced his hands on the arms of the swivel chair, rose like an aged man, and then ran like a boy.

Paula had seen him. He knew that. To look had been anguish because she had feared *not* to see him. As he had feared.

Porch. Screen door. Lawn. She was in his arms.

"Darling," he said. "Oh, my darling!"

She murmured, "Bill, Bill, Bill!" Then she yelled it: *"Bill!"*

Gaunt kissed her violently.

She began to cry.

"It's over," he said to her in a reedy voice. "Ended. We've come back to *now*." He realized she might not understand, suspected, suddenly, it had not happened to anyone but him. Stunned anew, he recalled and analyzed the fact of her equal shock, but he said, "I've had a sort of nightmare."

"Nightmare!"

"Did you—?"

He felt her nod against his cheek. "But it wasn't a nightmare! It was *real*. Oh, God!"

A few moments passed; she sobbed and they held each other.

Then there was Edwinna, coming through the screen door with Alicia in her arms. She stopped to kiss the child and stopped again. "Dad!" she called hoarsely.

Gaunt reached out a hand. Girl and child plunged into his embrace. Edwinna put her head beside her mother's. Tears like drops of rain ran down her face. Presently she whispered, "Dad. Were you—? Were the men—?"

"For four hellish years, alone—!"

"It was the same with us!"

Gaunt laughed in a high, wavery fashion. "Let's sit down, before all four of us collapse!"

They sat, then, hanging to each other, kissing.

At last Alicia spoke, perplexity in her childish voice. "I had an awful tummy-ache a while ago, Mummie! It went away. Can I pick a flower?"

Gaunt saw horror in the women's eyes and murmured, "What —?"

Edwinna said flatly. "It's the last thing she remembered. The pain." Her still-stunned eyes lifted to those of her father.

"Go pick a flower," Paula said softly. "Pick them all, if you like, Alicia."

"She *died*," Edwinna muttered. "Years ago."

They didn't seem to know what to say then. How to explain. "There was a hurricane—" Paula began.

"We had one also," he said, when his wife halted. "A couple of years ago. I was away at the time. It dropped a tree on the living-room eaves."

"*Here*, Bill?" Paula asked earnestly. "You were *here?*"

"A good deal of the time. Lately—on the keys. With Jim and Gordon—Teddy—and Edwin."

"*Edwin!*" both women gasped.

He said, "Let's just sit a minute. Let's—thank God."

Paula had moved so close to him that they touched from ankle to shoulder and Edwinna was as close on the other side.

The child plucked gardenias and piled them on the grass.

They looked at the sky where, presumably, God was.

They did not say anything. They did not know what to say.

It was Paula who finally made the attempt. "We are thankful for our deliverance. We implore it will endure."

Gaunt said, "Amen."

But Edwinna was not satisfied. Her handsome eyes probed the blue zenith with sudden fury. "And if You send us back, I will hate You through eternity!"

"We *can't* hate any more," Paula said reproachfully.

Edwinna's change was as swift as the coming of her rage. "I know. I won't. It's only that I had to tell Him how I really felt *then*."

A confused ululation came from the rear of the house.

"It's Hester," Paula said quickly, "having hysterics, poor darling! I'll go talk to her."

But Edwinna was on her feet. "*I'll* go!" She started, stopped, thought of taking the child along, and did not. The kitchen sounds quieted.

Wife and husband, father and mother, woman and man, grandfather and grandmother gazed eyes into eyes for a long space of time. The child brought the flowers to them and walked a little distance to watch a mockingbird splash in the scooped-out coral bath.

At last Gaunt sighed and said, "So you went through it—right here—the way we did. Alone."

"Yes, Bill. All those years."

"It must have been terrible." The faintest shadow of his grin showed evanescently. "Or was it a relief sometimes?"

She turned slowly and examined her home. "Don't make jokes." She looked out across the palmettos and spoke dazedly. "We cleared the whole thing. Yams grew out there. Pigeon peas. Colored women had log cabins beyond."

"The last time I saw it"—he plucked grass blades, tossed them, caught some on the back of his hand, threw them again and let them sift away on the mild breeze—"I was out there, myself, with a rifle. Killing men."

She had looked at him attentively, her thumbnail caught under the white row of her upper teeth. Now she smiled a little bit. *"You* did, Bill? Shot men?"

He nodded. "Several."

"Defending your home?"

"Which wasn't even home, really. A shambles."

"Did that happen—in many places?"

"Everywhere. For a long time men slowly degenerated. Finally, for a while, most of them behaved like brigands."

"You weren't hurt? Sick? You didn't?" She glanced apprehensively at the child.

"Die?" He shook his head. "Wasn't sick. Or hurt. You?"

"No."

"Edwinna?"

Another pause. Paula drew a deep breath. "Edwinna was magnificent! She had more courage than anyone. She was a Diana. She quit niggling and complaining. She went out in the Everglades and hunted for the whole community. When the cholera struck—"

"Cholera!"

Paula looked down. "We never could manage things well. Yes, cholera. A hundred families depended on Edwinna, finally, till most of them died—till all the rest of us moved away. In Minnesota she shot deer. She—oh—Bill!—she was splendid!"

Then, only then, Gaunt burst into tears.

Paula comforted him.

In a little while Edwinna returned, carrying two glasses. "Iced tea," she said. "Do you want it? Or a drink? Or anything? Hester's okay."

They took the glasses. Edwinna gathered up Alicia and fondled her.

Paula and Bill tasted the cold tea. They said together, "It's been a long time"—and they laughed.

Edwinna kept watching her daughter with a look in her eyes both tremulous and astonished, as if she had never seen a child before, never felt the indelibility of something of one's self recapitulated, alive and discrete, never thought sympathetically of *littleness*, never really known that Alicia was real, was hers, was herself over again. But while she watched—surprised, attentive—she picked up the words her parents had spoken.

"A long time?" Edwinna's smile was dubious. "*Is* it? Or is it—no time? Have four years passed? Or is it only half an hour later? The way you two drink tea—were you thirsty, before we vanished from each other—or is it that you've had no tea for such a long, long time? What do you think?"

Paula's face was puzzled; she turned to her husband. "Yes, Bill. What *do* we think?"

"Search me!"

"Haven't—either of you two—ever imagined it might be just like this?" Edwinna saw their heads shake. "I have. Often. It was a daydream. I always told myself, this is a penance. We asked for it; if we stick through it—keep our hopes quiet—then, some afternoon, they'll put us back the way we were."

" 'They'?" Paula gently repeated.

"He. It." The young woman waved a leisurely hand toward the blue sky and the topaz sun. "Up there."

Gaunt's eyebrow cocked. "I didn't know you were a Believer, Edwinna. In anything."

"I learned to be."

"In what?"

"Me." She said it almost demurely. "In me being able to do things."

A plane throbbed over the house, a small plane hurrying through the azure atmosphere as if its pilot had discovered there in the sky the evidence of some urgent business that needed his attention on the ground.

"I wish I'd thought of this," Paula presently said. "Because I'd have some idea of—how to take it. I haven't *any!* I'm just—hopelessly stunned. We probably ought to do something. Listen to the radio. See if it happened to everybody."

"I did," Edwinna answered. "Hester is. It happened. The radio sounds like New Year's."

"And we should go over and see Bella and Jim. How strange it'll be to see *Jim!*" Paula said.

Gaunt shook his head wordlessly.

"I just put in a call," Edwinna continued. "Before the whole world tries to use the phone. Before the operators cave in, or walk off duty, or whatever they will do. For Charlie."

Both parents glanced quickly, in amazement. Paula said, "You called *Charlie?* Good Lord, Edwinna! What *for?* Certainly not because he's behind on Alicia's—"

"—money?" Edwinna did not speak for a moment. She did not even meet Paula's eyes. But finally she said, "What a bitch, what a perfect bitch I used to be! Mother, you *know* I didn't plan to ask for money! You *remember!* Everyone must! That's why it *happened!* I called Charlie to tell him to come here."

"Here!" Paula repeated. "Did you? But—"

"He's Alicia's father, for one thing. He'll want to be with her awhile now. He may even want to be with me." She said it humbly. "He was a nice guy. I loved him, once; and half ruined him. I thought I was just a glamour-puss, for sale to the best bidder. I didn't think I had even a bad temper! I thought he was weak and *that* was unfair. And I thought the world was mean. I never tried to help Charlie. I didn't know what I had to try *with*. Now"—she raised her eyes at last to her mother's—"I do know. I ought to be quite a wife, for *any* guy! And I picked him *first*, after all. In some ways, some very important ways, Charlie was a *man!*"

Paula saw her daughter's tan arms stippled by the memory of ecstasy. "What about Billy?"

Edwinna grinned. "What about him? We're divorced. I wasn't his type. I want peace. I want kids. I want home. I want Charlie, if he'll have me again. And I bet I can persuade him to!"

"I bet you can!" Paula was sure.

"*I* always did like Charlie," Gaunt said. It was his only contribution to the discussion. Edwinna kissed him for it.

He wrinkled his nose. "I don't exactly understand what you mean—but I enjoy the way you say it."

"Ask Paula." His daughter smiled. "Ask her about herself too. Ask Paula what it means when a mother wants a boy and a father, too, but you're a girl, so she calls you Paula because you didn't turn out Paul. Then, when you marry, you pass it along. Edwinna. And Theodora. Ask her."

Gaunt blinked worriedly.

But he saw the two women exchange glances of understanding. It wasn't one of Edwinna's acid cracks; it meant something real and acceptable to his wife.

The door chimes sounded. Twice: for the front door.

"I'll go!" Edwinna hurried.

"Her date," Gaunt suggested.

Paula lay back on the grass and looked at the sky. "Come here, Bill. Kiss me. Really kiss me. You haven't yet."

He leaned over her. "If I really did I'd start a scandal."

"So what?"

At the door, trembling and disheveled, one black braid fallen and her small son's hand clenched firmly, stood Kate West. Edwinna's eyes were anxious. "Kate, this is no time to call."

"I'm scared! I found Georgie. I found myself home again! I want to see Paula."

"Not now."

"I gotta!"

"Look. I'll walk home with you. But you're not going to bother Dad and Mom right now."

Paula heard the voice, recognized it, sat up.

"What's wrong?" Bill asked.

"Kate West."

"You're white as a ghost, Paula! For heaven's sake! Kate was probably startled—came over to be reassured! She's a helpless little person, after all—"

Paula glanced incredulously at her husband and nervously walked toward the porch. This was a crisis precipitated cruelly soon. To reject Kate, to send her away, would be inhumane. Yet, to accept Kate would be to expose Bill to possible confessions or recriminations or accusations. Paula listened to the low-pitched altercation clearly and she knew, after another frantic moment, what she would have to do, irrespective of cost.

Edwinna shrugged and unlatched the screen.

The young woman and the child crossed the porch and walked on the front lawn. They stopped.

"Paula! I was frightened!"

The Gaunts were standing now. He thought: Here is still another *woman*. How beautiful she is! How innocent seeming! How desirable! What a marvel the mere being of woman is!

His wife's shock seemed incomprehensible, almost mean. It referred, he realized, to things that had happened which he did not know about. And there would be, in years to come, many such sudden, surprising episodes.

"Hello, Kate! Don't be frightened. We've gone back to where we were. That's all. Hello, Georgie-Porgie." Paula ruffled the little boy's hair.

Kate said, "Yes. I realized. But I *had* to come over, Paula! Higgie isn't home yet. I'll be so glad to see him." Her young, high breasts moved with her sigh. "And I felt so sorry about you."

"It's all over." Paula spoke with desperation. "Let's forget it. Let's be just neighbors, as we were. Two sets of married people living near each other, fond of each other."

"But I *am* fond of you, Paula! That's why I came with Georgie. *Really* fond of you. That's why I feel so ashamed. I mean, it wasn't your fault we got—mixed up. It was mine. Maybe it was my sisters' fault."

"Can't we just skip all that, Kate?"

The young woman looked warmly at Bill Gaunt. "I'm so *glad!* You're the first man I've seen, so far, except passing in cars!" She smiled. "And Byron, of course. He's just sitting still, under a cabbage palm!" She turned to Paula again. "I couldn't bear it if I thought you wouldn't forgive me. After all, we only—"

Gaunt saw his wife's dark flush. She looked at the ground. She looked despairfully at the trees. She looked, at last, toward him. "Kate lived with us, Bill. You might as well know now. There were no men, Bill. A lot of women had crushes on each other. Some of us didn't appreciate how masculine we'd always been until the fact was practically out of hand. I had to send Kate away." Her eyes begged.

The philosopher looked at his wife with disbelief. What surprised him was not the statement she had made; it was the anxiety that accompanied the statement. His hand went into a pocket. He fished out matches and a cigarette, moved his gaze down to them and put them back. He gazed at Kate and slowly smiled, walked up to her and took her chin in his lean hand. He lifted her face and kissed her lightly. Then he kissed Paula.

"Lord," he said, "women get upset by the smallest things!"

Paula began to sob.

Gaunt swung Georgie up on his shoulder. "Come on," he cried.

"We'll *all* walk Kate back home! Maybe Higgie will be there by now."

Higgie was there.

On the way back along the root-riven, jungle-arched street they encountered Jim, Bella, Gordon and Sarah, emerging from their yard.

Jim was marching solemnly. His head was up and his eyes flashed. He looked like a prophet at the moment of vindication, a martyr stepping forward for his reward, a soldier just decorated. And Bella wore her whole and perfect smile.

They stopped wordlessly. Soon they shook hands.

It was not enough.

They kissed each other.

"All over the world," Jim said in a hushed, dramatic voice. He repeated it, as if the phrase had a near-religious significance. *"All over the world!* With the scales off their eyes! They are looking at each other, men and women. They see what they are not, that they pretended to be. What they are, that they ignored. There is a passion in the hearts of all, the passion of peace. The passion of self-discipline. The glass they see through is no longer dark. They speak with the tongues of angels and it profiteth all, for they have love. The flesh of love, the golden flower and the spirit that abides in the flesh. The flesh that is the temple, defiled in the mind no more. They are purified, for to them *all* is pure!"

"Daddy," Gordon commanded, "stop talking like the Bible."

Bella laughed softly. "He's trying to say something, dear, that we haven't words for—yet."

Paula looked at a wet handkerchief and put it back in her damp pocket.

"Just cry," Bella said. "It washes out. It doesn't stain." She laughed again, lightly, self-reproachfully. "I used half a box of Kleenex."

"Magic," Jim murmured. "Sheer magic!"

Gordon, who had been eying Alicia, exclaimed, "She's cute!"

Gaunt chuckled.

Paula said, "Come over."

Jim nodded. "Afterwhile. We're going for a little stroll. Just the family. We'll be back."

Paula nodded and the Gaunts watched the family march up the lane.

She said presently, "Let's try to get a call through to Edwin, or a telegram."

"Let's," Gaunt said.

Bella ran back. "I've got stew, a lot, all made! Remember?"

"Do you think," Gaunt asked, "it will be safe to eat, after all these years?" His eyes sparkled. He felt he was beginning to catch onto the new rhythm, the new reality.

"I'll fix a salad and dessert. You bring the stew over to our place, Bella." Paula and the other woman nodded agreeingly at each other and Bella ran back to Jim.

Paula took Bill's arm. "Darling, we won't need to do anything for an hour or so—"

"I was thinking that."

All the round world over.

As the world turned, as the sun's curved light drove away the equatorial dark and the arctic dark, men woke and women to find themselves together again. Or near. Or woke without noticing the difference: the lonely few who had continued their solitary ways through the catastrophe. These, in some instances, did not learn for days or even weeks how the great and terrible dimension had contracted, effaced itself and brought a remembering species back to the moment when the sexes had been sundered. When they had begun to discover in hell what they had left undone and what they had done that they ought not. In hell: it is the place where there can be no love.

Later that evening, Paula and her husband drove toward Miami.

The Elliots had gone home long after everyone realized that even the most strenuous attempt with the most understanding auditors could not, in any one evening, convey the events that had occurred. For months these friends, like all friends old or new, would remember a fresh and salient fact, an untold episode, an emotional experience overlooked until then.

Gaunt had wanted to see how the city was reacting, and so had Paula. Yet neither had wanted to observe so much as to please the other; they had come by the discovery that they shared the same curiosity by such oblique suggestions and queries as are made by every husband and wife and always will be.

Paula had finally said, "Why don't we just go look? We'll be together, still. And we won't have to stay long."

"That feeling of being together," Gaunt said, as he turned into the jubilant traffic stream on Brickell Avenue. "Everybody has it, I guess. Maybe we're all afraid that this day is only an interval, a recess."

"Who doesn't think of that?" Paula looked at him in the vague, changing light. "It scares me."

"Don't you have any hunch about it? Any intuition? I do. I think it's over."

She replied quietly. "Well, so do I. In a way. I mean, I think it's over so long as we don't go back in the old ruts. If you *know* what I mean."

He hugged her in brief assent. "I was surprised Edwinna wouldn't come along. Jim and Bella would have let Alicia sleep with them."

Paula smiled to herself. "You don't understand a lot of things yet, Bill. Alicia *died!* For Edwinna this is a resurrection. Redemption. She's practical and realistic, heaven *knows!* But she just wasn't ready to stop looking at the child, even asleep. And then she's going to keep trying to phone Charlie."

Gaunt looked at slowed cars far ahead and turned, suddenly, into the schoolyard driveway. He parked where he had parked long before, on another dramatic night.

They walked up the bridge; they could see the center of Miami. Every light in the city seemed to be burning. Every person appeared to be on the streets. The parking yards were solid with cars. But no cars had been allowed in the main thoroughfares: there was no place for them; pavement and sidewalks were thronged with men and women and children. They were moving, milling, parading with linked arms a thousand all together, and dancing where a loudspeaker poured out music. Strangers shook hands, some gravely, some weeping, some hilariously; strangers embraced, strangers kissed.

Over a big bar a hand-lettered banner proclaimed, "It's free!" and there were many in the bar. Yet they noticed, as they came down the slope of the drawbridge and mingled with the crowds, that no one seemed to be drunk. No one wanted to blot out this experience.

An old man grabbed Gaunt's hand and wrung it. Two young men gravely approached Paula, smiled at Gaunt, said, "Pardon," and solemnly kissed her. Paula kissed them in return, putting her arms around them, letting them go with a fond look.

Dancers buffeted them. Old, young, middle-aged, whirling and stamping with the music, eyes bright, bright hair catching the many-hued glitter of electric signs.

The traffic lanes and parkways of Biscayne Boulevard were packed with people.

Gaunt thought of Jim's phrase.

"All over the world," he repeated.

Paula turned starry eyes toward him and nodded. "In the cities we saw burned. With the girls and the women we lost. In the cities you saw obliterated." She squeezed his arm harder. "Look at the park!"

For a moment, Gaunt was startled. The long, bleak years had not eradicated all of his self-consciousness.

As if by public consent, the park had been turned over to lovers, to couples wed or promised, or to strangers met but a moment before, and all these embraced in dusky reaches of lawn where night wind shushed in the palms and light exhaled by hotels across the boulevard was soft and filtered. There were flowers in the park, their colors faintly distinguishable, and the smell of the sea came from the far Gulf Stream.

Paula turned from the quietude of the throng to Bill. She started to tell him not to frown so disapprovingly. To ask him what else he would have expected—or wanted. But she held her peace and soon she saw his features change from consternation to a calm that was followed soon by a smile.

"Let's walk through," he said. "Nobody will mind. Nobody will even notice us. Others are."

"Looking for places to stop," she said hesitantly.

"So?" He led her into the park and they strolled in the happiness and dulcet laughter, the massive rhapsody. They came, finally, to the sea wall where waves splashed along the bulkheads, slapping, sucking, talking. A policeman stood there, his back to the park and the city, his eyes on the lights in the harbor.

He said, "Hello, folks."

They said hello.

He said. "Funny. An orgy."

Gaunt nodded. "Yeah." He breathed. "I guess it's the only happy orgy humanity ever had."

The policeman let go of his nightstick, spun it on its thong, and caught it again. "I had orders not to arrest anybody unless somebody was being hurt or making a protest—"

"And nobody is?" Paula smiled.

The cop's head shook. *"Nobody.* When I get off duty, I'm coming down myself."

"I would," Gaunt said. And they walked away.

A while later he began steering Paula with evident purpose.

"Where are we going now?" she asked.

"Where I went the first night."

"Were you downtown then?"

"Sure."

She said, "So was I. Late. All over yonder and out on the Beach the fire was raging."

They passed the tawdry, mustard brown arcade, working their way slowly through enchanted multitudes. They climbed the steps.

No one was singing in the imitation-Gothic cathedral. The organ was not playing. Connauth was not in the pulpit.

But lights were on; and people sat, here and there, in the pews. Gaunt stood with Paula at the head of the aisle. He saw again the ugliness of this effort to reassert, in structural steel and Portland cement, the sacred symbols of the Middle Ages. He thought fleetingly of how much brighter and purer Jim Elliot's "mandala" had been and he recalled Bella's account, which had so elated Jim, of how she had dreamed what the male world was doing while her husband meditated in his jewel-like "chapel." Not many persons were in the "cathedral." Perhaps twenty disturbed-looking individuals and a hundred couples who had obviously come in from the street not to worship but to be apart from the crowd, together.

"Hello, Bill! Paula!" The voice was tranquil.

Connauth and Berthene stood beside them. They had been sitting in the last row of pews.

Berthene and Paula embraced. The men shook hands.

"You were here that other night," Connauth said. The clergyman was not wearing his robes.

"I was, John."

Connauth looked down the pews, over the people, toward the

empty pulpit, then up along the arches and finally at the stained-glass windows where pulsing signs brought glitter, darkness, glitter. "A miracle," he finally said.

"No doubt."

"Did God do all this?"

Gaunt smiled a little and murmured, "You should tell *us*, John."

The minister's head shook. He spoke with hushed excitement. "How *can* I? *Bill!* Berthene's *forgiven* me! She always knew! And when she did it I suddenly found in her a different woman! A woman of burning passions. A love of me that was like holiness! Beneath that plain face, Bill, is this other Berthene! The pity is, we waited so long to learn it! Even physical love is more a thing of spirits meeting, blending—than the flesh—! I only learned."

"We *all* have flesh—" Bill answered.

He heard Berthene and Paula laughing softly, trying not to disturb the others in the church. He did not want to look at Berthene then. He would see her ponderousness, her mammoth homeliness. He wanted, instead, to share a moment of the Bishop's discovery, to add to his own impressions this one. He felt humble. For he, also, had been beguiled by surfaces and missed most of the experience of woman until this day.

John was watching him, a smile on his face. He glanced at his cathedral again. "I couldn't preach tonight, Bill. I couldn't even pray, except to say some shaken thanks. I couldn't don my robes. This seems no time for *costumes*. I felt a need to dissociate myself from ritual."

"I know."

"Not many came here, anyway. I regard that as a sign. There is something *wrong* here. We will tear down this edifice! This *mausoleum* of God! We will build a bright place, a simple place, and go in search of a *new* God. *Look* at them—!" The Bishop waved his hands. "A few vinegary ones who will not change because they cannot. The rest, they came in here to neck! Yesterday, whenever yesterday was—before the Disappearance—I would have driven them out! I would have called them defilers! But today I think my temple defiled *them!* We took away the sweetness of their bodies, their souls' temples. We kept them ashamed. We kept them sinning so we could own them through that hangman's rope of perennial repentance! We cut them off from nature. We built the barricade down the ages. We made what was one seem twain! There is only one sex, Bill! Woman, man, are halves. In all the rest of nature they are one. By dividing them we kept them conquered and subservient. I am ashamed of my doctrines!" Sudden tears filled his eyes.

Gaunt wrapped an arm around Connauth's shoulder and turned toward Berthene and Paula. There was a look in the older woman's eye like the emblazoned love he had seen in his own wife's, in Edwinna's, in Bella's, and everywhere that night. Gaunt impulsively put his other arm around her and he kissed Berthene.

"When you start that church to seek God, not to assert," he said to Connauth, "we'll contribute and attend!"

With Paula, he went out.

They skirted the human masses by taking quiet streets. But even here were songs, soft voices; here was the laughter of men, the flash of dresses, the rustle and murmur of love. They did not talk much until they came to the bridge again.

Someone had brought fireworks to the water's edge. Rockets and aerial bombs soared against the pale stars, broke and shook their scintillant confetti over the tumult. They stopped at the rail to watch.

"*Will* it go back to the way it was?" Paula asked in a recurrence of alarm. "*Will* we all forget?"

"How can we?"

"Won't people decide it was just a hallucination, or a collective dream—a tremendous, timeless moment of mass hypnotism, as you suggested at dinner?"

Gaunt followed a climbing rocket until it burst. "Won't they

—we—be afraid if we *do* 'go back' again we'll have the experience over? Won't *that* check us?"

"Yes," she said. "Yes."

"And then there'll be histories. And memoirs. A thousand written records of something awful and real that did but didn't happen and could again. Movies, telling both stories. Endless discussions. No, Paula. *We won't forget.*"

"Did God do it, Bill?"

He seemed only half attentive. "Well, who made God? I don't mean the real one that we have hardly tried to learn about. The God of the universe. Of evolution. Of instinct. Of the conscious mind and the unconscious mind. I mean, the squalid gods made in men's images that men worshiped. The gods as cruel and selfish and bigoted, exactly, as their devotees." He pointed. "Look! Silver pinwheels! I never saw a rocket do that before!"

Paula persisted. "I don't see *what* you mean."

He took her hand. "We made up our own religions and pretended they came from outside us. And that pretense finally split us apart. So, you can say 'God' did it. Man-made God. Now, if we try to learn what man is, we'll learn more of what the Truth is; the Truth we gave the bad name the old gods, then cheated. Just the way you are part of me, just as what happens in you *is* me, so we are part of whatever God really is. But the trick is to go on *learning* forever, not to *assert* God and *administer* Him. We don't own God, Paula. That's what John has just realized. We *are* God, I think, but that includes *all* we are, not just the special fragments selected by some doctrine or other. The *whole* thing—*man as he is*—Nature as It is. And we desperately need a new word, now, that means man-plus-woman and turns everybody away from the cockeyed idea that one without the other means anything—that there are *differences*—that there are relative superiorities and inferiorities. John saw that too! Others will. Millions. And more will *feel* it than think it, at first. But feeling's as accurate as thought and the new insight ought to overthrow the long blunder. The blunder of both sexes, that grew out of their insane sense of separateness!"

Paula sighed. "I guess I'm a feeler, Bill. I can't quite understand in my mind how it happened." She shook her head and then said, "Holy mackerel!"

"What's the matter?" In the light shed by the shining city he saw her alarm.

"My letters!"

He was still boyishly intrigued by the fireworks. "Letters? Did you write any?"

"Not to mail, you dope! Did you find them? The letters locked in my desk?"

"Oh." He turned toward her and grinned. "Sure."

"You *did!*" Paula's eyes were anxious. "You *read* them?"

"I read them." The dazzling sky no longer held his attention. "I was angry at first, too." His face relaxed; his eyes shone. "I had to know Teddy quite a long time, darling, before I realized he had the guts of a tiger, the instincts of a gent, the loyalty of a humble heart, and a decenter feeling about women than my own."

She said, "Oh!" After a moment, when he did not go on, she added, "Yes. Teddy's a very nice boy."

"In the end"—Gaunt stared at the sea now, ignoring the rockets and avoiding his wife's troubled regard—"Teddy made me perceive what you felt, that it never occurred to me any *women* really felt. So look, Paula. I don't *own* you. I *am* you. If, sometime, it isn't quite enough—if you add something else—for fun, from love, because of curiosity—so long as it isn't for revenge or from envy—I don't believe I'll notice the difference."

"But if I *am* you," Paula whispered, "would I *need* to?"

"It wouldn't be an important need. But you might."

"Bill!"

"Don't be mushy! This is a public place!"

They began to giggle.

He pointed. "Look at that! *Green* pinwheels!"

It seemed funny to them.

Later, when they had agreed that they would try to sleep be-fore dawn, Paula began chuckling. Gaunt, who had been lying in trancelike bliss, said, "You're awake too! What's the joke?"

"Pinwheels," Paula answered. "Green ones."

They laughed.

From far away came the sound of rain that soon swept across the city toward their immaculate residence. A spring rain, beginning early that year. And though they did not speak of it, each felt the other listen and knew what the other knew. Neither ques-tioned the cause of the peace that went with the knowledge, for there were many mysteries that night and many problems to solve and they were tired. But what both surely knew was this: that the morning would be beautiful.

In the Bison Frontiers of Imagination series